Robert Holdstock

Where Time Winds Blow

Pan Books
London and Sydney

First published 1981 by Faber and Faber Ltd
This edition published 1982 by Pan Books Ltd,
Cavaye Place, London SW10 9PG
in association with William Collins Sons & Co. Ltd
© Robert Holdstock 1981
ISBN 0 330 26759 0
Printed and bound in Great Britain by
Collins, Glasgow

To Fellow Voyagers:
Chris, Garry, Chris, Chris and Andrew

T'ung Jên!

Contents

PART ONE

Where the Time Winds Blow

page 11

PART TWO

The Phantom of the Valley

page 89

PART THREE

Manchanged

page 189

PART FOUR

Walking on the Shores of Time

page 217

PART ONE

Where the Time Winds Blow

CHAPTER ONE

Towards dusk, five days after they had left the city, Lena Tanoway led her small team through the rugged foothills of the Ilmoroq mountains, and out onto the narrow coastal plain that bordered the Paluberion Sea.

It had been an exhausting mission, and Leo Faulcon, the team's middle-runner, was tired, uncomfortable and very ready indeed to return to base. He could not comprehend the reluctance of the leader to turn for home; her seemingly endless enthusiasm for continuing the exploration was uncharacteristic, and bothered Faulcon, and he could assign blame to no other than the third member of the party, Kris Dojaan.

Kris was young, and had only recently joined the team. He lay back in the deep seat of his touring byke and whistled through his mask; he was saddle-blistered and sore, but the newness and excitement of this routine expedition had been serving as a balm for his various wounds for all of five days. Whilst this unconcerned attitude to physical discomfort disturbed Faulcon he could have coped with Kris Dojaan's immunity to pain if the youth would not keep making suggestions: why don't we try this, why not explore there? And Lena, with a finely misplaced, and long overdue, sense of responsibility was quite evidently determined to conduct this mission in a proper way, and for a proper length of time, something that ought to have been unthinkable.

Thus, after more than two days exploring the high hills and lower slopes of the Ilmoroqs, where the terrain was rough and abundant in dangerous life-forms, Leo Faulcon found himself sullenly agreeing to a tour of the ocean's shore, a last ride before the long journey home.

The coastal plain was a land dominated by giant blackweed, forests of tall, branchless trees that crowded so high towards the deepening red of the sky that their tiny, flowering tops could not be seen. But it was not the plant life that fascinated the travellers so much as the crumbling, calcite towers and arches of the land-corals that huddled between the trunks of this silent forest. Built by *skarl*, a tiny, winged life-form that had adapted well to these dry, pollen-rich lands, some of the castles were half as tall as the blackweed, their arches and passageways wide enough for a shuttle to pass. It was a crowded, shadowed land, and as Faulcon watched so a flock of *skarl* rose silently above their castle and streamed towards the distant, brilliant red-sheen of the ocean.

Riding her battered rift-byke along the easiest route, Lena Tanoway led her group in the same direction. Soon, the ground beneath them softened and they entered a landscape of dunes and tangled, grey plants. Megalithic fingers of sand-scoured rock rose high above the riders; in their lengthening shadows whole flocks of *skarl* fluttered in panic as the noisy machines passed by.

They rode across a ridge-back of harder sand and the wind hit them, brisk and cold. From here they peered down a slope, and across a mile of nearly lifeless shore, to the dusk-lit sea and its gently moving waves. An object gleamed there.

At first glance Faulcon thought it was some gigantic sea beast, stranded on the shoreline of this inland ocean; dead now, its corpse half buried in the darkening sands, it seemed to reach a stiffened limb towards him, scaly skin all-shining in the light of Altuxor. It had crawled there, perhaps, from the unfathomable depths of this dark and dying sea, and had expired in the red heat of the planet's day. And yet this thing, this rounded beast, was no beast at all, but a machine, an artifact of some other age, cast adrift on more than just the shores of a moon-torn ocean.

The team approached cautiously; during the last few days a time wind must have blown across the sea, and there was always the possibility that the beach would be swept by a breeze, scurrying across the sands to reclaim the wreck and the fragile beings who were exploring it.

Faulcon climbed down from his byke a hundred yards or so

from the derelict and walked across the dunes, following Lena Tanoway. It galled him a little to notice how strongly she stepped out across the heavy sand, how sure she was in every movement of her wiry body. Faulcon took no comfort from the fact that she had been on VanderZande's World—he disliked the new name, Kamelios—a good twelve-month longer than he, and was consequently more experienced than he, and far less cautious than she should have been. He found his feet dragging, his body labouring for breath; he was sure that some rudimentary element of survival within him was desperately trying to slow his pace. It was not fear, then, but survival tactics, and he shrugged as he watched Lena's shadowy figure vanish behind the machine.

Behind Faulcon young Kris Dojaan stumbled and fell face down in the sand. His swearing was muffled as grit clogged his face piece, and Lena chuckled as she realized what had happened. Faulcon watched until Kris was on his feet again, and he smiled at the youngster, though in the fading light the gesture was probably lost.

"How can you trip on sand?" Kris asked, his voice plaintive, hurt. *Sand* of all things. Faulcon laughed. A rasping sound, like the evacuation of a vacuum closet, accompanied Kris Dojaan's over-enthusiastic unclogging of the filter he wore. "Wait for me."

Faulcon held his ground as the new recruit floundered through the sand and clinging scrub to make up distance. He had lagged behind, perhaps dragging his feet as much with fear as with awe as he stared up at the ruined machine. If Kris was scared, Faulcon thought kindly, he could not be faulted for it. This particular discovery was very big business for a young man's first few days on this particular planet. (He had brought luck to the team, Faulcon realized!) The thought of the time winds both fascinated and terrified, and the balance between those two emotions varied, as if by some precise mathematical equation, with the distance one moved from the bubble-like security of Steel City, the mobile installation where the non-colonists lived on VanderZande's World.

Kris caught up with his team mate, grumbling about the necessity of leaving the bykes so far away. Faulcon reminded him that the bykes were filming the whole scene, just in case they all got swept up by a wind. Lena was standing in the deep shadow of the machine now, a tiny figure gleaming in stray light from the sun. Kris grimaced behind his mask, looking strangely insectile as he peered through the wide goggles, and continued to blow sand from the proboscis that was his filter and air-booster. They were ants, then, scurrying in their skin-hugging black suits across the dunes, dwarfed by the scarred hulk of the alien wreck.

It was a land machine of sorts, a fact evident from the enormous wheels and tracks. It had been blown out of time and into the ocean, and had crawled across the floor of the sea for weeks, perhaps, before emerging onto the shore and burying itself in the sand. The metal was pitted and scarred by the corrosive salts in the ocean; fragments of weed were still visible. There had been a storm raging about the Ilmoroq foothills just a day before, and the sand had blown across the dead machine and hidden it from the prying eyes of the satellites above the atmosphere; a regular prize, then, a prize for the ground team and not for the luxuriating men in the orbiting stations.

"I have a feeling we've done well," said Kris, palpably excited, his thin body shaking more than his voice as he peered upwards.

"We've done *very* well," said Faulcon. "And we shall live like kings for a seven-day or more."

"You've brought us luck, young Dojaan," said Lena as she hoisted herself up the ridges and spars of metal to obtain a view in through one of the windows.

"I guess I have at that."

In the deepening red dusk they stood before the metal creature and contemplated their discovery. Twelve convex windows, bulging outwards like gleaming silver blisters, gave the thing its animal appearance; sensory apparatus, extending forward like spider's legs, gave the machine a sense of panic, as if those spindly protrusions had tried to scrabble through the sand to free it from the clinging sediment. The hull was metallic, plate upon plate of heart-shaped armour: like scales, Faulcon thought, like the skin of a reptile. And here and there he could see hatchways, and incomprehensible painted motifs; and pipes and wires, weed-clogged and bent; and the bristling finery of antennae, broken now, and useless. There were scant signs of wind and sand abrasion, which confirmed their feeling that the machine had crawled from the sea only hours before. Glancing up into the sky, where three of the world's six moons were already high and bright, they searched for the winking orbital lights. There were none, although they could tell, by the haloes around the moons, that the organic zone was deep here, which would make such lights difficult to see. Faulcon, nonetheless, laughed with triumph. "We've beaten them!"

"They're going to be so *mad*," said Lena, echoing Faulcon's delight. "If I could wear you round my neck, Kris, I'd do just that." She fingered her charm, a jagged shard of green byrilliac taken from the first piece of time-junk she had ever touched. Faulcon involuntarily touched the leathery object that was his own amulet, mummified animal flesh from the corpse of a time-blown creature he had discovered in a cave in Kriakta Valley.

Kris watched the movement of his colleague's hand, and behind his goggles he seemed wide-eyed. "I don't have a charm yet."

"You're a charm yourself, boy," said Faulcon.

"But he needs a necklace," said Lena more seriously. "Everyone on Kamelios carries a bit of flotsam. Luck is finite, and the amulet extends it." They looked up again, up the wall of the alien. "A shard from this," she said. "It's all that will work. Get up there, Kris, and crack yourself a bit of the pre-historic."

Pale red light gleamed on hundreds of small windows, high on the flanks of the derelict. Kris Dojaan crawled his way across it, hitting here, hitting there, cursing as the metal failed to yield. "Are you sure this is such a good idea?"

Lena used her sand blaster to clear the ruddy grit from about the wide, salt-caked tracks. Faulcon searched for a doorway into the vehicle that would open: pressing, squeezing, coaxing, pressuring, kicking. Nothing moved.

"What can you see?" he called to Kris, and the youngster slipped a bit and polished up a window, no more than a foot across, and peered through. "Black. All black."

"Try another!" shouted Lena; she was across at the bykes, relaying a routine description of the discovery back to Steel City; they had registered the wreck some minutes before. Kris Dojaan reluctantly changed his position, high on the scaly roof of the machine. "Some sort of control desk. Ridges on the floor, and a face . . . that's me. I'm being reflected in something on the opposite wall."

"The floor," Lena pointed out as she approached, and Faulcon chuckled for no reason that he could fathom. Kris sat upright on the top of the vehicle and kicked frantically at a jagged piece of the outer structure. It didn't give.

Faulcon photographed the hulk from every angle on the ground, then followed Lena Tanoway down the shore to where the sea broke almost soundlessly against the land. A line of tangled weed, and oyster-shaped shards of rock, marked the highest tide-line. Kamelios had six moons, all small and insignificant lumps of rock that skipped and danced above the world to no one's great concern, although the pink, striated bulk of Merlin, being always partially occluded by silvery Kytara, had an appreciable effect on the seas, causing small but noticeable tides. Tharoo, a pitted and ugly moon, was the largest, and drew on the waters too; but since it rose and fell with the twins, only a single tide was ever seen clearly. Aardwind, Threelight and Magrath were pretty, but fleeting; there were human bases on all the moons.

"This is a good one," said Lena, drawing Faulcon's attention away from the indistinct discs that scattered the dusklight. She was turning a palm-sized shard over and over and touching the rippled green and yellow pattern in its matrix. She skipped the stone and Faulcon whistled approval through his proboscis as it made the eight-bounce and plopped out of sight.

Before them the huge red disc of Altuxor moved closer to the horizon; more stars shone through.

"I hate the dusk," said Faulcon, skipping; he only got five

18

, bounces, and kicked around the tide-line looking for a better shard.

"I like it. It reminds me of a time when I was younger, happier, prettier, richer and when sunset meant beach parties on New Triton, and more fun in one night than you can have in a year in Steel City."

If Faulcon had thought she meant it he might have wept mock tears for her. He noticed that Kris Dojaan had slipped down the alien machine and was walking slowly ... the gait and posture of disbelief ... towards them. His voice, as he called out to them, testified to his confusion. "What the hell are you doing?"

"He who gets the ten-skip gets the girl," Faulcon said, and Lena laughed.

"Unless she gets it first herself." Her dry voice was slightly muffled through the mask, slightly distorted through the transceivers. She skipped another stone, but Faulcon had turned round and was staring at the motionless youngster.

Kris took a step forward, then changed his mind, glancing back at the alien hulk for a moment. Red light reflected brilliantly off his faceted goggles; his eyes seemed filled with fire. "But the machine ... it's alien, it's ancient, it's wonderful."

The word "ancient" sent an unexpected thrill through Faulcon and he found himself frowning, staring at the ruined vehicle and thinking of the whole of time, the immensity of time gone by. But Lena's cynical laugh—a peculiar rasping until he turned round towards her—broke the flash of the spell, countered that brief return to the way he had once felt about VanderZande's World.

She was staring up the beach and Faulcon could see that she was slightly irritated. "But this whole world's alien, Kris. This whole world's ancient!" She swung round, skipping a shard out across the ocean, into the glare of the red sun. It went so far, the bounces becoming so low, that Faulcon lost the count. Lena wiped her hands on the tight fabric of her suit and watched the sluggish Paluberion Sea.

Kris was shaking his head as he walked back to the machine. Dwarfed by its bulk he leaned forward to rest both hands against the giant tracks. His voice was shrill as he said, "But this was made by intelligent creatures! It's a sign of the life that once lived here . . ."

"So's this ocean," said Lena calmly, almost inaudibly. Faulcon was walking towards the youngster, picking his way carefully as the shadows lengthened and the red light confused his senses. Lena was chuckling again. "Didn't you know that, Leo? They carved this ocean out of the crust . . . they filled it up with sea, then closed it off. We're skipping stones across the biggest damned swimming pool in the Universe."

"But the machine . . ." cried Kris Dojaan.

"Is just a damned machine."

Faulcon said, "You've seen one, Kris, you've seen them all."

"This is the first *I've* ever seen!"

"And in a year you'll wonder why you ever got excited about it," said Lena. "Go on, Kris, have fun, feel the thrills, feel the cold shivers. Why not? I did. Leo did. You have the right to that at least, to feel a certain *awe* . . ." she emphasized the word with effort as she flung a shard out towards the sun, ". . . for something dead. But in a year, mark me and mark me well, you'll think of this as cold, hard cash. Why the hell not? To whoever built this thing it's no more than a bicycle. Would you go berserk over a bicycle if you dug one up?"

"Yes! Leo . . . tell me it thrills *you*."

"It thrills me," said Faulcon dully. "I'll fetch the bykes." He walked past the youngster, trying not to think about how upset his colleague was, or of how dulled he himself had become by the cycles of change on VanderZande's World. If I could feel it, Kris, I'd scream along with you, and toss Lena out across the water head first. But I'm dying, and you'll be dying too. Don't fight it. The world is hard enough to beat.

One by one he led the rift-bykes across the barren land and into the lee of the machine, away from the ocean winds. Here, watched by the irritable figure of Kris Dojaan, he erected the survival tent, and pumped it full of sweet air. Darkness grew about them, stars shining, redness deepening to grey and a time when dusk was gone.

Lena came to the tent and they unsealed the outer lock, crawled in, crawled through. Re-sealing the small chamber they sat silently, for a while, and listened to the night winds. Faulcon activated the light and they all unclipped their masks; for the first time since early morning they scratched their faces and breathed air that was free of the choking organic poisons that soured the natural atmosphere of the world.

Lena was pale, her angular features drawn, her green eyes dark-rimmed with fatigue; she combed through her long fair hair and dabbed at her skin with a pad of moisturizing cream. She watched neither Faulcon nor the young Dojaan, but Kris watched her intently, almost studying her. He looked every bit as youthful as his speech and action indicated; his beard was hardly in evidence, and he was flushed and angry. He had tied his dark hair into a single, short pigtail, and a gleaming green jewel sparkled in the lobe of his left ear.

"Do you want to talk or eat?" asked Faulcon, reaching for the small case of food supplies. He shook the box and it rattled ominously. Opening it he peered in some dismay at the remnants of their mission supplies. "We have beef chews, three, halka chews, four, some nutrient paste still untouched—and who can blame us—and . . ." he held up a shrivelled red object. "I believe this is a carrot."

Lena smiled. "Kris here's the vegetarian."

Kris eyed the ancient vegetable with some distaste; carrots were an imported vegetable and very expensive. Faulcon had made up the food pack, and had included fresh vegetables for the new recruit as a special treat; but the items had, for the most part, not survived. Kris asked, "What's halka, did you say?"

"A local animal; the soft organs are very tasty; the chew is a concentrate of various bits and pieces—"

"I'm not hungry."

"You'll have to eat something. We shan't find edible plants until we get back beyond the Ilmoroqs."

Kris shook his head "Fasting's good for the soul. I'm really not hungry."

Faulcon, on the contrary, was ravenous. He carved himself a

21

slice of meat compress and settled back as it expanded in his mouth, chewing and swallowing and letting the day's aches dissipate into his extremities. Lena ate sparingly of the same compress. She had exhausted her anger at the way Faulcon had packed the box two days ago. In the mountains they could shoot olgoi, perhaps even halka, and feed better. The carrot was consigned to night's oblivion, through the small disposal chute next to the air-lock entrance.

For half an hour they relaxed in silence, listening to the wind, Kris apprehensive despite Faulcon's calm assurance that the chances of the wind being a time wind were reasonably remote ... well, unlikely, at least. Kris grinned humourlessly, eyeing the older man. "How many times have you been out this far?"

"Four," said Faulcon. "This machine is the first thing I've found. I had more luck to the north; it's colder up there, but at least the world looks like a world; it's richly vegetated," he explained as Kris frowned. "The southern hemisphere is mostly ocean, a few islands ..."

"Thousands of islands," said Lena, without opening her eyes, or moving any part of her supine body other than her lips.

"Thousands of islands," Faulcon echoed. "There are six other rift valleys, or canyons, like Kriakta Rift. Kriakta is the biggest, and the only one with a mobile city unit. It's also the most spectacular. Everything's watched from the satellite stations, of course. Have you been on one yet?"

"I've been here seven days," said Kris irritably. "I've hardly had the chance."

"That's odd, though. Most new arrivals spend a two- to six-week on the sat-stations, getting primed, learning the boring facts of the world's climate and geography."

"I obviously got missed out."

"You've missed nothing," said Lena, her eyes still closed. "Pollen week can be counted among the greatest moments of near-nausea in the history of the human race."

"Pollen week?" Unsure whether he was being teased or not, Kris had relaxed, smiling, yet looking from Lena to Faulcon with almost frantic regularity. As if a light dawned: "Oh, you mean learning about the organic atmosphere." He picked up his mask, put it down again, stared at it thoughtfully. "Without the chemicals we could use Kamelios like another Earth, isn't that right?"

"If it didn't have a habit of transporting you instantly into times gone by. Yes. I think you could."

"Or times to come," Lena pointed out.

"Indeed. Time, not being the simplest thing on Kamelios, it's hard to tell."

"There really is no future in it." Lena and Faulcon laughed at their shared joke. Irked, by missing the humour, Kris said, "Anyway, I think I'd like a look from orbit."

"You will, you will." Faulcon's gaze took on a distance; his face slackened. "I shall be up there in a six-month or so, and there I shall stay, unless I quit. Which I'm thinking of doing. It's the job I came to do, orbit-watch. I was adapted to artificial-weight living."

"I thought you looked thin."

Faulcon pinched his flesh through the tight suit. "I've been thinner. Lena was supposed to be sat-personnel as well. We got overlooked—it happens a lot. Steel City is run by the rules of Chaos. After the introductory period in orbit, everyone has to do a six-month on the planet. We came down, Lena first, me later, and somehow we didn't get recalled. I've been here a year, now—Lena's been here two."

"But you've been called back up . . ."

"Indeed we have. It's going to hurt. I don't think I could ever enjoy life up there . . ."

"It'll never happen, Leo," said Lena tiredly. "The only thing anyone cares about around here is the valley. As long as we keep working, we'll stay down."

"They'll be keener, now, since we struck lucky." And Lena said, "We've made it rich. Well, quite rich."

"There'll be a big bonus coming our way," said Faulcon. "And furlough; a few days off. Time to go upland, time to go hunting."

Kris shook his head in despair, saying, "Why this money fixation? My God, Leo, I hope I keep my sense of wonder."

23

"You won't," said Lena, and then more kindly, as she sat up and wrapped her arms about her knees. "But I hope it lingers for a while, Kris. I really do." She lowered her gaze to the food box in the middle of the tent. She was silently thoughtful for a moment, then laughed at some private joke. "You're right, you know. You're right, we've lost something very precious, something intrinsically human. I don't worry about it, it doesn't hurt, or ache ... but it's gone, and I wish I could remember how it felt."

Faulcon said, "We get over-exposed, I suppose. On a world where so many millions of years of past and future surround us, it's hard to stay interested. We're jaded."

"It's not over-exposure," said Lena solemnly, "I'm sure of that. It's the world. VanderZande's World. It gets in through the ears and eyes and nose and mouth and every time it changes it changes you, every time a wind blows through time it blows through your skull, and upsets things, changes things; like the *fiersig*, but worse."

"*Fiersig?* What's that?"

Faulcon said, "You'll see one soon enough, Kris."

"It's a dehumanizing world, Kris," Lena went on, "and if you had any sense you'd recognize that now and get the hell off. Except I think it's probably too late. You've got sand under your nails, VanderZande's World has got you, and I think you'll find it won't let you go."

Kris looked slightly apprehensive, glancing at Faulcon, his face creased into a frown; when the ocean-wind whipped about the fabric of the tent he seemed startled, hugging his knees tighter and nodding soberly as he ran thoughts and facts and advice through his head.

Faulcon, intrigued by the moody youngster, prompted him: "Why did you come here?"

"Why do people usually come to Kamelios?"

Faulcon glanced at Lena, then shrugged. "Curiosity, perhaps?"

"Not curiosity," said Kris quietly.

"Seeking ... searching ... chasing, chasing a dream."

"Chasing a dream," echoed Kris, and Faulcon saw the boy's eyes mist up, even though just the hint of a smile had touched the pale, mask-marked lips. "I'm certainly doing that. Chasing a dream—seeking." His gaze hardened on Faulcon. Lena was propped on her elbows, her long legs crossed at the ankles, between the two men. "Are you going to tell us what you're seeking?" As she spoke she exchanged an almost quizzical look with Faulcon.

Kris Dojaan shook his head. "I'm not ready to talk about it, yet. Will I really change?" he said more brightly, altering the subject. Lena smiled kindly, perhaps angry with herself for having been so blunt.

"Maybe you won't change as much as me," she said. She fingered her amulet. "And with your lucky shard maybe the world will treat you respectfully." She looked at Faulcon. "I think it's prayer time." She lifted the leather necklace over her head and placed the strangely patterned metal on the ground before her. Faulcon unslung his own piece of VanderZande's pre-history and placed it next to Lena's. Kris made no move and Faulcon said, "Where's your shard?"

"What shard?" The boy looked blankly from one to the other of them for a second, then, quite clearly, remembered.

"The piece of the machine . . ." said Lena, an edge of anger, of panic in her voice. "The lucky shard I told you to get from the derelict. Where is it?" But she gave Kris no chance to speak before she cried out, "Leo, he's not broken anything!"

Startled by this sudden change in Lena's attitude, Kris watched her curiously as she seemed to teeter on the verge of hysteria, twisting round to kneel up in the wind-swept tent. He said, "I'm sorry. I didn't know I had to get it so soon . . . I just couldn't break anything . . . I told you it was tough."

"He didn't get his charm, Leo!" Tears flowed. She stared at Faulcon, seeking an answer in his impassivity.

Infuriatingly, all he said was, "Calm down."

Lena reacted with open anger. The tears dried, her face went white, her voice coarsened. "You fool! Don't tell me to calm down! The kid's as good as killed us. He didn't break off a

25

charm, and he's done for us! I *told* you. I told you so bloody *clearly* to get an amulet. What do you think they are? Games? Little indulgences?" She raved openly, and Kris nearly fell backwards as she made to hit him. Her face had turned livid, her eyes bright, her lips wet as she shouted. Faulcon felt helpless because he felt so afraid, but he reached out and tugged the girl back from Kris, forcing her to sit. Her fists clenched up as she tried to control the terrible emotion she felt. "Damn it, Leo ... why didn't he do it when I said ... ?"

Kris Dojaan, confused, lost: "I'm sorry, Lena; Leo ... I'm so terribly sorry ... I just didn't realize ... what, I mean ... well, what's so important about them, about a bit of metal?"

"Luck," said Faulcon stiffly. "You brought us luck, Kris, by suggesting we came as far as the Sea. But the world will take it back, and us with it, unless we pin it down, pin that luck down by getting it into our life frame."

Kris shook his head, the hint of a smile on his face. "But that's nonsense—"

Lena wrenched herself from Faulcon's restraining grip, and struck at the boy with the open palm of her hand. The blow resounded loudly, and Kris's startled cry was almost a scream of confusion. But the physical violence seemed to calm Lena. She grabbed for her sand blaster and narrowed the focus until it was effectively a weapon. She thrust the gadget at Kris and said, very stiffly. "You get out there and blow something, anything, some piece of metal *off* that hulk. *Do it!*"

"I'm going. I'm going."

"Maybe it's not too late. What d'you think, Leo?" She turned, and was suddenly lost again, becoming tearful. Faulcon hugged her and watched as Kris strapped on his face mask.

"I think it'll be all right," he said. "It's not too late. If you can get a good shard, Kris, not too big, it'll bring that luck with us wherever we go. I think it'll be all right."

With difficulty through the improperly aligned face piece, Kris said, "And who's going to explain the damage to Steel City? I'm not."

"Just do it!" shouted Lena, drawing away from Faulcon and

using the back of her hand to slap the boy on the arm, a more friendly blow. Kris crawled through the lock and out into the night. Lena looked almost embarrassed when he'd gone, smiled at Faulcon and feigned the slapping of her own face. Faulcon laughed. "When did *this* happen?"

"What, the change?"

"All this hysteria, this insecurity. This isn't the real you."

Lena agreed. "I suppose it must have been that storm just before we left to come out here. Remember the change? I didn't see a *fiersig*; it wasn't that physical, not much of a light show, but there must have been one hidden behind the dust. I woke up from it feeling very on edge. I've managed to keep it under control quite well, until now. I'll change back, of course."

"I certainly hope so." But Faulcon knew she was right. Mood upsets were never permanent in their extreme forms, although each electric storm that brought the *fiersig*, the power-fields of change, twisted and distorted the stable mind just that little bit more, scarring the mind irreversibly in a way too insignificant to note at the time, but with mounting effect over the months and years. They were fools to stay here, Faulcon knew, but then what had he lost, how had he changed from the man he had been a year ago? He didn't get excited by ruins; he was no longer thrilled by the dead past. Not much of a change, he thought. Nothing to concern him as much as the more physical upset that might occur if he got caught by a time squall.

But he thought back to the storm that had hit the area of the valley, and the human installation, just before they had embarked on their seven-day prowl through the Ilmoroq mountains. Mood changes were not normally connected with dust storms, even if there was electrical activity about. There was always electrical activity in the atmosphere of Kamelios, but infrequently did it blossom into the spectacular *fiersig*, the drifting sky fire that worked its mysterious force into the minds of men and turned Steel City into a focus of human fear and desperate resistence. The storm had obviously concealed a small *fiersig* and the City had not realized its effect until the following morning, when patterns of behaviour were manifestly altered.

27

"I got away this time," said Faulcon. "I didn't really notice any change at all. Felt good when I went to bed, felt good when I got up." He grinned boyishly, and Lena touched a finger to the tip of her nose. *Get lost.*

"I don't know that you're good for me," she said. "Sometimes I love you, sometimes I don't. Mostly I don't. At the moment I particularly don't."

Faulcon grinned, but before he could speak there was the sound of a discharge, and a peculiar grating sound as of metal being riven. Faulcon called out, but the tent, and the wind, must have stolen his voice; Kris did not answer. "I bet he brings in a piece about six feet long, just to spite us."

"He doesn't believe yet," said Lena. "But he'll learn. I just hope he doesn't learn the hard way."

They waited for Kris then, in moody, contemplative silence. Faulcon felt very tired and wanted to sleep, but he wanted the ritual with the charms even more, and he grew impatient waiting for the youngest member of the team to return. After half an hour he abruptly felt uneasy, and picked up his face mask, activating the radio. He called to Kris Dojaan, but there was a static-filled silence, and he guessed that some sort of electrical disturbance was happening out in the cold night world.

"I'm going outside," he said, and strapped the mask on properly. Lena nodded agreement, but made no move to follow.

As he emerged from the tent the wind tugged powerfully at him, and as he stood erect so he felt himself flung heavily against the sheer wall of the derelict. He clung on for a second and watched, by Kytara light, as sand and shards were whipped up into scurrying vortices, and sent into the darkness by this "night breeze". He had never known such a strong wind blowing in such localized fashion, and though he knew the tent was safe with its deep "roots", he felt a moment's concern for the boy who might well have been caught off-balance and knocked against the metal machine so hard as to render him unconscious.

When the wind dropped a fraction, Faulcon leaned into it and made his way carefully about the wreck, until he saw the gleaming ocean, its sluggish movements highlit by two of the moons,

Kytara, of course, with its crescent of pinkness where enigmatic Merlin slyly watched the world below, and Threelight with its three shining dust deserts, higher and brighter than usual. Tharoo, he noticed through the swirling sand, was low against the horizon, half full, seeming to hover as if waiting its moment to sweep across the sky.

He called for Kris, and continued to call as he worked his way precariously about the entire perimeter of the hulk. He realized, with some concern, that Kris was nowhere to be seen.

Beginning the circuit for the second time, he soon discovered the place where Kris Dojaan's shot had struck the hull. The metal was twisted inwards, the side of the machine opened in a long and narrow split. The shot seemed to have half-caught an entrance-way, because Faulcon could see the twisted remnants of some intra-wall mechanism; beyond the hole was a passage-way, narrow and of pentagonal cross-section. He could see only a few inches into the interior, Kytara being bright but not sufficiently bright.

A wash of purple light made him stand, startled, and become aware that the wind had dropped. He looked up into the heavens and saw the tenuous flickering purple of some stratospheric activity. It was pretty, though not startling, and moved away to the south, discharging two magnificent strikes of forked light-ning down onto the ocean.

Lena's voice in his ears whispered, "Is he there? Has he got a shard?"

"I think he's gone inside the machine," said Faulcon stiffly. "He's opened some sort of passageway. I've tried calling him but he doesn't answer. Maybe he's screened somehow."

In the stillness, but still wary of a sudden squall, Faulcon backed away from the hulk and peered up at its tiny windows, hoping to see some movement. He saw nothing and felt a moment's thrill at the thought of where inside that vast ruin his colleague might have been, and what sights he might have been seeing. *I haven't lost it all; not yet, not yet.*

There was a sound down by the ocean and he glanced that way; it had sounded like an animal splashing in the water's edge

29

and his body chilled as he imagined something creeping up the shore towards him. As he saw movement in the darkness he felt a second shock, and backed away a little. The creature came between him and the bright reflection of Kytara on the ocean's surface, and he saw that it was a man; after a moment he recognized Kris, walking steadily towards him.

"I thought you were inside the machine," said Faulcon evenly.

"I got a six-skip," said Kris, laughing stiffly. And he held up his hand. "I also got my lucky charm." Light reflected weakly off a small fragment of opaque crystal, star-shaped and precise.

Faulcon said, "Then you didn't go inside ... ?"

Kris hesitated just briefly before he said, "No. No, I didn't go inside." And he walked past Faulcon to the tent.

CHAPTER TWO

It was the end of spring, and time for the city to move. Spring on Kamelios, whether in the northern or southern hemisphere, was a season, no more, no less, dry and windy than any other time of year. But for the last three Kamelion months—longer than a Standard Earth month, but the year on Kamelios was divided up into the same twelve units—there had been a noticeable darkening of the native flora, and changes in the behaviour of many of the beasts that inhabited the lands about the valley. And for three months, too, the crop-fields of the various human settlements, from Valley Edge and Chalk Stack, to Touchdown and Hawkman's Holding nearly two hundred miles away, had begun to show a rapid growth, and would soon be ready for harvesting.

For Steel City, the end of spring meant a change in position, a move of fifteen miles along the edge of the valley known as Kriakta Rift. It was mere ritual, and as such was never missed.

From a high ridge of ground, west of Steel City, where a tangled forest of the white and purple tree-form known as sun-weed made travel difficult and habitation all but impossible, Leo Faulcon watched the city rise on its engines, and hover almost silently above the blackened crater that had been its home for the last quarter year. Behind him, Lena Tanoway guided her byke through the snag-toothed trunks of the forest, and brushed blue and grey fragments of leaves and pollen from her black travelling suit as she stopped by Faulcon and watched the manoeuvres several miles distant. Kris Dojaan could be heard, distantly, cursing and shouting as he failed to ease his way through the forest. They should have come by the marked track-way, Faulcon knew, but they had been in a hurry to get home, and this short cut, close to the scientific station at Chalk Stack, had seemed like a good idea at the time. They had forgotten the date, and the ritual shift of base location; they would not be able to enter the city until dusk, and they could easily have taken the longer, more leisurely route along the edge of the valley.

To Faulcon's surprise, when Kris finally emerged from the stand of sunweed, dishevelled and covered with the fine, powdery exudate from the plants, instead of complaining he gasped in wonder. Climbing down from his byke, still brushing at his arms with abstracted gestures of his hands, he walked to a chalky outcrop of rock, stood upon it and gazed across the land laid out before him.

Faulcon recognized instantly what Kris was feeling, and realized that he had been right to suggest the short cut. Was he getting so jaded that he could overlook the simple pleasures of tourism? He smiled as he walked to join the youngster, and as he looked at the distant city, and the land surrounding it, he felt, for a moment, the sense of awe he could remember having experienced a year before when Lena had taken him up into Hunderag Country, to the foothills of the Jaraquath Mountains. There, close to the many territories of the manchanged, the view to the south, across the rift, had been even more startling than from Chalk Stack.

"You think it's so barren, round the city; when you're inside, looking out, it seems so desolate and dry. But it isn't, it's beautiful, it's rich, really rich. And that valley!"

Faulcon smiled, half watching Kris Dojaan's dust-and mask-covered features as the boy enthused, aware of the expression in his eyes, even though the goggles effectively hid his features from view.

They were not high enough to get a clear view into the valley, and they could not get a real view of the spread of the land; but they had sufficient vantage to see how wide the valley was, nearly a mile across, with its wind-scoured bluffs and ridges covered with all manner of gleaming, indistinguishable junk. It looked vegetated in parts, and Faulcon, through binoculars, observed that a wide spread of now-dying forest covered several miles of the valley's bottom, ripped there from a future time, no doubt, when the valley had been eroded away, and a stand of these high, tree-like plants had grown upon a marshier soil. Two spires rose from that green and brown foliage, and a movement upon one of them told Faulcon that a team was crawling about those ruins, logging everything. It did not make him want to be there, back in the valley; but it made him remember how thrilled he had been the first time his Section Commander, Gulio Ensavlion, had allowed him to join a Section 8 team shortly after a time wind had blown through the gorge.

The valley was two hundred miles long, in places so wide and low that it seemed like no more than open land between rolling hills; at the far end, the eastern limit, it was deep, narrow, dangerous; here, close to the western extreme, the "beach" was wide and shallow, marking the place where the east to west flow of the time winds blew themselves out. From their vantage point they could see some twenty miles of the valley's snaking form, as far, in fact, as Riftwatch Station Eekhaut, the ruined observer post that sat on the sharpest of Kriakta Rift's bends, at Rigellan Corner.

Along each side of the winding valley ran a ten-mile strip of

32

essentially uninhabited land, varying from a tangle of jungle life along most of the southern perimeter, to the more barren reaches of Gaunt's County, the western lands where Steel City spent most of its restless life, and across whose forested borders Faulcon and the others had just passed. Only installations from the military section of the Galactic Co-operative, or Federation as it was more familiarly known, were allowed access to this so-called Valley Zone, although there was a small and vital tourist trade, and for the purposes of more practical trade and communication there were trackways passing from the various counties beyond the Valley Zone up to the huge, brick-built Exchanges that were scattered along the border. Those counties were the neo-colonial settlements. Gaunt's County, Five Valleys, Seligman's Drift and Tokranda County were the nearest to Steel City, and the only inhabited regions that Faulcon had visited.

Here lived the first and second generation colonists, human settlers not prepared to undergo the same drastic engineering as the manchanged (which would adapt them, ultimately, to Kamelios in all its poisonous, pollen-saturated glory), but rather hoped to evolve a natural tolerance. The nearest of the manchanged lived in the high lands, in Hunderag Country, the foothills of the Jaraquath Mountains, and were rarely seen in the counties. These low lands were mainly devoted to agriculture, and quite intensively farmed; the fields made an octagonal checkboard of colour, and the darker shapes of the towns and villages were scattered almost regularly between the smallholdings.

The area of habitation ended at Chalk Stack, close by, with a sprawling scientific installation, built below, up and across several weather-worn pinnacles of a white and flaky limestone-type rock. The place was well known to Faulcon from a few months ago when, his relationship with Lena broken for the while, he had known a girl called Immuk Lee. She lived at Chalk Stack, now, with the station controller, one Ben Leuwentok, who had often induced sleep in Faulcon with his interminable, and no longer fascinating, seminars on man, moons, madness and the native life-forms of Kamelios.

33

Six counties, Faulcon explained to Kris Dojaan, and six major towns; at their edge, moving between them, using them for food and supplying them with consumer goods of a more idle kind, was Steel City, an immense, domed monster, overshadowing the townships, shifting restlessly as it crossed the border between Gaunt's County and Five Valleys, and onwards, along the rift, until it turned and came back again.

It began its fifteen-mile drift now, away from Faulcon and the others, towards a place in cleared land where already a site had been marked out for it. Through his glasses Faulcon could see the winking lights, the scurrying shapes of rift-suited men, and the bulkier, spidery gleam of digging machines. At this time of day the sun was high, more orange than red, and the land was bright and green; the rift valley appeared as a reddish and grey streaked channel, bordered by greywood forest and the more colourful jungle, a treacherous land that reached hundreds of miles into the hazy distance to the south.

"Time to go," said Faulcon, and they returned to their bykes, and the patiently waiting leader. Kris acknowledged her with a slight movement of his hand. "Sightseeing completed?" she asked, and Kris nodded: "It's a great view."

"Wait until I get you hunting," said Faulcon, "up in Hunderag . . ." He stopped speaking as Lena punched her byke into noisy life.

They trailed the city for several hours, passing around the gigantic crater where it had recently nestled. The city floated ahead of them, the whining of its motors growing in volume as they closed the distance. Soon they had to turn their heads to see the full span of the floating hemisphere, with its bulbous traverse units—five of the six—clinging to its lower half; where was the sixth traverse unit, Faulcon wondered idly, and as if to answer his question his eyes caught the flash of light on the tiny mobile installation, miles away, and crawling home, still a week away after some expedition into the far lands of the east.

From satellites, from air cars, on bykes and from segments of Steel City itself, from all these things was VanderZande's World studied and explored; an enormous team of men and women,

34

dedicated to following the time winds, and picking up the traces of those who had gone before—and those who would yet arrive on the world, at a time when Steel City had long since corroded.

By mid-afternoon the city had reached its new location, and settled noisily and chokingly to the ground, promising an earlier entry than Faulcon had at first believed; the cloud of dust and smoke remained about the installation for several minutes, and by the time it had cleared the Riftwatch Tower had emerged, sliding upwards from the central core, its disc-shaped observation platform already turning.

Faulcon watched the city as it settled and was still again. He lounged back on his byke, scarcely aware of the muscular control he exercised over the intricate and complex mechanisms of the speeding machine. Moving at more than a mile a minute was not a particularly hazardous occupation, but on this terrain, with its hidden clefts, and sudden gusts of wind, it was far too fast for common sense. This was why Lena and Kris were now trailing him, concerned over his obvious relaxation. Faulcon was fascinated by Steel City, though. He thought it was incredibly ugly, and with the gaping gash in its side where the crawling traverse unit belonged, it was both ugly and lopsided. He could never understand why so many thousands of people opted to live within its glassy shell (calling it Steel City was just a way of describing its anti-glare appearance) and had not set up town-ships within the Valley Zone.

Convenience, he supposed; and the sense of transience it brought to one's stay on VanderZande's World; that was why he himself had secured quarters in the city. Nobody with any sense ever came to this place intending to stay. Which was not to say that people who came to Kamelios ever left it.

The city, then, despite its hideous presentation, attracted Faulcon in an indefinable way. It also promised good food, proper rest, proper bodily hygiene, and a fat bonus, in old-fashioned credit chits, which he had every intention of spending with as much irresponsibility as possible. With Kris Dojaan on the team, he had managed to convince himself, they were the luckiest team on the world. When credit ran short they could always follow the youngster's nose.

The three-day journey home had been a reasonable approximation of hell. Food had virtually run out, and the expected catch of edible life-forms in the Ilmoroq passes had not materialized; meat compress and nutrient paste can become a most nauseating prospect when it is all there is to look forward to. He preferred to eat sand; he bitterly regretted the loss of the real carrot. Lena had seemed less bothered by the discomfort, but then she was a real old hand—or so Faulcon thought of her. Surprisingly, too, Kris had seemed unconcerned by the agonies of the return trip, and for one whose stay on Kamelios was still measurable in days, that showed remarkable self control. What puzzled Faulcon was that, for virtually the whole of the trip, Kris had done little else but complain—at not being able to visit the valley straight away, at the primitiveness of the masks and bykes—or gasp in awe, as when they had come through the Ilmoroqs, for example, and later, when they had hit the Paluberion beach. But from the moment they had started coming home he had seemed a different man. Certainly he had inquired almost endlessly about the human habitation and set-up on the world, and Faulcon had swiftly grown tired of exercising his own rather shabby understanding of how the world functioned commercially, and how it was governed. But there was nonetheless something curiously different about the boy, a sense of detachment.

In whispered tones Faulcon had confided his concern to Lena, who had agreed with him. There were two possibilities. That Kris had lied when he had denied entering the derelict, and that what he had seen inside it had upset him, or altered him in some way. Secondly, that a tentative, rather weak mood change had swept them during that last night by the ocean; whilst Lena, and Faulcon himself, had not sensed any subtle change in their psychological presentation, Kris Dojaan, raw and fresh, and untampered with by the world as yet, had been badly affected.

There was, in fact, a third possibility: that all this was pure imagination; that Kris's early awe and the sense of his being overwhelmed by place and discovery, had worn off; that he was a controlled and inquisitive young man, with a great deal more sense than credulity, in contrast to the way he had earlier appeared.

As they circuited the perimeter of the installation, waiting for an access bay to lower from the core, Kris's soft voice again crackled through Faulcon's mask radio, expressing disbelief that anyone could be so obsessed with luck that they would move a whole city.

Faulcon had explained the reasoning behind the location shift a few hours earlier, and even then had found himself laughing in agreement with the boy. It *did* sound ludicrous, no matter how you expressed it, that every three months, by Vander-Zande's time, the city should lift up its skirts and scurry to a different place on the cliff approaches. It did not in the least reduce the chances of being caught by a time squall. It *did* give observational access to a different section of the valley, and Faulcon supposed that there was something to be gained from watching the time ruins regularly from a different spot. But anyone—and he was thinking most emphatically of Mad Commander Ensavlion—anyone who wished to watch the valley with a curiosity bordering on the obsessional had only to climb into a rift suit and go down to the valley's edge. If you'd paid your money to come here you could do what you liked—within reason, rules and your own scant spare time.

Steel City, Faulcon explained as they rested, close enough to the building to hear the low, grumbling sounds of its various systems, had a second escape-ploy, should a destructive wind rear up and out of the valley and swoop towards it. The traverse units, the six mobile domes that were effectively mini-cities on their own, could move considerably faster than the crawl with which they circuited the continent. They could, if required, lift vertically at only just less than bone-breaking velocity. If the klaxons went—signifying a time wind's approach—the populace could drain into the six units in literally thirty seconds, through any one of hundreds of drop-chutes from the main city body. The longest drop was from the observation tower that was raised

37

so high in the air. Thirty seconds down, and the traverse units would explode upwards and away to safety, though the main city would be lost.

"A time wind," Kris repeated, the tone of awe back in his voice for the moment. He had seen a derelict, an ancient machine ripped from its own era and cast, lifeless, upon the shores of a red-lit ocean. But he had not seen the wind that had brought it, and he was impatient to witness such a phenomenon. Faulcon explained that in the year he had been on Vander-Zande's World he had observed a time wind on only a half-dozen occasions, although he had once come close to being caught in an eddy, the sudden appearance of a tiny, transient focus of distortion. But the main winds blew in the deep valleys, and in the nearby valley most of all. If he was patient, he would see his wind; but there was no predicting them.

CHAPTER THREE

Two hours after their return to base, Faulcon was comfortably attired, cleaned inside and out, and replete after an uncomfortably generous meal of charcoal-baked tongue and boiled vegetables. He sprawled in his small room for a while and considered the state of his existence. For a man of thirty-two, with—time winds permitting—more than sixty active years ahead of him, he had not done so badly. He owned this room, although it had cost him two K-years' service pay to acquire it. The first year had passed : one to go; and of course every bonus he earned was his to keep, and he rarely went short of anything. Being, in this sense, freelance, with no regular income, was a spur to his activities in the field—it made him work all the harder. It galled him sometimes to meet explorers, traders, dieticians, administrators, any and all of the hundreds of functionaries on VanderZande's World who had signed on for the same brief spell of service and who were already, after one or two years, regularly amassing small fortunes and would leave Kamelios rich. He himself would have nothing to sell save his room, and the value of that asset might have changed radically. His consolation was that on a world as insecure as Kamelios this nest of security, this huddling place that was unobserved, impenetrable, his and his alone, was at the moment of immense value to him, and not just in a financial sense.

He would marry Lena whether she liked it or not. One day, one year, they'd sort themselves out, and in the meantime they were two people with their own rooms in the belly of Steel City, who shared a lot of fun, a considerable amount of love, and who were both as blank about the future as each other. Except for the desire to live together eventually they looked forward to nothing beyond the excitement, and risk, of VanderZande's World. Lena had lost her awe of the place, and Faulcon was well aware that he himself was changing, becoming jaded. Lena had bought her room outright, with money left to her by her parents, both of whom had died in a fire on New Triton, a world they had come to from Earth when Lena had still been in her infancy. So perhaps it was the fact that he was *working* for his special possession, his forty feet square of apartment, that kept his regard for Kamelios somewhere in between the extremes of feeling represented by Lena and Kris Dojaan. Unquestionably he experienced the same lack of concern, the same indifference to the scattering of alien artifacts that had been dredged up by the time winds that Lena and all the long-termers on the planet had come to feel; but equally he had found himself sharing in Kris's excitement, his eager concern with the wonders of other times. Faulcon was the bridge between attitudes in the team, fluctuating between those extremes according to whose company he found himself sharing. Like Kamelios itself, like all who lived in Steel City, Faulcon was a unit of change, an unfixed

39

star, someone whose emotions could twist about in an instant for reasons other than the effect of the world upon him.

Despite the pleasurable anticipation of a small wallet containing his bonus—perhaps two or three thousand chits, the Kamelion unit of credit, on good, old-fashioned plastic notes—Faulcon decided he could not face Commander Gulio Ensavlion just yet. By rights, and by tradition, he should have gone straight to the section head to report on the expedition, and to answer questions. In practice there was always an hour or so delay before such debriefings, but Faulcon would have preferred to keep Ensavlion and his bizarre obsessions at bay for a whole night-day cycle. He called through to Lena but received no reply; checking with administration, he found that she had been summoned peremptorily to Ensavlion's office, and had been with the Commander for nearly an hour. As team leader it was not surprising that she had been called alone in the first instance, but it *did* mean that there was more to the mission than would at first seem obvious. It was not routine, Faulcon imagined, but he could not think what could have been so different about it that the leader should be summoned on her own. Surely not the discovery of just another derelict? Unless the damage that Kris had caused to the interior had got her into trouble, but that was most unlikely.

Suspecting that he might himself be summoned imminently, and still unwilling to face Ensavlion, Faulcon called the dormitory where Kris was billeted. The youngster also was unobtainable, but one of his room mates suggested that he might have gone up the Riftwatch Tower, to get the view from those wind-shaken heights before dusk settled.

So Faulcon left his room and made his way along the level until he came to the main plaza. Here there were colourful, spacious lounges, comfortable and quiet save for a distant susurration—the air conditioning—and the occasional drift of attractive, alien music. Voices were muted, though attention could be drawn across a distance by the careful use of speakers built into the ivory and jade columns; purely decorative structures, with no supporting function at all, the columns rose from the plush flooring into the hazy distance of the roof space, and served to give a sense of territory to the area. The lounges were crowded, and in one corner, muted behind a translucent screen, a celebratory party was occurring, with dancing and not a little drunkenness. Moving rapidly about, and giving to the plaza a certain sense of panic, were teams of repair men, and engineers, and a few medical personnel, hastening from damage point to damage point in order to seal and secure the city before the next Kamelion night.

Faulcon navigated this confusion, and resigned himself to the unpleasant sensation of the lift-chute in the plaza's centre, that whisked him from stable ground to a point five hundred feet above the lounge area on what appeared to be no more than a whim of warm air. But abruptly he was on a solid surface again, and stepping into the swaying platform that was the observation zone of valley and surrounding lands. A circular area that could support five hundred persons, it was now relatively empty, despite the city's change of location. Its motion had stopped and Faulcon walked around its inner path, away from the jutting windows; he was uncomfortable in the sun's glare, despite the fact that no harmful rays, nor distracting light, could reach him; but he had spent several days beneath the blinding disc—very unred in its passage across the heavens, and showing its age only at dawn and dusk—and he preferred to remain out of sight of that warming sphere unless it was absolutely necessary.

He spotted Kris Dojaan, and hastened towards him.

Kris was now robed casually in a short red tunic and thigh-hugging half-jeans. His feet were bare, and his hair was tied back in several elaborate ringlets, a fashion that Faulcon himself adopted. He was leaning against the restraining bars that kept observers from the thick, faintly tinted windows. His eyes were narrowed as he peered, without the aid of any of the several telescopes, at the distant valley.

As Faulcon came up beside him, the youngster turned and nodded acknowledgement, almost as if he had been aware of Faulcon for several minutes. Faulcon noticed the alien shard, now slung on a thin, leather necklet. Again he felt disturbed at the sight of the amulet, its regularity, its manifest deliberateness. Kris touched the tiny star and smiled, never taking his gaze from Faulcon's face. For a fleeting moment Faulcon had the sensation of being in the presence of a mischievous child. Kris had said that the object had been lying just inside the passageway exposed by his thoughtless discharge. He had seen it, grabbed it, become filled with a senseless panic, and had run down to the ocean, dropping to his knees and shaking for several minutes. Only Faulcon's arrival, searching for him, had calmed him down. But having taken the relic, nothing would make him give it back.

Now he fingered the object almost reverently. "It's warm," he said. "Here. Feel. It has some sort of inner warming mechanism."

As he held the amulet towards Faulcon, Faulcon found himself almost reluctant to touch it. But touch it he did, and he felt a thrill of fear, a shiver of apprehension, as his fingers communicated the information to his brain that the amulet was ice cold to the touch; ice cold.

After hesitating a moment, he closed his mind to the insistent voice that told him to say nothing, and informed Kris of the sensory contradiction.

"Cold?" Kris, who had seemed vaguely amused, now was puzzled for a second, stroking the star and staring at Faulcon as if it was taking some time for him to decipher the brief words. Then he looked away, out across the evening-lit surface of Kamelios. "I suppose that's not surprising. You're already cold towards this place. You're as cold as Lena, like all of this city. Something like this, like this piece of history, well ..." he struggled for words to express what was subsequently revealed as a garbled thought. "I'm sure that things like this star respond to emotional warmth. To a sort of feeling of wonder, a feeling of respect and love for this world as it once was. Maybe Lena is right and I'll lose it, but if this jewel is warm, I guess that means for the moment the world is on my side. Does that make sense, Leo?"

Faulcon laughed, a gesture not without humour, but with an edge of considerable regret. He bit his lip before answering, framing words carefully. "It makes as much sense as anything on this planet. But you're wrong to say I've lost my respect for the place. It gets covered up at times, but with you around . . ."

Kris grinned, and in his face and manner there was a disquieting hint of patronage as he prompted, "With me around . . . ?"

"It brings it all back," Faulcon concluded. "The sense of the ancient. The sense of the alien. The sense of excitement."

"Touch the pendant," said Kris encouragingly. Faulcon shook his head—a gesture of resignation—as he reached out and laid two fingers on the ice-cold crystal. Perhaps there *was* just a hint of warmth there.

Instantly afterwards Faulcon learned the reason for the relative desertion of this highly popular viewing platform: one of the traverse units was about to detach itself from the mother city, and the Riftwatch Tower would be withdrawn. The announcement had already been made and those who remained obstinately on the high level were now chased to the lift-chutes by several irritable security men. Faulcon hustled along with the small crowd, and when they were back at level four he dragged Kris by the arm and led him towards the museum.

Here, presented in something akin to organized chaos, was a cross-section of everything of interest that the time winds had dredged up on VanderZande's World, from the smallest "toy", a wheeled object that had perhaps been the model of some land transport carrier, to the largest coffin-shaped enigma, four hundred feet long, still sealed along all edges, and according to every sensory probe used against it, filled with nothing but an assortment of small, differently shaped boxes, all lying free. Function, like the function of nearly everything in the museum: unknown.

Kris Dojaan's amazement at many of the things he saw, in particular some of the human-looking artifacts, his almost boyish energy, had a dramatic effect on Faulcon, charging something within him until he not only recalled the near-hysteria that had accompanied *his* first tour of this junk yard, but actually relived it. He led Kris through the galleries, round the cases, up to and away from the reconstructions of the planetary surface,

43

as far as they had been elucidated by the enormous teams of geologists and topographists; and eventually, almost breathless, they arrived in the biology section.

In silence, reverent, awed, they peered at the main exhibit, the preserved carcasses of two carapaced, winged creatures that had lived upon this world perhaps fifty million years before, or which might yet be born to occupy it at some age long after Steel City had vanished into desert dust. Dredged through time these two unintelligent (it was believed) creatures had died quickly in the awful air of Kamelios. The rift team had lost two men to a following squall as their duty members had dragged the twisted corpses out of the deep valley.

Still staring at the largest of the two creature's enormous, dulled eyes, Kris said, "And they don't know where they came from?"

Faulcon shook his head. He was trying to imagine these beings in full flight above the rich, forested lands of primeval Kamelios. They looked heavy, the carapace being thick, and armoured, all wings and the long-necked head protruding from beneath it. It would have been difficult to make exaggerated flying motions—the drawings in the next display demonstrated that—but gliding was the most likely main motion of the beasts.

"The trouble is, you can't date things that are swept through time as new. The only way you can get an idea where they came from, or rather *when* they came from, is by looking at what gets dredged through with them. Bits of rock, perhaps whole rock scarpments, dust, things like that. The geological history of this planet has been reasonably worked out, and you can sometimes match a time-torn rock with a dated and recognizable rock formation close by. Again, the trouble is that the rift valley itself is such a mess, such a mixture of different ages, that any sort of dating work is just guesswork."

There were other creatures labelled as "extinct"; they were mostly small, insignificant-looking things, conforming basically to a "spring-limb" structure, with several scrabbling and holding limbs, often much modified, for example into the carapace of the winged creatures. And there were displays of the existing

44

life of Kamelios, animals that had been named in the early days of the colony: skarl, snake-hare, easiwhit, olgoi, and the gigantic gulgaroth, shown only in holographs, and frightening even so. There was too much information on life-style and symbiotic relationships—the strange olgoi–gulgaroth sexual relationship especially—for Kris, restlessly fascinated, to stay long at any one display.

Ultimately he was disappointed in the display of the ancient, extinct (or successional, as yet unevolved) life of the world. What was missing, of course, was any life-form manifestly intelligent ... Where the hell? ... Nothing? "No thinking creatures at all?"

They walked back to the tower, now that the traverse unit had departed. "There obviously *were* intelligent creatures here ... over a span of thousands of years almost certainly."

"Obviously," Kris repeated irritably. "What I meant was, where are they? Surely somewhere, *something* got caught by a time wind."

They had reached the chute and made the stomach-churning ascent to the top of the tower. "You'd certainly think so, but no one has ever found such a creature."

"Or seen? No sightings?"

Faulcon smiled and glanced at the youth. "That's a matter of debate. There have always been sightings, claims that are never backed up with hard evidence. Everybody would like to see an intelligent alien, and it's just too easy for the mind to fill in the missing image. Everything's been seen over the last few years, from God to giant squids; and some things that aren't quite as amusing as that." Faulcon ceased to talk, unwilling to volunteer what he knew without further prompting. He always hated to talk about the pyramid, and the sighting of a year ago. Why his mouth should go dry, why Ensavlion's unwillingness to drop the subject should upset him so much, he often found difficult to answer.

Kris, ever inquisitive, said, "Have *you* ever seen anything?"

Faulcon smiled and shook his head. "I've seen it all, Kris. And in a year, so will you. I see things in my dreams that ought

45

to drive me insane. And there are some who say that every waking hour on Kamelios is a dream."

"So you've never seen a real, live, indisputable alien?"

Faulcon couldn't help laughing at Kris Dojaan's eagerness. "Only one man on Kamelios persistently claims that privilege; usually the certainty of the sighting fades with time, but this one man ..."

"Tell me about it."

"I think not. I'll let the man himself tell you. It's more fun coming from him."

Kris sensed Faulcon's meaning instantly and looked suitably impressed. "Commander Ensavlion, you mean. That makes it tough, though. I mean, what I've heard about him isn't exactly flattering. Some call him mad, others deluded."

"A bit of both," agreed Faulcon as they walked to the edge of the platform, facing the darkening Kriakta Rift. "And it's the sighting that turned him. But as I say, he'll fill you in on the details, I'm sure. He's always glad of a new boy to talk to."

The plump man who had been using the telescope nearest to Faulcon suddenly swung the instrument round on its housing and walked away from the viewing platform. Faulcon moved swiftly into possession, and slipped a coding disc into the slot, pressing down on a small red button on the body of the binocular magnifiers. "As long as you like," he explained to Kris, "but if you take your finger off the button you have to pay again. Yes, I know ... it's like something out of an old film." Kris was looking vaguely horrified at such a primitive viewing system. "Everything on Kamelios is old-fashioned and clumsy. You'll find that out soon enough."

Before allowing Kris access, however, Faulcon himself took a slow and steady look at the distant valley, sweeping the field of view from the small, squat Riftwatch Station at the head of the gorge, right along to the distant gleam of some spiral structure which, rising a few yards above the edge of the cliffs, marked Rigellan Corner, where the valley curved round to the south.

As he peered across the mile or so to the rift, so Kris followed his gaze, squinting against the distance and the growing darkness. He said, "Why wouldn't they let me trip out to the rift? It was the first place I wanted to see . . ."

By way of an answer Faulcon swung the viewscope and focused on a jagged rise of purple rock and scree which seemed almost incompatible with the surrounding dun-coloured landscape. "Take a look," he said, and when Kris had looked, and was still staring through the binoculars in some confusion, Faulcon said, "That was once a Riftwatch Station . . . You can still see part of it. Between one windy gust and the next it had gone; that small crag, the result of some future movement of the planetary crust cracking the valley wide open, and then being eroded down . . . That lump of rock is all that remained. To go to valley's edge is to invite a wind to snatch you away."

Kris pointed out the hundreds of dark shapes moving darkly along the top of the valley, some of them quite obviously dropping over the cliffs and into the hidden deeps beyond.

"But they're all in suits," said Faulcon. "Rift suits—we call them r-suits. Have you had any practice in an r-suit yet?" He knew the answer of course.

"I tried one on," said Kris. "Why?"

"Because a rift suit is a life-saver. And it takes a lot of practice to learn how to respond to what the suit does. Until you've practised you won't be allowed within shouting distance of that wind channel down there. No one goes there naked. Not unless they're stupid. You're not stupid, are you Kris?"

Kris Dojaan's only reply was a contemptuous—irritated—snigger; but he kept his eyes to the viewscope, and Faulcon noticed him frown. "No one goes there naked, eh? Well, what about him?" There was a moment's silence. Faulcon sensed the sudden shock that struck Kris rigid. The boy said only, "It can't be . . . it can't be . . ."

"What the hell are you looking at?"

As Kris Dojaan drew away from the viewscope, Faulcon saw tears in his eyes, a frown of disbelief on his face. "It can't be . . . not so old . . ." as if imploring.

Faulcon had tried to stop the machine cutting out as Kris's pressure eased on the red button; he failed. He slipped his credit

47

disc into the slot again and peered into the distance. After a second he noticed what Kris had seen, and he couldn't restrain a laugh. "That's nothing to be afraid of," he said. "That's our phantom."

"I don't understand." Kris's voice was quiet, worried.

"Our time phantom," explained Faulcon. "Or at least, so it's said. He's wearing the remnants of a Steel City uniform, and he first appeared out there, by the valley . . . oh, I don't know. Before my time. Ten years ago? You can't get near him. Either he teleports, or there are hidden burrows that only he has discovered—or he vanishes into time . . . Nobody bothers him, and he doesn't bother us."

Even as he said the words, so Faulcon recognized the death of wonder in his statement. He felt a prickle of cold sweat as he glanced through the great windows at the wind-swept landscape, and the distant figure—indistinguishable from the waving vegetation in which he crouched—that was the phantom. Nobody bothers him, and he doesn't bother us. The words seemed to mock him. A man who could travel through time itself! But he doesn't bother us. Faulcon's gentle laugh was impossible to read. We don't understand him, and on VanderZande's World that's the same as losing interest! The coldness clawed at his stomach. He looked to Kris Dojaan, and might have said something about the sudden terror he felt, the sudden focus upon the process of dehumanization, but Kris was speaking, responding to Faulcon's words of the second or so ago.

"He doesn't bother you? That's nice. Well let me tell you, Leo, he bothers me. And it's a damned shame that he didn't bother someone in Steel City, because he might have been saved a lot of agony."

Puzzled, but aware that Kris was fantasizing about, or identifying with, the ancient relic of humanity that was crouched out by the deep valley, Faulcon focused again on the phantom, and reappraised the man. It was some weeks since he had last seen the apparition, and to be fair to Kris Dojaan, he *had* at first been excited at the thought of the man who had apparently conquered time.

The time phantom was an ancient, shrivelled figure; it was difficult to make out detail in the fading light, but he seemed to be staring straight at Faulcon as the viewscope peered down upon him, staring from shrunken eyes hidden in massive wrinkles of flesh and twisted facial muscle. His nose was squat, giving every appearance of having been crushed; it seemed to twitch as if he smelled Faulcon's scrutiny, but this was almost certainly imagination. His hair was lank, long, grey as ash—though there were those who said the phantom had hair of a different, darker hue—and from this distance seemed filthy; it blew, in the breeze, straggling and unkempt. By way of breathing apparatus he seemed to wear a corrupted respirator that covered the lower part of his face, held in place only by the pressure of his lips.

Suddenly he had risen to his feet. Stooped with age he began to lope along the edge of the valley. Now Faulcon could see that he was tall and withered, his arms skeletally thin when glimpsed through the ragged fabric of his clothes. When he crouched again he seemed to fold up into himself.

His garments were the fading remnants of a body suit, the clothing worn beneath the bulky rift suit. He could see no identification tag, nor any insignia.

The man was an enigma, and, excited by Kris Dojaan's freshness and the youngster's interest in all he saw about him, Faulcon re-experienced the thrill of mystery about the phantom. He was a man who no longer talked, who no longer allowed any contact from his fellow human beings, but a man who had undoubtedly once been of the city. He had been snatched by time and flung somewhere, somewhen, some place and time where he had screamed and not-quite-died . . . a prison where the walls were centuries, where time itself was his gaoler.

And despite all that, he was a man who had come back!

Whether he had been lost from Faulcon's time, or from a time several or many generations hence, it was impossible to know. The man said nothing, and always ran from company as it approached. He was to be seen only on occasion, and had the knack of vanishing into thin air. The belief that he *was* one of

49

the timelost was based more or less on this fact of his sudden appearance and disappearance, but it was true that he might well have been able to teleport; on a handful of colonized worlds such latent talents were more sharply pronounced than on Earth.

Faulcon cared to believe that the time phantom was just that ... a time traveller. He had been in Kriakta Rift a few weeks before when the man had last been seen by a crowd. All work had stopped, all eyes turned on the enigmatic, aged figure, as it had scurried along the base of the cliffs, darting between one piece of alien ruin and the next. There had been a slight breeze blowing, an ordinary wind, bearing with it no sign that it was concomitantly blowing through time. But abruptly the phantom had vanished, and the conviction was that a time squall had taken him. But a week later he had been sighted at the southern end of the valley ... more than three weeks' walk away!

Faulcon had found himself in considerable awe of the man, a man who could somehow ride the time winds, ride the whole of time itself.

Kris agitated for access to the viewscope, and Faulcon stood back, keeping his finger on the operating button. Kris, as he stared across the distance, was silent for a long time, although his breathing grew more pronounced and Faulcon saw that he had begun to sweat. All the while he fiddled with the star-shaped amulet, already developing Steel City superstition.

Quite suddenly Faulcon's body turned cold; he felt chilled to the bone and began to shiver. He wrapped his arms around his body and frowned, shocked by the suddenness of the sensation, then increasingly apprehensive. He took a step back from Kris, his gaze shifting between the stooped youngster and the haze of distance and dusk that bordered Kriakta Rift. He knew what was happening, not by virtue of any experience, but by having heard so often from older inhabitants of Steel City that this sudden awareness was one of the most frightening tricks that VanderZande's World could play.

Faulcon wanted to shout, but he kept determinedly quiet; he felt sick; his head was spinning, and cold panic began to drain the blood from his face. If Kris should have looked up at that moment he could not have failed to see the mask of shock that twisted his colleague's face. He would have asked pertinent questions, and Faulcon knew that he would not have been able to hide the truth from the boy.

Kris continued to watch the phantom, unaware of the deepening sickness in the man behind him. He himself was still agitated, upset by what he could see, recognizing, or identifying something about the distant figure, and Faulcon wondered whether Kris was gradually coming to realize just *why* he was experiencing that feeling of familiarity.

Faulcon began to walk quietly away from his team mate. He felt the rigidity in his face, the expression of bitterness (Kris was so young, it was so unfair!) and the deeper shades of unease. There was no question in Faulcon's mind, however, that those in Steel City who preached the strangeness of the world were right; there had always been those who held the view that within a few weeks of arriving on the world, certain senses expanded, certain sensitivities became more acute. It was said that you could tell the moment when a man's destiny linked with time, the very instant at which fate decided a man was to be lost into Othertime, even though the event may have subsequently taken a year or fifty years to come about.

Kris Dojaan was a marked man, marked out by the world to be swept into the greedy maw of years. Faulcon heard hastening steps behind him, realized that the boy was hurrying to catch up with him. But he wanted distance. He felt very sick, and there was a sharp pain in the pit of his stomach: tension. To be on the same team as a man whose death you have discerned is a terrifying ordeal, for once the team is formed it is formed until the end. Where Faulcon went, outside the City, Kris would also go, and Lena too, and one day a breeze would come, and perhaps as it took Kris Dojaan away into time it would spare a gusting afterthought for the others of the team as well. There was comfort in the simple action of raising the leathery piece of skin, his amulet, to his lips, wishing away the evil gaze of Old Lady Wind.

He stopped, then, and turned to face his colleague, not surprised to see tears in Kris's eyes. Not knowing what else to do he patted the youngster's arm, then began to walk with him towards the lift. "You know, then. You've realized . . ."

In retrospect Faulcon realized how cruel those words might have been, because surely Kris Dojaan had not had time to hear about the acuteness with which humankind on Kamelios came to be aware of time, and all its tricks. His words had been as cold, as thoughtless, as fleeting as a sudden bitter breeze.

He nodded his agreement, miserable, yet somehow resigned, now, to his new knowledge. They dropped to the lower levels, and began the lengthy walk to where the Commander of Section 8 would be waiting for them. Kris said, "I should be at least grateful that I've seen him, even though he's . . ." He broke off, shaking his head, perhaps shaking away tears. He slammed the amulet on his chest. "I was so sure I'd find him, and then I felt so elated—it never occurred to me that what I'd find would be . . . oh hell!" He laughed bitterly, then, and went on, "I came here in the desperate hope that I would find out what had happened to him. The letters we received were not very specific, but I think we all guessed what had happened. Someone had to come and find him again. I dreamed of him, one night, I could hear him talking to me, telling me to follow him to Kamelios. You can't just sign on for a stay here, but I found a way of getting accepted quickly, and I came out." He turned anxious eyes on Faulcon, who was by this time disturbed by the fact that he had misunderstood Kris's distress. He was also apprehensive, for he was aware of the youngster's fate when Kris Dojaan himself, it now seemed, was not. Kris said, "Leo, I must get out to the valley. He's alive out there and I suppose that's all that matters. I'm sure that's him, and I'm sure he'll recognize me. I must get out to the valley . . ." Faulcon saw him shiver, saw doubt touch his features. "And yet, I'm reluctant to. Deep down I don't want to face him, not like that. But I must . . ."

"Who are we talking about?" asked Faulcon carefully. His own agitation was growing. "Your father?"

"My brother," Kris said, as if surprised that Faulcon could

have thought differently. "My elder brother, Mark. He vanished nearly a year ago."

"Mark Dojaan," Faulcon said, and he felt clear-headed and ice cold as the name sprang out at him from among the lists of the timelost. In his months on Kamelios over forty men had vanished into time; incautious behaviour, perhaps, or the unpredictable time squalls that were the bane of the Riftwatch Stations, and the men who staffed them, catching them unawares. Faulcon knew all those forty names, could have written them out when drunk. You never remembered the names of those who had disappeared before your arrival on Kamelios; but you never forgot the names of those who disappeared while you were there.

So Kris was now convinced that the time phantom, the wizened enigma out by the valley, was his lost brother Mark; and Faulcon thought he knew for sure that the phantom was Kris Dojaan himself, thus accounting for the boy's sense of familiarity with the dimly seen figure. Both beliefs, both ideas, were unreasoned, unreasonable, unshakeable. Faulcon felt torn as to whether or not he should tell the youngster of his feelings, and whether he should tell him tactfully, or bluntly. One thing, he realized, was essential, and that was to take Kris out to the canyon as soon as he could, to let him get as close as possible to the man he believed to be his brother.

Another part of the strange lore of Steel City was that a man who is about to die at the whim of the time winds can always sense it, out there where the cliff walls dropped steeply to the alien lands below. He can stand there and hear the wind that will take him. When Kris Dojaan heard it he would know, of that Faulcon was sure. Kris was a man destined to be lost, and perhaps to be found again, found as an aged and withered creature whose movements and existence baffled and frustrated Steel City's security.

Faulcon wanted to be with his colleague, and yet he was afraid to be near him. This was the terrible paradox of Steel City, and the time wind teams; the terrible irony of friendship on this strange world.

53

CHAPTER FOUR

Between and above the six domes of the traverse units, the central city core was a great bulbous construction, divided into twenty-four levels, each with an area of a quarter of a square mile. Each level was equipped with its own scattering of lounges, "open space" illusion, tight-packed living quarters, and less cramped administrative centres. Winding corridors linked extremes of each level, interlinked levels themselves, and connected the whole city mass with the traverse units, and with the utility sections in the wide stem of the central core. From most levels it was possible to look inwards and outwards across the vast, central plaza.

Steel City was crowded, often claustrophobically so; only 5 per cent of its population ever ventured out to the alien world with any real regularity. What had drawn them here, what kept them here, what motivated the fact of their contentment with VanderZande's World was something Faulcon had only vaguely ever understood. And even though he sensed it might be important to understand the reason for this massive commitment of human energy to such an apparently worthless existence, he had long since lost that natural inquisitiveness that might have led him into deep, psychological waters.

This was not to say that everyone on Kamelios, or in the city, or out among the neo-colonial towns, was kept here for no apparent reason. The communities were genuine long-term settlements, granted by Federation Charter, supplied by Federation ships, listed with the Galactic Health Organization, and granted full rights under Galactic Law. The same was not true of Steel City, which was officially a "military installation", still part of the same Federation, but responsible to a different Earth-based Committee of Interstellar Affairs. And even in Steel City itself, among that aimless population of clerks and cooks, cleaners and doctors, musicians, writers and entertainers of every sort, maintenance engineers, troops and the rich élite who had spent a fortune to buy the boredom of the mobile city on VanderZande's World, even here there were those who knew exactly why they stayed, whose whole lives depended on, and functioned because of, the quirks and mysteries of the planet beyond.

Commander Gulio Ensavlion was, among these few, the most manic, the most obsessed, the most fascinating.

As leader of Section 8, the exploration and monitoring section of which Faulcon was a member, Ensavlion lived, brooded and planned in a vast semi-circular office on level nine. One side of the room was a single, tinted window, overlooking the land between Steel City and Kriakta Rift. The curved wall seemed taken up not with gentle pictures, or soft, relaxing colours, but with maps, designs and charts: contour maps, detailed and precise, of practically every square mile of the main continents of the planet; satellite photographs of the world; meteorological charts of the wind flow, cyclone distribution, rain belts, earthquake zones. Colourful, confusing, convincing, the man was surrounded by VanderZande's World in so much detail that it was doubtful if he could ever finish the exploration of his walls, let alone the real world outside.

One map display above all dominated the room: a one to ten thousand aerial map of the rift valley, all two hundred winding, enigmatic miles of it, taking up yards-long rows across the middle of the wall. The map seemed blurred at first, until Faulcon realized that each display was in fact several views of the valley taken at different times, showing the effects of each of the really powerful time winds that had blown through it over the last few years. The regular geometric patterns that laced the valley were the ruins, the structures of other times and other beings. Of some of these Ensavlion had pictures and plans: the towering temple-like building that had popped into view almost two whole years before, only to be snatched away a month later; the cubes, and spires, the domes and twisting, unaesthetic structures, hollow and more often than not empty, sometimes filled with such meaningless garbage that might be

55

found in any building—containers, vessels, objects of decorative nature, supporting structures and a plethora of incomprehensible, ostensibly functionless trivia. Ensavlion's office was filled with such things, many in cases, some on open display. He even had models of a few of the more elaborate ruins in the valley.

As Faulcon led the way into the room, at last summoned by the Commander, Kris Dojaan's eyes lit up. There was something even more exciting about seeing such junk in Ensavlion's office than in scrutinizing a carefully labelled display in the museum. It was as if the fact of its presence in the room of a Section Commander lent an aura of importance and mystery to the objects.

The door closed silently behind the two explorers. Faulcon relaxed, probably the effect of some ease-inducing chemical in the air, and smiled at Lena, across in Ensavlion's small interview area, away from the enormous desk where he worked. She was stretched out in an easy chair, legs sprawled, hands behind her head. She looked bored, tired, and extremely irritable. She raised a hand and waved at Faulcon, but her face never changed its expression of total fatigue. No doubt Ensavlion had been questioning her with great enthusiasm. The hazards of leadership.

Kris Dojaan, Faulcon noticed, had eyes only for Commander Ensavlion; he did not even acknowledge Lena. And to Faulcon's mild surprise Ensavlion himself seemed to find the young Dojaan an object of irresistible interest. The two exchanged a long, intense, mournfully solemn gaze. Abruptly Ensavlion smiled. Kris, who had seemed in awe of the older man, gave a quick little bow from the neck and his face hardened. Faulcon thought he saw a hint of anger there.

Gulio Ensavlion was an impressive-looking man, not particularly tall, but strong in build; his legs, in particular, were noticeable for their musculature, and though Kris could not yet realize the fact, Ensavlion's physique showed all the signs of one who spends hours, even days, in a rift suit. Older than his visitors, Ensavlion was nonetheless of indeterminate age. Faulcon thought he might have been in his sixties, on the declining side of his prime, but with a good forty or fifty years of active life before him. His face was drawn, deeply lined; his black hair was greying; swept back, and tightly bound in a small, greased plait, it seemed to shine darkly, strongly. He wore his green undersuit, an outfit designed as a wear-anywhere, but which was particularly designed to be worn underneath an armoured rift suit. Kris was no doubt puzzled—whereas Faulcon was slightly impressed—to observe no insignia of rank, of achievement, sewn upon it.

"Welcome, gentlemen," Ensavlion said, extending his hand to each of them. His grey eyes regarded each in turn, a nervous, hesitating gaze, and though he smiled he was apparently uneasy with them. "Follow me, will you? We'll eat the cream before talking about the cake."

Faulcon echoed Kris's empty laughter with a nervous smile of his own. He fervently wished that Ensavlion could relax more. But then Ensavlion had isolated himself so much from the human community that perhaps there was no hope of him ever regaining human attitudes.

Lena rose to her feet as they gathered at the main desk, came across and courteously shook hands with Faulcon and Kris, something they never usually bothered with. Ensavlion picked up two red plastic folders, slapping one into Faulcon's outstretched hand, and the other into Kris's. He laughed abruptly, staring at Faulcon who was greedily weighing the fat wallet and its traditional, plastic chits. "Heavy, huh?"

"Generous," Faulcon agreed, wondering what value was coded into each strip. It would have been improper to check the value of the bonus here and now; fifties or hundreds, certainly, and therefore five or ten thousand g.u.'s. Faulcon could scarcely bring himself to accept the possibility of the higher figure, but when he glanced at Lena she flickered her eyes heavenwards, and made a facial expression implying she was overwhelmed.

Ensavlion had slapped Kris on the shoulder, a hesitant but friendly gesture, and waved him to a seat. "Sit down, Leo. Lena ... Mister Dojaan." He waved to a third chair. Sitting behind the desk, and leaning forward with his hands clasped on the work top, he looked at the two men and nodded. "Very good work, gentlemen." And to Kris Dojaan. "May I assume the liberty of calling you Kris?"

"By all means," Kris answered, while Faulcon winced: *may I assume the liberty!*

Ensavlion relaxed for the first time since they had walked into the room. He looked through slightly narrowed eyes at Kris. "I've heard a lot about you. It's good to have you on the section. Good. Need vigorous young men, people with an interest, a compulsion . . ."

A compulsion to what he never said, but spent a moment nodding thoughtfully and appraising the youngster. "I remember your brother. A good man and a tragic loss."

It was possible to tell, from the way he chewed at his lip and sat up, that Kris was about to interject something on the subject of the phantom. Faulcon caught his eye and gave the merest shake of his head. Kris frowned, but relaxed again. Ensavlion said, "I know you've come looking for him. I know that's very much on your mind. Well, maybe you'll find him. I can say this, Kris . . . I hope you do. I hope you find him, and I hope . . . I hope things work out fine."

Faulcon noticed a certain shared grimness between Kris and the Commander. He glanced at Lena who was staring across the room at one of the maps; aware that Faulcon had glanced towards her she raised an eyebrow in query, but Faulcon shook his head and turned away. Ensavlion was saying, "Always the need for young recruits, coming here from other worlds, distant worlds. We have an important job here, a vital job . . . a job that needs to be done, and I guess it's true that . . . I think that young men and women bring freshness, young ideas. And that's important if we're ever to . . . if we are to complete our mission here, and find out just what they are, these . . . these creatures, these beings. We need all the ideas we can get, all the good ideas and insights because, you know, they *are* there, they're out there, out there in time, and we need them, and we know that they watch us sometimes and know we're here, and maybe as I've often said, maybe that's because they need *us*." He laughed suddenly, briefly. Falling solemn again, he stared across the room at his wall charts and diagrams. "They need us, gentlemen . . . and Lena. I beg your pardon. They need us, and that's something other section Commanders . . . well, they forget the mutual need aspect. We can help, we can exchange . . . ideas, you understand; cultures, insights. We *have* to find them again, and I think that . . . I think that if we can just get out there and be . . . and be positive, then maybe we'll benefit, maybe we'll advance our relationship with the Galaxy."

He stopped talking, pushed three fingers across his brow and looked at the moisture he had rubbed off onto them. He was embarrassed, and suddenly in a state of extreme tension. Kris looked horribly uncomfortable, and Faulcon sympathized with the lad, wishing that somehow he could convey to him that Ensavlion always broke out into a sweat when he talked about *them*, and that there was nothing to worry about.

Ensavlion laughed suddenly. "Hot," he said. Faulcon agreed. The room was indeed stifling, but now that Ensavlion had finished speaking, had got this routine speech out of the way, an air of relaxation descended.

Ensavlion knew full well, of course, that he was regarded in a variety of ways by other Sections, even by his own: with amusement, or with contempt, with frustration or apprehension, and very occasionally with interest. There *were* those who believed he had seen what he claimed to have seen, the time-travelling creatures from the ancient days of this world. But the believers were few and far between.

It was a paradox that Faulcon occasionally found nagging at him. With a valley full of relics, and a land surface that was forever presenting new junk, new time debris to the inquisitive minds of men, it was difficult to comprehend how people could deny so aggressively the passing through of those who had once lived here, and who had constructed some of those objects. It was as if all the artifacts of another age were no more than toys to a child, a child who would find it hard to comprehend the stages, and hands and minds that were once occupied in constructing the playthings.

Behind Ensavlion, where the wall was blank over a fairly large area, a light flickered into existence, and a moment later, on the blankness, appeared a map of that part of the continent that included the vast inland Paluberion Sea, and the Ilmoroq mountains, with their dense forests and deep gorges. Ensavlion turned, reaching for a light pointer, and flashed the tiny arrow onto the screen, waving it in a wide circle. "Recognize the view?"

Faulcon found himself nodding thoughtfully, but disturbed by something. He realized abruptly that the vast stretch of fairly featureless land reaching back from the foothills of the Ilmoroqs had been omitted, so that the end of the rift valley, the western beach, seemed far closer to the ocean than it was. A huge, multi-branched arrow was drawn across the ocean, its path curving both up and down. "This is a prediction of the time flow that caused your machine to appear. Based on surface disturbances, and a more intense look at the sea bed now that you've drawn attention to the likelihood of a wind in this area, it looks as if we have a dual-channel flow. The machine could have come from either of them."

Lena asked, "Are there other ruins, traces on the sea bed?"

"None," said Ensavlion. "No traces at all, in fact, except for some strange topographical features. But no remains."

"Just our derelict," said Faulcon, suddenly realizing the full importance of the find. Normally such a discovery, leading to the prediction of a nearby time-flow, would be the first discovery of hundreds, or thousands, as full survey and excavation teams moved into the area. With the ocean, of course, they would be submarine teams, from one or more of the units that crawled along the ocean's edge, working in conjunction with deep-water orbital surveying satellites.

Ensavlion had turned about, and looked at Faulcon, something of a smile, something of concern on his face. "Not *even* your derelict," he said.

All three reacted with surprise, Faulcon leaning forward, and Lena shaking her head in bewilderment. "I don't understand," she said.

Ensavlion touched the small button built into his desk and

60

the map view of the continent vanished, to be replaced by a satellite photograph of the shoreline. The tracks of their bykes, practically obscured by drifting sand, were none the less clear. Where the machine had been stuck in the rise of the sandy shore now there was nothing. Faulcon clutched his wallet of money tightly, wondering whether its continued association with him was now in jeopardy. He had actually stared at the machine-shaped impression in the sand for some moments before he became aware of what it was, and he relaxed.

"It went away, then," he said. "Good God. It must have crawled away again after we left, back into the sea."

Another photograph appeared on the screen. This one clearly showed the hulk, and the marks of the three explorers who had walked so excitedly about it. Faulcon felt safe, now. The extra bonus was no doubt a personal gift from Ensavlion for their having found something that actually *functioned*.

"It had gone between one orbit of the viewSat and the next, a period of thirty minutes. Something went wrong with the geo-synch as it moved into place, the morning you left; it made another loop, and when it got back the thing had gone. No tracks left, but the wind might have obscured them on the ocean side of the ridge. Did any of you get inside the machine?" How confident and clipped Ensavlion could become when not indulging his encounter with the aliens.

Faulcon shook his head, then dropped his gaze as he waited for Kris to respond. Kris, however, denied having been inside the derelict. Faulcon glanced uneasily at Lena who shrugged almost imperceptibly. Then Kris said, "But I'm afraid I damaged the side of the thing, trying to . . . trying to clear sand. I set my blaster too high and gouged out a piece of the hull."

"Did you enter it?"

Kris said no. He touched his amulet almost lovingly. "I removed this from just within the confines of the machine I reached my hand inside to do so."

Ensavlion sat back, staring at the youth. "It's possible, then, that your damage triggered some mechanism that eventually set the machine into motion. Is that what you think?"

"Delayed action . . . up to ten hours later, following a freak shot?" Kris shook his head. "That doesn't sound very likely to me."

Ensavlion was staring at the amulet. For the first time he was realizing that the regularity of the shape meant it was an artifact, and not a shard. And of course, it was all that remained of the derelict. He drew a deep breath, selecting his words carefully, then leaned forward, hands clasped before him. "Kris, you're new on this world, and we have codes of behaviour, and ways of doing things that may seem a little strange at first. I expect Leo has been filling you in . . . telling you all about it. That's why you're on his team. You've broken a code of behaviour out of ignorance . . . I should be angry with you, Leo, for letting him." Kris paled, Faulcon noticed, but kept calm. "You've taken an artifact as your charm, and not a shard. Artifacts are commonly taken as charms when there are several of them. Single artifacts are not." Kris fiddled with the necklace, shaking his head almost imperceptibly : *you're not taking it away from me*. Ensavlion went on, "However . . . once a man takes his charm, it's taken. It belongs to you. To deny that would be so deny your right to life. There is nothing that can . . . nothing that will be done to, do you understand, pressure you into allowing an examination of that piece of history." He was beginning to sweat again, his coherence going as he succumbed to discomfort.

Kris had immediately caught his drift, however, and was obviously eager to co-operate now that he knew he would not have to lose the jewel. Had Kris so quickly become ensnared in the world's superstition? He said, "But if I *allow* a study . . . that's all right, is it? And I get the charm back?"

Commander Ensavlion nodded his agreement. "Would you be prepared to do that?"

"Yes, of course." Kris made to remove the amulet; he seemed vaguely amused by the whole discussion. Ensavlion quickly stopped him from lifting the necklace over his head. "No, no. Don't take it off. Never take off your charm, Kris. Always wear it, keep it close, keep it soaking up your life spirit, guarding you.

62

We'll conduct an examination *in situ*. I can only thank you for your help."

How strange, thought Faulcon: over the last few minutes, except for the occasional moment of discomfort, Guilio Ensavlion had relaxed more than Faulcon had ever seen him relax in all his time on Kamelios. He obviously liked the boy, was recognizing, or reacting, to something about Kris Dojaan; this was good for Kris, and it was good for this tiny team. It was also good for the Section, because it had long been the considered opinion of the thousand persons who comprised Section 8 that Ensavlion needed someone to bring him gradually, delicately, but firmly back to the harsh realities of life on this confusing, changing world. Maybe Kris Dojaan could do it. Maybe the boy was a walking focus of luck.

Ensavlion slapped his hands together, then laid them flat on the table, staring at his knuckles. As Faulcon watched him in the silence he suddenly realized that the Commander wore no visible amulet. It had never occurred to him before, but now that he thought of it, he had never ever seen a shard or a necklet on the man. Before he could take the point further in his mind, Ensavlion said, "The question is, to return to the problem at hand . . . was it the jarring effect of the shot that sent the machine moving again; or was there someone . . . or something . . . on board. We'll never know, I suppose. The machine hasn't been spotted in the ocean . . . it's a big ocean, mind you, and the bed is craggy and scored with deep, overhanging rifts. It could be hiding down there. More likely, it got caught up again in a flow of time. The ocean seems to be an active place, despite its quiet surface motion and unspectacular tides. Gentlemen . . . Lena . . ." He settled back in his chair, his gaze going beyond Kris to the wall maps. "I think we may have encountered the travellers again."

Oh dear God, thought Faulcon. Not the lecture. Please not the lecture.

Faulcon's fervent prayer was heard and granted. Ensavlion rose from his seat and gestured to Kris to follow him across the room. "Come and see this, Kris. The others are probably fed up with hearing me talk about it, so they can start thinking of the report they'll have to make."

He led Kris away across the room, to stand before the diagrammatic map of the present valley. Faulcon heard him describing the rift, pointing out the ruins of past, and some that were thought to be future, showing him the paths of the time winds, and the gullies and crevasses where squalls of time flowed and scurried almost constantly. He described his own visits to the interesting buildings, and to the less interesting structures; he stabbed at places where strange, living animals had been seen—always elusive—and where dead ones had been concerned him most, the place where the pyramid had come and gone in the twinkling of an eye, and yet in that twinkling . . .

Although others had seen the structure, only Gulio Ensavlion had glimpsed, through the wide, unsymmetrical window, the movement within the machine of intelligent beings, the creatures who had once owned the world, who had left their ruins in abundance, and who journeyed through all of time to see what had come after them . . . and perhaps to monitor it with some unknowable purpose in mind. They had paused in the valley for just a second, stepping through the shimmering walls of their vehicle, perhaps aware, as they journeyed on, of the human eyes that watched them from the cliff tops . . not staying to exchange greetings.

Ensavlion's audience of one was watching and listening, fascinated, mouth open, Faulcon imagined, eyes wide. Lena came over and sat next to Faulcon, whispering, 'Six thousand g.u.'s!'"

"Six thousand!" Faulcon shook his head, almost in disbelief as his wildest dream came true. "And for a machine that walked found . . . And all the time he circled about the one place that away! The old man must be crazy. Crazier, I mean."

Lena laughed quietly, then nodded down the room where, to nobody's surprise, Ensavlion was telling Kris in great detail the story of that sighting he'd made, just less than a year back. "Many good men lost out there, Kris. Good men, brave men. Seeking the aliens, seeking to make contact with them, and some of them went out once too often and never came back.

64

But we've got to find them again, we've got to flag them down, so to speak. Man has learned to live on this planet, Kris; he's learned what to expect and how to react; there are no surprises except . . . except what's in the valley. There's danger there, certainly, and yet there's a goal there that makes no danger too great, no loss too heavy to bear. The valley, Kris. Have you been out there yet?"

"Not yet. Apparently I have to train first." There was a hint of irritation in Kris Dojaan's voice as it drifted through the stillness to the silently listening Faulcon. And then an abrupt change of subject that caused an awkward exchange of glances between Faulcon and Lena. "Commander . . . about Mark."

"Mark?"

"My brother. Mark Dojaan. You know, the man who was such a tragic loss. Mark, for God's sake!" The sudden anger disturbed Lena Tanoway who turned to watch Ensavlion's reaction. Like Faulcon, all she saw was a stiff embarrassment on the Commander's face.

"What about Mark? A good man."

"So you already said. But your letter told us nothing. Just that he was lost, dead . . . but how, why? Who was with him, Commander? Did he go bravely? If you thought he was dead, couldn't you have said that he had died without pain? You can't know the agony that letter caused . . ."

"Mister Dojaan."

"No! I'll finish!" Ensavlion's face was red, now, and his skin gleamed with sweat. To Faulcon's surprise he stood his ground, watching the youth, watching the anger, taking it. "You told us nothing, nothing but his death." Kris suddenly relaxed, glanced at Faulcon. "He's not dead, you know."

"Isn't he?"

"I *know* he's not. But that's not the point. It's taken me months to get here, months even to start to find out why he failed to 'survive', when you could have been so straight with us from the beginning. Mark was a strong man, a clever man; he was a natural survivor. So what happened, Commander? What went wrong for him?"

As if suddenly aware of the two listeners, Ensavlion glanced down the room at Faulcon. Faulcon and Lena rose from their seats and made "about to leave" gestures. It was appropriate; they would have to submit draft reports within twenty hours, and there was a lot of writing involved.

Ensavlion gently propelled Kris back across the room. "Kris, I can understand how upset you are. I really can. For the brevity of my letter, I apologize; and for failing to patch the information into the GHO network, yes, I apologize for that too. To be truthful, one gets forgetful . . . so many good men are lost here. . ."

"Right! You forgot about him. He was nothing to you but a name and a rank, that's the truth of the matter, isn't it? A routine loss. You don't even remember him now—you just checked his records."

Angrily, no longer prepared to tolerate Kris Dojaan's emotion, Ensavlion silenced the man curtly and authoritatively. Kris fell sullenly silent, and when Ensavlion said quietly, "That will do, Mister Dojaan. That will do," he began to look slightly abashed. Ensavlion relaxed again, smiled nervously as he moved with the group towards the door. "The sooner you get out to the valley the better, I can see that. Get in a few hours' training in a suit, and get out there. Look for your brother, if you really think he's still alive, and look for the travellers. Watch hard, watch constantly, watch carefully . . ." he glanced towards the darkness beyond the window, ". . . because they come and go, fleeting, like a breeze."

The door slid back, squeakily. Cooler air from the neon-lit corridor was refreshing to Faulcon. Ensavlion shook his hand. "Look after the boy. Talk to him, explain to him. He's bringing luck to Section 8—if a little impatiently." Faulcon forced a laugh at the strained jokiness. "And maybe we'll catch a glimpse of the travellers when he's around. I've waited a long time, long months, and I've waited patiently; and now all of a sudden," he shook hands with Lena and Kris, "I feel they're just around the corner. Goodbye, gentlemen. Lena."

CHAPTER FIVE

"Are you always so tactful?" Lena led the way into a credit registration booth, barely wide enough for the three of them to squeeze in together.

"I don't want to talk about it." Kris Dojaan watched as Lena operated the automatic teller. "This is a really stupid routine," he observed as she slid the thin chits into a slot labelled with the same denomination and watched her credit tally mounting on a screen before her. She punched instructions—20 per cent to be transferred to her personal account on New Triton, 10 per cent to her tax account, automatic settling of her dream-dome bill.

"We like it," she said.

"We certainly do." Faulcon kissed his wallet, pocketed one of the smaller chits—"for a souvenir"—and shuffled round to gain access to the register. "That's the trouble with progress; it forgets that people *like* the way they do things." He started to register his bonus. "If I were you, young Kris, I'd salt some of those g.u.'s away for a windy day."

"Why? I'm not going to need it."

Sullen, depressed. Faulcon looked at him, and at Lena, who shrugged.

"It's going to be a real fun evening, I can see that." He punched buttons.

"Ensavlion's a fool."

"Yes, well there are those who say he is, and those who say he isn't. Whatever you've got against him, somewhere there's a man who would disagree with you—violently. So I'd keep my irritation to myself, if I were you. Your go."

A while later they stood outside the registration console and watched the bustle of life within Steel City. Kris was fascinated by peering upwards through the vast central well of the core,

67

to where the different levels could be seen; for several minutes he was content to watch the movements of men and machines, passing around the huge open space above the plaza. Lena suggested they ate dinner together after night-fall, to celebrate their new luck. She had had no time to herself as yet; she scratched her torso and murmured something about a dream trip, a quick freshening up of the dye of her hair, a long bath—did Faulcon want to join her? Was he sure? Okay, she wouldn't press—and they could meet in the Star Lounge at chime nine, nine-thirty. Faulcon and Kris were agreeable, although both had stuffed themselves with junk food at the first opportunity earlier that afternoon. Faulcon explained that the Star Lounge was deliberately set aside as being too expensive for more than the very occasional visit, dealing as it did mostly in exotic imports and expensive trivia. It was Steel City's most attractive prospect, at least as far as food was concerned, and it was the quickest and easiest way of recouping a bonus into City funds.

Lena slipped away, into the crowds; Faulcon thoughtfully watched her tall, lean shape, her body moving with the stiffness of fatigue, her long hair gleaming, blue-tinged gold, in the bright, artificial light. He felt a momentary pang of some emotion as he realized that because he had refused to go with her, now, she would probably spend time with someone else. He couldn't help feeling that their relationship was getting a little too casual.

He turned back to Kris, his unease with the lad effectively damped by the protective walls of Steel City. His first panic gone, it was nevertheless with some misgivings that he anticipated the external training schedule that he would have to undertake with the new recruit. "Do you want to be alone until we eat?" Faulcon enquired, not certain, because of Kris's quietness, whether he was intruding on the youngster's solitude. Kris shook his head, and declared quite brightly that he wanted to get drunk. Drunk straight away? Or first laid, and *then* drunk? Kris thought for a moment, wiry body hunched as he looked about him at the restless population, perhaps seeking inside his mind and body for some stirring of interest at the prospect of going up to the dream-dome. He decided just drunk

68

would do fine, so Faulcon led the way up to a sky bar, with an outlook towards the gloom-shrouded valley. Kris sprawled out in the quiet and relaxing lounge, watching the lights of the world come on, while Faulcon acquired two bottles of a green, translucent liquid that he told Kris was *baraas*, a rare distillation and among the most expensive drinks in the Galaxy. They tucked in with enthusiasm, although after a while decided that *baraas* would taste better flavoured with lime.

During the evening Kris met a handful of Faulcon's acquaintances and section colleagues and exchanged increasingly slurred pleasantries with them. He perked up quite noticeably when Faulcon introduced him to a dark-haired girl called Immuk Lee, who sat for a while and shared a glass with them. She was an old flame of Faulcon's, and Kris was quite evidently attracted by her. Down from the biology station at Chalk Stack, she was staying overnight. She'd brought in several specimens of gulgaroth body fluids for a more detailed analysis in the laboratories of the City. Kris Dojaan, for thirty minutes, discovered an amazing interest in the blood of native carnivores. When she left she invited them both to visit Chalk Stack. Kris watched her go, then slumped in his chair, mournful and distant. When he recovered from what he revealed had been an incapacitating surge of desire he began to ask questions, many of them conversational (and about Immuk), a few of them to answer things that had puzzled him since his arrival on Kamelios.

Why, for example, did Lena speak so peculiarly, so liltingly? Faulcon had long since ceased to think of Lena's speech as being unusual, but of course she *did* have a strong accent, and that accent was colonial New Triton, her planet of origin. New Triton was a world where InterLing was spoken with reluctance, the main language being that primitive version of inter-Lingua, French: she had come to the Galactic language with facility, therefore, but had never bothered to try and work away the clipped, lilting accent of her natural tongue. Some people, Faulcon hinted strongly, found that trait attractive. He was slightly disturbed when Kris declared emphatically that he did not.

But why, he asked, did she wear her hair so long, like a man's, with those ridiculous transplanted side-burns curving nearly to her cheeks? The way he described them, in an exaggerated, almost comic fashion, made both men laugh. But Faulcon pointed out the high incidence of transplanted cheek and chin hair on the female population, some worn bushy, some shaved very close, and he made it clear that Kris's awareness of Lena's modishness was only because he was more aware of that one woman among all the hundreds who inhabited Steel City.

Faulcon spent a while instructing Kris in the arts and versatilities of Steel City tastes, and how attitudes and clothes, make-up styles and hair arrangement, changed not from year to year, but almost from a fourteen-day to a fourteen-day. Sometimes a group aestheticism would emerge from the chaos of styles and modes, and then it would linger longer, and permanently establish a group of men and women who would forever wear that style, for although fashions changed frequently, there were always minority groups who settled for one "look". At the moment, Faulcon explained, pointing out examples in the bar to illustrate his words, the mode was for women to wear their hair long, like Earth women, and to seek skin grafts with bright orange or red hair on them, to give their side-burns an interesting contrast to the green or purple staining of their natural locks. He pointed out the high incidence of male pigtails, with natural colours being more obvious than the occasional streaking of silver, an outdated fashion that had lasted several months, about a year ago. Body hair, of course, was dyed in personal choice colours, and often grafted or shaped into elaborate patterns. Faulcon opened his shirt slightly, and showed Kris the abstraction of his own chest hair. Kris laughed, frowned, and swallowed his *baraas* quickly, refilling his glass almost as if the stimulant would make him immune to Steel City's bizarre behaviour. He had led a very sheltered life on Oster's Fall.

He was glad to hear from Faulcon that, whereas on many civilized colony worlds voice and pigmentation transplants were

70

common, on VanderZande's World such extremes of body art were frowned upon.

Gradually Kris brought the idle conversation round to the subject of the great valley, and its ruins, and in particular its human ruin, the phantom. He repeated his feeling of urgency that he should get out to the lip of the canyon and look for that fleeting figure against the wreckage-strewn landscape. He glanced at Faulcon. Could he go out the next day?

Faulcon shook his head, concerned for the youngster, and concerned for the flaunting of Steel City rules. "I'm afraid not. It takes several days training in a suit . . . You can't just put an r-suit on and away you go. And the rules of the City are quite explicit about it; we had a lot of difficulty clearing the Ilmoroq mission so soon after you joined us, but we never underestimate the danger of the valley.'

Kris looked first crestfallen, then angry. "But Commander Ensavlion said I should get out there as soon as possible."

"Which is a three-day at least. Two if you really work hard."

"Ensavlion implied quite strongly that he thought I should go out to the valley *today! Tonight!*"

One glance at the impetuous Kris told Faulcon that this was a lie. Besides which, he'd heard no such implication, although he *had* heard Ensavlion encouraging the boy to train quickly so that he could become a fully fledged member of the team.

"Steel City has the final say, not Ensavlion." And by way of changing the subject and bringing the pressure down, Faulcon told Kris something of the team he'd joined.

When Faulcon had arrived on VanderZande's World, Lena had already been here a year. He had come with more than a hundred other rookies, a very bad error of application on his part, since it meant he had been assigned to a large, inexperienced team, led by one old hand, well-satiated with the wonders of Kamelios. It had taken a month to get his first circuit of the valley, and two months more before the team was allowed its first run down to the cluttered lower slopes of the rift. Thereafter, for a few weeks, he had worked as part of Ensavlion's ten-man team, the Commander at that time being head of Section 3.

At his own request, and against Lena's better judgement, he was finally taken on in Section 8, assigned to the team that had Lena as middle-runner and a man called Rick Kabazard as leader. By coincidence, Ensavlion transferred command at the same time.

Most of their trips down into the gash in the crust were for the purpose of investigating "hollow boats", the City nickname for any building or structure with an r-suit-sized opening in it, and a very dark maw. Most of his work, he told Kris, had been spent walking or crawling in dark and cramped corridors from one boring end to the other, or perhaps to a dead end at which point, frustrated, the team turned round and came out again. Where entrance-ways were tight it was traditionally the middle-runner who climbed out of the r-suit and squirmed in naked.

There was precious little by way of bonus for that sort of work, and Faulcon, and indeed Lena herself, began to get very restless. In fact, what was happening to them was perfectly common, and their feeling of being a bad-luck team was shared by virtually every other team in Section 8. Then, just twenty days or so ago, a time squall had thrown up several oblong structures, piled in random, chaotic fashion, and thought at first to be crystal formations of geological interest only. With a geologist from Section 14 the three of them had "run the rift", dropping down into the canyon some way from the object of exploration, and moving towards the destination in a wide line, wary for the sort of swirl of wind and time that had thrown the artifacts out of past or future. The obsidian crystals were some four hundred feet long, and forty wide, and were piled in threes, so that they towered well above the team. It was immediately apparent that the smooth surfaces were pitted in an artificial way, and that underneath, where the juxtaposed faces were not always aligned, there were knobs, buttons and panels.

Kabazard and the geologist discovered a low entrance-way, where the squall had unevenly fetched the object from its natural time; part of the back of the structure was sheared off, exposing thick, crystalline walls, and for men in r-suits an uncomfortably narrow tunnel-way in. The two men had entered, despite Lena's protestations that because this was not a geological

72

feature it should be she who went inside with the leader, and not the man from Section 14. Her protests ignored, she and Faulcon had continued exploring those parts of the outside of the feature that the view-probes in orbit and on the canyon-lip could not see.

The squall came back, a rising eddy of air and dust, and the dizzying blurring of features, and flashing of colours about an area of total black, that tells of the opening of the time gate. Faulcon could not forget Kabazard's screaming as the first eddy had sheared part of the structure away, and part of the leader's body. Faulcon was already hundreds of yards away, his suit obeying his unconscious instinct to run, and since he was now under total control of the cerebrally-linked servo-mechanism, he was able to turn and watch as the obsidian enigma was again swallowed by time, but in two bites, as if it were too large to be ingested in one go. And for that terrible instant, as the eddy veered away and then back, he saw Kabazard's bloody figure, cramped up inside the warren of tunnels that penetrated the structure, his right side sheared clean through, and the suit jerking spasmodically as it tried to function and failed. A second later he had flickered out of sight. By that time their r-suits had taken Lena and Faulcon well out of range of that danger spot.

"We didn't know it," he said to the silent, attentive Kris, "but Ensavlion had just accepted your application form, and logged you down for Section 8; you were already on your way, of course."

"I don't understand . . . I don't understand the connection."

Faulcon grinned. "Your luck, man! Your luck. It had reached across space and wrapped its arms around me. By rights it should have been Lena in that object, with the geologist waiting outside. By rights both Rick Kabazard and Lena should have died. And on this world we have special rules, as Ensavlion tried to tell you. If two of a three-man team get swallowed up by time, well. . . "

He had stopped, but Kris had comprehended. "He has to go too; he has to sacrifice himself."

Faulcon nodded. "It's a tradition that has grown up over

several generations; it's a rule of the game, a code, an unbreak-able code."

"But it's unhuman! It's stupid!"

"It's an inhuman world, Kris. It's a hard world and makes hard rules."

"I didn't say *in*human, I said *un*human. It doesn't sit right on man to agree to such self-sacrifice. It's wrong for man."

"This whole world is wrong, Kris. It's a world of constant change and it changes man along with it. If you spend long enough here your body and mind will be twisted and torn until sometimes you'll be walking when you're sitting and awake when you're asleep. Unless you fight it, like we've all fought it. Resist it, resist the change, resist until sometimes you'll want to scream. We've adapted to Kamelios, all of us, all the survivors. We've worked out our relationship with VanderZande's World, and we've mastered it. And the changes are all superficial, Kris —they don't get in deep down. Like Ensavlion said, we've learned how to live here, what to expect, how to react. Now we can get on with the business of exploring the alienness."

Warmed and slightly dizzy from the *baraas*, Faulcon felt a peculiar sense of pride in being on the world. Kris Dojaan watched him carefully, perhaps looking for some facial gesture that would belie the words. He said, "So man has no fear of Kamelios, or of time, or of the ruins."

"There is a gut fear of the time winds—they're dangerous.You don't treat danger in a casual, careless fashion. I'm afraid of the time winds, I'm afraid of being swept away—and I behave care-fully, respectfully. That's how I behave with loaded weapons, with gulgaroth, with everything that has a dangerous potential; especially with the winds. Nobody wants to go into time."

Kris's eyes lowered and he swirled the drink in his glass. "No-body?" he said. "Surely there must be a few adventurers, men sufficiently disillusioned with our world to kiss it goodbye and go to other ages."

Faulcon said, "You might think so. I think I remember think-ing so myself. I think. To be honest it's hard to remember, but it certainly seems a ludicrous idea to me now. And a terrifying

74

one. You'd literally have to be out of your mind to risk being swept away . . . The evidence of what animals we pick up in the valley, and where other winds blow, is enough to tell us that the atmosphere of Kamelios has altered vastly over the ages. You'd have to be mad."

"Or obsessed?" Kris was looking hard at his team mate, his youthful features tense, almost agonized, Faulcon thought. Was he referring to Ensavlion?

"Commander Ensavlion wouldn't risk it," he said. "The man is obsessed with his aliens, but he wants to see them here and now; he wants to invite them to Steel City for drinks and supper. He wants the glory, and you don't get glory if you're stuck a billion years in the past, or embedded in primeval sedimentary rock, with just your face plate gleaming through as erosion works its way down to you. There is such a corpse, Kris. It's at the farthest end of the valley, and it's been there a long time. I tell you, one look at that 'fossil' is enough to put anyone off stepping deliberately into the path of a squall; it lets you know that the time winds are death winds . . . when they take you, you *die*. Forget the romance. I can't forget Kabazard." Faulcon hesitated, conscious that his voice had risen, and his speech had begun to slur. "Besides," he said, "back to Ensavlion for a moment. He believes in the travellers, the alien time-travellers. Why risk death in the unknown when the travellers could teach us all we want to know? It's neat. That's why Ensavlion is not alone in his belief."

Silence, then. A brooding silence, despite the babble of conversation, and clatter of glasses in the extensive bar. Faulcon was thinking of Mark Dojaan. Was it Kris's brother who was emerging from the valley wall under the eroding influence of rain and ordinary wind? Most unlikely. And it was not Mark who was scurrying darkly about the canyon, Faulcon was sure of that as well. When Kris found the fact out for himself, what would his next step be? Faulcon was almost certain that it would be a step into the path of a wind, a deliberate suicide in the hope that it would not be suicide, but rather a mission of rescue.

Which of course it would not be. It *could* not be.

"How do you know", said Kris quietly, "that hundreds of men and women, trained people, people fully aware of the dangers, and the certainty of being forever lost, how do you know that there aren't hundreds such going out to the valley every night and slipping away into Othertime?"

It was a disturbing thought, and Faulcon felt the hair on his neck prickle as he tried to picture such teams slipping out in the darkness, descending the canyon walls, and stringing out, grabbing squalls and winds with joy, popping out of sight, some perhaps being sheared completely in half, or losing limbs, or bits of protective clothing. He had been out at night, and had never seen any such movement. There was no talk in Steel City about such events. But the rift valley was hundreds of miles long, and there were stations along its rim every twenty miles or so, stations big enough to accommodate a large population if that population was just passing through. And some of them had landing sites for the cargo shuttles from orbiting supply ships.

He said, "I give up. What's the answer?"

Kris laughed. "You don't know, is the answer. You can't know. Nobody in this steel-hulled hell-hole knows anything about what's *really* going on on VanderZande's World. You get up, go out, get a bonus, get drunk, get laid, go to bed . . . sleep. And in the night the world could stop, do a somersault and spit a hundred explorers into the world's Cambrian, and in the morning Leo Faulcon would still be thinking of *money* for *artifacts*, and how to survive another day, and what's he going to have for breakfast."

Faulcon poured himself another drink and wondered what was coming—hysteria, contempt, anger? It was difficult to gauge a man whom he had only known without a mask for a matter of hours.

He said, "I'm sorry if you're angry, but that's the way it is. I don't believe in your moonlight missions, because I don't believe that Steel City has a secret side to it. We hear about everything that goes on—"

"And don't give it another thought, right?"

"That's as may be," Faulcon agreed mildly, settling back and staring hard at the boy. Kris's face was white, his lips pinched, and Faulcon guessed that it was a recurrence of the grief he had felt at losing his brother, a grief now tempered with desperation . . . and yes, maybe a little contempt for Faulcon's mercenary, easy-going attitude. "That's as may be," he repeated, "But the point is, we've heard nothing. There are three-man teams, there are eight-man teams, there are solo riders, there are sections set up for liaison, for geology and chemistry, and there's a section kept ready for that much desired first contact. There are no time-travelling sections. I could account for every room, every level, every section, every Commander, every man, woman and child in Steel City and its environs. I could stop *anyone* and get a response from them as to what they're doing on the world, and it would fit with the routine scheme of things. Kamelios is not the last great frontier, Kris. There are no pioneers here, no covered wagons heading through the misty wall of years, back into the untamed lands of yesterday . . ." he briefly shared Kris's smile at the purple shade of his prose, ". . . the planet is an anomaly. The people here are monitoring that anomaly. A few are trying to understand it. Earth awaits their findings with interest, but hardly with baited breath."

Kris Dojaan shook his head, as if in sympathy with Faulcon's short-sightedness. "I can only assume that something about this place, or the society of men in Steel City, blinkers people like you. I hope it doesn't happen to me. I shan't be around long enough to find out if it will."

Faulcon waited quietly, watching his colleague. "What does that mean?"

"I mean, when I find Mark I'm going home. That's Mark out there . . . old, frail . . . maybe no longer the brother I knew in mind, or experience. But it's Mark, and I've come to take him home. To find him and take him back, because that's what my family wants, and it's what I want, and it was what Mark said to us before he left. He said to find him if anything went wrong, and when it went wrong he called to me and repeated

77

his plea." Seeing the quizzical expression on Faulcon's face, he shrugged. "We have this thing, this contact . . . a talk-space in our heads. As kids we played chess across half a planet's distance . . . we lived apart for a while, when our parents were split up. I'd always know the move he wanted to make, and he'd know mine. We're not twins, we just have talk-space. I heard him, Leo. I don't expect you to believe me, but believe that I *think* I hear him . . . he communicated with me, he called to me. And I've come a long way, and practically signed my life away, to get him back."

Quietly, Faulcon said, "Is a brother so important then?"

Kris's eyes were tearful. "Yes, he bloody well is."

Faulcon thought: what do I do? What do I say? The man is right to be wary of my motives, to be contemptuous of me. But what do I say to him to convince him he's being foolhardy? Kris Dojaan had reached across and was draining the *baraas* into Faulcon's glass. He smiled thinly, almost ashamedly. "I'm sorry, Leo. I shouldn't take it out on you. It's not your fault. I'm sobering up too fast. Let's have another bottle—this stuff's good."

Before he could turn to attract the attention of a waiter, however, Faulcon said, "That's not your brother out there, Kris. That's not Mark."

"You've implied that before." Kris was not hostile, just quiet, thoughtful. "If it's not Mark, then who is it?"

Faulcon stumbled on the words, not really wanting to antagonize the boy, to spoil the evening's celebrations; he was aware that Kris would probably react scornfully to the idea of Faulcon's truth, but he was afraid that the boy would be contemptuous, almost aggressive at what he might see as Faulcon's delusion. Before he could verbalize that truth he felt he should tell Kris, Kris said, "It's Mark. I just know it is. Mark had that survival streak in him, you know what I mean? He was a winner, a natural winner. It made me mad, sometimes . . . jealousy, envy, call it what you like. But others fed on his strength. You talk about luck, and me spreading luck; with Mark around, as kids, even in national service, everything went right; he was so confident, Leo. He made life a challenge, and he made it rich. And if anyone came back from Othertime, it was Mark. That was the sort of man he was. He was a winner, Leo, an absolute, survival-oriented, winning-streak of a man." He smiled. "That's why I know instinctively that it's Mark . . . he came back, Leo. He was lost, and he came home again. And he communicated to me . . . mind power, his mind power reaching across all those light years."

"Is he talking to you now?" asked Faulcon, but the dead tone of his voice was a sufficient indication of his cynicism to make Kris's face darken. The point went home. Faulcon moved quickly, sensing that it should be now or never, prepared for as many reactions from Kris Dojaan as he could foresee. "Kris, that's not your brother out there, it's you. You. Kris Dojaan, the young man of twenty who, in a few weeks' time, or a few years' time, will be snatched away by the winds, and will somehow make it back. The time phantom is you, yourself."

If Kris was momentarily stunned, laughter soon swept through him "Me? *Me*? Oh come on, Leo, come on. That's nonsense and you surely know it. Don't you think I could have sensed myself out there. . . ?"

"You sense your brother," Faulcon said stiffly. "But what you sense is something personal, and you are rationalizing it as your brother."

"I don't believe it. Anyway, what makes you so sure it's me? What makes you so sure it's anyone? I've got an empathy with Mark, and whilst I wouldn't call that any sort of *psychic* power, it's strong enough to . . . you know, it's an *affinity*. That's what I mean, an affinity, a spiritual affinity between us. . ."

"Talk-space."

"That's right, that's what we called it at home. And it communicates in some way other than by senses. But what are you using to be so damned sure it's me, and not Mark, or you yourself?"

Faulcon almost shouted with frustration. He placed his glass down on the table, glanced around guiltily as he realized that Kris's outburst had caused an embarrassed silence in this part of the bar. Gradually heads turned away, conversation resumed, and Faulcon faced Kris's aggressively triumphant features. The boy was drunk, that was clear enough. He was also getting very angry, very concerned. Faulcon didn't want to talk seriously in conditions such as this, but he felt he had no choice.

"Look, Kris. On the one hand you're claiming powers of empathy, on the other you're denying them. If you can believe an affinity between two brothers, living light years apart, why can't you believe in a heightening of extra-sensory powers on a world like this one, whose second name is Kamelios, think about that . . . Chameleon, the inconstant one, a world of changes, a world where nothing remains the same when it gets here. And that goes for people too. I came here thick and dull, sensually that is. Within a year my senses are sharp. I can hear better, I can see better, I can smell better even though I wear a mask outside, and I can *sense* better. Everybody here can do it. No, that's not true. Not everybody, perhaps not even half. But so *many* people experience it that it is a definite phenomenon. We develop special senses. Come on, Kris, it happens all over the colonized galaxy. Worlds have auras, and those auras impose different psychological constraints or enlargements upon an alien population."

"I know about that," said Kris, testily. "Homing, the shroud, all of that stuff."

Faulcon had not thought of Homing for a long time, and now, just briefly, he experienced it again in all its clenching, nostalgic, desperate sharpness—fields, cities, the smell of earth, the aura of Earth: the earth shroud within which man had evolved, the aura of the world that had become so deeply interpenetrated with the cells and substance of the animal body. It had marked humankind as belonging to a single world, and when they left that world the tie of the shroud was only broken with difficulty —it tugged at heart and mind, and could break spirit; it could destroy, and yet it could be destroyed itself. Homing. Homesickness. The voice of the earth, weakening, but always there.

"All that stuff," Faulcon echoed quietly. "That's right. And how do I know it's you out there? I felt a strong sense of

80

familiarity myself. I felt it suddenly, and agonizingly. A little voice in my head told me that you were doomed. I'm sorry to be so blunt, but it's one of the phenomena of this world that when someone gets 'marked down' for taking by the winds, when fate decides you're going to be lost in time, it communicates to some of those around you. It really does, Kris. I can't explain it, all I can say is that if you're here long enough you may well come to feel it yourself."

Kris stared at Faulcon, expressionless, but obviously intent. "What are you saying, Leo . . . that suddenly, a few hours ago, you felt, you *sensed*, that one of these fine days I'm going to slip into Othertime?"

"And the coincidence of your own familiarity with that phantom . . . it seems to add up, Kris."

"What I want to know is, why didn't you sense the impending doom of Kabazard? Your old leader."

"Rick Kabazard. Yes, a good point, and one I did wonder about . . . briefly. A man like Kabazard, doomed, doesn't sort of 'radiate' his fate; perhaps I gave that impression. There is a moment when your life takes a turn, links up with Kamelios. It's at that moment that you can 'feel' his fate, sense it. It had happened, with Kabazard, before I met him, before I spent time with him. He knew it, he must have known he was doomed, but he said nothing about it."

"All right, Leo. I'll accept that. I don't want to talk about it now, but Leo . . ." he smiled and leaned forward; the amulet swung free and struck against the glass he held with a short, ringing sound. Kris raised the star to his lips just briefly. "Leo, it should be *obvious* to you that I'm going to slip into Othertime. For God's sake, that's the whole reason I came here. I've got to find Mark. I came quite prepared to chase him through Othertime, to seek him out. I still am, and I know that I may have to pursue his withered body through the years, to give him the confidence to return. I shall do it. So of course you sensed my impending 'doom'. But what makes you so sure that the *phantom* is me? I don't understand that."

Faulcon shrugged, *baraas* dimming his vision and his facul-

81

ties. How to explain that sudden surge of understanding, that moment's intuition? And how often that intuition had been proven wrong. "You identified with the phantom, I identified you as fated to be lost to time. I think two and two make four. I agree, we could both be very wrong. You *want* to find Mark, and I don't comprehend the way VanderZande's World affects my mind. Or anybody's mind, come to that."

"Here's to madness!" Kris, having replenished their glasses from a new bottle of *baraas*, raised his drink towards Faulcon, who responded, smiling. "To madness."

The long Kamelion dusk ended, the light outside Steel City deepening from red to grey as the ancient sun was swallowed by the mist-shrouded mountains of the west. The nearby land was an eerie nightscape of scattered lights and winking green signal-points, marking danger zones and trackways through the jagged rocks. Steel City was a brilliant jewel, glowing with internal light, yet still reflecting the redness of Altuxor; a fire-lit ruby, the installation entered its evening phase. From the bar where Faulcon sat he could see the warm glow of life in the cabins and restaurants below them, and in shops and work-places in two of the traverse units. But as yet, though he tried, he could not see the stars.

At the musical disturbance of nine chimes they rose from the bar and made their way to where Lena Tanoway had just arrived in the Star Lounge. She was dressed more casually, now, in wide trousers and a green, many-layered shirt, the folds of cloth tumbling across her breasts most erotically, as far as Faulcon was concerned. She had trimmed her hair, and tightly curled it about the rim of her skull. The sideburns that Kris found so idiotic were hardly in evidence. She smelled faintly of musk, faintly of soap, and Faulcon felt his mouth go dry. Raw jealousy, the belief that Lena had been up to the flesh farm since he had not gone with her, made him angry with himself; the drink made him emotional; his maleness made him resentful.

82

Inside he twisted up as he said, with affected relaxedness, "It's good to see you. And you look gorgeous."

Lena smiled at the compliment, and as they took their places in the lounge she cast a cynical glance at Faulcon and said, "One bottle or two? Each?"

Faulcon made a gesture with his hand: more than one, less than two.

"You reek. Both of you. I'm surprised you're still standing."

"We've been arguing," Kris observed politely. "And now we're friends again. Isn't that right, Leo?"

"Kris won't believe that we sense certain things," explained Faulcon, and Lena stared at him hard. "Won't he?" she said, and it was apparent to Faulcon that she was less bothered by the cause of the argument than by something in Faulcon's demeanour, his behaviour; he sobered quite abruptly, met her gaze coolly. *Please don't say anything, not yet, not yet.* She said, "That's enough of that, anyway. I want to eat, to talk about our next few days—we have to train Mister Dojaan here to ride an r-suit, but on the other hand it *is* our vacation, and only three days to offload a vast number of g.u.'s. That's going to take some organization, gentlemen." She looked at Faulcon again, but the hardness was gone; Faulcon felt himself go tense, and then warm with love. She was smiling very faintly, but her eyes communicated more than she ever allowed her words to say. "After dinner, Kris, you will excuse us I'm sure."

"I suppose so," Kris said glumly. "But haven't you got a sister?"

They toasted a good week's work. The two meat-eaters ate snails in their shells, imported from the farms on nearby *Cyrala 7* and cooked in garlic and tasselroot sauce. Faulcon indulged himself, then, with a white meat called *beliwak*, from a non-terrestrial animal with an analogous amnio-acid structure to Earth animals (the *beliwak* had probably been seeded in the early days, and no record kept), which had a strong taste, and made Kris blanch as Faulcon offered him a morsel. He said it smelled rotten. Faulcon explained that it was allowed to deterio-rate in a special liquid containing herbs and bleaching for nearly two months. Kris blanched even further. He himself, being a principled vegetarian, ate a spiced dal made from lentils grown in the colonial communities hereabouts. He was particularly taken with coddleneep in red wine sauce, a native root plant and a recipe acquired from the manchanged colonies, high in the foothills of the Jaraquath mountains. Its flavour was not unlike strong game-bird (although only Faulcon recognized this fact). Kris thought it was excellent, and seemed doubly delighted to be eating an "alien" plant, since on Oster's Fall everything was earth-seeded.

The meal for three came to eight hundred g.u.'s, ten times what they would normally have expected to pay.

Kris excused himself eventually, and Lena and Faulcon walked hand in hand down to the occupation levels, and to Faulcon's quarters. Lena was warm, communicative. Perhaps the tension of leading the team for a seven-day had drained away, leaving her relaxed, aware of those parts of her body and mind that were not concerned with VanderZande's World, and work, and aliens; parts concerned with love, and Leo Faulcon.

In the soft light of Faulcon's room her body lost much of the hardness imposed upon it by training and life on Kamelios; they stood in each other's arms, close, warm, eyes shut, lips playing gently on each other's skin as they fed on the peace and tranquillity of this first embrace since the mission.

Lena kissed Faulcon on the mouth, then said, "You followed me to this world. . ."

"I wasn't going to lose you. I was determined about that."

"I know. You followed me here, I suppose it's only right that I should follow you away from here, to your own world."

Faulcon smiled. "I don't mind where we go. The problem is, how can we break with Kamelios?"

They drew apart and hand-in-hand stood by the window, looking out across the brilliantly-lit slopes and surface walks of the city. The nightscape beyond was visible only as a series of red and green lights; their own shapes moved, ghostly, tenuous, in the glass. Above the land Merlin showed its face from behind bright Kytara, the two planetoids skipping ahead of tiny, pale-

84

faced Aardwind—the moons were insubstantial half-discs, seen as in a pond.

"Do you realize", Faulcon said quietly, "that we have just acknowledged how trapped we are by this planet?" It was something they had never discussed, something, a knowledge, that all on VanderZande's World denied. Faulcon realized, now, that the denial of this particular reality had been a barrier between them, indeed, was a barrier between all men on Kamelios.

Perhaps trapped was the wrong word, with its connotation of imprisonment and desire to escape. Lena said, "We've become masters of Kamelios, we've learned to live on the world, to use the world, and we've changed. We've both changed, Leo. Our ambitions are the ambitions of just about everybody who ends up in Steel City, and not on the farms: discovery, investigation, the finding of *something*. . ."

It was a feeling with which Faulcon was well familiar—the sense of having a goal, of seeking something, even though he could not voice, or articulate, exactly what it *was* he was seeking. And the thought of leaving Kamelios was terrifying—the thought of distance between himself and the valley and time and ruins. What contrary creatures we are, he thought—on the one hand cold, contemptuous, uninterested in time's derelicts, but trapped by the need to discover something within those remains.

"Perhaps we should just go—right now," he said. "People *have* left Steel City. We should just drive out to the landing strip and wait for a shuttle. What do you think?"

Lena said, "That would be the only way. Just up and go. Don't think about it, don't think of the valley. Just leave; Leo, I truly want to leave here, to go somewhere dull and simple, Earth perhaps, or any farming world. Why don't we do it?"

Faulcon found himself in the grip of a sudden panic, a claustrophobic sensation, the room closing in, the air straining his lungs, the beast of blood through his head loud and physically violent. "We should do it tomorrow," he said, and there was no real heart to his words. "Why don't we see how we feel in the morning?"

If Lena felt like laughing she restrained it well. Hugging Faulcon, she agreed quietly. "We change our minds so often, Leo—we really will have to move fast when we move."

"We've adapted to the world, as you say. We're in control here, but the price has been heavy, very heavy."

Sometime during the early part of the night a *fiersig* drifted from the hills, and across the valley, causing a change to pass through Steel City. Faulcon felt it without realizing what it was for a while; the shivering sensation, the sudden change of mood, the sudden feeling of irritation, excitement, a quickening of heart and mind, a livening of the spirit.

Immediately he began to breathe deeply, heavily, his eyes shut, his mind fixed on the idea of permanence. With each second that passed he felt the vaulting, tumbling mix of emotions, a confused and frightening jumble of anger and fear, of humour and indifference. He bit the flesh inside his mouth as he resisted the probing fingers of the *fiersig*, fought to keep the mood of love and determination he had shared with Lena just hours before.

He began to groan, then cry with the effort of resistance, but he was winning—he sensed he was winning, he *knew* he was beating it. His cries woke Lena. "It's all right," he said, and then was quiet, deciding against further words, for words were dangerous while the *fiersig* passed.

Lena sat up, not looking at him, disturbed by the change herself. Faulcon stepped down from the couch and dressed. His mind was fresh and alert, as it always was during a mood disturbance; he left the room without a glance back, aware of the sounds of Lena's efforts to block the change, and walked up to the Skyport at the top of the Riftwatch Tower.

The strange lights in the alien sky were brilliant, and crowds of people were drifting up to the lounges to observe them: streaks of red and green breaking across the night and fading, then the spirals and circles of yellow, sparkling gold, zigzagging between the stars, racing across the nightscape from one horizon to another, it seemed, in the twinkling of an eye . . . more reds, breaking and dividing, curving about and dissipating in startlingly bright explosions; then winking, flashing purples, drifting between the gold and red-streaked chaos in serene fashion. The whole fiery display of atmospheric energy passed above the city and away into the night in a little over half an hour.

Faulcon heard laughter, then, and some shouting: the usual heated debates as to whether the *fiersig* might be intelligent life-forms; the usual empty arguments. The restaurants and bars were closing down as temperaments altered and relationships shifted in the delicate balance of intellect and instinct that had brought people together a few hours before. People needed time to adjust, time to think. Clothes were shed, bodies and souls bared to the unseen, unknown fingers of Kamelios, defying them to try and wreak change upon the individual. Figures walked naked, unsure, through the corridors and across the softly undulating floors of the relaxation lounges.

Faulcon saw Lena there, moody, depressed. He walked across to her, and tried to speak to her, but she shrugged him away and walked back to her own quarters, all her earlier energy dissipated in an instant.

PART TWO

The Phantom of the Valley

CHAPTER SIX

An immense black shape, manlike yet not a man, passed out through Steel City's southern gateway and moved swiftly across the brightly lit land surrounding the silent installation. Within seconds it was entering darkness, its form visible only by the occasional reflection of light on its smooth metal bulk. Soon it was gone.

An r-suit could move fast under direct human control, but at night the terrain between the City and the deep canyon was hazardous, and the man moved slowly, following, after a while, the lines of green and red lights that marked out smoothed trackways to the lip of the gorge. In the windless night the servo-mechanisms of the suit made distinct whirring sounds, but as he drew near to the valley a fresh and gusty breeze blew up, and only the fleeting glimpse of a tall shape, or a momentary rattle of rocks, told of the passing of the stranger.

At length the alien canyon yawned before him, and even the suddenly activated light from the helmet of the suit showed only blackness. Bright stars, and the glow of the moon Three-light, permitted glimpses of the structures below . . . Here a gleaming, greenish plate, there a twisting spiral of blue and silver, fragments of sparkling red catching the eye from among large, amorphous areas of nightblack.

The man turned and began to run his suit along the trackway that bordered the canyon's edge. Soon the city was a long way behind, an area of bright yellow light that reached up into the sky, and gave the horizon behind him an eerie glow. In the distance, on both sides of the valley, were the smaller, less inviting lights of the Watch Stations. A sedately moving light in the sky, passing across the Kamelion constellation of the Axe, was the great orbiting refuge known as Night Eye Station, but it was well to the west, and its banks of cameras would not be directed here, not so far away from its present route across the world.

The rift suit moved on, seemingly of its own volition. The man inside relaxed physically, but remained watchful for movement on the canyon's rim, and for movement and light in the darkness below him. The suit had run this route many times before. It reached into the man's mind, snatched its instructions from the imprinted repetition of activity it found there. It powered the legs and the helmet, it kept the arms comfortable, and it sniffed and probed the ground ahead, all in the twinkling of a star, each movement a co-ordinated movement, happening between mind and machine, taking the man on his circuitous pilgrimage about the gorge.

Soon it stopped, bracing itself almost at the very edge of the drop. Although viewing from within was easy through the wide, outwardly curved face plate, the helmet turned. Through the darkness the man could almost see the shapes and shards that crowded the deep cut in the world, the cubes and spheres, the girders and jagged edges of once-proud, once-living structures. But to his eyes, and to his immediate awareness, there was only blackness.

And yet not so long ago. . .

His eyes, and the helmet of the r-suit, found the place where the creatures had come, where the golden glow of their machine had lit the dusk with a different fire to the red light of Altuxor. The emanation had seemed to fill the valley, to radiate to heaven itself. The glow had been warm. His r-suit had consciously adjusted its temperature to maintain the comfort of the startled, overwhelmed occupant within. Then the shapes had gone, the golden machine had vanished into time. The moving creatures, glimpsed so quickly, so imperfectly as they stepped through the sloping side, had taken their minds and their awarenesses elsewhere in the cosmic vastness of the single world; to times beyond.

Darkness. He watched that darkness, and hours came and went, and soon he moved on, further from Steel City, disappointment drying him, and choking him, nagging him as it always nagged him, distracting him as it had distracted him a hundred times before. They had not returned; but surely one night they would. They *had* to return, they *had* to.

And so as he ran, as the darkness passed him by, as the r-suit plundered the miles. its monotonous movement regular and steady, so his mind went out: upwards to the stars, downwards to the earth, sideways and inwards to the rift, to the unconscious minds that he *knew* must be listening from the eternal void of time.

I'm here, I'm here ... please show yourselves ... please come back ... please communicate...

But Kamelios answered him as it always answered him, with wind, with stillness broken by a gusting breeze, with the cold light of stars, with the chasm and the dead things that lay therein.

He passed widely by the ruined Riftwatch Station Eekhaut, and returned to the edge of the world of man. Suddenly he began to run faster, looking away from the valley, away across the hills to the north where—had he the necessary magnification on his face plate—he might have seen the tiny lights and fires of one of the human townships.

And gradually the suit stopped, and turned back to the gorge, though the man inside the machine was anxious to pass on. And yet he had sensed it would stop, just as he sensed that there was some meaning to the sudden hastening of the suit's progress whenever he passed the ruined Riftwatch Station.

It stood there and watched the darkness of the deep void, and the man watched that same darkness, and felt the suit's arm raise and point to a place in the emptiness where he knew he had been before.

Aloud he said, "Move on," but the suit stayed still, its arm pointing, its helmet turned sideways, looking down, so that he could stare through the clearest part of the visor at the place where the wind ... where the screams...

He could hear the screaming now, a banshee wailing, the sound of awareness of death, the sound of a drowning man.

"Move *on!*"

Standing silent and still, the r-suit disobeyed the verbal order, but in truth it disobeyed nothing, for it drew its power and its commands not from the voice but from the mind, and in his mind the man did not want to move; he wanted to stand here and remember, and re-live, and become aware again of that thing which he had forced from his mind, that inaction that he had expunged from his existence, and had thus taken from that area of responsibility and morality that dictated to his conscience.

The time winds broke distantly, booming and thundering, darkening the sky. They swept close, bringing time and change, bringing destruction and creation, driving away the ordered ruins in a fleeting moment of visual chaos, only to vanish westwards up the gorge leaving a new order, a new stillness. The arm of the suit pointed in the darkness, the stiff metallic finger an arrow of guilt drawn tense in the bow, ready to discharge itself into the man's heart. Through the dark quiet he could hear the wind, he could see the struggling shape of the man, caught in the tight angle of two alien structures. Through the suit receiver the voice was hysterical, fear-filled, terrified: help me, for God's sake don't just stand there, help me!

They might come, they might come behind the wind

Help me!

I saw them before, golden creatures in a golden machine, they came behind a wind for

For God's sake!

a second, they were there, a second, golden, creatures, second

Don't just!

after the wind, watching me, watching them, intelligent time-travelling beings

Stand there!

I must watch, I must watch, I can't go down ... the wind too strong too fast ... I can't go down . . get free, wriggle free ... creatures coming, golden machine

HELP ME! HELP ME!

I can't. I won't! I might miss them!

The arm of the suit dropped. In the stillness the man's voice was a strange keening, that broke into the sound of sobbing, that suddenly cried out through the dark night, that gave vent to its frustration and fear and guilt. "He had to come! He had to remind me!"

The suit moved away, running fast and furious, the man's legs drawn up to his chest so that he rode within his machine in a crouched position, the mechanical legs pounding the cliff top at speeds faster than a human limb could tolerate. He tried to race his shame, to outrun his fear, to leave behind the need to tell the boy, to say something, to tell him how his brother had died, and how he had seen the death, and how he had stood there and done nothing. But all these things were carried by the suit as well, and the faster he ran, the faster they span in his mind, and blurred his vision, and dulled his senses.

But soon his blood cooled and the tears on his face no longer tickled their message of weakness. The suit slowed, and stopped, and turned about, facing the distant glow of the city, staring there now because the man wished to stare there. And when it moved it was because he wished to go home.

CHAPTER SEVEN

Kris Dojaan's impatience to go out to Kriakta Rift, and seek out the time phantom, made him a willing trainee, a hard worker, and an exhausting student; it also boiled over, on several occasions, into an anger of frustration, against which Lena was forced to pull her rank. Much of the next two days was spent in silence, the sullenness almost physical. And Kris was tired, too, Faulcon couldn't help but notice that, the weariness and pallor in the youngster's cheeks. Yet he worked hard, and could give his team mates no cause for dissatisfaction.

Lena and Faulcon took it in turns, three hours a session, to teach the boy the function, structure, use and dangers of the rift suits, the protective armoured mobile-environments that were often all that stood between a man and the endlessness of Other-time.

The suits were not just bulky, they were immense. Even a largely built man seemed no more than a stick insect within the voluminous confines of the machine, his arms padded and cush-ioned in the severally-jointed upper limbs, his body supported naturally and comfortably within the body space, surrounded by tubes, the ridged coverings of crystalline power transmuters, the brightly marked "organs", each the dispenser of some survival in-gredient. Inside the suit it was soon easy to forget that you were riding a structure half again as high as your own body, with five times your body's volume; your legs dangled free and comfort-able into the cavernous thigh of the suit—the "idea" of walking was enhanced by the slight pedal pressure available if a normal walking action was undertaken. The silent, swift response of the suit, walking as you wished it to, belied the power available to it if escape action was needed: at two hundred miles an hour it gripped you somewhat more firmly, pulled your legs up to your chest, free of the limbs which now moved like pistons, almost blurringly fast, taking the body away from danger as an athlete sprinting for the finish line.

On the first day, after completing their mission reports, they introduced Kris to his personal r-suit, sealed him in, and let him experience the frightening disorientation, and uncoordination, of a machine that was overwhelmed by his conflicting conscious orders. They were in the special environment, in one of the low levels of traverse unit *Pearl*. Kris's preliminary running-falling-turning-tripping activity was hilariously funny to watch, al-though Kris himself was less amused. Nevertheless, that first training session helped to lighten the moodiness that was still residual from the passage of the *fiersig*, the night before. Kris had been violently affected by it, he said, and had thought he

was going out of his mind. Perhaps that accounted for his tired-
ness, Faulcon thought, and reassured him.

Within a day, after that shaky start, Kris was making good
progress, at ease with the suit, and with the irritating skull con-
tacts that always pressed harder than expected, and which could
become a source of intense itching, or aching, or other psychological manifestation of newness and new awareness.

On the second day, again ignoring Kris's protests and claims
that he was ready and able to go out at least *near* to the rift, they
took him on a south run, through the hills and stumpy forests of
Tokranda County, and along the wide, stone roadways that
linked the townships. Immediately on passing out of the protective walls of Steel City Faulcon felt his unease at being close
to Kris Dojaan surface again, the awful fear of time's grasp that
can infect men close to one whose fate has been ordained. But
as they put distance between the rift and themselves, the concern fell away, itself outdistanced, perhaps.

Kris had little time, as they ran, to observe the sprawling
areas of wood and brick houses, smoke rising from primitive
chimney stacks, animals and men practically indistinguishable
against the muddy backgrounds of their communities; even
their clothes, skin and farmhouses seemed stitched into the
visual fabric of Kamelios. The towns were often this primitive,
although they drew much in the way of luxury and services
from the Federation installations around them, in particular
Steel City itself.

The people who lived here maintained close links with their
home-worlds, and the governing and economic bodies that had,
in part, financed their colonization. The simple use of primitive
building materials was as much due to the smallness of those
financial contributions as to the widely felt principle that it was
important to build using the world and its resources, and not
depend from the outset upon the imported materials that could
make an air-tight, heat-tight living unit. It was true, also, that
most external finance was channelled into medical supplies, for
while the hundreds of tiny communities in each county could
support themselves from their hunting and farmlands, they were

unable to produce that natural resistance to disease organisms and pollen that the manchanged (whom they loathed) could achieve. These lowland communities had opted for the middle ground, a toughing-it-out type of colonization, more integrated with Kamelios than the "instals" of Steel City and its associated supply and watch stations, but not prepared to undertake the violent, and grotesque, bio-adaptive processes of the manchanged, whose territories were well away to the south.

The lowland farmers wore breathing and eating masks against the organic ravages of the world, but within their houses they took advantage of technology to maintain a tolerably low organic level, and by generations, and agony, would come to terms with the environment.

The mountain road through Tokranda County meandered through the settlements, then turned to run, no more than a track, along the edges of the dusty, white-wood forests. Faulcon led the others along this track, in a suit-programme designed to test each and every reflex in their new team mate's body.

Kris ran and walked and became adept at living within his suit; he became expert at controlling it. He learned to relax as the suit's internal mechanisms gently manipulated his body . . . Turning, for example, made him feel as if four hands were pushing him into the direction of the turn. Starting to run gave a sensation of being lifted bodily. To slow gave pressure on chest and back, and made him feel as if gentle hands gripped his skull. The final practice on the run-back that second day was allowing his body to be squeezed into the crouched position preparatory for a rapid run. His suit was not yet programmed for that, but he went through the motions of snap-shutting his eyes, opening his mouth and letting his legs be painfully pushed up out of the thick, highly-motored legs of the machine. Each time this happened he found his knees jarring agonizingly on the front of the thigh region of the armour. Buttock to knee he was two feet in length, and the suit, built to accommodate the longness of this body section of his, was dangerously close to inefficiency with its mid-quarters so bulky.

The mechanism demonstrably worked, however, and when

the suit decided to move Kris out of danger, it would work again; it would skin his knees, maybe even break them (this was not unknown); that discomfort, Kris was assured, was far better than the alternative.

As they moved at forty miles an hour, back through the farmlands in the hills, towards Steel City, Kris complained bitterly that he would have to spend a third day training, this time at the bone-wrenching speeds of 150–200 mph. But, since there was no escape from a time wind in an upwards direction, this was the suit's primary function, and it was the hardest function to live with.

He was still bitching when they crossed the dirt trackway that skirted one of the townships and came suit to face with a straggling band of manchanged.

"Who the hell are they?" rasped Kris, the surprise and revulsion clearly evident in his voice. Faulcon was still moving along the track, towards the hesitant group. Now he stopped, turned, and snapped at the youngster, "Keep your mouth shut, Kris. These are manchanged."

The manchanged were a group of twelve individuals, six males, four females, and two drawn-faced rather ragged children. Faulcon thought he recognized the leader at once and lifted a hand as a gesture of greeting.

The whole group stopped, visibly tensing. Enormous, bulging eyes stared at Faulcon, mouths opened and closed, taking tiny gasps of breath. Skin, white and unpleasant looking, flushed slightly, a bluish grey colour, not the red flush that Faulcon was used to. They looked, otherwise, perfectly human, and of course that was exactly what they were. Humankind, changed to accept the organic poisons of the world, to be able to see without their eyes melting away, to breathe without corroding the linings of their respiratory tracts.

The sight of three towering, threatening armoured-suits was discomforting them greatly. Manchanged were rare visitors to the lower lands, especially to the communities and installations along Kriakta Rift. They brought sun-dew, of course, bright yellow crystals that formed in the deep earth, and were useful—

99

though not essential—to the power supplies of Steel City. It was diplomatic trade, and the only reason for a manchanged group to be this far north.

Faulcon saw the several sacks of the precious substance, carried by the men. It would have been a long walk from their plateau. They would be glad to get rid of the crystals.

Switching on his exvox, Faulcon said, "I'm sorry if we startled you. Please don't be afraid. We're only training."

The older man who led the group stepped forward and raised both hands. "We're not afraid. Just startled, as you said. We're taking sun-dew to the City."

"So I see." The nagging familiarity of the man's face made Faulcon strain to remember where he had met this particular manchanged before. "Are you the man Audwyn? I seem to recognize you."

The manchanged smiled; his face could not show surprise. "Yes, I am. I am Audwyn." He came right up to Faulcon's suit and stared into the helmet. "The gulgaroth hunter—is it you in there?" He seemed pleased.

"Leo Faulcon. Yes. Hello again."

As best they could, manchanged and armoured-suit shook hands. Much of Faulcon's unease slipped away in those few moments. He stood and stared at the strange man before him, half wanting to get away from the unpredictable creatures, half remembering the occasion, those months back, when his presence in the foothills of the Jaraquath mountains had marked a meeting of destinies, his and Audwyn's; his snap-shot had caught the rogue gulgaroth in mid-leap, saving the unsuspecting manchanged from the particularly hideous death that the beasts imparted to their human prey. Gulgaroth did not usually feed on man, but somewhere in the half-awareness of their brain-masses they felt resentment for the alien intruders on their domain.

Behind Faulcon, Lena murmured, "Let's go, Leo. We have a lot to do. Come on."

Perhaps Audwyn sensed the restlessness, the discomfort of the group of rifters. A hint of a smile touched his lips, making

Faulcon feel at one and the same time both guilty and irritated. There was little love lost between the two types of human— didn't rifters refer to the manchanged as "manks", a particularly unpleasant epithet—and little trust. The manchanged were withdrawn, hostile to outsiders, and hid away in their plateau-based communities, learning their own rules about VanderZande's World.

"Would you carry our crystals to the City?" asked Audwyn. "It would save us a day's walk, and your suits. . ."

"Can carry tons. Yes, of course, we'd be happy to. But don't you want paying . . . trade?"

Audwyn said, "This is final settlement for several boxes of metal shapes. Thank you." And he turned from Faulcon, gesturing to the rest of his band. The group turned and began to walk back towards the far mountains.

There were five sacks of sun-dew and Faulcon carried the single, largest. They continued on their way towards Steel City, just visible in the distance, beyond the band of tall, twisted chalk formations that was Whitefinger Row. The nearest of the colonies to Steel City lay the other side of the desiccated area, on ground that rose slightly towards the edge of the canyon. As they ran, Lena queried the occasion on which Faulcon had previously met the manchanged. "I didn't know you went off alone so much," she said, as Faulcon described the unexpected turn of events during his routine stalking of a male gulgaroth that had left its forest haunts and climbed into the foothills.

"I like to be alone at times—"

"Don't I know it."

"I went hunting more in the early months. I found it relaxing."

Lena made a sound like a laugh, but without humour. "You didn't seem very relaxed when I came with you."

They arrived back at the City in mid-afternoon, all three of them sweaty with effort, although the suits had kept them otherwise comfortable. They powered into the shedding lounge and switched off suit power. Instantly the three towering structures froze into silent stiffness. The backs opened and with difficulty

Faulcon hauled himself out into the cool room, shivering as the fresh air around him made the clinging sweat of his woollen undergarment cold and clammy.

When Kris was with him Faulcon stared up at the r-suit helmets and said, "Are you beginning to get the idea that if Steel City regards these monstrosities as necessary for survival, then the rift valley is not quite the day-trip, picnic-view area that you seem to think it is?"

Kris grimaced as he stared at the suits. "They're so damned ugly."

"You should have seen the man who designed them," said Lena coldly. She was still moody, and slightly depressed, but the worst effects of the abrupt changes brought about that evening, two nights before, had mellowed as her real personality inched through again. Faulcon himself felt tired, short-tempered. He had not slept well, mainly because he had been eating rich foods, and drinking too much *injuzan*, an alcoholic drink with a high caffeine content. Similar indulgence was possibly the reason for Kris Dojaan's weary features, and his constant, nagging complaints about the continuing denial of his access to the valley area.

Later that day, during the slide show in which the final structural and functional suit mechanisms were explained to the bored and drowsy recruit, Commander Ensavlion stepped into the room and stood silently watching the small company. When Lena noticed the man she switched off the projector, and Faulcon and Kris rose to their feet, uneasy with the intrusion.

Ensavlion had been a frequent observer during Kris's training. On the second day his loping form, r-suit clad, had dogged their tracks for several miles before vanishing, presumably to change course and head back to the valley, to stand and watch, awhile, for a sign of the travellers. The Commander had said nothing and in no way interfered, but it was apparent that he was taking an immense interest in the new recruit, and equally apparent that something about him was disturbing Kris.

"He makes me shiver," Kris had confessed the evening before, whilst they were still out on a short run. "He just watches me, and never smiles, just frowns. Then he waves and walks away."

"He's taken an interest in you," said Faulcon. "He's not the only one. The story of the luck you've brought our team is quite widespread now. You're a minor celebrity."

"I don't think it's anything to do with the machine we found," said Kris quietly. They had been resting, still in their suits, and were preparing to make their way back to the City. "I think it's my brother. I think he knows something more about Mark's loss into time and he doesn't know how or when to tell me. It has to be that, doesn't it, Leo? He was Mark's Section Commander, and it was Ensavlion who wrote to my family, telling us of Mark's heroic death during an assignment. Now he seems to fight shy of even mentioning my brother's name; but it's obvious he hasn't forgotten him. I know you only knew Mark in passing, but can you remember anything that happened back then, anything between Mark and Ensavlion?"

"It's easy to forget things on VanderZande's World," said Lena quietly; she was uncomfortable with the discussion.

Faulcon laughed bitterly as he agreed. "And when you forget caution, you forget everything. But you may be right about Ensavlion. It may well disturb him that you've come. One man dies, and his brother comes almost to take his place . . . I'd imagine the old man is feeling the responsibility he may have to bear if you fall foul of the winds."

It was Kris's turn to laugh. The pale features that regarded Faulcon from behind the gleaming face plate seemed almost stretched into a smile. "Do you realize you said 'if' and not 'when'?"

"So I did. I must be taking you for granted."

Now, in the Visual Education room, Ensavlion waved Lena back to work: "Please carry on with the programme. Leo, would you step outside a moment, please?"

As the room darkened again, and Kris settled glumly back in his seat, eyes fixed on yet another cutaway of an r-suit, Faulcon followed Commander Ensavlion into the passageway, and the two men walked slowly towards the main through-way.

"How's the training programme going? Well, I hope."

"He's very adept, very keen," agreed Faulcon. "He's half an inch too long for total comfort in an r-suit."

Ensavlion seemed slightly amused. "Cumbersome bloody things. And so damned impractical."

"So Kris Dojaan has been pointing out to me for two days. He's overwhelmed by how primitive much of Steel City is . . . masks, bykes instead of air-platforms, force-fields only on the entrance-ways. You'd think he came from Earth, the way he misses technology. But the r-suits, they annoy him most of all."

Ensavlion shook his head. "He has a dream about how advanced it's possible to be; he'd never even experienced space-flight before he came here, and he's disappointed not to be able to float around as if by levitation. And he has no idea of cash flow in the Galaxy. He thinks force-fields grow on trees. As for the suits, there'll be a new design up from Base Seventeen soon; hopefully it'll be less restrictive—and smaller in size." He was silent for a moment, and Faulcon wondered whether he should stop his slow amble, indicating his wish to return to the VE room. But Ensavlion said, "What stage is he at?"

"Kris? He takes a fast run with Lena, tomorrow."

"And the canyon the day after?"

"Or later in the day. He's itching to get out there; he can't understand the delay and our refusal to let him just go and see it, to peer over the edge."

Ensavlion slapped his hands together behind his back, turned to Faulcon as he stopped walking, and Faulcon saw the mixture of pleasure and concern in the Commander's face. "That's good," he said. "The boy has a good potential. But you won't let him go to the canyon until he's fully ready; you won't flaunt the rules, will you, Leo?"

"Of course not, Commander." He didn't add that it had been Ensavlion's encouragement that had given Kris high hopes of a rapid access.

Ensavlion looked back towards the room. "I wouldn't want anything going wrong. I don't think he fully comprehends the danger, and the nature of death on this world, not yet, not fully.

You'll help him understand that. You didn't mind taking over the training yourselves, did you?"

"Good heavens, no," said Faulcon, but Ensavlion was carrying on along his own train of thought: "I trust you, you see, Leo. I trust you to look after him. I don't want us to lose the man."

Ensavlion's stare was hard, and yet Faulcon detected the concern behind the grey eyes, a more personal concern than just a Commander worried for the well-being of an impetuous recruit.

Faulcon knew his own face was pale, and he could taste bitterness himself; the blood seemed to have stilled in his body as he stood with the Section chief and contemplated the nature of Kris Dojaan's tragedy. Finally Faulcon said, "With respect, Commander. . ."

Ensavlion silenced him with an abrupt shake of the head, and a hint of a smile. "I know what you're going to say, Leo. I must talk about his brother Mark. I must take the boy aside and talk about Mark Dojaan, and let him know that we *do* care, that we *do* live with our responsibilities; and our tragedies; and that a man like Mark Dojaan isn't wasted for nothing. Have you said anything to him yet? About Mark?"

"Very little. He seems to be expecting more from you."

Faulcon saw the alarm in Ensavlion's mind, a brief glimpse of the passionate unease that he wore with such outward calm. "I'll be frank with you, Leo. I don't know how to do it; I am afraid that the words will not come, and I dare not show weakness to the youngster. You and I, Leo, we know each other; not well, but we have worked together, and we have seen through each other's masks. But Kris Dojaan has come here with an image of his brother, with a belief in his brother's strength of spirit, and we must keep that belief alive, for his sake; and he must not see Kamelios and Steel City as they really are until he has come to comprehend the nature and facts of his brother's death. But how do we explain to him without shaking his belief in the orderly and directioned existence of his race on this world?"

Much of the agony that Ensavlion was attempting to communicate was lost on Faulcon, who had concerns of his own, and he let a long moment pass when the Commander had finished speaking while he tried to divine what was the best course of action now. He finally decided to tell Ensavlion of Kris's belief in the return of his brother Mark as the so-called phantom. Ensavlion was surprised by that, and then concerned again. "It's not possible. Keep an eye on him; the phantom is still about, so I heard. . ."

"The phantom is *always* about. Somewhere, someone sees him. . ."

"Right. And if Kris hears he might take it into his head to slip out this evening. I will have to hold you responsible for that if it occurs. . ."

Dully, Faulcon said, "Yes, sir. I understand." And slightly angry at that condescending flourish of authority, he turned and walked back to the room, and his colleagues.

CHAPTER EIGHT

At the end of the session they made their way to a small restaurant and ate a light meal, relaxing for an hour afterwards before picking up one of Kris's barrack mates, a jovial, blond-haired, Earth-born youngster called Nils Istoort, and playing some sport, two rounds of handball, a twenty-one of badminton. Quietly, when he had an opportunity, Faulcon mentioned to Nils that it might be a good idea if he kept a close eye on Kris Dojaan for the next few hours. The two of them had planned to go up to the Sky Lounges and drink some of Kris's bonus, anyway, and Faulcon and Lena thus found they had a few hours to themselves. They went immediately to Faulcon's quarters. For a while they sprawled out on the cushioned floor and talked.

"What did Ensavlion want?"

"He told me to keep an eye on Kris. He doesn't want him rift-running before he's ready."

Lena shrugged, disinterested, tired. "From what you say he's on his way in any event. Do you trust that other kid to look after him?"

"I think so. Besides, I'm meeting them both later—"

"Oh I *see*! This is just an interlude in your drinking!"

Ignoring her, Faulcon went on, "Meeting them! For talk! And I don't propose to let Kris out of my sight until he crashes out. I don't think he'll disobey me, though. He has a sense of responsibility, and he knows he'll be a free agent as from tomorrow."

"A sense of responsibility," repeated Lena, and laughed as she mocked Faulcon, "Just like you?" Then, more seriously, she said, "What's Kris doing to you, Leo?"

"How do you mean? Doing to me? He's not doing anything to me."

"Yes he is." She moved off her cushion and wriggled up next to Faulcon, unclipping his shirt and stroking his chest. "He's having quite an effect on you."

"What sort of effect? I hadn't noticed anything."

"For a start, I've only ever once known you to spend so much time with a person other than me—"

"Don't talk about that, Lena. Please."

"I wasn't going to. Kris is a very different person. I know you're sympathetic, and I know you're trying to relax the boy, and make him feel at home—but Leo, after a mission we *always* spend time together!"

"And we didn't this time. I know—Lena, I'm sorry about that—"

"I don't need your sorrow, Leo. I'm a big girl. I just need you to recognize that Kris has far more of a hold on you than you seem to think."

"As you say, I'm trying to welcome him, that's all. To make him feel easy. To be a friend to him." Faulcon took Lena's roving hand and lifted it to his lips; she watched him warmly and he asked, "Moodiness all passed?"

"Thank God. Don't change the subject. What's going on in your head, Leo? What has our young man from Earth done to you?"

Faulcon didn't answer for a moment. He stared across the room, trying to find some order in the confusion of thoughts and emotions that was conjured to mind whenever he tried to assess his relationship with Kamelios. "It's excitement, I think. That sense of excitement, of wonder. The sort of feeling we had at school when people talked about other Galaxies, and all the worlds in our Galaxy that had only been recorded, never explored. It's imagination, the feeling of mystery that you get when people tell you stories about distant islands, hidden asteroids, secret locations, secret lands where things are strange, and where we're infiltrators, or strangers. There's something so magic about the unknown, and I remember that it was the sense of the unknown, and the desperate need to penetrate that unknown just a little, that brought me out here. And then it went, and everything became so routine, and the canyon was just a canyon, and the aliens were just aliens, and so what?"

"And then Kris Dojaan. The child, his eyes filled with awe, with wonder, and Leo Faulcon finds his humanity again. I understand. You're very lucky."

Lena was quiet. Her hand rested on Faulcon, but she no longer communicated her desire for him. She lay staring away from him, and he put his arm around her shoulders, gently stroked the soft skin of her cheek. "You think you're too dulled, is that it?"

"I was dulled a long time ago. I can't feel that wonder. But I sense the loss, do you know that? I do sense the loss . . . of something, of a part of me. This is a killer of a world. We have to get away, Leo, before it kills us completely."

Faulcon squeezed her tight, and she looked up; her eyes glistened with tears. Faulcon kissed her on the nose. "I love you, Lena. I really love you."

"Say it again."

"No." He grinned. "That's your ration for tonight."

"Cheapskate."

She lay back on his chest. It was pleasantly still and silent in the room, and after a while Faulcon's eyes closed.

Later he checked on the young Kris Dojaan and found him sleeping soundly in his bunk, his barrack mate finishing a bottle of *baraas* and quietly reading. Faulcon took a midnight stroll about the Sky Lounge, but it was a quiet and dark night, and there was little happening. After a while he found a deep arm-chair, leaned back and slept.

In the morning, shortly after the huge red-haloed disc of Altuxor had crept above the eastern horizon, he made his way back to the barracks, intending to fetch Kris—who no doubt would complain at the earliness of the hour—for breakfast, a good feed before the final, most intense part of the training.

Kris was not there. His barrack mate, Nils, was still asleep, sprawled half out of bed, snoring loudly; the place reeked of drink. Faulcon stood for a while wondering where Kris might have gone, what he could possibly find to do at such an early hour. Watching the dawn was one possibility, or already at breakfast. A thought nagged at him. It wasn't possible, was it, that he could have decided to take an early morning walk . . . out through Steel City's public ramp. . . ?

He suddenly realized that he was being paged, the voice a soft and insistent repetition of his name, almost lost against the growing activity and bustle in the barrack corridors. He glanced around and saw a wall phone. When he picked up the receiver and identified himself there was the briefest of pauses before Lena was on the line, telling him curtly, almost angrily, to move himself down to the suiting and shedding lounge.

He ran down the levels, and burst breathlessly into the room, pushing among the lines of r-suits, seeking Lena. The ramp was out, leading down to the planet's surface, and only the faint whining of the preservation field across the opening prevented Faulcon from diving for a mask. A bulky shape stood there, a rift suit, its legs braced apart, the details of its insignia lost against the bright light of the outside world. But behind the tinted face plate it was obviously Lena. When the suit moved, deeper into the lounge, he saw her face inside the helmet. She looked tired, almost exhausted. And she obviously had bad news.

Her voice rasped on the exvox. "Suit up. Our child team member, despite his *fine* sense of responsibility, has gone out to the valley."

"Surprise, surprise," said Faulcon dully.

"And he's gone out in a touring suit! We'll get docked our bonus and more if he gets himself caught by a squall, or even breaks a limb. Suit up. Don't just stand there gaping."

All love was gone in the face of professional anger. As Faulcon hauled himself into his suit, wincing at the stinging of the control probes easing into his skin, he thought for the thousandth time that he must have been mad to have accepted a position in the same team as Lena. Mad. It was difficult enough to love the woman with mood changes upturning relationships every five minutes. When she was forced every day into a position of leadership, into a command position, it put an often unbearable strain on them.

Which was not, he silently acknowledged to himself as he sealed himself in, totally true. He was tired, she was tired, their moods were bad. Most of the time they worked well together. It was times like this that he could do without.

And Kris was going to get a rift glove slapped across his face, Faulcon was sure of that.

When Faulcon was ready Lena turned and raised an arm to the monitoring technicians. The preservation screen collapsed, lights winked on; in his headphones Faulcon heard Lena's instruction to move out of the city. He followed her up the ramp, and down onto the planet, and when they hit hard ground they began to run.

Lena led the way at a compromise speed of ten miles an hour, not uncomfortable, but involving some actual physical effort to control the suits. They dropped down into a flat-bottomed gully, which was crowded with transport vehicles of various kinds, taking supplies and specimens between the city and the Riftwatch Stations. After a few minutes they were pounding along the valley road, parallel to the rift, but some way below the rocky approach slopes.

They passed by several Watch Stations, including the ruins of Eekhaut, and Faulcon began to wonder what Lena had in mind. Before he could voice his question, however, she abruptly changed course for the north, up the approach track, and close by to Riftwatch Station Shibano.

At once Faulcon found his heart beating fast, his mind and body light, a sensation of floating. He had seen this valley so many times . . . but he suddenly knew that he was going to see it differently, or more accurately, that he was going to see it again as he had first seen it, through the eyes of wonder, with the imagination of the young.

They were at Rigellan Curve, where the canyon turned to the north, widening and deepening and boasting its most fabulous array of ruins anywhere along its length, a fairground of Othertime, extending miles into the distance. Within seconds they had reached the edge of the rift. In silence they looked at the breathtaking view.

Here was such a farrago of alienness that Faulcon found himself growing dizzy every time he shifted his gaze. He always found it hard to convey the baffling impression of lights and shapes, the jagged and the smooth, the towering, twisting, stooping structures of another race and a thousand other times, all interlocked and tangled in ways for which they had never been designed. His attention lingered on several, translucent towers, their enormous heights shaped and beaten by wind and rain, sparkling and glittering in the bright, red-tinged light of high Altuxor. He was fascinated by an immense, sprawling spider's-web, complex in design, its broken strands jutting and quivering as if they sought that part of the web that had been lost to them. He could see wide, half-familiar roadways, one raised above the ground on steel pillars: this road began and ended abruptly, and it had been shifted by wind and change so that it had skewered the web at its mid point. The other end rested awkwardly upon a cubical black structure, in and out of which moved several city-robots, no doubt documenting and removing the contents now that a human team had been inside. The whole valley below them was a junk-yard of alien buildings and huge half-severed, half-alive machines, snub-nosed and wide-winged, or on tracks or wheels, upturned to display their gaping rocket jets, or plunged nose first into the substrate of the valley so that just their ends rose into the still, cold air. Shimmering walkways trembled in physical breezes, spiral structures that ended hundreds of yards in the air.

Most of the remains were clustered at the very bottom of the canyon, on a wide, scoured plain, where once, perhaps, a river had flowed. Now it was substantially forested, the colourful, confused afforestation that results from the overlapping of native species from different ages; predominant were the thrash-ing red and green masses of broad-flails, not native to present-day Kamelios, and expanses of the white and hornified plants known as skagbark. On the wide ledges that separated the several scarpments of each cliff side, it was scagbark that dominated, roots twisting out into the void in their search for water in the thin soil of the slopes. Above the ledges the pattern of stratification rippled, twisted throughout the valley in a geo-logical jigsaw. The deep rift meandered into the distance, into haze and obscurity. And Faulcon and Lena Tanoway were minute black shapes against that vastness.

Faulcon suddenly realized that Lena was talking to him; her voice had been gently insinuating itself into the sensory con-fusion in his mind, and now he looked at her and saw her point-ing across the canyon. Faulcon turned up the magnification of his helmet and the bulky shape of Commander Ensavlion ap-peared clearly before him, recognizable from the insignia on his armoured suit. He stood close to the rim, above a sloping escarpment, below which were the covered tents containing the dead life that had come out of Othertime, unintelligent forms, of course, mostly animals, with a smattering of organisms that were unclassifiable in terrestrial terms. Ensavlion stood stiffly, his head bowed as he scanned the valley bottom. He seemed unaware of the team that regarded him from more than a mile away.

Faulcon knew that Ensavlion came to the valley every day, sometimes for just a few minutes, sometimes for hours. He came and he stood and he watched, and one day perhaps he would again see that small, glowing pyramid; it would flash into the canyon, appearing from nowhere, and the tall, hovering shapes would materialize through its walls, moving about the valley for a minute or so before returning to their machine and vanishing into time. Although the travellers may have been constant visitors to this place and time, only once had they materialized before a group of men, one of whom had not been running when they came, a man whose memory of that event was so distorted, by time and the need to review the occurrence, that the pyramid had increased, in his account, to something twenty times as large as it had been, and the creatures had become almost godlike, manifestations of the super-race he so obsessively sought in the Universe.

As Faulcon watched Commander Ensavlion, strangely disturbed yet fascinated by the man and by the turmoil of feeling that seemed to be plaguing him since Kris Dojaan's arrival, so the distant figure turned and vanished below the approach slopes of the canyon. Faulcon switched off his helmet's magnifying plate and returned to the task of seeking his team mate.

It was nearly four hours before they spotted him, seated on an outjutting of rock, some hundred yards down the sloping inner edge of the valley. He appeared to be contemplating the infinite, his head turned, his gaze obviously somewhere out above the distant reaches of the rift. His knees drawn up, his arms tightly folded around them, he might have been any sightseer on any gorge on any world. The irresponsibility of his behaviour incensed Lena, and she almost shrieked at Kris, but the boy remained motionless, and perhaps his tiny face-mask radio was not operating.

Faulcon remained on level ground while Lena, her rift suit sliding in what seemed to be—but was not—a most precarious fashion, came up behind the youngster. Kris turned at the last minute, but did not seem alarmed. When the r-suit picked him up as easily as if he were a cat, he remained motionless and un-bothered, and waved at Faulcon as he came up the slope in the arms of his team leader.

Lena deposited him far less gently than she had picked him up. Faulcon eased down the volume of his radio as the woman's voice shrieked angrily through his head-set. Kris said, "Ease off. I'm safe, aren't I?"

Before Lena could react with a possibly damaging blow—and Faulcon felt such an event was looming—he stepped in and said, "Let's get him to the nearest station. Maybe Ensavlion need never find out."

"Good idea," said Lena, and they picked Kris up between them and ran the mile or so to Riftwatch Station Shibano.

In the warm, spacious interior of the station Faulcon stepped out of his suit, and helped Lena from hers. The two on-duty station crew, ageing, rather unsociable men, remained at the Valley Monitoring Console, listening, always listening, for the sudden atmospheric crack, the electromagnetic symphony that heralded the abrupt appearance of a time wind. The winds did not begin at one end of the valley and blow through the gorge to the other. They could form anywhere, and though they usually blew east to west, they had been known to blow in the opposite direction as well. The valley was watched constantly and with great concentration.

"That was a stupid thing to do," said Faulcon. They sipped hot soup and sat in a small circle close to the wide window overlooking the valley; the thick glass was tinted in some way, and the dome's interior seemed slightly blue. On Kamelios, where the ageing sun cast a red shadow across everything, the effect was slightly disturbing.

"It was a bloody irresponsible thing to do," snapped Lena glaring at Kris. "On my team you obey the rules. You've not only put your own life in danger, you inconvenienced and endangered *me*, and I resent that."

Kris, quite pale, seemed unrepentant. He drank his soup, holding the cup in both hands, and stared out through the overlook. Finally he said, "I guess I'm sorry."

"That's a shame," said Lena stiffly. "If you'd known you were sorry I'd have liked you a lot better."

"I *am* sorry," Kris amended, looking at her. "It was dumb of me. I'd ask you only to crawl inside my head for a moment, to have a sniff around and see what's there." Imploring eyes turning on Faulcon, reasonableness oozing from his youthful features. "You've got to know what it's like . . . what it *was* like . . . to have come so far to find Mark, to see him, and to be denied access to him because of . . . because of a *danger*, a dangerous thing, that in my days here I haven't seen, or heard, or even got wind of, if you'll pardon the feeble joke."

Lena dismissed the levity with a contemptuous glance. Kris tried to ignore her and looked at Faulcon. "I saw the phantom, Leo. I really did."

"A lot of people have seen the phantom." Faulcon could recognize that something in Kris's expression testified to more than a distant sighting. He wondered how close the man had got, but he didn't want to push Kris for information, not in the present hostile atmosphere.

Distantly the two observers laughed at some shared joke; their console had been making crackling sounds, the sound of communication with something or someone out on the planet. Faulcon watched them for a second, then let his gaze drop back to Kris Dojaan, who was chewing at his lower lip, distracted and thoughtful.

"I know a lot of people have made sightings from a distance," he said, "but I've been right up close."

Now Lena looked interested too. "How close?"

"As close as this," said Kris. He was being infuriatingly unforthcoming. "The first night I didn't get very close—I saw the figure and it ran away."

Faulcon was horrified. "The *first* night? You mean you've been out every night since we came back?"

Kris grinned. "Do I get my wrist slapped?"

"Imbecile," said Lena quietly, and Kris shrugged.

"I'm not the only man from the city who goes out at night. The first night I saw someone in a rift suit, running like a mad thing along the edge of the canyon, and yelling, I think. I could hear sounds coming from the helmet. I was a long way away, and he didn't see me. I was hiding. But he *was* in a rift suit and if he was looking for the phantom he was destined to be unlucky. A rift suit moves too fast and the phantom doesn't take a chance. Me, out there practically naked, well, I was trusted."

Lena said, "I doubt he was looking for the phantom. A golden pyramid more like."

"Commander Ensavlion, you mean? Yes, that makes sense."

Faulcon watched him solemnly, quietly, and finally said, "What about the phantom? What did you learn?"

"Too much," said Kris quickly, not meeting either gaze. When he had said no more for several seconds, Faulcon prompted, "Was I right, then? Have you come to understand a little more about this world?"

"Do you mean is it me out there, running around in rags?" Kris neither smiled, nor frowned, but his voice became sad for a moment. "It isn't Mark, at any rate. I was so sure it was Mark, and it wasn't, and so I've still got to go after him. But that's all right. That's why I came here, to Kamelios. It's in my contract."

Faulcon and Lena exchanged an uneasy glance. In his contract? His work contract? There was surely no such clause that required a man to sacrifice his life into Othertime. But Kris was not elaborating.

Putting that last cryptic statement aside for the moment, Faulcon persisted: "If it's not Mark out there, who is it? You must know if you've spoken to him!"

"I'm not sure that I do know," said the boy. "And I'm not saying what I think. Don't press me, Leo. Please. I really don't want to talk about it."

Exasperated with him, Lena stood, smoothed down her tight-fitting undersuit and shook her head. "I'm going back to the city. There'll be a cargo transport passing here in two or three hours, so I'm told; you'll ride back on that. Is that clear?" Kris nodded. Lena looked at Faulcon. "Are you coming?"

"Later," said Faulcon, and Lena was puzzled for a moment, watching him curiously. When he made no effort to explain further she turned abruptly and went to the alcove where her suit was standing. Before Faulcon could rise and help her she had swung into the machine and was walking to the airlock.

"I really don't want to talk about it," said Kris as she went, looking at Faulcon with an expression of slight embarrassment. He had obviously assumed Faulcon had stayed because he thought Kris was uneasy with Lena. He hadn't. Faulcon smiled at his team mate, and observed how tired Kris looked.

"I'm dog tired. It's true. The training—the sleepless nights—is taking its toll."

"Then sleep," said Faulcon, and Kris walked to a couch and curled up gratefully. Faulcon watched him for a while, then rose and fetched the face-mask from his suit. The two observers watched him sourly as he strapped the face piece on, and one of them said, "Against regulations to go out there without an r-suit."

"Report me, then," said Faulcon bitterly. "But first, let me out, will you?"

Reluctantly the station crew obliged.

Running. It was like running through time. It was an exquisite freedom, and experience so terrifying that it was almost intellectual; the relinquishing of responsibility, the dispensing-with of the protective suit, the running through this backwater of time's great river was a religious thing, and Faulcon wanted to sing its praises, to scream the sweat that covered his body, to sing the tension of the wires that moved him.

He went down the canyon slopes, and the sun was lost to him; the cloak of deepening red became a darkening night, a land of shade, where structures and decay were highlit, then brightlit, then redlit, then instantly in darkness; and as he moved through alienness so he found an incomprehensible

117

beauty in the moving of one ruin against another, the red crystal spire that was suddenly a towering dark shape, moving across his field of vision and showing him the wonder of mindless cubes and pyramids of green and red-lit colours of the rainbow.

Deeper; darker; a shard of life in the barren sediment of time, running through the ages of the world, crawling down the eons, the rocks and fossils of the strata scattering and crumbling and making their own way from some para-permian to a sterile cambrian, and deeper still, to the scar-ridden flat lands in the deepest part of the half-lit gorge.

Before he reached the bottom, more than an hour since he had started his descent, Faulcon's resolve gave out, the thrill of fear overwhelming him, and he sat down heavily in the stillness. The smile behind his mask was of triumph—to have got so far, to have overcome fear to this extent! All his unease at being so close to Kris Dojaan had gone. The fear he faced was that terror of anticipation of being lost in time that had haunted him since his first days on Kamelios. Naked to the winds he could gauge the extent of his courage; in his months here he had never before dared to approach the valley without a suit, and gradually that suit had become a mask to his apprehension, a crutch that had almost grafted itself to his body. For the first time in a very long time he was starting to find out how it really was between him and VanderZande's World. He felt the gusting, tugging fingers of some natural breeze that heralded the coming dusk. With a view down the valley, into the western distances, he sat as Kris had sat, and contemplated the farther wall of the canyon, and the minds that had designed this carnival of ruination; and he examined, too, the nature of his fear, and the sense of ecstasy, and excitement, that had suddenly greeted his contemplation of the alien land before him, a land he had observed so many times before, and always with a bored indifference, a mercenary-seeking of anything that might pay well.

Yes, much of the coldness was the fault of the rift suit, the stable environment, the human-made machine enclosing the fleshy thing that was the intelligence, and bearing it about its business secure in the knowledge that the suit was increasing its survival chances, to such an extent that the odds were highly favourable. And when the sense of danger goes, perhaps the sense of awe follows. A full appreciation of mystery demands the linking of the soul, and the r-suits cut off the soul as hard and definitely as they cut off the wind, the air, the waves of energy, the very breath of time itself.

He was free now, and his soul and his heart soared out across the void of the canyon, settling on this structure, then that, winging its way from city shard to city shard, never knowing whether there was a billion years of difference in the simple visual hop from a spire to a stone arch and back to the ground again.

Where are you then ? Come on, show yourself. I haven't got all day.

A long time passed and Faulcon remained still, searching the canyon and the buildings for any sign of movement. The day grew redder, darker. He knew that soon he would have to move back up the slope or risk spending the night in the valley, exposed to any time squall that might whip up over the next few hours, and exposed to the terrible night chill of Kamelios. His undersuit would keep him warm or cool within moderately intense fluctuations. But night would creep through the fabric with steady, ghoulish cold.

A movement, distantly, made his heart stop. He peered hard to the west, towards Steel City, seeing some few miles up the canyon before the curvature of the valley cut off his view. He gradually realized that the movement was caused by twelve riftsuited figures racing across the canyon bottom, and disappearing into some invisible structure on the far side. Faulcon could not imagine what they were doing here. He had always thought that all missions returned to a station or the city when dusk came down.

He had managed to worry over the distant figures for no more than a few seconds when he heard stones tumbling, and the unmistakable sound of something moving across the ledges above him. He remembered, with chilling hindsight, that this part of the valley was a favourite hunting ground for the male gulgaroth, and that unprotected humans were by no means outside the range of such creatures' tastes if they had not fed for several days. He stood quickly, turned, and stared hard against the sky, seeking the sleek, gleaming shape of the creature. As he did so he suddenly felt his skin crawl, imagined for a moment that he was being watched from the deeper valley. The presence was so strong that he cried out, but when he turned there was nothing to see and the sensation faded. He looked back up the slope. For a moment he saw nothing but the rising cliff, and the waving motion of sparse vegetation clinging to the easier slopes. Then something, too small for a gulgaroth, darted off to the left. He thought it was another animal at first, but when it slipped slightly, and stopped, he realized he was staring at a man, an old man, wearing the ragged uniform of Steel City and a small survival mask. Faulcon knew without hesitation that it was the man he sought. He shouted for the figure to wait, but his own face mask inhibited the sound. He waved. The man turned to watch him briefly, then ran along the slope of the canyon, behind a jagged outcrop of sparkling rock.

Faulcon went in pursuit, up the incline, and calling as loud as he could. The phantom scurried away from him, but Faulcon came close, closer than he would ever have thought possible. Whoever this man was, he was reluctant to invoke the mechanism of his vanishing trick. He wanted Faulcon to come close, and yet was afraid to confront him, to face him.

"Please wait! You spoke to my friend, speak to me. For God's sake wait. . ."

Why am I so afraid? My eagerness is fear, isn't it? Of course it is.

Quite suddenly the phantom was before him, cowering, crouching, hands lifted to face, fingers spread and hiding those features of the aged face that the mask did not conceal. Faulcon wondered if he looked frightening, inhuman in the narrow mask he himself wore; perhaps to remove it, to show his full face, would emphasize to the phantom that his concern was genuine. He removed the faceted goggles, gagging on the atmosphere of

Kamelios for a second before he could get the respirator back into his mouth. Now he could breathe but not talk properly. "I'm a friend!" Patronizing words, and difficult to achieve: remove respirator and speak without breathing; respirator back; blink away streaming tears; rack with the choking sensation induced by whatever organic compounds made the Kamelion atmosphere directly unbreathable. The cowering figure of the man was silent, all the whimpering, strangely animal noises gone.

"Who are you?" said Faulcon, learning how to speak and breathe without choking. "Please tell me." Breathing. "I'm not just inquisitive, I really care."

The shape turned away from him, the fabric of the tattered suit stretching tight across its back. The phantom held up a wrinkled, trembling hand, held it out towards Faulcon, stretched his arm for the most direct and fervent gesture possible: please stay away.

Faulcon approached, only to hear the phantom cry out, a strangely old, high-pitched voice, the voice of a very, very old man, almost child-like, almost desperate. The hand shook, then was snatched into the body, and the figure seemed to shrink even further. Faulcon drew his hand across his eyes, trying to clear his vision, horribly aware that less than a minute of exposure to the Kamelion atmosphere could start to corrode the cornea.

He realized he was about to lose the time phantom, and even as he shouted, "No, wait, please . . . I must know who you are . . ." so the figure blurred through his tears, seemed to dart out of sight, and was gone as abruptly as that, as cleanly, as completely as any fleeting breeze, Faulcon found himself staring at bare rock through his goggles, still in an attitude of appeal, still working to fix the mask on properly. He straightened and looked around. Bitterly disappointed, and yet elated somewhere inside that he had achieved so much more than for years had been believed possible, he began the slow climb back up the cliff.

A long while later, in the last hour of Kamelion's rich red

dusk, he re-entered the dome of Riftwatch Station Shibano, and dabbed a special ointment to his weeping eyes. Through his blurred vision he noticed that Kris Dojaan was not in the main lounge. He asked the crew of the station if the cargo-transport had taken him back to Steel City and was told that the transport had been delayed.

A pang of disquiet silenced Faulcon for a second and he regarded the observers with blank features. "Where is he, then?"

"One of the Section Commanders turned up. Just came, just this last few minutes."

"Ensavlion?" asked Faulcon, and the man grinned.

"The very same. He's been out looking for aliens, and he's popped in for a drink."

The observers found that very funny. Faulcon remained impassive. What was Ensavlion doing here? Coincidence? He would certainly have known that three of his team had checked in, the observers would not have broken regulations and *not* reported the arrivals. Or had the Commander followed them yet again? And what was he saying to Kris that he felt he had to hide away from the main lounge, and the possibility of being overheard?

"They're back there," Faulcon was told, and followed the man's glance to the relaxation and tv room, now lit up. The door was slightly open and Faulcon walked quietly across the floor to stand just outside, carefully peering in.

Kris was seated, his back to the door. Commander Ensavlion was leaning against the ebony box that housed the tv player, looking away from the boy, and away from the watching stranger outside the room.

CHAPTER NINE

"I should have spoken to you before, I know that. I'm sorry about it. I was glad when Leo Faulcon suggested you go straight out on a mission. I thought it would help settle you psychologically to Kamelios, to come to understand the place to a certain extent. Then I thought it would be easy to talk to you about Mark, about the mission, about me . . . about why Mark died when I could have prevented it. But it wasn't easy. I should have spoken to you when you came. I must confess that I am afraid to speak to you even now. I wonder what you must think of me. . ."

Kris sat stiffly and watched his Commander. For some minutes the conversation had been strained, and trivial. Ensavlion seemed incapable of looking at Kris Dojaan, but cast furtive, fleeting glances at him; and furtive, fleeting smiles, as if always divining for sympathy, always trying to elicit a warm and friendly response from the young man who sat so solemn, so passive, so embarrassed. And Kris *was* embarrassed. And he was also angry. He was confused, and this world and its people confused him worst of all. If Ensavlion would come out with his statement it would be so much easier for all concerned. If he would say: I let him die, I was irresponsible, I am to blame, I shot him, I pushed him . . . if he would just say whatever it *was* that was eating at his soul, the atmosphere in the room could become sweeter, and Kris would relax; and maybe then they could talk sensibly about a brave man, about a "dead" man, more accurately about the man who had gone into time . . . and had not come back. Mark had *not* come back; he was not the phantom. It had been a stupid dream, a clutching at straws of the first magnitude. Mark, nonetheless, was the survival type, and if anyone could survive the hostile future—or past—Kris was certain it was he. Mark's survival instinct was far greater than that of either Leo Faulcon, or Lena Tanoway . . . far greater. He thought of Faulcon for a moment, a fleeting moment, a distracted instant in the silence following Ensavlion's stilted, awkward confession. Poor Faulcon. Poor man. He felt close to Leo, close enough to regard him as a friend. He felt a sympathy for him that he could not have felt for Lena. Sweat prickled on his face and he tried to put the terrible thought aside, let his attention swing back to Commander Ensavlion.

"I sent him out, you see. I sent him out when I knew it was unsafe. There hadn't been a full scale wind for weeks, but there was a spate of squalls, sweeping the valley; totally unpredictable. Quick, clean, the flash of an eye. They often herald a major wind, and there were structures appearing in the valley that were lasting only a few hours before vanishing again. I wanted so desperately to see everything, to get a glimpse of everything that was time-flung. I sent a lot of men out, and most of them did an hour in the rift, then fled. Mark was a strong-willed man, and he behaved by the book. I told him to go out, and he went out, and when the wind came he was stuck . . . he got caught." Ensavlion glanced at Kris, his face white, his eyes dim behind tired lids. "There was nothing anyone could do. I'm convinced of that. There was nothing. Please believe me. If your brother could have been saved, then, as I'm sure you know, he would have been. I'm sure you know that . . ." He was staring at Kris queerly, a steady gaze, now, a searching stare. He wanted comment from the boy. He wanted his psyche patted better, a kind word, a forgiving gesture.

Kris, comprehending that it was unfair of him, nonetheless did not feel that he wanted to put Ensavlion at his ease. He could scarcely credit that this trembling, weak, fearful man before him was his Section Commander, and the leader of the mission that had brought Mark seven hundred light years to participate in; and which had brought Kris himself along the same interstellar route to join in place of his brother.

He said, "I'm sure everything was done that could have been done. I don't understand your feeling of failure."

Ensavlion paced awkwardly in front of the seated youth. "He

knew I was wrong to order him out. But he went out, him and others . . . I forget exactly who, now. Afterwards we tried to forget about it, to put it from our minds. I had no cares for his safety, but he never found the words, or the disobedience, to correct my instruction."

"That's a mistake of war, Commander. Every Commander is responsible for the life and death of his men, but it isn't as if you stuck a knife in him. You were wrong, and my brother was caught off-guard; if I was convinced he was dead it might make me more bitter towards you. But he's not dead. I know he's not."

Ensavlion laughed in a way that suggested relief (at the change of subject, perhaps) and just a little appreciation of Kris's dogmatic adherence to what must surely have been a lost cause.

"You mean the wizened phantom of the valley . . . well, I appreciate your enthusiasm, and your imagination, but you really should start to think—"

Kris cut in. "Not the phantom. Not the phantom . . . I know that now, and I realize I was wrong, and I'm angry at myself for being wrong. Not the phantom . . ." he touched the amulet about his neck, drawing reassurance from its cold, smooth feel; Ensavlion followed the minute motion with his eyes. "Not the phantom, but something the phantom said . . . I know my brother is alive. But whether I can find him is another question."

Kris was amused by the expression of shock that touched the otherwise dull and expressionless features of his Section Commander. Ensavlion pushed himself away from the tv unit, his hands behind his back. Dramatically he turned round, peered down at Kris. "Are you telling me you've spoken to this person?"

"Not exactly spoken. Exchanged shouts, snatches of words, sentences. A rather unforthcoming piece of time flotsam, the phantom. Enough exchanged, though, for me to shed a tear or two, one for grief, one for joy. What I sensed about the phantom was not the actual identity of my brother, but the transmission of that identity. When I was on Oster's Fall, my home world, when we got news of Mark's death, I had already been dreaming of him, and when the news came I dreamed harder. I heard him speaking, I'm convinced of it. It was something similar when I first came here. There were moments when I felt Mark calling to me, desperately loudly. He was alive, but trapped. The phantom was relaying that telepathy—"

"Telepathy?"

"Or whatever. I appreciate my senses, Commander. I don't try and constrain them with reason. If I smell something I smell it, I don't start questioning whether I smell it in my nose or my olefactory lobe, or even whether I've smelled it at all, but rather am smelling something because of a visual association working subconsciously. If something stinks, it stinks. If something speaks in my mind, it speaks in my mind." He frowned, then laughed as he noticed Ensavlion's cynical expression. "What I'm trying to say is that I'm a slave of my sensory input, and I don't worry about it. It keeps me going, as it has kept many a so-called crank going, through the centuries when people laughed at teleportation—remember that?—and now certain planetary environments enhance that power, right? And through times when people thought that there had never been animal God creatures on Earth, and now there's been communication with the creatures on Earth, which live out of phase with humanity, the same beings who inspired all those legends and myths, right?" Ensavlion was nodding in agreement, conceding the point. Kris said, "And of course, through times when people scorned time travel."

Ensavlion's eyebrows rose slightly. "We still don't have that, you know. There is nothing to say that the phenomena we are observing in the valley, on VanderZande's World, are not in fact something else, some perception trick, or spatial orientation trick."

"Do you believe that? Do you believe in cosmic tricks?"

"No, I don't," said Ensavlion, wiping a hand across his face, and smoothing back his hair; he was hot again. "I don't because I've seen them, the causes, the travellers. I've seen their machine. But despite what my colleagues say, I am not blind to their argument, and indeed to those who argue against a point

126

blank acceptance that the time winds are time *travelling* winds."

Kris felt smug in his special knowledge. "It *is* time travel, and you are right and they are wrong. I'm convinced of it, and I've spoken to someone who has hopped through time with the same ease as you or I might hop into a car. That's why the Catchwind Mission is so important. That's why I'm puzzled as to why it hasn't happened yet."

"Ah," Ensavlion turned away again, considering the statement with something akin to embarrassment. "Yes, you are quite right to query that. Your brother was part of the original team, and he was here for some months, and we did not go; and it is months since he disappeared and still we haven't gone."

When it seemed that Ensavlion would be content with stating the obvious, Kris prompted, "But I keep seeing men out in the rift. When I was out last night I saw movement. Not the solitary figure that keeps running along the valley's rim. That's you, I guess."

"Me?" Ensavlion smiled. "I do spend rather a lot of time out there, I must confess. But go on, you've seen men. Men in rift suits?"

"Of course."

"Men and *women* in rift suits, to be precise. That's the team. Every few days when there is a sort of wind eddy, or dark cloud, or electrical disturbance that sometimes, but not always, is associated with a time wind . . . out they go. But they would abort the mission without instructions from me."

"And that's happened several times."

Ensavlion looked horrified, then angry. He took a step towards Kris and his face flushed with suppressed rage. Then he smiled grimly, slapping his hands behind his back and looking away. "By God, Mister Dojaan, you've been nosing around to an impressive degree. Out on the rift where you oughtn't to be, not yet, and asking questions that by rights should be unanswerable."

"Are you angry?"

127

Ensavlion considered that, calming during the few seconds of silence. "I don't think I am, now."

Kris decided that he should tread prudently and pick his words with care. "I thought I might have touched on a sore point. I haven't been nosing, and that's the truth. I was talking to one of the Section during my suit-training, and I suppose he divined that I was the new Catchwind recruit. Maybe something I said, or did, or implied, gave it away."

"Your name, probably."

"He told me straight that we're not supposed to talk about the mission, but also that he was part of it. That they'd been waiting for over a year, and they'd always been available when the wind blew, but that you've never given the word. And you never explain why. And they're getting very fed up waiting, which is why there is such a need for replacements."

Ensavlion watched the boy and hardly a sound was heard, hardly a breath was drawn. Kris felt the terrible imminence of the question, and his heart began to stammer as he wondered what he should say when it came.

"They say, I suppose, that I'm afraid. Commander Ensavlion is scared to death of the mission, and because of his streak of yellow is denying the Universe the possible benefits of the first organized and considered venture into Othertime. Am I right, Kris?"

Kris said nothing, did nothing, but sat in embarrassed silence. "They think you're scared," he confirmed after a while. "As if they're not scared themselves."

Ensavlion obviously appreciated the softness of that, the generosity. If it was not totally honest on Kris's part, and if Ensavlion realized this, nothing was said, only, "Everyone's scared of course, that's only natural. But those men and women were prepared to risk death; they signed on for the Catchwind mission, and they were prepared to go through with it, exhausted with fear, damp with fear, sick with fear, they'd nonetheless have done it."

"Why *are* you so afraid?" asked Kris, aware, now, that all ice was broken, and that Ensavlion and he had grown closer than was good for two men of such different ranks and such different age; but close they had grown, and there was no denying or escaping it.

The Commander shook his head. "I've never fully understood, Kris. One day I watched a time wind . . . a magnificent sight. I can't begin to describe it. The most fabulous, the most incomprehensible sight in the whole Universe, an art form so distinct, so natural that it fills me with joy, such joy that I want to sing with that wind, always sing, always become a part of it. And for years I fought, and argued with the Federation, with the financiers, with the governing body of this Sector to allow a 'suicide mission' into time. I got volunteers and I said it was madness not to send an expedition into Othertime. They always came up with the same argument: no one has returned, and therefore no one will. No information has been received from Othertime, and therefore no information will."

Kris was momentarily confused. "That makes no sense."

"I agree. They argued that any successful expedition would indicate a control of the random time-flow in the valley . . . Do you see what I mean? That time would flow from specific point to specific point, and everyone going *into* time would follow the same path. If such control existed then men, lost or expeditionary, would have turned up, and been turning up for years. . ."

"One did."

Ensavlion laughed. "I don't think the phantom would have been very good support for our cause. In any event, the council eventually agreed to the formation of a small task force, to be maintained in strict secrecy, everyone working a normal job, and waiting for *their* say-so, for *their* word to go. Then, when I saw the pyramid—and I was not alone although I am the only one left alive who saw the travellers—official opinion was swayed sufficiently. I was put in charge of the mission, with full authority to call the task force out into the valley. Secrecy was maintained. After a few weeks the interest in seeking the golden pyramid declined, and I became . . . I don't know, a laughing stock perhaps? That wouldn't be so far from the truth." He smiled thinly. "Then two things happened, two terrible things.

In fact, perhaps a third thing happened, a change on Kamelios, one of those electrical storms that addle the minds for a few days and impose different personalities upon us. I don't know. Perhaps world and fate conspired to take the steel from my nerves, but whatever happened, the confidence was suddenly ripped away from me. Though I was afraid for myself, I was as afraid for the people I was planning to take into time with me. Suddenly I couldn't do it."

"What happened? Or is it too. . ."

"Is it too what? Too difficult to talk about? Not any more. It was at first, which is why I didn't. Oh yes, your brother's death was one of the things. You should know that."

"But not the main thing. . ."

"I don't know. Who can quantify these things? And what good would that do, anyway? Mark's death happened two days after I'd led an expedition up the valley to a place called Ridge Seventeen. You can't see it from here; it's forty miles or so to the east, well away from Steel City. There are Watch Stations there, but that's all they are, Watch Stations. They monitor the winds, and give us warning of time squalls, electrical upsets. They're not equipped to send men down to the valley, at least, not on more than preliminary surveys. Something interesting turns up, out goes Section 4 with the scientific groups, then my section, 8, with its three-man, careful-study groups, then the big Sections with the scientists again. All very complex, and often not adhered to. Well, just before your brother got swept away I'd gone down with one of the eight-man teams, a rapid survey group attached to geology, to see some particularly fine structures, and formations, thrown up by a time-eddy—that's a persistent flow of time through a small area; it has no physical manifestation, beyond the sound, a sort of high-pitched screaming. Time flows fast and furious and all you can really see is sensory impression, and feel the occasional vibration through the ground—you know about that, about the fact that the valley seems physically separate from the land around, although it is apparently connected. We went down into the valley a few hours after it had fallen quiet. Experience teaches us that these rapid-flow time fluxes burn themselves out. I was with the geology group and I saw what looked like a fossil in a stratum of sedimentary rock, and, as you've probably been told, fossils are rare. I went up closer and thought I was looking at a crinkled, pitted shell-form. It swam into focus suddenly, the same colour as the rock around it, a sort of smoky grey; it was a rift suit helmet. When you looked hard you could make out the vague shape of a suit lying horizontal as you'd expect. It was very crushed, but clearest of all was the shape of the five-fingered glove, curled up. You can look at that shape and argue for hours as to whether it *is* a rift suit. All the features are much obliterated, and the face plate lay turned into the cliff from the valley. We were looking at the back of the helmet. It's still there. No wind has touched it since. No one's ever gone and dug it out."

"Why?"

"Why? Why won't a man go out without his amulet? Why does the loss of a team member result in an elaborate ritual of exorcism for the others? Why does every rifter scrub the dust off his suit before he leaves the vicinity of the valley? Because to do otherwise would be bad medicine. Because on Kamelios we don't invite Old Lady Wind to supper. Because we respect the dead, and we respect Othertime even more."

"I understand that," said Kris, and added, "You don't wear an amulet, I've noticed."

Ensavlion smiled, just briefly. "I don't need to, Kris." He touched his skull, above his eyes; by looking hard Kris could see the thin line of a surgical operation. "I wear my shard inside."

There was a moment of silence. Kris thought of rifters turning up from other times not as phantoms, but as vague outlines in deep sedimentary strata; crushed and twisted by planetary forces, they outlived, in their new stone form, the flimsy, fleshy shards of life that busied themselves over the monumental trivia and enigma of the alien ages that filled this deep cut in the world.

He thought of Mark.

"And a few days later, to add to the deep concern this fossil human filled you with, you pushed Mark to work the valley and heard that he had perished."

Ensavlion looked grim and cold as he silently agreed. "That's about it. When I heard that Mark had been swept away I was upset at first, then angry, then just very, very depressed. I couldn't spend a night without thinking of him. It took me three weeks to write the letter to your parents—I couldn't bring myself to use the direct link—and what a terrible, and trite, letter that was. I'd written such letters before. Of course I had, many times before. Section 8 is a spear-head, a dare-devil group; they go everywhere and they die everywhere. I've written letters to a thousand worlds, and a thousand homes, and a thousand men and women who I have never seen, and who, for all I know, never got those personal notes, but found out the details by u-fax. But all of those dead went out on missions that were approved, and sanctioned, and they knew the risks, and they took the risks voluntarily; it hurt when they were lost, but there was a greater stake, and it was easy to be cold."

"But Mark knew it was wrong to go out, and he made you know without objecting at all. You forced him, and he obeyed. He was a fool."

"He trusted me. Don't you understand that, Kris? He trusted me, he obeyed me, because, even though he sensed the risk, the danger, he decided that I was a man to be trusted; he could not find it in himself to doubt that if I was insisting on him going, then I knew something, or I had a different, more rational, more experienced instinct. Your brother went into the valley because I had as good as said that nothing would happen to him; my credentials were experience, my rank. And there was no experience. He died. I wonder if he died thinking of me, wondering if I had done it on purpose, if in some way I had felt contempt for him that I could waste him so. And I didn't. He was like you, Kris, like you in many ways. And as I feel a bond with you, so I felt a bond with him. Rank meant nothing. We shared an enthusiasm, an awe of this place. A sense of the alien, a gut-wrenching sense of wonder that people usually lose on this world, like Lena and Leo, your colleagues. They're dead, like

132

steel, polished, sharp, but cold, cold. Not you. You are not sharp yet, and not too polished, but the vibrant energy in you is almost tangible. You came looking for Mark, and you found a world that thrilled you. I could sense it in the sweat smell of you the first time we met. Pungent, aromatic, the most wonderful stink in the world, the stink of excitement. It was the same with Mark. But I pushed that poor bastard, I pushed him because I was half afraid to do my own work. I sent him to the valley whenever I should have gone myself, if anyone was to go at all. Because the valley is our enemy; it is our death; it is to be respected, and there are rare moments when it is totally safe. There are too many moments when it is comprehensively dangerous. I abused his trust, and his awe. I killed him."

Kris watched Commander Ensavlion, feeling a terrible cold chill deep inside. He could not think of his brother as a man who would mindlessly obey; his brother was a survivor, all the Dojaans were survivors. And Mark would have had the instinct to know when not to go to the valley. He wouldn't have trusted Ensavlion so, not such a weak man. He would have seen that weakness and questioned that order. And yet, he believed in obedience. He hated rank, but always respected sensible, genuine, considered rules; and orders were rules; orders drew on the rules of a place, or a game, or a situation. He might have been torn, then, torn between his contempt for Ensavlion—for surely he could not have respected this sweating, trembling man—and his respect for authority, for rules. Could Mark have made a mistake? Could Kamelios have so affected him that his judgement had been dulled? It was a possibility too reasonable to deny. Kris felt anger, now. It was irrational, certainly, but as Ensavlion wiped a pad across his face, soaking up the great sheen of wetness that had formed from hairline to chin as he had spoken, so Kris heard a voice saying, "Kick the bastard, kick him now, when he needs you to kick him! Get it out of your system." But he remained quiet, and still. He obeyed the rules. He sat stiffly silent, sensible that on VanderZande's World, with its never-easy double name (the confusion of identity stretching to the very world itself!), he must always keep his emotions, and his reactions, in tight check. You beat this world by always comprehending the nature of the forces that worked through you. He knew that, now, and all he needed was the experience of those forces. He would make a start by allowing Ensavlion no let-up in his embarrassment, because he would not melt again, he would not show tenderness again. Survival was what it was all about, as Faulcon had said to him twice during the training. Kamelios hates our guts, and wants to mentally castrate us. Fight it. Shout at the devil and you win. The meek shall inherit the time winds, the unwary shall inherit a body sheared in half by a gusting squall.

Ensavlion had sensed the hardening of Kris Dojaan's spirit; he seemed uncomfortable again, on edge. He leaned back against the tv unit and the look on his face was one of considerable uncertainty. But he had committed himself, now, and the story was finished. He had laid his soul bare to the youngster—or at least, had appeared to—he had expounded the factors of his fear, and perhaps, by so doing, had expunged them. Kris said nothing, sitting quiet and straight-faced, his gaze as near unblinking as was humanly possible, and fixed upon Ensavlion an arrogant gaze, a contemptuous consideration of the elder man. When long moments of this strain had passed, Ensavlion looked away, looked down.

"Well, Kris, now you know. I don't blame you for being a little surly, but perhaps when you have been on Kamelios a short while longer you will be a little more sympathetic to the pressures of responsibility." The stiffness in Ensavlion's voice, Kris realized, was a reaction to his own hostility. He must have been sitting there looking melodramatically grim, and he tried to relax. Ensavlion was right. This world was an important factor in any assessment of men and the value of the experience they might have acquired. It was unnecessarily harsh, and naïve, to judge Ensavlion as if this were Oster's Fall. ,

"I apologize, Commander. I suppose . . . I suppose it's hearing about Mark, and seeing how the world itself has had a hand in his fate. It makes me go very dry, very tight."

"I know. I can imagine."

"And perhaps it's also a reaction to the silence on Mark since I came here. I really thought that the moment I stepped from the shuttle someone would come up to me, take me by the arm and say, I knew your brother, great guy, tragic death, lots of friends, come and have dinner, talk about him, see what we can do about him. You know, a sort of 'friendships formed in the teeth of tragedy'; people *caring*."

"People don't care, on Kamelios. At least, not after they've been here a while."

Kris shook his head, "That's not always true. You care; you plainly care. About the world, and about your men, and about the possibility of tragedy."

Ensavlion conceded that. "Yes, you're right. I was generalizing of course, but even so, even I, even Leo Faulcon have been dulled by the world. People get *control* of VanderZande's World —we can become its master, but at a cost, a terrible cost."

"You said Leo was sharp, just now."

"Sharp in a different way. Sharp instinctively. Sharp in that he has got a nose for the planet, and a reaction time to it. I imagine, though, that he had forgotten much about Mark before you came, and then probably felt as awkward as I, talking about it."

Now Kris was confused. For a second he tried to remember what Faulcon had said, those earlier days, out in the mountains, and more recently during their long, lazy chats. "I don't think Leo Faulcon knew Mark at all. He'd heard of him, of course, but he didn't seem to know much about him."

"That's strange," said Ensavlion thoughtfully. "What's Leo playing at? I agreed with him that for the first few days he would say nothing about Mark, giving you time to settle into the world, and get to know Leo himself. But I thought I'd made it quite clear, the other day, that I wanted him to talk to you about their friendship, to break the ice a bit. Perhaps he misunderstood me."

Kris had risen to his feet, frowning, taking a step towards Commander Ensavlion, and then stopping, crossing his arms as he let the full impact of Ensavlion's words sink in. "I don't understand this at all. Leo and Mark were *friends*?"

"The best of friends," said Ensavlion quietly. "I wonder why he said nothing?"

"He not only said nothing, he specifically and adamantly denied knowing Mark. Why would he lie so intensely?"

Ensavlion shrugged. "As I said. . ."

"No! I don't believe that. For the first few days, yes, perhaps he would have thought it best to let me get acclimatized. But we've spent so much time together . . . we've talked, we've got drunk, we've trained . . . he's had ample opportunity to say something to me when the moment would have been right. Are you *sure* he was friends with Mark?"

Ensavlion was uneasy, yet firm. He gave a barely perceptible nod. "Of course. You'd better ask him about it. The whole reason I assigned you to his team . . . kept he and Lena waiting for a recruit for several weeks . . . was because I knew you were coming . . . the whole reason was so that he could help you understand what happened, and get a sympathetic picture of Kamelios, so you could comprehend what Mark had signed to do, and what you have signed to do in his place."

Had Ensavlion used the young replacement as an excuse for holding up the mission into Othertime, Kris wondered, as he followed his Commander through into the main lounge of the station. Only the observers were there. Had there been a whole string of excuses, and delays, each and every one sounding terribly reasonable, in fact just a mask to hide Ensavlion's own fear? But why had Faulcon said nothing to him? There had to be a reason, and because it was possible that Ensavlion was right, that Faulcon had wanted his young colleague to discover certain truths and certain facts about his brother on his own initiative before talking to him in more personal terms, Kris reluctantly decided that he should approach Leo Faulcon with care, and consideration, and not with fists flying.

CHAPTER TEN

At first they thought it was some gigantic sea beast, seen through the night lens of an immobile camera and barely visible as its decaying, scaled bulk settled deeper into the sand, deeper into obscurity. But when the projected image was sharpened and brightened it could be seen for the machine it was, lying slightly askew on the uprise of the shore. The ocean was a glimmering spread of movement in the far distance. A figure walked across the red, blurred image on the screen. It passed across the field of view from right to left, and vanished; then it came back, further from the camera on the byke and stood, its head turning and lifting as it stared all about the hulk.

"That him? That must be Dojaan, right?"

The disembodied voice startled Leo Faulcon. He felt Lena's sudden start as she sat beside him, eyes fixed on the well-remembered scene of their discovery. Faulcon said aloud, "That's right. He'd forgotten to get an amulet shard and Lena —Leader Tanoway—sent him out. We were angry and upset and he went out fast."

As he spoke Faulcon glanced around, and by the projected light from the film room he could catch glimpses of the rows and rows of white, impassive faces behind him. It was impossible to tell who had spoken.

They were deep in the heart of Steel City, somewhere below the great plaza, at least half a mile beyond the restricted-travel barrier on level four. This was an administrative centre that Faulcon had only guessed at before, a silent, solemn area, well guarded and uncomfortably clean. The people he had seen working here had all worn prominent identity tags. He had not seen many amulets.

The same voice behind him said, "He is unaware of the camera? You're sure?"

"Almost certainly," said Lena testily. "He was unfamiliar with normal routine at that time."

"Besides which," added Faulcon, "it's very easy to forget normal routine procedures—I forgot I'd been filmed until we got back."

On the screen the shadowy shape of the youngster, moving in an exaggeratedly jerky way, blurred even more as he obviously went down the beach and around the machine. For several seconds there was stillness before their eyes, the strange, gentle motion of the sea being difficult to focus on, causing confusion —was it a photograph or not? Suddenly there seemed to be a flurry of motion before the camera eye. The wind had begun to get strong again, and sand swirled in brief-lived vortices about the derelict. The camera eye trembled slightly. Faulcon couldn't remember if the bykes had fallen during the night, but he felt sure they hadn't.

"Has he gone inside?" came a woman's voice. "What the hell are we looking at?"

Faulcon exchanged a mocking glance with Lena. They decided comment was unnecessary.

Difficult to see against the dark, rising wall of the machine, Kris eventually reappeared, holding onto the metal hull, and inching his way back into camera shot. His body seemed thinner, more ghostly through the redness and the haze of sand. For a long while he stood, irritatingly at the edge of camera view, and stared at the hulk. Then he seemed to fumble with something in his hand, staring down at it but casting quite apparent glances towards the nearby tent. He raised his hand and the screen flared briefly as he discharged a bolt of energy into the wreck. The hull splintered and fragmented; a brief cloud of smoke was rapidly swept away by the wind. Kris edged forward and dropped to a crouch, peering in through the gap he had made.

"Watch now. Watch carefully. The film gets a bit dark here and we want to be absolutely sure we are agreed on what happens." The voice, alien to Faulcon, was worrying in its implication of how often the attached mentality had observed this strip of film.

On the screen he could see Kris Dojaan leaning into the hulk, but his body and the machine were difficult to distinguish through the raging storm of sand and wind. Faulcon glimpsed the boy's figure by brief, dull reflections from his faceted goggles as he looked towards the tent, and by occasional, more clearly resolved, movements as he leaned back and looked up the wall of the wreck.

Suddenly he was gone. "There," said the same voice. "He went inside. Did you see that? He went inside."

Faulcon felt cold. He had instinctively known that Kris had been lying about not having entered the hulk, but here, before his eyes, was the hard, blurred evidence. And yet, when Lena whispered, "What's all the fuss about? So he went inside. So what?" he had to admit that his feeling of anxiety was irrational.

For several minutes the room was heavy with the concentrated silence of its occupants (save for the coughing, shuffling and nervous whispering of those only peripherally interested in the events); the screen remained a view of an ocean, a wind-swept shore, and an alien machine that seemed to change its appearance the longer the gaze was fixed upon it. Faulcon grew hot. Lena, beside him, touched his hand, but any meaning, or shared sympathy, was lost on him. Eventually there was a rapid, startling motion on the screen, something huge passing in front of the camera, out of camera-shot, and then back into view. Faulcon himself, coming to find out what had happened to his young team mate. He battled against the wind, round the hulk, and back into vision again, then peering into the hole in the machine's side.

"Has anybody seen any activity to or from that gap until now?" The voice was the woman's voice, and Faulcon cast a quick glance backwards and saw the person sitting on her own.

There was a murmur that signified "no". Faulcon watched

himself back away from the hole and look around, at the tent, at the ocean, up into the night sky, then back at the machine. And quite suddenly there was Kris, rising from the shore, a dark shadow, insignificant, moving and standing and achieving a significance of high priority. The figure ambled towards Faulcon who suddenly saw it, manifestly jumped with fright—which caused a ripple of mirth among those who perhaps had not seen the film before—and then walked a few paces to meet the boy.

There were a few seconds of motionless, silent communication, and then Kris held out something towards Faulcon.

Brilliant blue light washed across the screen, ceasing abruptly and leaving an intense after-image on Faulcon's eyes, although the Faulcon on the screen—several days ago—had been unaware of any emission from the star-shaped shard that Kris had shown him.

The film was stopped there. The lights in the room came on and Faulcon and Lena swung round in their bucket chairs. Now they sat in the initial arrangement, as part of a square, facing a desk behind which sat two men and a woman, making notes and murmuring quietly to each other. The room was filled with doctors, psychologists, geologists, section Commanders (Ensavlion was not among them), and the dark-suited figures of two Galactic Commanders, the overseers of all planetary colonies. These two men said nothing, and would probably continue in the same vein. They were here as observers, and the only function they served was to take information back to the Federation. But they worked closely with the tripartite structure that controlled VanderZande's World, representatives of which were the three stony-faced individuals who sat before Faulcon. The woman was from the offices of the *Magistar Colona*; she was youngish in looks, with fine features and carefully plaited hair, and she spent a while reading through her notes before she said, "Did Dojaan give you the impression that he was lying?"

"About going into the machine?" Faulcon thought back, trying to remember exactly what it had been that had made him uneasy with Kris Dojaan's behaviour out by the ocean. "Yes, I think he did. He hesitated. He seemed guilty. And it seemed unreasonable that he should *not* have gone into the machine."

"But you didn't go inside yourself," said the sallow-faced man who sat on the right of the woman from the *Magistar Colona*. He was from the Office of the Provincial Secretary, and as he watched the proceedings his face hardly moved; Faulcon was hard-pressed to observe him blink.

"I felt afraid," he said. "And I was looking for Dojaan outside."

"Guilty? Or confused. Dojaan." This contribution was from the other man, older, grey-haired and very overweight; Faulcon had seen him before, Marat Inhorts, adviser to the *Magistar Militar*. "Could he have been confused? Addled? Unsure of what *had* occurred to him?"

"Yes . . . yes, I suppose he could have been."

A nameless psychologist said, "That would fit with the speech and behaviour pattern that Faulcon reported. He may have deliberately entered the machine, and subsequently been confused, perhaps even mind-blanked."

Faulcon said, "He was certainly not possessive towards the amulet, the artifact that seems to be linked with his entry. He was quite prepared to give it to Commander Ensavlion so it could be analysed."

"But Ensavlion stopped him taking it off," said Lena. "I think it was analysed *in situ*."

The council all nodded as one, and the woman held up a sheet of paper, staring at the words written upon it. Behind her, as she touched a small desk button, appeared a trans-ray photograph of the star, showing a jumble of small tubes, circular structures and geometric—crystalline?—formations. Under higher power, it could be seen that the internal face of the star was literally covered with small scratches, linking and crossing, a micro-circuit perhaps, of crude and clumsy design.

Inhorts said, "As you can see, the artifact has a detailed, mostly incomprehensible, internal structure. It is apparently very inferior to our own technology, a crude mechanism for producing energy at all wavelengths, and under a sort of external pressure and heat control; these microcircuits are quite alien to us, but very crude; the crystals fulfil a sort of channelling and reverberation function and are unnecessarily enormous. It's a child's toy. A stupid thing, functionless."

The woman said, "Shortly after the encounter between team and wreck, the machine vanished. There is a generalized belief that it crawled back into the ocean, and then disappeared into time, perhaps in an undersea current, or squall, or perhaps by its own volition. The lack of track marks, and the failure to observe any small disturbance whatsoever in the ocean during the hours following, also suggests the possibility that the machine may have vanished from the site of its shore-line presence. There is, again, little sign of any disturbance of the shore. We have to consider the possibility that this was a deliberate contact, for purposes we can't understand." She held up a photograph, which Faulcon thought might have shown Kris's amulet. "Surely not for this, this toy. Although . . ." she shrugged, placed the picture down, and looked abruptly at Faulcon, her face hardening. "One question that intrigues us, and this is the real reason for your presence here, the question of coincidence: the fact that you, Faulcon, are now the only person we know who has—apparently—been exposed to the monitoring life-form twice."

As the words had come so Faulcon's head had started to ache, and the room had seemed to close in about him. Beside him, Lena's presence grew out of all proportion. He could hear every breath, every heartbeat, every frown, every silent query, every flush of anger and confusion. When he looked at her out of the corner of his eye she was staring straight ahead at the council, but her cheeks were bright red, and her chest rose and fell rapidly, a sign of the emotion she was feeling.

Trying to ignore Lena, Faulcon said, his voice not steady, but hopefully under reasonable control, "I don't really understand the meaning of that . . . What are you implying?"

The woman laughed humourlessly, as if she had only contempt for Faulcon's defensiveness. "We're not really implying anything, rifter. We have here a satellite plot of your route, the three of you, during that last mission. We have your instruc-

142

tions as well. For several days you explored the mountains and part of the desert, approaching the northern shore of the ocean; abruptly you changed direction, south-west through the forest lands, a very large change in direction and one that takes you arrow-straight to the alien derelict, even though at the time you could not possibly have seen it; and even though, as best we can see from the scattered, rather disinterested satellite shots, the hulk was not in evidence for several days before you came . . . it wasn't there. It seems to have come out of the sea to greet you. Whose idea was it to change direction?"

The room was almost totally silent. All eyes were on Faulcon, all faces solemn, all solemnness belying the deep mistrust and inquisitiveness that beat in thirty breasts around the room.

"I don't know," said Faulcon quietly. "We just did it on impulse, I think."

Before there could be any response to that, Lena said quickly, sharply, "In fact it was Kris Dojaan's idea. He wanted to see the ocean, and we knew that the view from the north was across salt flats. We changed direction while we were in the mountains and just followed the sun. When we made the discovery we attributed it to our luck, brought on by lucky Kris Dojaan."

The council talked quietly together for a few seconds; and during that momentary pause Faulcon tried to attract Lena's attention. Irritatingly, and worryingly, she remained staring steadfastedly ahead; but she was aware of Faulcon's worry, he could tell that. She was freezing him out, and he knew exactly why.

"Rifter Faulcon?" He dragged his attention back to the council, to the woman who had been insistently calling to him for several moments.

"Sorry. I was miles away."

"Something has to be explained to you, we have decided, to both of you, in view of your relationship, and Leader Tanoway's existing security clearance. This world, this time, this whole installation, is watched. Who or what is watching us we can only guess. Why they are watching us is something else we cannot at this time answer. It seems, however, that they do make

143

contact; they make contact in a variety of ways, or at least, we assume they do. The amulet may well be an example of one form of contact, a subconscious calling to a site and a sort of 'handling' process . . . in this case Kris Dojaan, although almost certainly both of you were scanned in some detail while you were there. The visual sightings are another contact; or so we assume. And there are other suggested ways that we needn't go into here and now. We know, of course, that you have officially denied seeing the travellers—" she was addressing Faulcon direct. "Or indeed their machine. At the time your section Commander saw both, and when others of the team, now dead or insane, also made visual contact, you claim to have been unconscious. The fact that you are neither obsessed, nor dead, nor indeed committed, suggests that you are telling the truth; your story holds up. We know, of course, that you are lying, your scan-debrief following the incident told us all we needed to know, that you saw as much as Ensavlion—"

Again Lena caught her breath sharply; no doubt she was wondering what would come next, what other falseness and deceit would be revealed. Faulcon could only sit in hot, terrified silence. He had not even *known* they had scanned him at his debriefing. He felt angry, hostile at the invasion of his privacy.

"—Ensavlion's obsession, his public bragging, is an embarrassment, but is also useful. There is an impression that only he has seen this structure, and the travellers, this visitation, but in fact it is a well-documented, and often-sighted phenomenon. Whether or not the travellers are fact or fantasy we can't judge yet. . ."

"Why don't you scan him, like you scanned me." Bitterly, the blood hot in his cheeks.

Inhorts shook his head, "You gave permission on your arrival form that if you made a contact we would scan you. Ensavlion did not. We don't abuse our technology and our position of responsibility, rifter. Although I can see you don't believe it."

The man was right! He *had* agreed to *viscan* debriefing if he should be unconscious, or incapable following a mission.

"Besides," said the woman, "we are not so concerned as to

144

what you saw as to whether or not what you saw is real."

Lena said, dully, almost mechanically, "Did you *viscan* Kris? Did you peer into his skull to see what *he* saw?"

Inhorts nodded thoughtfully, staring at her. "He gave permission. Nothing but intense, high-resolution images of his brother, and the ocean . . . the Paluberion Sea. It was impossible to tell if he even went into the derelict. The images were not helpful. . ."

"What the man means is . . ." the woman in the middle, almost sardonic. "Kris Dojaan appeared to be deliberately blocking his mind to us."

What *are* you up to, Mister Dojaan?

"We're telling you all this, rifter Faulcon, Leader Tanoway, because you are now part of a greater project." As Inhorts talked, he slowed his speech, enunciating the words with almost comic clarity, as if anxious that their full import should sink into the minds of the commoners before him. "You will continue your work with Section 8. Although your commanding officer is security cleared, henceforth your orders will come from us; Commander Ensavlion will not be aware of the fact."

Aware of its pointlessness, Faulcon half-heartedly protested: "I'm not full military; I'm freelance; slightly."

"Not any longer. Law forbids us to watch you, to monitor you in private—unless you give permission? No, I didn't think so—in public, however, you will be overseen constantly. You know the routine: if you have any objections they must be received on tape, by Central Judiciary, within five days, supported by a representative of Section 8. Incidentally, you are forbidden to mention any of this to any representative of Section 8—" a sense of humour, thought Faulcon, and actually smiled himself. "What you have heard here today, what you now know about Kamelios, and the valley, all of it is classified. If you talk about it, if it is suspected that you have talked about it, you are liable to transport and confinement in solitary. I hope that's clear. As you leave pick up grey security identification discs. Carry them, concealed, at all times."

Faulcon nodded dumbly, watching the impassive faces of the

council. The woman said, "This is the first time you have been before the council. It is also the last. But we shall never be very far away."

Faulcon rose and followed Lena to the door. "That's very comforting," he said, as he stepped out into the cool passageway beyond.

CHAPTER ELEVEN

Bright sunlight filled the central plaza of Steel City as Faulcon and Lena walked quickly and silently through the milling crowds, towards the sloping corridors that led to the living levels. There was a fair taking place, probably a trader fair from one of the older colonized worlds, bringing strange goods and strange acts. Faulcon could see two highly colourful men balancing on a tightrope and fighting each other with mock swords. The plaza was a vast arena, and there were hundreds of people gathered by the open spaces; it was difficult to make out more than just a flash of colour and movement.

As they walked up the sloping hill, winding round the outskirts of the plaza and glancing down to the soft green floor below, Faulcon became very aware of the tiny dark spots that were the traffic-monitor eyes; he had no doubt in his mind that those same eyes were now linked to his personal profile, and the relevant views being passed to a bored official in some sprawling, white, personnel-watching room, somewhere in the deeper layers of the city. Lena was also super-sensitive to the idea of being constantly regarded. When Faulcon tried to speak to her she shut him up with a curt and angry comment. She strode ahead of him, tense and upset. Faulcon, not even knowing if she would let him into her room, followed resignedly, assuring her that she was overreacting, expecting nothing else but the silence he received by way of answer.

She opened the wide door of her suite and turned to prevent him entering. Faulcon took a step forward. "Lena, let's talk about this—"

She cut him short with a vicious, and painful, slap across the face.

"You *stupid* bastard."

"I knew you were going to do that." He forced a smile as he tenderly touched his cheek.

"Well, aren't you the clever boy. But lying and deceit isn't clever. Lying is stupid. *You* are stupid. You've lied to Kris Dojaan, and you've lied to me. I thought we were close, Leo. . ."

"It's such a trivial thing, such a small lie—"

Her voice was choked with rage. "Small! Don't you even understand now? It's not the lie, but the fact of the lie. Suddenly I don't think I like you very much."

"Let me talk to you, Lena."

She slammed the door in his face.

There seemed no alternative but to get out of Steel City for a while. He knew Lena well enough to recognize a full day's sulk, and there would be no reasoning with her until the next day at least. He was wrong, he knew; her anger was fully justified. What made him furious was the frustration of being unable to account for himself to her, to put her in the picture. As he made his way carefully down the levels, until he entered the walkways around and above the plaza, he reflected ruefully that now, more than at any other time, was the right moment to say the things to Lena that had haunted him for so long. And she had slammed the door in his face. He would have to wait, and it made him apprehensive when he entertained the possibility of the rightness passing, of the moment becoming wrong again; of the haunting continuing.

For a while at least two things were for sure—he had no Lena to turn to, and he had to avoid Kris Dojaan. If it would have been appropriate to speak to Lena at this time, the same could not be said for Kris. The lad was full of questions, full of restrained anger, full of resentment. And Faulcon could not blame him for that either. But what he had to say to Kris could not be said now, not until he had exorcized a particular ghost. Not until the past was cleared in his mind.

The most sensible thing at the moment seemed to be to take his leave of Steel City, a byke ride perhaps, a night-trip out to the hills and back. An escape. First, though, he ate in a tiny, out-of-the-way bistro, then dialled his apartment recorder for messages. Kris had called twice. And there was a message from Immuk Lee. Was she still in the City then?

Immuk. Faulcon thought of her warmly, and of the help she had been to him before. They had been very close, shortly after Mark Dojaan had been taken, at a time when Faulcon had needed a good friend; they had been lovers in an unsatisfactory way, ultimately deciding not to continue the affair, but remaining close, almost amused at the failure of the sexual dalliance. Lena had been distant from Faulcon at that time. He had not even tried to turn to her. He had known intuitively that it would be a redundant effort.

Immuk Lee, yes; it would be good to talk to her. The only thing that worried Faulcon was that Kris had shown great interest in her. Were they together now? He decided to take a chance. She was down in Biolab 5, and he began to make his way there.

Immuk was on her way out of the science complex as their paths crossed. "Leo!" she said brightly, and stretched to kiss him. Her oriental eyes sparkled as she looked at him, but she withdrew a little, apparently concerned. "What have you been doing to Lena?"

"You've seen her?" Immuk nodded.

"There's a confrontation looming," Faulcon went on. "At the moment she's upset."

"At the moment she's probably still in the Sky Lounge getting drunk. I saw her an hour ago; I spoke to her and she eloquently told me where to go."

"She's in a bad mood."

"I'd never have guessed. What are you doing now? You need a talking post?" She smiled.

"I could do with one. But more than that I just need to get out of the City for a while. I need to get my mind off its current preoccupations. How long are you staying here?"

"I'm leaving right now, although I'll be working here permanently from the end of the seven-day. I'm going up to Overlook. Ben's up there, Ben Leuwentok—"

"Yes I know. The olgoi watcher."

"He's doing some good work, Leo. And not just on olgoi. I've got some charts for him, information on the moons. Why don't you come along up?"

Faulcon required less than a second to agree. "Thanks. That's a very good idea."

Within the hour they had checked their bykes out of the hangar and were speeding west, away from the city, following a route close to Faulcon's return route of a few days before. But Immuk suddenly turned inland from the valley, and up the steep, chalky hills that led through Chalk Stack, to the wind-eroded bluff known as Overlook. The station there was a cluster of dull, cubical houses, grouped around the taller dome-shaped laboratory and observatory building. It looked very run down, and very quiet, but as they drove into the compound, and turned to get a good look at the forest spread out below them, Faulcon heard the sounds of revelry from one of the huts, and gradually became aware that the place was humming with activity.

Ben Leuwentok was a man in his middle age, weather-worn and grizzled; very tanned. The area of his face that bore his mask, when outside, was a striking white streak across his nose, above his eyes and reaching into his cheeks. Faulcon couldn't help chuckling as he saw the strange colouration. He had forgotten that Altuxor emitted a good deal of UV light, and that at the equator a tan was almost as easy to achieve as on Earth, where legend held that pale skin bronzed in hours. But what Faulcon noticed most about Leuwentok was his intensity. His brown eyes gleamed as if with their own light; his face, lean and hard, was never still—he laughed, regarded intently, thought, then broke into rapid chatter, explaining his work to Faulcon, taking immense pride in what he was doing. His hands were as restless as his body, secure only when thrust deeply into the pockets of the green lab-coat he wore.

"The main work we do here is on the native life of Kamelios. My particular interest is the olgoi-gulgaroth symbiosis."

"Symbiosis?" Faulcon was following Leuwentok through a narrow corridor and into a foul smelling, but spacious, animal room. There was a sudden fluttering, darting action on all sides as creatures, large and small, reacted to the intrusion. "I thought the gulgaroth *ate* the olgoi, except when they send them up the hills to feed the females with their seed. Where does the symbiosis come in?"

Leuwentok had busied himself cleaning trails of evil-smelling excreta from the walls of the lower environments; the exudate had dripped from higher, open-fronted (but barred) cages where the sullen, beady-eyed forms of four olgoi squatted, watching the humans. "Somebody'll get sent back to Steel City for letting them get into this state," he said irritably. And to Faulcon. "Symbiosis—well of course—have you ever tried to capture an olgoi in the lowlands? They're protected, they're fed, they're kept warm, they're transported to where their females are. There's a lot of life on Kamelios that would enjoy an olgoi for dinner. But when half a ton of razor-clawed and dagger-toothed arachno-form comes as dessert, you think twice. The olgoi are only vulnerable during the six-moon run."

"That only happens for a few weeks of the year, doesn't it? I know there's a limited hunting season."

Leuwentok looked appalled. "Are you a hunter? You hunt olgoi—shoot them?"

Faulcon shrugged, glancing uneasily at Immuk Lee. "Why not? They're good sport, and good eating. You can't get olgoi in Steel City, the communities won't touch them because they're taboo, and the manchanged don't kill enough even for their own use."

150

"That's disgusting." Leuwentok was quite sincerely appalled. It had genuinely never occurred to Faulcon that a preservation instinct prevailed on Kamelios with regard to the fleet-footed little animals that scampered, for a few summer weeks of the year, up into the territories of the female gulgaroth. He decided against mentioning how his main reason for hunting was to get gulgaroth trophies—claws, teeth, shearing plates, and the coloured gulzite crystals that their bodies manufactured for decoration. Leuwentok went on, "I suppose I shouldn't expect any different from a rifter. But it's bad enough that the man-changed set traps in the high country—Hunderag Country is one of the four main route-ways of the species, and manchanged colonies intercept as much as 20 per cent of the betweenings!"

"The betweenings? What's that, slang for migrating olgoi?"

"Very perceptive," said Leuwentok grumpily. Immuk smiled at Faulcon from across the animal room. The largest olgoi made a keening sound and came to the front of its cage, chewing the bars with the four, triangular cutting plates in its round, decep-tively weak-looking mouth. Faulcon thought its four tiny eyes were all swivelled to watch him. "Aren't they beautiful crea-tures?" Leuwentok continued, suddenly relaxed.

"Yes," said Faulcon. "Do they bite?"

"Do they bite!" Leuwentok glanced, half amused, at Immuk. He held up his left hand; the little finger was missing, and still obviously healing, and there were deep, red-rimmed scars in the palm and on the meat at the base of the thumb. "Just occasion-ally," he added.

And yet, despite these appalling wounds, the man abruptly opened the cage and shot his hand inside. The olgoi all hugged the back of the environment, but the bold one, the one that had come forward, was firmly grasped by its neck. Leuwentok closed the cage and held the shrieking, defecating animal up to Faul-con's face. The smell was unbelievable, a richly chemical odour that turned his stomach—sweet, sickly, overwhelming. Leuwen-tok laughed. "You've probably never noticed, but that's the way the world smells; up here, in the forests, at least." The olgoi, in its ungainly attitude, dangling from the biologist's hand, reminded Faulcon of a green and blue plucked chicken, save that its feet were viciously clawed; the animal made high pitched sounds of objection.

"That smell", said Leuwentok, "is not its own. It's gulgaroth. I caught this one as it began its run. Every year there's a small percentage of olgoi that begin to move up into the mountains when only five moons are dancing. Merlin is the main influence, of course, but only when all six are thirty degrees or more above the horizon do the really big changes happen to the fauna here. I think it depends on the gulgaroth more than the olgoi. The olgoi are just carriers, as you know, and they're programmed by the symbiont. When a male gulgaroth discharges its seed into the olgoi, the olgoi takes off, no matter how many moons are up."

He held the creature close to Faulcon again, and pulled apart the muscular orifice that ran the length of its underside—Faulcon found himself looking at a slick, purplish grey cavity, covered with yellow-tipped nodules, and coated with a translucent and highly unpleasant jelly. "You know how many gulgunculi are in there, how many thrashing sperms? About four. Ridiculous isn't it? Germ plasm in the throat, and four sperm; and they can't even be bothered to inseminate the female themselves. How the hell do they expect that to work biologically?"

"But it does."

"Of course it does." At long last Leuwentok released the olgoi, which ran, panic-stricken and senselessly, around the cage. "Any eco-system that is literally programmed by the movements of six moons is bound to be weird, and bound to work in a weird way. This reproductive process, using a go-between, works— quite what would happen if a male and female gulgaroth ever got together is something I'd dearly like to know."

Immuk had slipped out of the room, Faulcon noticed, and now Leuwentok led the way back to the cluttered workbenches. Coffee was stewing in a conical flask. Coffee! Faulcon bent to sniff the imported drink, and found the aroma to be everything he had imagined of such an expensive luxury—weird, but wonderful of necessity. He declined a beaker-full, however (he didn't really understand why), and watched as Leuwentok sipped a half-glass himself. Immuk came into the room, holding several rolled charts which she placed on the small desk at the end of the room. "I hope these are what you wanted. They have to be returned within a two-day."

Quite suddenly Faulcon felt out of place, an intruder. He had got away from Steel City, and for a while had forgotten about Lena and Kris Dojaan. But now Leuwentok had work to do. Faulcon excused himself and walked alone across the station grounds, and up the chalk bluff. He decided against risking a quick smell of the real, raw atmosphere. He sat there for a long time, watching the sun creep down towards the horizon, watching the wide land redden and darken and take on a very different appearance, somehow more alien than the familiar world of the day. At dusk he began to sense movement below him, in the forest, and in the deep shadows of several of the towering crags of white rock. He was on the point of returning to the station, for safety's sake, when he saw Immuk a few hundred yards away, darting between the seemingly petrified trunks of ancient skagbark, among the strands of powdery sunweed. He rose, stretched, and scrambled down the easier slopes until he was on the spongy land that approached the thin forest. He couldn't see her among the trees, but Altuxor's red disc made a part of the forest unseeable, setting everything into silhouette. He shouted through his mask, calling her name, and her answering cry was almost frightened. "Leo? Is that you? For God's sake go back to the clear land!"

"Where are you?" A breeze had confused his senses. He wasn't sure he knew where her voice had come from; in these conditions the mask's small ear-plugs, designed not to affect sound reception, could not have helped. He stood among the skagbark, conscious of the darkness, aware of the surreptitious movements of small animals. It suddenly occurred to him that he was being very foolish indeed, and that he was unarmed. He had never, in all his sorties through these forests, seen a gulgaroth—but he had never been through at dusk.

He turned back to the bluff, intending to walk up to its top and wait for Immuk to come to him. He continued walking towards the cliff, noticing the dark area at its base, and thinking for a second that it was a shallow cave. The sound, as of several twigs snapping, brought him abruptly to a halt. Blood drained from his face. His heartbeat quickened. It was a familiar sound, that snapping sound—claws clicking out of their pads. The next instant an olgoi shot away from the patch of dark, shrieking horribly. Faulcon was so startled that he felt he had been punched; he froze. He was partly aware that he should be reaching for his holster, partly aware that he wasn't wearing it, mostly aware of the huge shape that was rising onto eight, spider-like legs, and turning its head towards him.

Several eyes sparkled in the forest of black, spiky hair that covered its head; sensory tendrils on the bloated, shiny body quivered frantically, sniffing him out; a gaping hole opened in the face and cutting edges passed silently across each other.

The gulgaroth made a throaty, rattling sound, and took several rapid steps closer to Faulcon, then stopped and began to weave from side to side, its head turning from Faulcon to the sky. It should have attacked instantly, Faulcon knew. The male gulgaroth never hesitated. It should be chewing its way through him by now, not eating, just killing. It was twice as tall as him as it stood on four legs, its other limbs reaching towards him, stroking the air between them.

Behind Faulcon the forest rustled as two human forms darted out of concealment. The gulgaroth made a deep sound, a click-spitting noise. It took a step back! Faulcon heard the sound of a hand-weapon being made operational, and Leuwentok's voice, "No. Don't shoot it!" The man sounded disturbed as he called loudly through his mask.

"Are you mad?" Immuk; angry.

"Don't shoot it!" Leuwentok insisted, and a moment later he tugged on Faulcon's arm. "Move slowly, round to the right, and up the bluff."

"Why doesn't it attack?"

"Look behind you. Easily, not jumpily."

As they edged away, the gulgaroth hesitantly turning with

them, Faulcon looked over the forest; in the dusk sky five moons formed a diamond pattern—tiny Aardwind at the top, the heavily pitted twins Kytara and Tharoo at the sides, and green-glowing Threelight below; nearly fully emerged from occlusion by Kytara, the striated red disc of Merlin was an unfamiliar, and brilliant, addition to the pattern.

"It's beginning," said Leuwentok cryptically. They had put distance between themselves and the gulgaroth, and Faulcon noticed with some relief that the giant animal was slowly turning back to face in the direction of the moons.

"Saved by magic," he said.

"Merlin's magic," Immuk murmured, expanding Faulcon's point unnecessarily. They climbed the bluff—the gulgaroth had vanished by the time they were peering over the cliff for it—and watched the double moon slowly break away from the pattern, Merlin's disc paling quite noticeably, and shrinking a little as Kytara came to cover it again. A few minutes later an eerie howling rose from the forestlands that dipped down towards the barren area of chalk stacks and scrubby, brush-like vegetation. Darkness was approaching quite rapidly, now, and the moons were assuming more dominance in the sky, only pale Aardwind dropping away to the horizon and losing distinction. Magrath was just visible to the north.

Leuwentok said, peering downwards, "I think that's our gulga —quite a long way off. Let's go back to the hide. But go quietly, and keep your eyes open. These masks don't let us smell a gulgaroth like the other creatures can."

The "hide" was a small, pre-fabricated hut, double-walled and strong enough to withstand an attack by the giant animals it was designed to observe. Grey stippling was its only attempt at camouflage. Inside was a single, spacious room, with wall bunks, desk area, eating area, and a closeted convenience that Faulcon used with much relief. When he stepped back into the main room, Immuk and Ben Leuwentok were sitting close together, poring over some figures. They were holding hands. Faulcon was aware, again, that he was still intruding. He wished he could be back at Steel City, and he wished above all that he could talk to Lena, right now; get her back on his side.

"You take the top bunk," said Immuk suddenly, and in that moment all thoughts of leaving the hide were taken from Faulcon's mind, although he said, "I'd thought of riding back to the city. . ."

"With Merlin showing so much of his face? I shouldn't." It was Leuwentok who spoke. "It's coming time for the moons to part, and that's hunting time for all you trigger-happy rifters—it's also problem time for the gulgaroth. They'll guard their little go-betweens quite savagely once they've broken Merlin's spell. Like that fellow out there, right? High on Merlin, but only for a few minutes. You're safer here. We don't mind."

So Faulcon found a chair and sat with them at the table. He was hungry, distracted by the gnawing emptiness inside him. As if reading his mind—or perhaps hearing the rumbling of his stomach—Leuwentok grinned and said, "Vegetable stew. It's heating up; won't be long. Meantime, come and look at this."

As Faulcon moved around the table, to look at the several graphs, Leuwentok looked at him quizzically. "You're hiding out, Immuk tells me. Is that right?"

"Lying low for a while. Personal difficulties."

"I thought you might have been checking up on us. Steel City occasionally sends people out to see if we're coming up with anything really *interesting*. Intelligent life, in other words. But you're just curious, right?"

Faulcon shrugged. "Fascinated. Curious. Intrigued. It seems much more alive out here than the science section in the city."

"It is," said Leuwentok, in a tone of voice that suggested he had little more than contempt for the city scientists. "We're a part of Section 2, the peripheral part. Oh, the city's data is useful: migrations, sightings, specimens. But the real work is done here, in the field."

The sheets of statistics were all concerned with the movements of the six moons, related to single and multiple behaviour patterns of the olgoi, gulgaroth and assorted other creatures. "The moons are really important—that's something I never really understood; I *knew* it, but it had never sunk in, if you see what I mean."

"Merlin is most important of all. Quite why I don't know." Leuwentok searched through the sheets until he found a plot of olgoi mating activity, related to the various emergence phases of Merlin from behind the disc of Kytara. He made his points one by one in rapid succession, stabbing the paper with his finger, giving Faulcon no chance to think hard about any single fact: that a hormone called *attractin* increased dramatically in the olgoi body fluids when Merlin was first seen as a crescent in the early spring months; that male olgoi responded to the first half-face of Merlin by producing quantities of germ cell fluid; that females held fertilized embryos in stasis until Merlin was more than half obscured again, in late summer, but that the final trigger for development was the first time that all the moons were in alignment, vertically, following the Merlin factor. And the gulgaroth, too, showed physiological and behavioural changes all closely related to the occlusion, waning and waxing of the red moon, in particular their seed-mating as Merlin was almost fully seen, the ritual insemination of the olgoi occurring —and there were many results for this conclusion—the moment Merlin's full disc had emerged, and at a time when the olgoi's own reproductive cycle had finished. Some, like the pair they had seen this evening, behaved differently, early, futilely, responding to a wrong sky-sign, perhaps.

"The moons form a highly intricate and complex programme. The pattern of movement is identical year to year—I can show you correlations between the colour change of whip-weed and bladderlash fronds and the distance above the horizon of Threelight. I can show you a thousand correlations—life on VanderZande's World jumps to the pull of the moons' strings, and does so to a degree that is quite staggering. But Merlin most of all—that's the main force. Perhaps for no other reason than that it's hidden for so much of its year. Certainly there are no measurable, or should I say yet-measured, rays from it, no forces reaching down to grapple with physiology. Visual cues are supplied simply by its appearance and disappearance, and

Merlin's combined gravitational tug with Kytara probably acts as a non-visual cue." Leuwentok sat back and looked up at Faulcon, who shook his head, partly in bewilderment as he scanned and rescanned the columns of data, partly from a sense of guilt—after all, Leuwentok had explained all this during those early seminars—and partly from a sense of surprise. The question he had been burning to ask at last found voice.

"There's nothing here about man. Do we escape?"

Leuwentok chuckled. "I could see that question coming a mile off." He moved papers aside until he found what he was looking for. "This is a correlation between the so-called *fiersig* and the position of the moons. Inasmuch as *fiersig* affect man, the moons affect man. You can see that we get spates of the activity when there are four moons high. *Fiersig* tend to pass south-north as you know, they come from the direction of the mountains, and drift away across the valley. As they move they follow a line towards either Aardwind or Tharoo, changing direction as their target moon sinks or rises obliquely. And don't ask me what any of this means, because I have no idea, and I don't think anybody ever will—if we were going to demonstrate that the *fiersig* were life-forms I think we'd have done it by now. The whole thing is cosmic linkage, moon to world, moon to life. Earth experiences a similar linkage, but in a much simpler way since it only has the one moon, and most life on Earth is programmed by daylight. But that moon does have *some* effect—dogs howl at it, physiology can be shown to fluctuate with it, sea-tides are much the result of it. On Kamelios we have all of that six-fold."

"That's why there are no dogs here," said Immuk knowledgeably. "They howl themselves to death."

Faulcon frowned as he looked at her. "Really?"

She looked embarrassed. "It was a joke, Leo."

Leuwentok went on, "Incidentally, there is no correlation between moon and the time winds—not as far as anyone has determined. Nor between moon and the time squalls, or eddy currents or swirlwinds—whatever governs the flow of time through the valley is responding to something other than the obvious climatic and environmental triggers."

"And the sightings of the pyramid?" Faulcon felt a moment's unease—he had stayed quiet about the pyramid for so long, tried to put it from his mind so totally, that he felt himself fighting against a powerful internal resistance to even mentioning the subject.

Leuwentok stared at him thoughtfully, and with just a hint of apprehension. Guessing what was the matter, and taking a chance that what he was doing was not against regulations, Faulcon drew out the small security disc. At once Leuwentok rose to his feet, walked up to Faulcon and took the piece of plastic. "Good God—he's got a grey clearance. How did you get this? You *are* a rifter. . . ?"

"I made a sighting. I've been sworn to silence on anything I see, hear or do, on pain of isolation."

"Well, don't take too much notice of that," said Leuwentok, and showed Faulcon his own clearance. Immuk waved hers. "A grey clearance doesn't mean much; it does mean I can talk to you about the aliens. Even so, nothing you hear on the subject of sightings should go out of this room. Olgoi, gulgaroth, moons —that's fine, that's education. But someone in Steel City doesn't want the sighting, or our ideas on them, talked about. They're trying to keep it all to rumour level; no hard facts. What they don't want is a generalized *belief* in an alien presence. Not yet, at least."

"Do you *know*, then, that Commander Ensavlion's sighting— an alien machine, with travellers aboard—is a genuine sighting of genuine creatures?" Faulcon was hot, the flush in his face burning him.

"Have you experienced them?" asked Leuwentok quietly. "I mean the aliens, not these so-called humanoid creatures, these time-travellers. I mean the *real* aliens. Have you sat in that valley and sensed them?"

What do I say, Faulcon wondered, and his head whirled in confusion. Did he admit things or not? Did he make the decision now that the experience of the alien in the valley the previous evening—something he had felt several times before, but only when naked to the world, at times such as his hunting trips—that that experience was real? Or was it just imagination? He said, "I've felt something—something close. As if I was being watched. Yes."

"Have you seen the phantom?"

"Certainly. More than once."

"How about the timelost, the shadowy figures crawling up the side of the valley?"

For a moment Faulcon was puzzled; he had not even heard of such sightings, and said as much. Leuwentok agreed. "They're a rarer sighting, and they tend to be very disturbing. It only goes to show that more is going on in the world than even an old-timer like you knows about." Faulcon had heard that before, somewhere. Leuwentok pressed on, "What about the whirli-gigs?"

Faulcon had heard talk of the whirling forms that swept through the valley occasionally, but he had always thought them to be tricks of the light, or a form of the *fiersig*. He had never seen one. Leuwentok nodded thoughtfully, asked quietly, "What about God?"

"God? The white-robed man? That's just nonsense—that's a joke, a Steel City joke." The tall, rather arrogant-looking ghost that walked through the ruins, his feet hidden in a swirl of dust. Faulcon had shared the joke—on Kamelios you get to see everything if you wait long enough, even God!

"They're no joke, Leo. They're genuine, and terrifying, sightings. The old man himself, his arms outstretched to welcome you into his kingdom. And a surprising number of people go—and get lost." Faulcon said nothing, watched and waited. He was now beginning to feel a little dizzy. He had *seen* the phantom, but he had never thought anything at all of the wild reports of spiders, gods, whirling shapes, spirals and shimmering alien forms that made a man feel nauseous to see, so indefinable and confusing was their appearance. It was Kamelios folklore, the sort of nonsense that accumulates on any world.

But in the next few moments Leuwentok put him straight on

that particularly blinkered attitude. "You'd be surprised what people report that they've seen—in the valley, on the edge of the valley, in the hills and faraway. A lot of it is classified. A lot of people have left Kamelios in a disturbed state of mind; most just keep quiet. The people who live in the township, miles from the valley, well, perhaps they keep quiet too—but regularly there are medical teams go out and, so to speak, 'cure the manias' of a few townsfolk who have seen things, or who feel compelled to undertake irrational, or dangerous tasks—long walks seeking an enlightenment, or a rendezvous with something, or someone from their past lives. The townspeople are all affected in one way or another by a conviction that others of their family are on the world, and waiting for them, lost, alone, frightened, perhaps crashed in one badland or another. It's very strange."

"I'd never noticed. They always seem calm, disinterested, learning to live with the world in their own way, rather unconcerned about us and our valley-edge city."

Immuk spoke for the first time in several minutes. She had been poring over the charts, making marks by certain figures. "Most of the community folk are fed huge doses of some form of repressant, something to stop them being as restless as we are —something to stop them wandering off in search of their dreams. It's all official; they asked for the treatment."

Leuwentok laughed as he watched Faulcon's solemn face. "And that's it, Leo. Dreams. You feel an alien presence because that's what interests you. We are all at the mercy of some form of desire fulfilment. We see lost kinfolk, lost friends, lost images from our past—we see treasure, aliens, religious manifestations, and mostly we see enigma, we see things that excite us because of their mystery. It holds us here more strongly than gravity. We are not conscious of it because consciously most of us become dulled, disinterested, as if incapable of excitement. And yet, deep down, we can't give the world up—we can't run out on our need to see those images, to visualize our dreams, or our fears."

It did not ring true for Faulcon. "This is just your idea?"

"Just my idea. Except that—you asked about the effect of the moons on man—well, the number of reports of sightings of different images fluctuates quite remarkably—it correlates with Merlin's appearance. As Merlin shows from behind Kytara, M-Z-alpha neural activity increases; so does leucocyte mobility in the tissues, but I don't suppose that's important. At the same time, man sees the ghosts of the Kriakta Rift."

"Some of those ghosts have been holographed—the phantom, at least."

The point was not lost on Leuwentok. He hesitated a moment. "That's true, of course. The phantom may be a different phenomenon. . ."

"A time-travelling phenomenon, perhaps?"

"Maybe. It is the only image that *has* been holographed. The so-called pyramid, which on hypnotic description turns out to be a much less pyramidal structure than you might think, has been photographed several times—only nothing showed up. That shape is a very powerful human symbol, more powerful than people often realize. And gold is a powerful symbol too— it isn't surprising that they show up in combination as an enigmatic sighting by people searching for just that."

"And yet it is not a pyramid at all—is that what you said? Why would people imagine one shape, and be aware of something different?"

"Dreams," said Leuwentok. "Deep desire, deep-seated images—no alien has been seen, despite that one man's claim. And yet something is dreaming along with man. I believe that. The pyramid is the dream image of something non-human, the alien presence that we all seem so aware of on a non-intuitive level. We share its image—we change it to our own; but we're not only chasing our own dreams on Kamelios, sometimes we're chasing something else's."

CHAPTER TWELVE

Faulcon travelled back to Steel City in the morning, having slept fitfully and uncomfortably. Leuwentok had worked late, and was still asleep at dawn when Faulcon made himself a small breakfast and left the hide to pick up his byke. Immuk, sleepily, wished him good luck.

Lena was in her apartment, still in night attire despite the lateness of the morning. She had spent a night every bit as restless as Faulcon's; the anger, and after-effects of excessive drinking, showed clearly on her: rimmed eyes, dishevelled hair, listlessness. She opened the door to Faulcon, stood silently for a moment looking at him (he said nothing himself), then stepped aside to let him in.

"I went up to Overlook," he said as she closed the door, but she ignored him, walked across the room to her small window and stood there, sullenly looking out across the sloping surface of traverse unit Opal, watching the activity of hull engineers laying external cables. If she had behaved differently Faulcon would have known he had lost her; but this stiff disappointment was an invitation to speak for himself, to convince her that she was wrong to be so angry.

The trouble was, Faulcon reflected quite grimly, she was absolutely right.

He went to her dining ledge and sat down, hands clasped before him. He could watch her, and also gaze ashamedly at his hands, depending on how he felt. "Okay Lena, I can understand your bitterness. Honesty is what we promised, even if the *fiersig* turn us head over heels. It's never easy to keep a grip on everything that happens inside, especially here, on Kamelios; but somehow we always managed. . ."

"*I* managed,' said Lena stiffly, not moving from the window.

"You led me to believe you were Leo Faulcon. But you're not, you're a different man. You have the same name, but you're not the man I've known for five years, on and off Kamelios."

For a second Faulcon was sufficiently confused to think she was implying something far more significant than she was: that he was in some way a substitute, had killed the real Faulcon and slipped in in his place, a spy, an infiltrator. His grasp of the metaphoric way she spoke reasserted itself and he wondered how to begin to tell her that he loved her, that he loved her very much indeed; that he had not always loved her, but that was not his fault, that was Kamelios playing games with him; that if he couldn't explain to her what had happened to him here he would be heartbroken to lose her, because increasingly she was the focus of his life, and he had looked forward to the day they quit VanderZande's World for several months, now, and had even made preliminary application for a place on the non-established colony of Tyrone's World, not so very far from New Triton.

No words formed to explain all this. How could something so familiar, so easy, so true, be so difficult? He knew the answer. Mark Dojaan. Bloody-minded, star-forsaken Mark Dojaan. She didn't even know him, had probably only seen him in passing when he had worked with Faulcon. And yet he was interfering in her life just as he had interfered with Faulcon's; and just as he had interfered in everybody's life, wherever he went, and no doubt, knowing Mark, *when*ever he went.

Unexpectedly, Lena walked back across the room and sat down across the dining ledge from Faulcon. He had been miles away, running through the rift valley, sharing—and this is what still shamed him, despite the other shame—sharing Mark Dojaan's destructive enthusiasm, caught in the whirling vortex of his mercenary vigour as he prowled and kicked-over and up-turned and sneaked-inside the structures and ruins.

Lena said, "So many lies, Leo. So much deception. Do you blame me for going off the handle? I keep asking myself, what next? What else? You know me, Leo. I can't cope with things like that. I have to have my life straight, orderly, above board. I need honesty like I need food. I not only depend on it, I thrive on it. I suppose I've been aware of the lack of honesty in you for months; I didn't know what it was was, but I've not been thriving. I've been wilting. You've commented on it yourself, that I've seemed moody, depressed, too easily upturned by the mood ripples."

"There are no more lies to confess to," said Faulcon quietly. He reached out and took Lena's hands across the ledge. She didn't pull away, but she didn't respond either. "There are elaborations, insights, facts that come out of the lies. But there are no more deceptions, nothing waiting to spring out at you."

"Thank God for that. Leo, I'm not at all sure that I want you to tell me any more about it; and yet I know that I'll not be able to relax until you do. You'll have to explain at least why you felt it necessary to deceive me. And then I suppose you should tell Kris about his brother. He's been here twice, looking for you, asking questions. I said nothing of course, but the time has come to admit you were friends with Mark."

"That's going to be hard. He has an image of Mark, and I've got to crack that image. Kris idolizes his brother. I'm not so sure I don't have the power to crack him wide open himself. I'm just not sure."

"You shouldn't have lied to him about knowing Mark. That was stupid. I knew you wanted to keep it from him out on the mission, but I assumed the reason the two of you wanted to be alone that first evening back— remember?—was so you could talk to him about Mark. It never occurred to me that you hadn't. If we hadn't spent so much time rift-suited up I'd surely have dropped you in it inadvertently. Then Ensavlion did it."

Faulcon managed a half-hearted laugh. "I thought my head was going to explode. I really did. I left that station on tiptoe. I thought that if Kris caught me there he'd do violence before I could get a word in."

"You are the most god-awful coward." But she liked that, because she was a large percentage coward herself. That's why she and Faulcon were still alive, when men like Leader Kabazard were dead. Cowardice, caution, the same side of a coin, and Leo Faulcon and Lena Tanoway were also on the same side; Faulcon knew that, unless he said something tactless, or got self-righteously angry, or unless a *fiersig* hit the city during the next few minutes, he had got Lena back.

Drawing her hands away from his she pressed a small panel on the wall by the uncomfortable dining ledge. The wall blinked open and displayed the well-stocked drinks cupboard. She knew Faulcon's taste in drink and drew out two small containers of *baraas*, nicely chilled. "Here's to the worst liar in the world . . . about to come clean." She filled and raised a glass.

Faulcon responded, and said bitterly, "Here's to Mark Dojaan. May he rot in the swamps of VanderZande's Cretacious."

As Lena sipped at her *baraas* she watched Faulcon carefully, thoughtfully. "I had no idea you had such hate in you, Leo. I had no idea that you and Mark were such enemies."

"We weren't enemies," said Faulcon, "My hate came after he was swept away. Reflected hate, reactionary hate."

She nodded as if she had somehow divined the darkness in Faulcon's mind, which of course she could not have done. "Tell me about the travellers, anyway. That's what's made me angry. Mark Dojaan is your problem with Kris."

"It's all connected," Faulcon said, and drained his glass. The *baraas* went through him like fire, made his muscles tense for a moment, then over-relax. He stepped back those several months as easily as he might step across a threshold; vivid, detailed memory projected before his mind's eye after months of being hidden away, repressed. He went white with cold. Lena said nothing, and in his own time he told her of that first mission.

"I'd been out to the valley before, during training. But I'd not been given clearance to go down, so I spent a lot of time staring at the view, and watching the ordinary winds and the men grubbing about among the ruins. I exepected that at any given moment a time wind would be blowing, but I never saw one. People described them to me, and most of all they described what happened to people who got caught at the edge of them. I began to feel as if I *had* experienced a wind. But I also started to jump every time it gusted strong on my naked skin. . ."

"I remember. You were really on edge for the first few weeks."

"That's right. On edge, because I spent so much on *the* edge, looking down into the valley. The anticipation, the suspense, was agonizing. People talk about time winds as if they blow fresh every day, with autumn breezes every evening. I sat or stood or ran and I watched and I watched, and inside I was getting more and more twisted. I asked you why I was going through this and you said, 'adjustment'. We all go through it, you said, and I was too glad to hear those words to think that you might have been making empty platitudes. No, don't interrupt. Just listen. I need you to understand something. I need you to understand what happened the first time I went down into the valley. For God's sake, Lena, it's as if it happened yesterday again; I feel just like I felt then, all the tension, all the fear, all the guilt and confusion. So let me explain it, and try and understand it."

"I'm sorry, Leo. Go on. I'll keep quiet."

"I hardly knew Ensavlion. To me he was a man in a rift suit who gave orders. I was training with a Section 3 team, stripping removables for examination, but at first I wasn't allowed more than two-thirds of the way down the valley walls. Ensavlion was with the section, as Commander—you remember that—and he was *never* out of that valley. He was always there, and he even went down with other sections. He was obsessed with the idea that one day there'd be a sighting of the intelligence that made these ruins; they'd find a body, or a message. He was convinced that somewhere in all that junk they'd find a living Kamelion, still eating breakfast. Nobody thought in terms of controlled time-travelling; or at least, if they thought of it they kept quiet. It seemed a huge jump from natural time distortion to free and safe travel through time. You've experienced this yourself, you know how it is. Madness, maybe, but that's the way minds work on Kamelios. A particular day occurred! I was to go down to the valley floor for the first time. There were about ten men from the section with me, following Ensavlion, while many more spread out up the valley. There had been two squalls, apparently, and several new structures had appeared during the night. Even as we reached the bottom of the canyon there were warning sirens going. We all stopped and listened, and in the far distance you could actually see the sky darkening, and those immense purple flashes of light over the far horizon. There was some debate as to whether or not we should get the hell out of there, but the older team members thought that was stupid. We had rift suits, and we could clear the area easily . . . why all the fuss? You got several minutes warning of the wind channelling down the valley. Ensavlion agreed and we started to move fast. I ran in the middle and I was scared as hell. That darkness seemed to be getting closer, but it must have been miles and miles away. What was of interest, what Ensavlion wanted to look at before it was swept away again, was a whole house. I mean, that's what it was. You've seen the pictures, I expect, a real brick house, with a roof, and obvious doors and windows. Nothing like any house you've ever lived in, mind you, but a house, a real dwelling place, ancient, all closed up and all intact. You could almost hear Ensavlion thinking, there might be a couple of aliens in there, still in bed, still in *coitus tempora interruptus*. We approached it like a pack of wolves, staggering and powering between walls of rock, and round the ruins, and through damn near sheer gullies, some still with water in them. The whole place was a geological nightmare. You couldn't even glance to one side without seeing something that didn't fit with something else, some stratification, or sedimentation, or boulder, or glacial deposit that just didn't belong where it was. How the crust survives these upsets I just don't know. But this was nightmare valley, and even the rift suits were having a job keeping balance.

"And there was this little brick building, really weird, standing askew, it must be said, and obviously beginning to crack where the stress had broken its main structure. The team gathered round the place in something like ecstasy. And in they went, with me photographing outside, and Ensavlion calling stupid instructions like, 'If they're there, be courteous. Back away and make no sudden moves.' I mean, it was really pathetic. It was still calm in the valley. Ensavlion reckoned we had almost ten minutes. But the rift suits let you know every breeze and draught and that was something I wasn't used to. Every time it gusted, my stupid heart stopped with the whining noise the wind on the sensors evokes. I was a nervous bloody wreck. I don't think I've ever been so scared in my life.

"And then a hell of a wind sprang up. Not a time wind, there was no klaxon blare, no darkness; just a healthy wind, the sort that you expect to precede a time wind by several minutes. Nobody reacted. They went on working, and over the radio I could hear them laughing, and talking as if there was no danger . . . and I suppose at that precise moment there wasn't. But at the time I had no idea . . . I saw that dark pall in the distance, I heard the racket in my headphones, the sensors, and I went crazy. I went so crazy that I must have screamed my panic, and so confused the rift suit that it whipped my legs up into rapid-motion position, but started to run around in circles. There I was, berserk in a berserk r-suit, and the rest of that team just howling with laughter. They stood there, watching me, and you'd have thought they'd never seen anything so funny in their lives. And they probably hadn't. Ensavlion stepped in; he came over and shot a tranquillizer from my suit into my arm. I felt the sting. I was still yelling. As the suit calmed and I calmed he said, 'It's all right, son. In a few weeks you'll get your own back on some poor rookie who'll do just the same. Let's get you up to to the cliff top.' I felt, you might say, something akin to a fool. In fact I felt quite suicidal. Maybe the drug had something to do with it—it was certainly giving me blurred vision—but the sight of those r-suits swaying about as their occupants laughed at me was crippling. I was crying when Ensavlion got me to the top of the canyon, and it was a reaction to that awful fear, the feeling that a wind was going to snatch me at any second! And then guess what happened. . ."

"A time squall, of course," said Lena. Throughout Faulcon's

narrative she had sat stiff, silent, solemn, slightly irritated by the way he filled in on detail with which she was well familiar—that much was often apparent to Faulcon—but perhaps piecing together in her own mind the events of those many months back. "A time squall?"

"A swirlwind," said Faulcon, "The first and last I ever saw. Maybe I had some survival sense working, I don't know. But that wind came out of time in a flash. Those poor beggars down in the valley had about eight seconds warning, long enough for those closer to the ledge system to bounce up out of the valley. Three men got out. I forget how many died. I saw two go up on jet power, straight up into the air. It didn't work, of course, they vanished into the squall . . . no, not like a squall; it was like a real wind, a real time wind, but generating out of nowhere and spreading out in both directions. To us, it seemed like a time wind that had come without warning. The brick building vanished. I dragged myself away from the edge, and all I could hear were screams, and the whining of the wind, and the exploding sound, the booming of atmosphere. It was so dark, like being trapped beneath a blackening sky. Ensavlion stood on the cliffs, looking down, watching the men die.

"Then the whole air was filled with a sort of golden glowing. It was like a bonfire at night, the radiant light filling the darkness, but not pushing it away. Ensavlion was saying things, incoherent things. I could hear him, but I couldn't understand him. He kept standing there, staring down into the canyon. I crawled towards him, unable to get the rift suit to stand properly. I was still shaking, still crying I suppose, my eyes blurred with tears and dizziness. And I looked down into the valley and yes, I saw it: a tiny, tiny pyramid, giving off an immense amount of yellow light. There were shadows and movements in it, nothing I could discern, but then you often get that in the ruins that are time-swept . . . you know, decorative, or the way the light passes through the different densities of crystal in some structures. I looked at that pyramid and I was watching it as it vanished, really abruptly, vanishing from that great swirl of confusion and time change happening around it. You couldn't help thinking that it was the pyramid that was causing the wind, dragging things through time with it as it was afterwards talked about. But at the time I didn't think of it as a time machine, or any sort of machine. It was just a magnificent, and beautiful, and awe-inspiring piece of time-junk.

"I backed off from the cliff edge again and managed to get the rift suit up to its feet. Ensavlion came running over to me and I realized the golden glow had gone. He started to shout at me, 'You saw them, you must have seen them!' I shook my head. I said I'd seen nothing. Everything about that vision was becoming just that . . . a sort of vision, a dream-like memory. I found myself not believing I'd seen anything. The sky brightened, a faint pink again. The sound of the wind had died away and my head was throbbing and felt slightly unreal. I watched Ensavlion standing, staring back at the rift. He kept saying, 'Somebody must have seen them. Somebody, one of the others.' At this time I didn't know that more than half the team had been lost. He came up to me and started to question me about whether I'd seen anything. I agreed that I'd seen a golden *light*, but for some reason I didn't admit to seeing the pyramid. I suppose I thought I hadn't really seen anything, and didn't want to get involved with what I detected as being an obsessive interest in this man, even then. But Ensavlion had seen more. He'd seen godlike figures, moving in and out of the pyramid through the very walls. I didn't see any such thing, all I saw was shadows. But he insisted that those figures had appeared there, and he kept on about it, and sometimes, when I think back, I can resolve humanoid shapes from those shadows, and I wonder if he was right; but the more he insisted at the time, the more I hid what I'd seen. I kept thinking, I knew it was going to happen. I could have warned them, I could have shouted; or perhaps I did, and they died because they took no notice of me. I survived and they died. Every day that passed I got more ashamed. People kept coming up to me and asking me why I'd survived, a rookie—always the first to go—when their mates had been taken. Was I in the canyon, or skiving? I lied and lied. Others asked if I'd tried to help. I lied and lied.

Others had heard about my panic, and they thought that was really funny. Ensavlion kept on about those stupid figures. The other three who'd survived had only seen the pyramid—so they said. And within a week they'd all got lost, one of them going up to the canyon's edge and falling in. He hadn't gone to find the pyramid, he'd just lost his mind. So it was Ensavlion. And me. And even Ensavlion came to believe I'd seen nothing. But I'd been close, you see . . . close. And so I got taken under his wing. Just like you saw him with Kris, so he was with me. Protective, friendly, fatherly. Concerned. And just like he was with me, so he had been with Mark Dojaan, and continued to be so after the event."

Lena looked a little surprised. "I've gone adrift—wasn't Mark one of those killed by the swirlwind?"

"He wasn't with us that day. I met him a few days later, through Ensavlion. You were on the islands, remember? Poking around down there with some section or other, digging up fossils and not contacting me."

Lena smiled thinly, rose from the ledge and walked to the soft vastness of her couch. She flopped down and put her feet up, staring at the ceiling. Faulcon watched her, wondering with irritating insistence what life would be like without a Lena featuring in it. He said, "The frustrating thing is, it probably wouldn't have made a damn bit of difference if you'd known that I was scared silly, and saw that pyramid. Not a bit of difference."

"You're undoubtedly right. I thought the revelation would hurt, but why should it? There is nothing nasty in it, nothing too shameful, nothing to make me think less of you, nothing to make me think that for those events alone you'd have kept quiet about it, told me nothing, upset me because of the *fact* of the deception, which of course is at the root of my anger. In other words, Leo, that's not the whole story. In other words— and I realize you haven't actually said 'that's all'—I expect to hear something else from you, something that makes it seem sensible that a man would deny even to himself the memory of such an event as glimpsing an alien time machine." She raised her head and peered at him, then after a moment shuffled onto her elbows. "I imagine Mark Dojaan is about to rear his handsome head."

"Mark Dojaan!" Faulcon exploded with bitterness as she spoke the name. Perhaps the *baraas* had reduced his emotional responsibility, but suddenly he was desperately angry, and the glass in his hand seemed functional only to be cast against the far wall of the room. The sound of the shattering vessel was wonderful, shocking. Fragments glittered and scattered about the room and Faulcon felt some of the tension drain from him. "I'm so sick of hearing that bloody name," he said, his voice soft, icy. He stared at Lena who shrugged non-committally.

"It means very little to me. I hardly knew him."

"And yet . . . though you didn't know him he's still there, behind you, overshadowing you. He's in your life whether you like it or not. He's like this bloody planet, always there, always watching, always with a finger firmly up the rear-end of your life. Mark Dojaan! How I wish to God he'd died before I knew him."

Faulcon's sudden anger fed Lena's. She swung her legs off the couch and stood, walking to her sleeping closet and stripping off her night clothes. "No more lies, eh Leo? No more deceptions to be revealed." Faulcon watched her coldly, partly wanting her as he stared at her nude body, partly afraid of her.

"There's nothing more," he said, but he knew she could hear the silent prayer he offered with that awful statement. She turned, dropping a flowing kaftan across her shoulders and billowing it out. There was no love in her face, no understanding. For a second she was silent, then she said, "What is it you're so afraid of, Leo? That he might be listening from Othertime? Is that it? Are you afraid he'll come back and dominate you again, make you feel like an idiot, laugh at you? That's what he did, isn't it? He got you under his thumb like a good little dog-like friend. Here Leo, there Leo, do this for me Leo, that's not funny Leo, enter your ten-minute embarrassment phase. You followed Mark Dojaan about as if you were on a chain. Did you think I hadn't seen? Do you think I'm blind?"

"It wasn't like that. For a while we were close friends—"

Lena's laugh was bitterly cynical. She walked towards Leo, standing in the bright light of the Kamelion day, and the expression on her face was malice. "You fool. You star-struck fool. Friendship? Do you know, do you *really* know what friendship is? Friendship isn't coming back time and time again and forgiving. Friendship isn't seeing who can vomit *baraas* furthest over the edge of the rift. Friendship is sharing the private part of you; *sharing*, Leo. Not giving, not taking, but exchanging. Friendship isn't one way, one giving, one taking. And that's exactly what you and Mark Dojaan were. I know that, Leo. I could feel it in you, and I heard it. I kept clear of you during that 'friendship' because I was afraid that if I tried to interfere he could damage what you and I had far more than I wanted. Perhaps something inside of me *was* afraid of Mark, though I didn't know him, perhaps I was warning myself against him all the time. Maybe you're right, Leo, maybe he was more powerful than most people ever realize. He had his doggy friend, giving his all—did you give your all, Leo? And you were too friendship-struck to realize that he was using you, and baiting you, and making you do things that your better self must have been screaming objections to. And this is why you hate him now, you hate him because you loved him, and you loved him because you were afraid of him, and in awe of him, and you rationalized everything about your relationship by calling it 'close friendship', and there's something about that bastard that lingers on, you're right, Leo, it's here, it's all around, the power of his mind, because you're standing here, your face white, your body shaking, your heart thumping, and you're defending someone and something that just moments ago you were screaming hate for. He's got you head over heels, Leo; you haven't shaken him off even now." She reached out and touched his face gently, then reached round to stroke the back of his neck. She came into his arms and felt the despair in him, and the rapidly surfacing tears.

"I loved him," he whispered.

"I know you did."

Faulcon involuntarily squeezed her tighter, and though she couldn't see it his eyes were tight shut, and his teeth crushed together as he drowned out, and fought against, the sudden furious desire he felt to scream and hit out and cry like a baby.

Lena said, "I've been waiting for you to find the way of getting this off your chest. This is why I was so angry Leo, I'm sorry. I knew you had this terrible thing weighing on you, and even though you should know it's not so terrible for me . . . I'm from New Triton, remember? Everybody believes in love without constraint there. But I knew you didn't, and I knew this was hurting you, and I could see you had blanked it out. But I'm human too, Leo, and I couldn't help wondering what else, what other deceptions were being gradually erased, buried in your super-active unconscious."

Faulcon relaxed his grip. He drew away from her and kissed her lightly on the lips. She smiled and kissed him back, long, hard, trying to express in that simple action the depth of her love and regard for him, no matter what, despite all.

Faulcon walked up to the window and leaned his forehead against it, staring out across the city, looking at the activity, but not seeing it.

"He was a criminal; he was a mercenary, merciless, power-struck kleptomaniac son-of-a-bitch. He looted the valley and he got me to loot it too. We used to go in there in our suits and hide anything small, and commercially saleable, in the spaces in the legs and body. It made the suits difficult to operate, but we walked carefully out of the valley every time and over a few weeks we got quite a little export trade, working through another friend of Mark's, a shuttle pilot operating a food drop, the sort of thing that gets a dismissive glance from the port guard. God, he had that so well worked out. It seemed such a good idea . . . give the Galaxy a bit of VanderZande's World . . . Why the hell should it all be stuck in one city, with only a fraction on display in the museum. By what right did the Federation prohibit the removal of artifacts off-world?

"And then one day we were working a standard rip-off, ostensibly part of our routine examination of ruins, and as usual we'd slipped ahead of the team a bit, and I went up the slope keeping an eye on the leader, while Mark darted in and out of the ruins, looking for removables, And a bloody wind came. Well, we had the usual notice, several minutes. I was damned glad to be up the side, and I called the warning down to Mark in case his suit was being screened from the sirens. He popped out of the ruins he was in, looked into the distance, checked my estimate of time before it struck—we reckoned five minutes—and went back in. He'd found a pile of small objects that looked like they had machinery inside them. He was loading his suit. He took two minutes. The sirens were going and I could see the rest of the team making an orderly ascent of the canyon. Mark was easing himself out of the jumble of metal and crystal structures when suddenly he called out that he was stuck. 'What d'you mean, stuck?' I shouted. 'Get the hell out of there!' 'I can't,' he shouted back. Some of the junk had dropped through his suit and was jamming a mechanism somewhere. He was caught there, in his suit, unable to move. I just stood there feeling sick, feeling terrified, and thinking to myself, the travellers ... they might come back, Ensavlion's godlike creatures. In a split second I became obsessed with seeing the pyramid again, following in the wake of the wind. Mark's screaming faded away, just like the sirens, and the clatter of wind-sound on my suit's sensors. That bloody wind struck, and the moment it struck I turned away. I didn't even watch him go; I can't even remember what abuse he was shouting as he was cut off in mid-word."

"So you killed him, and you killed your guilt, and then you had to live with what you'd done, and you killed that too."

"I guess so. It hardly took any time at all to erase Mark Dojaan from my mind, to put what I'd done aside, to regard it as a dream. Then Kris came, and it all came back, really intensely and frighteningly. I felt so torn with him, so close on the one hand, and so afraid, so distant on the other. And I sensed his tie with the wind, when it happened, a few days ago, and that hasn't helped."

Lena put her arm around him. "I think it might perhaps be

as well not to tell Kris any of this. You're right when you say he has an image of his brother, a good image, the image of a man of courage and honour. Kris shouldn't be punished for Mark Dojaan. What do you think?"

Before Faulcon could answer, however, there was a loud, almost angry knock at the door. Faulcon turned, puzzled, and Lena shrugged and walked to the door switch. "Who is it?" she called.

"Kris. Let me in, will you?"

Exchanging an uneasy glance with Faulcon, Lena nevertheless opened the door to her apartment.

It all happened almost too quickly for Faulcon to comprehend. Kris swept into the room, his face white, his whole body rigid with tension. "You bloody lying bastard!" he screamed, and ran at Faulcon. He punched Faulcon hard on the mouth, then slapped him about the head until he sank to his knees. "You're a liar! A bloody liar!" And he kicked viciously up at Faulcon's chest, sending his team mate toppling back towards the window. Lena was suddenly behind the youngster, and one jerk of her arm had Kris sprawled on the floor. He jumped to his feet and smiled with a sort of triumph. There was blood on his lip. Faulcon had stood up as well, clutching his chest and breathing with difficulty.

"Get out of here," said Lena to the boy.

"Mark was a good man," said Kris, speaking slowly, deliberately. "I don't know why that bastard said all those things, but they're lies, and he's a liar, and he's hiding something, and if he says one more word about my brother I shall kill him. And you'd better believe that, Mister Leo liar Faulcon."

Lena took a step towards him and slapped him hard and stunningly on the face. "I told you to get out of here." Kris turned about and ran from the apartment. Lena swore softly and went to a drawer, searching around among the junk until she found a small metal box, a detector. In second she had found the small needle, fixed above the door, with which Kris had heard their every word.

"How the hell did he get hold of that?" said Faulcon. "Unless Ensavlion gave it to him."

"Damn," was Lena's only comment as she snapped the needle. "He must have hidden it there when he came looking for you." She looked anxiously at Faulcon. "Do you really think Ensavlion would have okayed him eavesdropping?"

Faulcon eased himself down into a chair, clutching his stomach and dabbing at the blood on his lips. Lena suddenly mobilized into action, shedding her kaftan and taking out her grey overalls. "Never mind your aches. You deserved every punch. Much more to worry about is that we've just done a stupid thing, letting Kris go like that. He can put you in the disembowelling chamber if he decides to tell what you just told. You may have learned to live with the fact, and kept it quiet, but you are guilty of a crime against the Federation—and I doubt if you told council about it? No, I thought not—right, you're guilty of criminal abuse of the responsibility assigned to you when you were allowed to the world. We've got to talk to Kris, and we've got to secure his silence. And don't forget, the council will have eyes on us, now. So behave calmly. Clean up and let's get after him."

CHAPTER THIRTEEN

After searching in lounges, corridors and exit stations for nearly an hour, Faulcon did what he should have done at the outset; he checked with the suiting lounge and learned that Kris Dojaan had suited up and gone out to the valley. Furious with himself, and taking that anger out on the technician in the lounge— "Didn't you ask for his identity? Didn't you check that identity and find out that he hasn't been fully *trained* yet? Are you stupid or just lazy?"—he climbed into his own suit, waited impaitently for Lena to prepare, and then ran out into the red-tinged afternoon.

The canyon was a mile away and they arrived in less than two minutes, having broken the law on speeding, but not by much. After watching the activity in the area for a minute or so, scanning each rift-suited figure for the clue that would identify Kris, they decided to move along the valley rim to the east, to where the phantom had last been seen. Faulcon was sure that Kris had come back to find the time phantom again, perhaps for reassurance, perhaps to find out how to travel into time himself.

Lena was not so sure; she was worried about Kris's safety, even though she felt more irritable at this repeat of their earlier pursuit of the boy. As team leader that safety was her responsibility, and she was proving inept at the job. She accepted the fault, but was determined there would be no consequences for her. Kris was going back to Steel City if she had to sling him, rift suit and all, across her shoulder.

They passed two stations, contacting the observers only to learn that they'd seen nothing. They asked about winds, or signs of squalls, or atmospherics: nothing yet; and so they passed on, Lena less worried now, but Faulcon deeply apprehensive of being close to Kris Dojaan inside the volume of the valley itself.

The canyon widened, the valley walls sloping more gently. Wind and rain had scoured strange formations from the rock sections of the valley wall, columnar pinnacles of yellow rock that widened towards the ground and were lost in the heaving strata of some lake-bed sediment, perhaps, that swept about the pinnacles and seemed to be consuming them. Jewels glittered here, small structures, some crushed beneath the rock, some embedded in it.

And something moved.

Lena saw it first, the fleeting movement of a human figure, far down in the canyon, and lost behind the twisting walls of a leaning tower. As she saw the movement, Faulcon spotted the rift suit, standing on a narrow ledge where the canyon walls were less steep than usual; the suit's arms were extended, and the back hatch was open. Kris had used it to descend almost to the bottom of the valley, and had abandoned it before entering the canyon's deeps.

"He's a damned fool," said Faulcon loudly, and he recognized the anxiety in himself, the worry for Kris, despite the throbbing ache in his jaw and ribcage.

"There! See, Leo? Right down there."

Faulcon followed the direction of Lena's raised arm and after a second glimpsed Kris; now he was crouching watching something that neither Faulcon nor Lena could see from on high. A moment later Kris looked around, looked up, the sun flashing on his mask. He must have seen the two stiff, bulky figures above him, because he suddenly rose to his feet and made efforts to conceal himself.

"Let's go," said Lena, and she jumped from the ledge, using vertical power to descend the first steep hundred feet, to land on the natural trackway below. Faulcon's suit obeyed his similar unvoiced instruction. He landed lightly, ran a short way, and then followed Lena over a much greater drop; the ground fell up towards him, the tangle of alien buildings sweeping in an arc towards his slowly turning body; he felt himself guided between quivering girders and jagged projections that tried to snatch at him, and after a moment the suit deposited him jarringly on level ground, and returned main control to him.

There had hardly been time for him to reorient himself, and to accept and ignore the irritating pain in his knees, before his head was filled with the siren screeching of danger.

He froze, staring into the distance, to the growing darkness. The sound went through him like a knife, cutting his body into neat pieces, penetrating to his every cell. Whining, throbbing, rising and falling, the voice of panic, preceding the voice of the wind.

"Leo . . . move it!" Lena's voice was sharp, angry. He realized she was standing near to him, the rift suit braced ready for action, her face a white blur behind the face plate. "What's the matter with you?"

Faulcon powered forward, far too fast, forcing himself to slow. The whining siren made his heart race, made the sweat break from him as he moved through the ruins. He couldn't wrench his eyes from the gloom in the far distance. I'm afraid, he thought. I'm terrified, but I'm still here. I'm not running.

He saw movement to his right and Kris was there, fleeing between the crowded walls and girders, and rugged shards of rock. Faulcon couldn't follow him exactly, and nor could Lena, and they moved where the suits would allow them, getting deeper into the morass of channelled space between the time-flung ruins.

"Kris!" Lena's voice was shrill as it came through Faulcon's headphones. "Stop running, Kris. Give it up. We've got to take you back, and you know you've got to come back."

Kris's sour laughter was unmistakable. Faulcon stopped, looked around him, between walls, panels, girders, rocks . . . He saw Kris just briefly, the insectoidal mask flashing light as he turned to look at Faulcon.

"Can't you hear the sirens?" shouted Faulcon.

"Tricks is it, Leo? Trying to trick me out? Why don't you just leave me be. Go back to your fantasies."

He slipped away and Faulcon had to retrace his steps until he could move through the junk yard again. With a sudden awful comprehension he realized that Kris did not have the siren-tuner, the special receiver that carried the siren wavelength so that it would not interfere with the ordinary voice communication.

"Lena!" he yelled. "He can't hear the wind. He'll never get out of here, we'll chase him until it hits."

"Then we chase him until it hits!" she shouted back.

Raw panic surged through Faulcon. He started to shake and the suit behaved badly, not yet ready to take over the survival function, confused by Faulcon's lack of control. He looked into the distance, saw the darkness rising higher into the pink sky; he could see the moving shapes in that darkness, currents of air rising and falling, sweeping about as if the very clouds lived and writhed as they crossed the centuries.

"We've got to get *out* of here," he screamed, and the suit began to run, struck a wall, bounced back.

"Calm! Leo, *calm*," came Lena's voice. "If you throw a fit you're dead for sure."

Kris's baiting laughter; his voice: "Calm, Leo, keep calm. Don't be scared, poor little Leo. Just get out of the valley and go and stand and watch and see people die, just like you saw my brother get swept away. . ."

"Shut up, Kris." Lena, anxious, the edge of panic in her own voice.

Relentlessly: "Poor Leo, so shit-scared his rift suit is all fouling up. But don't worry about me, Leo. I'm all right. You can watch me without helping me any time because I don't want your fucking help. Go and stand and tremble and remember how it was when Mark called out for help, and you were too scared to lift a hand, too shit-scared to find out if you were really a man, so you just stood there while my brother called for help when his suit failed him, and got swept away. A brave man, Leo, and a man with all the instincts for survival. Just think about that, think about how it is to trust someone, to make the mistake, the noble mistake, of putting your faith in someone who isn't worth a damn. Just think of it, and think of all that fear-crap deep down in your belly, and think about all those times you go running at night, and stop and scream your fear when you look down and remember how fucking shitless you were that day. Oh yes, Leo, I know it was you that I saw running that night, running and screaming and vomiting your fear. It wasn't Ensavlion, like you tried to make me think. It was you! How many nights, Leo? How many hours screaming, how many buckets of tears?"

Faulcon moved towards the movement he could see. Kris's voice was a grating whine; it had jarred and stung, and then it had angered and hurt, and then it had become just the voice of a man in deadly danger, a man who was clinging to a dream, who needed help just like his brother had needed help, and maybe more so ... There was nothing wrong with Kris Dojaan, except that he didn't know what was about to happen to him.

Faulcon moved after him, now, and the pathways between the crowded ruins widened; abruptly he was out into the open, running down a slope, and into an area of area of high, misplaced rocks and crumbling brick and stone walls. He glimpsed Lena some way away, but moving in the same direction. The siren wailed, and he forced himself not to look into the distance; already his suit was beginning to sing its wind-song, the rattling whining of surface sensors reacting to the physical wind that was building up outside.

"Why don't you just leave me to myself!" cried Kris, and Faulcon imagined that he was addressing Lena; there was anxiety there, not hostility.

"Can't you see that darkness?" came Lena's voice. "Wise up, Kris. Your life is in danger."

"I want to go. Just leave me ... I'm going after Mark. .."

"The hell you are."

Faulcon listened to the interchange and felt terribly cold. Now he could hear the booming of the wind, the deep thunder of atmosphere being wrenched and twisted against the fabric of stable time. His head span, his mind became nothing but dizziness and determination; he seemed to run in a dream, his legs hardly moving. Even if he'd wanted to he felt he could not move fast enough, now, to escape that wind.

He saw Kris run out of sight behind a sphere of translucent green material; he could see the boy *through* the structure, standing there, breathing hard as he tried to think where he should run to now.

Faulcon moved after him, and quite abruptly he came face to face with the time phantom, the ragged, wretched figure, now standing beside him, staring at him. He stopped and stared into that wizened face, saw beyond the mask of age and into the very soul of this timelost. In the instant of indisputable recognition he felt a sobering shock.

His stomach heaved; sour bile rose into his mouth, flooded down his chin. His stomach clenched, stopped the vomiting, hurting as the muscles contracted and tugged and shrank, pulling his body down against the resistance of the rift suit. He was a man shocked to immobility, and the suit took over.

The time winds boomed again through his headphones, louder now, seeming to approach far faster than was usual; the siren was a persistent and frantic reminder that somewhere in the valley, men and women were scattering like frantic herds, that Steel City was swinging its observer stations round to watch, that photographs were being taken, that cars and trucks and shuttles were shifting into positions to get as much from the winds as they could, that teams were being called up, suited-up, instructed ready for the swift mission following in the wake of the time winds; and above their heads, in the deeps of space, satellite crews were swinging out of hammocks, crawling down to their cameras and view-stations and monitoring consoles.

And somewhere nearby, perhaps, Operation Catchwind was moving into place, waiting for the word from Ensavlion, the word to go.

All this was happening, and Faulcon stood and stared at the time phantom, remembering Leuwentok's words, but unable to make any sense of what he remembered, conscious only of that face; he felt his body moved finally by the gentle suit, moved away, moved almost out of eye-shot, just sufficient vision remaining so that he could see how the phantom appeared to fade away, to become insubstantial, ghostly.

He took control of the suit, conscious that the machine, itself aware of his shock and growing hysteria, had not relinquished full control to him. He moved out of the clustered rocks back into the open spaces, and Kris darted from hiding, and stopped, staring at him. There was something about the boy, something about his bearing, his posture . . . he was exhausted, his chest rising and falling heavily, his skin, the naked skin of his hands and cheeks, glistening with sweat; his mask was dirty, his vision impaired by dust. Lena appeared close by and began to run towards him. He heard her and started to move again; whatever he had been thinking as he had stood, staring at Faulcon, Faulcon would never know. Kris Dojaan

184

took two steps away from Lena when he noticed something beyond Faulcon and stopped again, this time turning fully round, then backing away, his body cringing, his face creasing with a sudden, shocking fear; he ripped the mask from his face so that he could see better, and his voice was almost hysterical as he screeched his panic, choking as the words came, "Oh *God*! What's that . . . Oh my *God*!"

"Get him, Leo!" shouted Lena, and moved in on Kris. "Come on, Leo, come on, for God's sake. My suit won't let me hang around much longer. *Leo*!"

Faulcon had turned. He could not hear her. He was listening to the screaming gale, the frightful booming and wailing, the thunder of the physical wind that came with the silent wind of time.

And he was watching; above the valley hung a great black cloud, rolling and breaking and flowing towards him, a hideous rolling caricature of the most fearsome night imaginable. Below it the valley was changing faster, more confusingly than the eye could follow—the land and the structures upon the land rippled and distorted, twisted and vanished as they were swept into some unimaginable future, Faulcon watched as white towers winked out of existence, to be replaced by moving spiral shapes that radiated redly as they turned. He watched as an immense spider's web of girders was torn from vision, flickering a moment as a time squall knocked it into Othertime and back, and then it was gone and a hideous shape stood there, the carved, gargoyle-decorated gateway of a primitive era. Then that too had been swept away and its place taken by bulging domes, then decayed concrete block-houses, then a vast tree-like plant, its branches laden with green and juicy fruit.

Everywhere in the valley the shapes were changing, the valley walls themselves shifting in colour and texture and dust rising from the incredible conflict of time and matter that was occurring.

And this terrifying storm of change was gaining on Faulcon, overreaching him, perhaps the most powerful wind that had ever been witnessed on Kamelios. . .

Faulcon's rift suit took command; perhaps it had comprehended the danger, both from the wind and from Faulcon's frozen fear stance. It turned him round and began to run him away . . . faster and faster, until his legs were jerked into the rapid run position and he was carried forward at an almost bone-breaking speed. In a matter of instants he had passed Lena and the petrified Kris Dojaan. If Faulcon heard her voice, "Leo, stop and help . . . help me carry him . . ." he could do nothing about it.

But after a moment as the terrain fled past, as the suit whined and groaned its effort, Faulcon snapped out of his shock and twisted about. He saw Lena running after him, the limp form of Kris Dojaan cradled in her arms, the towering dark, the flickering wavefront of change, close behind her. She was still screaming at him, still calling to him. But his suit would not stop; his suit had only one thing in its mechanical mind: the survival of its occupant. It was running him to safety, to the safety of the sheer wall up whose length it could leap in four or five jet-powered bounds. He was a passenger in that man-shaped survival machine, running forwards, looking backwards, watching appalled as Lena's suit, not prepared to live with the encumbrance of its passenger any longer, let Kris drop to the ground. Faulcon's ears blanked Lena's horrified scream from his mind; one glimpse, one imagined view of the disgust and helplessness she must have felt, was enough. Kris sprawled on the ground, then scrabbled to his feet. He looked about him, anywhere, everywhere but at that sheer wall of dark that was reaching above him. He began to run, and as if it might somehow protect him from the wind he had so quickly come to fear, he flung himself into the lee of a cubical grey building in whose translucent walls automatic shapes moved as they had moved a million years distant.

An instant later the wave front of distortion swept across him; the cube vanished, to be replaced by a towering crag of rock, Kris flashing into Othertime and a spinning, gleaming, indefinable shape appearing in his place, the dust of the ground a different hue, and where he had cowered, sensing death so close, just the swirling of dust, and age, and time. . .

Lena's yelling changed to the genuine screaming of her fear. Faulcon joined her, the flood of panic dissipating in a few welcome shrieks of terror. The wind boomed, the suits moaned as the wind tickled their sensors, Lena gained on Faulcon, and the edge of the canyon, the safety point, seemed to get no closer to either of them. Faulcon could see dark shapes scattering up the canyon walls in the very distance, suits mostly, but a few two-man craft rising vertically, and earning their price for their drivers. He could see the sparkle of light on steel, and knew that the monitoring cameras were in place all along the ridge. And as he looked into the distance, so it appeared before him in the winking of an eye, the pyramid, the time machine of the enigmatic creatures that Ensavlion believed policed this world out of sight of those who watched. Faulcon's suit veered to the right and he was powered past the faintly vibrating golden structure in a few instants. But as he passed so he turned to watch as a figure seemed to rise from the ground before the machine, a wrinkled caricature of a human shape, rising to its feet from a crouched position, a figure he recognized, having seen it only minutes before.

Faulcon could only assume that as the phantom rose to its feet it met the eyes of the woman who raced towards it, and in that terrible instant of recognition the shock, the surge of confusion and of comprehension that passed through Lena must have stopped the motion of the suit. Faulcon was half a mile beyond her as he strained to see backwards and saw her sprawling on the rocky ground, the time winds swirling around her and taking her in the gusting of a sudden breath.

Abruptly Faulcon's suit was veering to the right even more, running diagonally across the approaching wave-front of the wind. He reached the canyon wall and rose up, his body twisted and jarred by each rocket-powered ascent and every clumsy impact on ledge, or outcrop, or less hostile slope. Screaming for speed, helpless, fearing that he would not make the canyon's rim, he was stumbling across the lip of the valley before he knew it, tumbling end over end, being braced and grasped by helping hands. The time winds swept past in the canyon, darkness overtaking him, thunder, lightning, and the screeching of wind turning the safelands into a nightmare of their own.

It was gone then, and there was quiet, and the darkness lifted as it sped away to the east. Faulcon lay in his suit, on his back, for a long, long time, staring up at the afternoon sky, waiting for the shaking to begin and the tears and the shock. Somewhere he was sure he could hear the phantom laughing, her voice so horribly familiar to the man who imagined it.

PART THREE

Manchanged

CHAPTER FOURTEEN

He realized that he had never known true loneliness. He experienced, now, an aloneness, a discontinuity, that physically hurt him until he cried, or vomited, or dulled his senses with alcohol and drugs. There had been many times in his life when he had categorized the particular feelings of frustration and solitariness that he had been experiencing as "loneliness"; now he accepted that he had merely been in transit from one moment of aliveness to the next, and that what he had been feeling was impatience. Loneliness had never truly entered his life before, and now he found that he could not confront it, only succumb to it; the loneliness washed through him like the change winds, poked icy, mocking fingers into every nook of his body, shouted to him through the echoing void inside his skull. He was alone, totally alone. There were people around him, but they were not with him; there were two Universes of sensation that overlapped, theirs and his, but there was no communication. He was a Galaxy away, literally a Universe apart. When they smiled at him, those ghostly participants in Kamelios life, the smile was not for him, for he was no longer the body that people saw. He was carried by it, but he was not a part of it. He was alone even from himself.

For five days he haunted the corridors and plazas of Steel City, drifted through bars and lounges, and finally curled up in his silent quarters. After a while he became aware of the feelings of hostility being directed towards him. Abruptly he realized that the early expression of sympathy, in regard to his personal losses, had somehow transformed to an expression of anger that he was still not lost alongside of them. The rituals of Steel City came back to him with startling clarity, filling him with the coldness and bitterness of fear. He recognized that his presence was not only resented, but his death was rapidly required.

Fear and loneliness combined to empty his mind of everything but panic, and on the sixth morning, at the break of dawn, he left the city; afraid for his life, he was pursued every step of the way by the silent guardians of Steel City ritual, the angry few who remained unseen as they followed him, but whose presence he could discern quite clearly. They hesitated round corridors, hid among machinery, and hovered among the limp suits in the suiting and shedding lounge. He signed out his byke, rather than his r-suit, and rode out into the gusting dawn wind. The moment he was out of easy eye-shot of the city, he turned away from the rift.

He rode up into the wide lands to the south, through the limestone and chalk drifts, then travelling beyond the sprawling forests to Hunderag Country. In the foothills of the Jaraquath mountains he came to a high plateau where a large and thriving settlement of manchanged had long been established. The journey took five days and he did not eat in all that time. His only drink had been mouthfuls of warm water from a flask. Hunger had been an insistent pain every ten hours for the first two days; now he was aware only that he ought to eat to sustain his strength. The only hurt was the hurt of his loss.

So he approached the settlement, his byke making low noises as he crawled between fences and areas of cultivation, wondering where he should stop, and for how long. In the distance he could see the clustered buildings, white upon white, rarely more than two storeys high. The houses were huddled together about a wide compound as if they were insecure, unsure of themselves, and had not yet found the courage to spread outwards a little, to find their own space. He could see people working in the fields of green and purple crops, and as he rode past they glanced up, but quickly turned back to their work.

He was always discomfited by the appearance of these fourth and fifth generation inhabitants of the high plateaux, their bulging eyes shining unnaturally, their arms ridged where the purifiers beneath their skin showed through the lean flesh of their arms. They had not yet achieved full independence of technology; Kamelios was still a strange land to them, but slowly they evolved in the modern way, and soon men would walk about this hostile place and be able to say that they truly belonged here.

Faulcon stopped his slow ride some hundred yards from the township. He had not yet seen the only manchanged he knew. He dismounted and walked through the buildings into the compound, aware that he was watched from windows, conscious that he was causing something of a stir. Few rift-folk ever came this high up into the mountains, and Faulcon knew that he was not welcome. And yet he was abruptly surprised as a slim, dark-haired young woman walked from a barn-like building, through the doorless exit and into the compound, waving to him as she came, and smiling. Behind her appeared a tall, muscular looking man, his hair turning white, his skin weather-beaten and leathery. Behind his mask, Faulcon smiled as best he could.

In this way, grateful for the persistence of the human faculty for friendship, despite the adjustments to the alien, Leo Faulcon made the proper acquaintance of Audwyn, and his young wife Allissia.

"I wasn't sure if it was even the right plateau," he said, nervous and uneasy. "I need food, that's all. Just something to eat, and a little rest, and then I can be on my way."

"You'll stay until you go," said Audwyn with a smile, leading Faulcon into a small, claustrophobic house, two-roomed, with a table, bed and cooking area, and precious little else; the toilet was outside.

"Well, that's very kind of you," said Faulcon. "If you're sure. . ."

"Try doing otherwise," said Audwyn with a chuckle, and waved Faulcon to a stool at the table. "It seems to me you rifters believe everything you hear about the 'manks'. . . That's what we're called, isn't it?"

"I assure you that it is," said Faulcon, leaning on the table and watching as Allissia began to cut thick slices of grey meat from an unappetizing-looking joint. Audwyn himself drew drinks from a wooden barrel, three clay mugs of a green liquid that smelled sweet and tasted sweeter. With the steaks taking

care of themselves, Allissia sat down. Faulcon was less relaxed
with her than with her husband, and he knew this was because she was a lovely-looking girl below and above the enormous, sheathed eyes. But as he regarded her he noticed the
flexing of her nose and the glisten of hard, yellow substance,
the poisons and dusts of Kamelios that were gathering within
the cavity. During the next few hours he grew quite accustomed
to the way she and her husband would turn to the left and
delicately eject the hardened, colourful mucus onto the floor.

Before they ate, Faulcon fetched his gear from the byke, and
pushed the machine into shelter. He approached the task of
eating with some apprehension, since the mask was not an
efficient filter when it was being used in this way. He ate very
little, and felt queasy even as he was finishing; but his digestive
system was able to cope with the native meat, and two mugs of
the sweet, alcoholic drink helped enormously. He was amused,
as he ate, to notice the flickering of light in the room that told
of the surreptitious staring-in of the locals. Whenever he looked
up they had vanished, but he felt their watching eyes and
minds.

After the meal Allissia watched him sympathetically, assuring
him that if his stomach rejected the food she could find vegetables that might be less poisonous. Faulcon thanked her, but
declined, and after a horrifyingly sweaty and cold few minutes
the nausea passed away and he relaxed, replete, and grateful for
the dizzying effect of the drink.

"Why aren't you working?" he asked Audwyn, and was told,
"We are. We were settling calcas, a fleshy root crop we grow
up here. Settling means we were burying it in worm-soil. In a
few weeks the worms will have processed the roots into a more
digestible and solid cake which we then use both as a winter
staple for ourselves and our animals—we even have a few
adapted terrestrial animals, pigs, horses—and also for making
the brew that you appear to be enjoying." Faulcon smiled as he
leaned back in the only straight-backed chair in the house; he
raised the mug appreciatively to his lips and felt a shock of
revulsion as he saw the bloated shape of a small worm floating

close to the bottom. Flavouring, Audwyn said, apparently inno-
cent of the appalling effect such detritus could have on off-
worlders. Faulcon carefully picked the offending corpse out of
his mug.

"Now that you've come we're still working, being hospitable.
Only when the fields need furrying—that's clearing them of
parasites—do we have to be out all day. How about you? What
brings a rifter so far from his metal womb?"

Faulcon wondered quickly what he should say, how much he
should say. When the silence had begun to embarrass him he
murmured, "A friend of mine died. I had to get away from
Steel City, get out of myself for a while."

As he spoke he was not unconscious of the almost amused
glance that was exchanged between his hosts. Whatever it was
they shared they didn't share it with him, and he wrote it off
as part of the strange behaviour of these mountain farmers.
Only later did he discover what had tickled them; he was introduced to a younger man, a cousin of Allissia's, when he was on
his way out to the fields to participate. "This is Leo Faulcon,"
said Audwyn as Faulcon and the youth shook hands. "Mister
Faulcon is only partly here, some of him is still down by the
valley. There's enough of him to work, though, so show him
how to furry-up pulp-scab, and perhaps root-up as well."

Faulcon enjoyed the work he undertook for the next two
days. It was hard, and the pulp-scab parasites that crawled
through the crops were small and elusive. There weren't many
of them, but they were highly destructive to the maturing crops.
Faulcon came to understand how delicate and dangerous was
the balance up here between success and starvation.

The work enabled him to shed his tears inside, and in silence.
He fought against crying out loud, but too often for his liking
he gave in to emotion, feeling ashamed and embarrassed as he
realized his weeping had been heard by others around him. He
noticed, however, that they took no notice, and made no sympathetic gestures. Occasionally he would stand, leaning on the
wooden-handled furrying tool, and stare across the plateau to
where the lands to the north were green and grey, rolling and

rising from hill to mountain, the valley forming a recognizable
network back towards the crop-lands around the canyon where
time was master. As he stared at those distant, natural sights,
he saw Lena; over and over again he saw her, walking towards
him, or sitting quietly and moodily, trying to shake off the effects
of a *fiersig*. He missed her with all the pain in his body, and all
the reaction of the nerves in his torso, and all the coldness that
his spirit could muster. He worked hard and furious, letting
anger rule him, enjoying that anger, and shouting at the parasites that wriggled in his grasp as he squashed them between
thumb and forefinger, letting their sticky juices spread their
stink across his flesh.

Each night, as he shuffled around in the blanket roll that
Allissia had provided for him, he spoke through the open door
between the two rooms to his hosts, themselves quite comfortable and unbothered as they lay or loved in their own bed.
"I'd better not impose another night. I'd better leave."

Audwyn said, on each occasion, "You're welcome to stay until
you leave, Leo. One thing's for sure, there's not a chance in a
million that you'll still be here after you've left."

On the third day he cut his hand very badly, and walked up
to the village to find Allissia. As he made his way between the
houses he was again uncomfortable, the stranger in this tight
and unfriendly little community. He had met only a handful of
people and they had been friendly and communicative, but he
sensed their distance, their unwillingness to commit themselves
to him; they were friendly because that was the way to be. But
they watched him, and wondered about him, and many of them
resented his intrusion here. He knew he would have to leave
soon, because he knew he was upsetting the delicate balance
of life in the community.

He found Allissia in the small forge, working on a complex-
looking tool whose spirally curved blade had sheared in two.
The forge was hot, the brazier of organic rock glowing bluely
as she operated a small bellows with her foot; she was hammer-
ing the metal blade with remarkable proficiency, and Faulcon
stood and watched her work until the thin line of the join had

vanished and she seemed reasonably satisfied with the job. "It'll do for now," she said, smiling at Faulcon. She noticed the blood on his hand and said, "You've been using your fingers and not the furrier."

"That's right," he said. "You have some vicious stones in your soil up here."

"They're sun-dew crystals, and they're quite rare in the fields. Show me where you were working, later, and we'll dig the thing up and send it back to the City with you."

He followed Allissia into the small house and found Audwyn hard at work riveting a large, skagbark barrel. He was unsympathetic towards Faulcon's wound, but Allissia smiled at him as she cleaned the gash and bound it with a dark, rather pungent linen. "Have a drink before you go back out," said Audwyn, banging the last rivet into place and reaching for the mugs.

Faulcon said, "You'll have to give me another job. I'll have to rest this hand for a while." He sat down at the table.

Audwyn smiled as he splashed the sweet drink, which they called *calcare*, into the earthenware mugs. "Defeated by a shard of crystal, Leo? It amazes me that with an attitude to life like that, you could have reached the age you have. I'm surprised you didn't succumb to the first discomfort that ever got the better of you."

Faulcon was grateful for the warming glow of the drink; the plateau was cold and exposed. As he savoured the drink, alert for worms, he said, "I couldn't operate the furrier if I wanted; my hand won't grip at the moment."

Audwyn laughed and shook his head. "You rifters. . ."

"I'm an off-worlder."

"That's even worse!' Don't you know that you can do anything if you really want to? Don't you know, didn't anyone ever tell you, that a man is bigger and more magnificent than a piece of dirt? I guess they didn't, eh Leo? Pain, discomfort, irritating circumstances, they're all bigger than you, aren't they?"

Unwilling to provoke an argument, despite the throbbing pain in his hand, Faulcon said, "I can certainly try and hold the furrier. . ."

"I don't want you *trying* to do anything, Leo. If I try and talk to you I don't talk to you. If you try and hold the tool you don't hold it. If you *hold* the tool you hold it. I don't mind you doing that. I don't mind you doing what you're doing, but it seems pretty pointless to try and do something that you're not doing if all that's going to happen is that you're going to go on not doing it."

"Give me another drink," said Faulcon dully, and watched, frowning, as his mug was filled. His hand hurt like hell, and he was feeling silently angry at what seemed to him to be an un-forgivable carelessness on Audwyn's part. "Are you saying that you'd go out and work again with a four-inch gash across the palm of your hand that is stopping your hand clenching, and causing you considerable agony, and stopping you being efficient?"

"Well, why not? If I trip over I don't lie there saying, 'I've been overwhelmed by Mother Earth who has thrown me down, so I'll just lie here for the rest of my life and acknowledge that I'm insignificant against the huge presence of circumstance.' I don't do that, Leo."

"I hardly do that myself, but—"

"You've been doing that all your life, Leo! The hell you haven't. You've been totally content when you were happy and totally discontent when you were miserable; you've evaluated the moments of your life into good and bad, and you, and the billions like you, have never comprehended that there are no good and bad moments, only moments when you're alive, moments when you're experiencing life, being *with* life, no matter whether you're in pain, or pleasure, or depression, or solitariness. It's extremely easy, as you will no doubt be the first to acknowledge, to be happy when you're happy; but it's so damned hard to be depressed when you're depressed—you've always got to fight it, right? You've always got to treat depression as something to be got rid of, to be resisted, when in fact it is a commonly known truism that nobody is ever not depressed when they're depressed. Nobody ever has a pain in the hand when they don't have a pain in the hand. The point is, are you bigger than that pain; are you prepared to shrug your shoulders and say, so I've got this throbbing, hurtful, agonizing pain in my hand, so what? You see, Leo, that's the way we lead our lives up here, and we find it works rather well. We do things, we don't let things do us; we get hungry, but we don't let hunger get us. I can tell you with absolute certainty, Leo, that there's not a man, woman or child on this plateau who isn't hungry when he's hungry. The difference between us and you, Leo, is that here on the plateau hunger is a part of our experience, part of the life we lead, part of living; to you it's an ache that has to be satisfied in order to make it go away. Hunger gets you every time you get hungry . . it distracts you, it nags you. Up here, when we get hungry we get hungry, and later on when we eat we eat, and when we sleep we sleep. Do you follow me, Leo?"

Faulcon drained his mug, adjusted his mask afterwards. He felt bitter, quite angry. He didn't like this nonsense talk from the frog-eyed man who sat so smug in front of him; he didn't like Allissia's self-congratulatory smile, the way she watched him from a point of total subjugation to her husband's words. He said, "How can you pretend to know so much about we ordinary mortals?"

By way of answer Audwyn rolled up his sleeves, then pulled apart his robe at the chest. Faulcon stared at the hideous scars, the swollen, lumpy inclusions in the man's body, far greater than he normally associated with the process of manchange. "I was not born a manchanged, Leo. I lived among men, in the lower towns, in your city, for several years. I'm no older than Allissia—" Faulcon was taken by surprise. He looked twice her age. "The process has an ageing effect upon a matured body, which is something I know, something I accepted. I *chose* to come here, a first among the fourths and fifths. The gatherers brought me when I was alone and wandering in the mountains. I don't regret a day in my life. I don't regret the waste of time when I oversleep, I don't regret the missed opportunity, the lost love, the failed work. My memories of man are of a constant process of dissatisfaction, of regret, of resistance to anything

199

that does not seem as if it's going the expected way, of not *living*, Leo, of not ever being 100 per cent a part of *life*. I remember men as being a breed forever resisting its very humanness—its weakness, its flaws, its failures, its imperfections. Such resistance is the quickest way to self-destruction. It's the easiest way to become trapped by the very weakness you try to avoid."

As Audwyn arranged his clothing again, Faulcon said, more angrily than he intended, "If you're so damned alive up here, why are you so bloody unfriendly?" Restless, he rose from the table.

Audwyn exchanged a curious glance with Allissia. She said, "Who's unfriendly, Leo? Haven't we made you feel at home?"

"You have, and I'm more than grateful for that. But these mountain communities are so insular, so hostile to strangers. Why the hell do you think so few people come out here? It isn't because you're all leading natural, content lives, it's because you're inbred and suspicious of strangers. Maybe you can't see it from where you sit, but it has certainly been very apparent to me."

Audwyn rose from his stool and followed Faulcon to the door. "I must say, Leo, that from where I sit I see only that you came into our community and we made you welcome . . . I know we put you to work, but we do that to everybody who comes out here; if you want to stop work, then that's fine by us. Please feel free to do just what you want. But Allissia and I have opened our house to you, I've introduced you to several others. I don't see where this hostility lurks that you seem so conscious of."

They were out into the crisp day. Faulcon's skin-tight suit was uncomfortable in the strong wind, but he noticed that Audwyn was shivering slightly inside his patterned jacket and grey pantaloons. He was watching Faulcon curiously, staring at his eyes behind the glasses that covered the upper part of his face. Faulcon waved a hand around at the houses huddled about their small open space. "Why didn't they come out and welcome me, then, when I drove up? Why did they hide away as if they were afraid? I walked in here and I felt every eye on me, I saw people peering at me from behind the windows. I came here and I scared everyone to hell; a man from the lowlands, an outsider. And in the days I've been here I've not changed, I'm still the outsider, and I'm still distrusted to the point of fear."

Audwyn laughed, "Except by myself and Allissia. Everyone in the town is terrified of you, except two of us. Wouldn't that make us outsiders too?"

"You're part of the town. And I don't suppose I mean terrified . . . uneasy, suspicious."

"We're a part of the town, Leo, yes indeed; but we're a part of life. Tell me, are you uncomfortable when you're on your own, walking out through the houses to the fields? Are you uncomfortable now?"

Faulcon tried to flex his gashed hand and failed, looking around him as he did so. "I feel I'm an object of curiosity and suspicion, yes. I'm not exactly uncomfortable because I'm with you. But it would help if there was some life and communication going on here, if people weren't shuttered up in their houses."

Audwyn said quietly, "Leo, there's no one, not one soul in any of the buildings. A handful of us have remained here, to pick away at the lower fields; most people are up in the high fields, and in the game forests. This is Moondance Season, a time of hunting. When you came here a few days ago there was just myself and Allissia and those few out in the fields. You were welcomed by the only two people around to welcome you."

"Are you telling me I was imagining being watched?" Faulcon looked around him, disturbed by the implication of what Audwyn was saying. The houses looked as they had looked three days ago, deserted, lifeless, empty . . . and yet he had sensed the eyes watching him, the furtive movement of people, insecure now that their territory had been invaded by a lowlander. "I don't understand, I'm sure there were people when I came, when I walked past the houses."

Allissia laughed, and laid a gentle hand on his arm; Faulcon thought he recognized the humour in her wide, staring eyes, but now he was not sure. She said, "How lovely to be able to see people when they're not there. How sad to be able to see only frightened people."

"What other sort of people should frightened people see?" said Audwyn. "Poor Leo, so afraid that he frightens himself. So uneasy with the world that there can be no world in his eyes that is not uneasy with him."

"You make me sound like a victim . . ." Faulcon tried levity, but somehow there was nothing in what Audwyn said to make light of. "I guess we're all like that, down by Kriakta Rift."

Audwyn nodded his agreement, watching Faulcon earnestly. "That's the first step in getting rid of your status as victim. Keep working on it, Leo, and soon you'll see that you don't have to be victimized by anything, least of all your own shadows, and you do have shadows, don't you, Leo? So many shadows. Allissia and I have seen so many shadows crawling around in you that sometimes we thought the lights had gone out. There are more dead bodies in your past than there are in the time valley . . . all those friends, eh Leo? All those people you let down, deserted, denied, deceived. We can see them, and we can hear them, because they're all you, they're all your own illusions, just as we are your illusion, and the people that were watching you were your illusion. You make your own ghosts, Leo. Nothing you can do or say is going to change one molecule of anything in the damned Universe, so is there really any point in brooding about it, or worrying about it, being beaten to death by it?"

"I suppose not, except that I'm a rifter, remember? I eke out my existence down by the valley where the time winds blow. My whole life is about survival. The moment I give into inevitability, which is what you do—"

"Which is what you *think* we do. I've never said that, Leo."

"Okay, you've never said it. But what you're telling me is that there's no point in worrying about anything because everything is inevitable and nothing can be changed, so don't even try."

"That's what you *think* I said, Leo. That's how you've interpreted it, but that's all right. Everything's all right as long as it's the honest and real you. We don't mind what you feel, or do, or say as long as you are completely *you* in the feeling and doing and saying of it. You see, we like *people*, Leo, not 'roles', not 'labels'—not survivors or victims, or manipulators or aggressors. We like people and the reason this township is so alive is because there are no masks, there are no denials, no hidings . . . if we're afraid, that's fine. Did you ever know anybody who wasn't afraid when he was afraid? But you've spent all your life *trying* not to be afraid when you're afraid, denying yourself the opportunity to experience your real and mortal fear, and by so experiencing it, and allowing it its full expression and place in your life, by doing that, to be its cause, not its effect, to rule *it* and not vice versa. Your whole life is fear, even your shadows are afraid, even your words are afraid. Survival. That's it to you, isn't it? Kamelios is a world of change and sudden death, and so the off-worlders who come here have to immediately take it on, survive its changes, survive its hostility."

"If we don't survive we die."

"Exactly. Have you ever known anyone who wasn't dead when he was dead? No, of course you haven't. So what's to survive? Do you think that you can do anything, anything at all that will delay your death by even a millionth of a second? Is there something you can do that when the moment comes that you drop dead you can stand there a few seconds longer and say, 'Well here I am, dead as a doornail, but you'll notice I'm still alive.' Of course not. A survival machine, Leo, is surviving until it doesn't survive, at which moment it dies. There's no such thing as a survival machine, there are only machines with short and long life spans before they die . . . death machines. You approach Kamelios as if by doing what you do you can stop or delay something that is going to happen when it happens whether you like it or not. You survive, you take it on, you scream and struggle, you hide and deceive, and you have talked yourself into the idea that by doing this you can delay death, but when death comes, you're dead, and nothing you've done has changed it one iota."

"Except delayed the moment at which it comes."

"How in the hills do you know? How in the world do you know anything about what hasn't happened yet? And besides, don't you see that by delaying death, if that's what you believe you're doing, you're eking out your existence from the point of view of fear of death, rather than from experience of life? You exist because you're being buffeted about by just about every circumstance that the Universe can throw against you. We *live* up here because we create our own circumstances, we accept responsibility for everything. You fight against the inevitable . . . if you're going to walk into the time winds, do you think you can do or say one thing that will change that? Of course you can't. So why fight it, why be dragged fighting and screaming through the inevitable, only to emerge on the other side bloody and breathless, saying, 'My God, I made it through.' Don't you think you'd have made it through anyway? And how much more enjoyable the passage would have been if you'd relaxed and experienced what was happening to you."

For the last few seconds Faulcon had not been listening; he felt shocked and surprised at the reference to walking into the winds, and now he could not help himself saying, loudly and vehemently, "How the *hell* did you know that? I never said a damned word."

Audwyn smiled and shook his head. "Don't fight it, Leo. How did we know? People like you don't come up to the high plateaux very often, you've remarked on that yourself. When they come here, to one or other of the communities, they are coming here to think, and what they've come to think about *always* involves the winds, and their relationship to the winds, and the necessity of their destruction by the winds. Leo, you're one of many, and we've seen you all."

"Enough," said Faulcon, disturbed and dizzy with the calm statements in favour of inevitability. He had wanted to be alone with the agony of his decision, to come up into these hills and think, and instead he found himself transparent to the people he had come among, and he wasn't sure if he liked that at all. Allissia smiled reassuringly at him as she turned away to her work again. Faulcon flexed his hand and walked silently through the deserted town, out into the fields, to where he had left his furrier. As he passed by people they acknowledged him, but they were tired and sweaty, working hard and furious, and had no time to talk.

He worked into the red dusk, almost until the last edge of Altuxor was below the far horizon. His hand was hurting him but he had ignored it, and the hurt was no longer a threat to his work. He had learned how easy it was to operate the tool with his left hand. He had dug out the crystal shard that had cut him, and stood for a while turning its exotic shape over in his hands, and seeing how the deep-grained colour changed with movement, an attractive thing as well as a useful thing. He touched the small, leather amulet around his neck, held it before him and stared at it, wondering whether or not he should remove the one and replace it with the crystal. There was a fear inside him that to take away his luck, even for a second, would bring death that much closer, that much quicker. And yet he was half convinced by Audwyn's quiet, simple argument that if he was to die he was to die, and why fight it, why resist it? But the amulet was strength; around his neck it interacted with him and was strength. To remove it now would be to act against his genuine wish, and so he left it around his neck, pocketed the crystal and resolved to wait until he felt the time was right to change his charm.

He heard his name called, and when he looked through the twilight he could see the slim figure of Allissia, stretching up and waving to him. He shouldered his furrier and with a last glance to the north, to the place where Steel City was an occasional transient gleam during the brightest part of the day, he walked back along the winding ridges between the crops and to the trackway that led to the town. Allissia waited for him, and as he drew near he realized that there were many more people around, both in the compound and still walking in from the hills that rose beyond the community; the hunters were returning, and he could see that several of them carried beasts of varying sizes slung across their shoulders; he numbered three olgoi among this prey, and looked around quickly in case Ben Leuwentok should be watching. His attention, as he did so, was snared by the full face of Merlin, red and bright, its twin a paler gold beside it. The moons were rising.

"Is the hunting season over so soon?" he asked Allissia, as she took his arm and walked with him towards the village. She was smiling.

"No, no, not yet. This is Moondance Eve, the time of celebration for what the earth and the air have donated to us. The hunters return, the gatherers come in, and those in the fields abandon their tents for the one night. They bring animals, samples of the crops. If the Grey House has a lonely man in residence he comes out, his first contact with us."

"A lonely man? Grey House? What's that?"

Allissia frowned slightly. "The Grey House is where we are born, Leo. Surely you know that. Birth for a manchanged is a little different from birth for you. It's a hospital. A lonely man is like Audwyn . . . one of your own who has wandered away from the city. The gatherers watch for them throughout the Moondance Season, and bring them back to be manchanged if that's what they desire. No, this isn't the end of the hunting season, it's the beginning. At the end of Moondance Eve everyone goes back to work. Audwyn and myself will go up to the high fields this time and another couple will take over the job of settling, and holding the town."

"Waiting for people like me, who come here direct, eh?" She squeezed his arm. He was a little disturbed by the affectionateness of her, wondering whether this was the way with these people. Where he himself came from there were restraints on public demonstrativeness, especially between a man and his hosts's wife (or husband). But Allissia clung on to him firmly, walking beside him, her body in close and quite intimate contact. As they approached a great brazier that was burning in the compound, Faulcon saw Audwyn working huge chunks of meat onto a spit and laying them across the fire. He acknowledged Faulcon with a cheery wave, a cry of "How's the hand?" and a laugh when Faulcon replied that he'd hardly noticed it all afternoon.

They went into the house and Allissia took Faulcon's wounded limb and removed the dressing. The gash was congealed and ugly. It hurt as he became aware of it, but Allissia now had a thick blue ointment, highly unpleasant on the nose, she said, and Faulcon grinned behind his mask. She washed his hand again, and smeared the balm along the cut. It hurt for a moment, and then tickled. Allissia laughed as Faulcon winced with the strange feeling. "It's a root pulp that I prepared this afternoon; it will help the skin and muscle to knit together, and it will also make your hand more flexible. We'd run out earlier. You see, we do have medications . . . We don't walk around in pain or with disease when we can do something about it."

Faulcon said nothing. He was very aware of the girl, now, and although by his eyes she was hideously ugly (because of *her* eyes) he found that the ocular features of her face could not detract from the warmth he felt for her, and the strong feeling he had that he would like to kiss her lips. His respirator allowed him to notice that her breath was very sweet on his face as she laughed, and she had some simple body perfume that was subtle and intriguing. Beneath the colourful tunic he could imagine her body, small, girlish, not full, yet manifestly womanly.

Perhaps Allissia was aware of the beginnings of his arousal. She seemed embarrassed for a moment, glanced towards the door then down to the floor as she knelt beside the chair where he sat.

"I'm fifth generation," she said, and her wide, staring eyes fixed upon him, and he knew this was a question: are you aware what that means?

"Fifth of the manchanged, you mean. I understand that, yes."

She shook her head. "It means I was not born like I am, changed for the world . . . physically changed. You know we are not *really* changed, not the people that we are. We change our clothes, and we change our bodies to live here more comfortably, but the people inside are not changed. I came from the womb of my mother and I was altered in the Grey House, where all the machines are locked away. A lot of me was born genetically changed . . . a lot of the altered me was passed from my mother to me through the genes. But not everything, not yet. They think it will be the tenth generation who will be born pure. I shall be long dead."

"I don't understand how these things work, but I always thought they programmed the mind to accept the form, the new form . . ." He had imagined she was distressed because she was abnormal in appearance, compared to the appearance of Faulcon, the natural human form. He had even thought: "So much for acceptance."

Allissia said, "They don't. Part of the adaptation is to evolve psychologically. Here on the plateau, in all the communities in the high lands, we have come to accept what is, and we live and we are alive, and when we have doubts and fears we accept that we are doubting and fearful, and experience it. Nothing about us is so contrived that we cannot cry, or feel an agony at the ugliness we must appear to people like you. And I feel it very badly, Leo. I had to tell you this, I am so afraid of what I look like to you."

"You look . . . lovely," he said. "Your eyes are not lovely, but *you* are lovely." It was true, he thought. It's what I've been feeling.

"You are like gods to us," she said, and reached to touch his face. Faulcon waited for the gentle touch on his skin, and realized the moment he sensed her fingers on his mask that what she was seeing was a man in glasses and breathing tube. He frowned, wanting to remove the mask for a moment, but there was an expression of such passion in Allissia's face that he made no move; she moved her fingers over his cheeks and the glasses, across his hair, and the leathery binding of the mouth-piece; she curved her fingers about the ridged pipe that extended two inches from the mask, where the filters were housed; she seemed to caress something that was to her more erotic than lips.

"I dream of faces like this, real faces, the faces of men," she said.

"I'm a man wearing a mask," he said. "The real me is underneath."

"In our stories the great men are masked, the masks are golden or red or black or white, and some of them are strange, and some look like faces over faces; but this is how we remember the time of the first men, unrevealed, and yet unchanged by the masks that conceal them, just as we are real and unchanged. You are beautiful, Leo, and I am going to miss you so much."

"That sounds perilously close to regret, Allissia. I thought regret was frowned upon."

She shook her head, "Not regret, Leo. Just honesty. Just true feeling."

I look like an insect, he thought, and this is how she knows me, and this is how she will remember me and miss me. I must show her my face, all of my face . . . not once while I've been here have I taken off my mask. . .

He reached up to remove the eye-covers that kept the stinging atmosphere of Kamelios from his sensitive corneas; Allissia made a sound of panic and raised her hand to stop him taking the action.

Faulcon took her hand gently and smiled, wondering if she could see that smile, wondering if she had ever realized he had smiled. "There is a greater distance between your people and mine than even you admit. . ."

"Perhaps."

"You would never come to Steel City, never mix with rifters." It was neither question nor statement. There was something of regret in his tone.

"No, I don't suppose we would. This is our living place. When we trade we go on the long walk down, and if any of us felt like staying, then he would stay. Usually we just want to make the long walk up."

Faulcon leaned forward, close to the strange eyes that regarded him with such warmth. "But can't you see how frustrating it is—how difficult—when you stay up here, and we stay down there, and come to regard each other with fear and contempt?"

"Speak for yourselves, Leo."

"But you have things to offer—life to offer, warmth, experience. Don't you ever regret that no one can share the experience of your life, the love of life?"

"We don't regret it, Leo. What more do we need than you to take our life beyond the plateau? You share our lives for a while, and experience our love and our minds and our traditions, and you go from us and take that with you. You will never lose it. What more could we need? What more could we ask for? A few people carrying our lives in their hearts."

Outside there was a great cheer, and laughter, and the two of them turned towards the door, the intimacy suddenly broken, the night of celebration stretched before them, suddenly demanding their attention. They both laughed, nervously, perhaps with a certain relief. Arm in arm they went out into the compound; the fire burned high, blue and yellow, with the occasional licking of a deep red flame into the night. Sparks flew up to the stars, and the skagbark crackled and charred, noisy and alive. Faulcon wished he could smell the wood, and the sizzling joints of meat, but his mask allowed him only a hint of a smoky odour, and a continuing memory of Allissia's perfume.

And so they celebrated Moondance Eve, the night of the hunter's return. The meat they ate was exquisite, like nothing Faulcon had tasted before; it was not the grey meat he had eaten for several days, nor was it the meat of imported terrestrial food animals; it was, he was told, the flesh of some creature they called a pathak, a large, fleet, man-eating predator that had been evolved for Kamelios from the stock of old-earth cats; it was an experiment in domestication that had gone wrong. Faulcon ate so much of the non-poisonous meat that he was sick anyway, leaning against the wooden walls of the house as he held his mask clear and voided his stomach contents with an amazing force; Allissia laughed at him and wagged a finger at him for his unnecessary indulgence. The drink was good, too, mostly *calcare*, but supplemented by three large china flagons of *baraas*. He threw up some more, and his mind grew euphoric with happiness, alcohol and a clearer understanding of what he was and what he had to do; he would experience everything, from the revolting sensation of nausea, to the final, heart-pounding moment when he stepped into the path of the time winds. Not a moment would pass when he would not be alive and aware of the simplest, most transient sensation. He would go to his death more alive than he had ever been in his thirty-two years. And when he died he would be dead, and there would be no resistance, there would only be fear, and that fear he would experience and know that he died Leo Faulcon, and not a man denying the innermost agony of that final moment when he found out what really lay beyond Old Lady Wind. Perhaps not death at all, but a new freedom; and Lena.

The fire was burning low, and all the meat had gone; the drink was as bountiful as ever, probably because half the community were slumped quietly, or chattily, about the brazier, or in shadows, by the houses. It was well after the mid-night hour, and Faulcon was on his back, close to the dying warmth of the skagbark bonfire, half listening to Allissia talking to her husband, half watching the incredible spread of stars, the wide, white band of the galactic centre, the twenty dazzling blue stars that were the Twioxna Lights, a cluster with an abundance of inhabitable worlds. He was just deciding that he would close his eyes and sleep, right there beneath the sky—even though he would wake up dew-covered and frozen—when distantly there was the low rumble of thunder, and the terrifying crackle of an atmospheric disturbance. Above him the stars seemed to ripple for a moment, as if seen through a pool of water.

"A *fiersig*," he said aloud, and sat up, then stood up, staring into the night, watching carefully until at last he saw the purple glow, moving towards them across the hills. It was a wide band of flickering light, with golden and red whorls chasing each other in frantic displays about the night sky. Below the activity, the land was eerily lit with an iridescent green, that changed to yellow and blue each time the thunder rolled and the leaping shards of lightning struck down to the earth.

Around him the manchanged had fallen quiet, and slowly,

one by one, were standing, watching towards the south and west. But as Faulcon looked around him he realized there was none of the apprehension, or fear, or defensiveness that he would have expected as these strange manifestations of Kamelion interference approached. People watched as if impatient, as if the approaching phenomenon, and all it implied, was something that was interfering with their celebration, and which they would be pleased to get over with as soon as possible. Allissia was still murmuring quietly to Audwyn. Audwyn noticed Faulcon watching them, and a moment later Allissia turned as well, and the two of them rose to their feet to approach him.

"Are you afraid?" Allissia asked, and Faulcon said, "Not at all. But it will end the pleasantness of the evening. These changes hit so hard that it's easier just to go off alone. I'm disappointed, that's all. I was enjoying the tranquillity."

"Don't resist it," said Audwyn. "Just let it happen, let it pass. It's irritating that one of these things has to come tonight of all nights, but so what? It's here, let it pass through. The best part of the celebration is yet to come . . . at dawn, you'll love it."

Faulcon thought to himself that at dawn there wouldn't be a person in the compound talking to anyone else, because there was no way of resisting the ferocious, mind-tearing effects of these electrical storms. But he said nothing, turned back to the thunder, and the flickering lights in the heavens.

Faulcon's skin began to tingle; he felt a wave of change pass through him, the alertness, the freshness, the turmoil in his head seen through a crystal glass; he held onto his amulet, focusing upon it, concentrating on it. At once he felt bright and cheerful, then a wave of sadness, then a sudden terrible panic, emotion piling upon emotion, over and over again panic insisting its way into his heart so that it raced and his palms began to sweat coldly. Around him there was silence for a long while and he was aware of the community watching restlessly as the lights swept steadily towards and above them, the centre passing out across the fields, but the full sweep of the flickering area of the disturbance taking in the clustered houses and huddled peoples of the plateau.

Quite suddenly they began to wail, the sound starting softly, a few heads hanging forward, only a few voices participating in the rising wave of despair; the wailing grew louder as more of the manchanged joined in, and soon Faulcon was in the centre of a howling mob, resisting his own emotional upheaval and fascinated by the racket that surrounded him. He saw Allissia, her head thrown back, her eyes closed and bulging against the thick lids, her mouth open, her voice lost in the greater sound of screaming. But Audwyn, standing near her, was angry, shouting, his voice insisting its way through the noise so that Faulcon could make out his words, the incoherent babbling of his fury; others still were laughing, or weeping, but over all there was the whining sound of a hundred manchanged experiencing some common feeling, and as Faulcon thought of this so he began to understand what might have been happening.

The change passed over and left Faulcon alert, slightly apprehensive, a small alteration to his previous mood of relaxed acceptance. He was nervous as Allissia, smiling broadly, came up to him and suggested a drink. Around him people were shuffling back to the fire or the places where they had been sitting, and the sound of laughter and chatter was loud and unexpected. Even those who had been crying were wiping the wetness from eyes and cheeks, and talking as if they were doing no more than brushing a stray hair back into place.

No lingering after-effects, he thought. They went through it and emerged unchanged.

When he said this to Allissia she frowned and shrugged, "Why do you always question things, Leo?"

"Because I'm puzzled, and interested. You seemed in deep despair, but now nothing has happened to you. I feel all tight and on edge. I know people in Steel City who would have been knocked out by that change; for days. I know, I know . . . people in Steel City are not the best examples in the world."

"You said it," said Allissia, and added, "I feel a little tense, now, but that doesn't matter. It'll pass away in a few minutes; most of it passed through me as the *fiersig* passed overhead.

213

These changes aren't permanent, but the more you resist them the longer they stay."

"But in Steel City it was proved that if you didn't fight the things you got addled for weeks—upset for weeks . . . There must be a reason. . ."

"Reasons!" Allissia snapped the word, a touch of that residual tension emerging in a moment of frustration. "You can work out reasons for anything, Leo—it's the human facility. Reasonableness can kill you quicker than anything. Reason is a liar."

Faulcon said no more, nor asked another question. Allissia drifted away from him to talk with friends, and take part in a quiet, almost sleepy dance in the dying glow of the fire. Faulcon crept into the house and curled up in a corner, sleeping quite heavily; at dawn he was woken by the sound of laughter, and, peering out of the window, watched the manchanged dancing almost frantically, carrying colourful paper, or cloth, streamers. He did not feel in the mood to join in, and returned to sleep, his last wakeful thought being of the time winds, and of Lena, and of the way he would go to follow her soon, and of the excitement that he was suddenly feeling, the determination to fulfil the terms of his agreement without fear, without restraint, without tears.

He slept late into the morning and rose to find the house and the village deserted. The hunters had moved back into the hills again; the fire still smoked greenly, a wide patch of charred ground and ash showing where it had spread beyond the metal brazier. There was no sign of Audwyn or Allissia, and Faulcon felt quite pleased about that. He wrote a brief note on a piece of torn paper he found in the house, and then walked to where his byke stood in the shelter of a small, empty barn.

The noise of its motor must have resounded about the silent village, but no one appeared to watch him go. He rode slowly through the fields, winding along the tracks towards the wide, dirt road that led to the steep, descending path to the lower lands. Several manchanged were working here, and those that saw him stood and waved. He waved back, increasing his speed all the time. The last of the villagers that he saw was a woman, bent to her work, her back to him, her body slim and small beneath the wind-whipped garment she wore. She remained unmoved by the sound of the byke, and Faulcon remembered that Allissia was supposed to be working in the high fields. He waved anyway.

PART FOUR

Walking on the Shores of Time

CHAPTER FIFTEEN

At the first break of dawn Faulcon rose from his damp and chilly sleeping place and walked to the edge of the canyon. Here he stood for a few minutes, staring down into the gloom of the valley, discerning the shapes and structures, watching as the slow rise of Altuxor brought shades of pink, then yellow, to the alien confusion below and beyond him. The wind was fresh on his naked cheeks, and the dampness of night's sweat was obtrusive and cold beneath his outfit. He watched the heavens as the stars expired, noticing that the last to vanish behind the red-streaked day were the winking lights of the geo-stationary satellites, watching the rift valley, probably watching him.

He felt no fear. He ached for Lena.

In his hands he held his old amulet, the small fragment of leather, smoothed and worn by his constant touching. He had carried this object of art around his neck for far too long; it had come to embody Mark, he realized now, and to throw it from him would be to detach one of Mark's fingers from their frantic grip upon his arm. Around his neck, now, he wore the crystal shard, carefully contained within an unobtrusive, platinum holder and slung upon a strip of the dark linen that had once bound the gash in his hand. He was not a man to spurn the slightest sentiment, not Leo Faulcon. Allissia was in his mind, and she was slightly in his heart. In the days since he had left the manchanged, she and Audwyn had grown in his life. They were warmth to the planet's cold; they were certainty to Vander-Zande's uncertainty; they were resolve to the inner fear he acknowledged, experienced, and realized could not control him.

And yet he could not cast away this strip of leathery skin, this piece of him, this part of his past. He dearly wished to consign it to the oblivion of the canyon, to watch its fall into the vast unknown, to await the next time-sweep of wind from beyond.

"Throw it you fool; break the spell once and for all."

Faulcon had been unaware of Ensavlion's approach. He turned, now, and saw the man in similar garb to his own, an off-white service outfit, reasonably warm, designed for less risky environments than the canyon edge. Ensavlion's rift suit stood awkwardly a few hundred yards back along the track; Faulcon could see it, standing twisted as if staring at him.

"Commander," Faulcon acknowledged. "What brings you here?" Yet another chance for the Catchwind mission missed, quite obviously, but Faulcon said nothing.

"You, of course," said Ensavlion, his face working behind the thin mask, his eyes clearly narrowed behind the goggles he wore. "I tried to find you in the City, but you must have spent only a moment there. I wondered where the hell you'd got to these last few days."

This declaration of Ensavlion's concern for one of his junior rifters disturbed Faulcon; what he had to do, what he faced, was something solitary, something that no man could be a part of. But he said, hoping to pacify his commanding officer, "I took absence without leave."

"That I know. I signed papers giving you official leave. You're off the hook, but where did you go?"

Cynically Faulcon glanced at the older man. "You mean you genuinely don't know? I thought you had eyes everywhere, Commander. You certainly had them in Lena's room."

Ensavlion appeared unabashed; the area of cheek that showed beside his mask did not flush; on the contrary, Faulcon thought the man was positively amused. Ensavlion said, "I heard nothing myself. I make no apology. Consider us to be square, me for allowing Kris Dojaan to eavesdrop your conversations with Lena, you for taking unofficial leave. Where did you go?"

"Up to the lower plateaux, in Hunderag Country. I stayed at a manchanged colony. They made me realize the foolishness of bending to fear . . . of bending to anything. They made me aware that I, Leo Faulcon, am ten times bigger than fate. Fate may call the tune, but I dance the way I want to dance."

Ensavlion clapped his hands together three times, slowly. "Bravo, Leo. Three cheers for the man who has stood up to destiny. And still you'll jump into the path of a time wind, and still you'll be swept to an unimaginable future. What you mean is, the persuasive, and hallucinogenic ways of the manchanged have rid you of apprehension; no, not even that. It's made you accept that things are the way they are, that nothing will change, and you might as well go time-swimming with a smile on your face. I think that about sums it up."

Irritated at the tone in Ensavlion's voice Faulcon said, as coldly as possible, "I think you're right, yes, that sums it up. Why the sarcasm, Commander? The approach a little too simplistic for you?"

Ensavlion prodded the leather amulet in Faulcon's grip, his glassy eyes meeting Faulcon's and doing their best to communicate reasonableness from mask to mask. "Simple or complex, who the hell cares? All I wonder about is a man who professes such acceptance of the inevitable, such control over circumstance, who stands fondling the one thing that promises to trip him butt over elbow the moment he takes a step. Throw the damned thing away. Don't you think it's been a weight about your neck for long enough? Throw it away, you fool, now, quick ... quick!"

And Faulcon, his heart racing, drew back his arm and pitched the amulet out into space, watching the leather thong twisting behind as it plummeted out of sight and clattered off a ledge, somewhere below.

Faulcon returned to Steel City on his byke, following the towering form of Ensavlion's r-suit. He reported to his section to terminate officially his unofficial official leave, and waited a few minutes in the lounge, aware that the silence in the place was the silence of embarrassment. He remembered the mistake he had made in the plateau township, the belief he had that he was regarded with hostility, a stranger, a threat to them. So he walked to one of the older Section men, who sprawled in an easy chair reading a news sheet. He acknowledged the man who looked up at him without a flicker of a smile and said, before Faulcon could initiate a conversation, "Get lost, Faulcon. And I mean lost."

"In my own good time," said Faulcon stiffly, feeling the flush rise to his cheeks. Around the room others, men and women both, had looked towards him, their faces pale and angry. The man he had addressed said, "We lost young Cal Reza to a wind because of you. The sooner you go the better. There's not a rifter in this room can walk safe while you're alive. If I had my way, you gutless wonder, I'd kick you over the canyon myself."

A man whom Faulcon only vaguely recognized said, "You made an agreement, Faulcon . . . your integrity is on the line; you're betraying your very humanness!"

"Do it, for God's sake, Leo," said a woman behind him. Faulcon felt instantly cold as he turned to face Immuk. She came into the lounge area and sat down heavily in an easy chair, spreading her legs and gazing up at him coldly.

"Do you think I don't intend to?" he asked. She said, "I don't give a damn what you intend to do, just do it. The sight of your face makes me want to throw up. I'll like you a whole lot better when you're dead." She grimaced in disgust. "You're such an appalling coward. You'll end up with your neck being broken and your body being thrown over the edge, and I shan't shed a tear for you, not one single tear."

"It frightens me to hear you talk like that. It makes me realize how much this world has got into our blood, has changed us."

Someone sniggered and Faulcon felt his face flush. Immuk said, "That's fine, Leo—you didn't think that way before, a few months ago when you helped escort Opuna Indullis down to the valley. But when it's you who has to show the colour of his courage, oh it's a different matter then. It suddenly seems so reaonable to remember that we have peculiar rules, peculiar rituals, and to invoke them as a sign of our madness. You make me bloody sick!"

Before Faulcon could retort, two section wardens appeared

from the other end of the lounge. Faulcon turned away at the sight of their yellow uniforms, unwilling to make a scene, or be the cause of one. As he walked towards the door he was aware of the two men running quickly after him. He had hardly decided to turn before he was pushed hard in the back, and flung heavily against the wall, a hand on the back of his head making sure that his nose was blooded painfully before he was kicked twice in the groin and unceremoniously bowled out of the lounge, into the public way.

"See you in hell, Leo," was the last voice he heard, Immuk's voice, followed by her cruel laugh and the thud of the door sliding back into place.

He brushed himself off and limped to a san-closet to attend to the blood that was gushing from his nose. When the flow was staunched, and he had sealed the small gash in the membrane that had split, he went to his room, changed his clothes, and then made his way to Ensavlion's office.

Gulio Ensavlion was expecting him.

"Can you blame them?" he asked, after Faulcon had briefly described the attack. "A rifter called Cal Reza was swept away by a time wind because of you, and these things escalate, as you well know."

"Cal Reza was caught because he was careless," said Faulcon bitterly, touching his nose tenderly. "He *must* have been careless. I'm beginning to despise all this 'lucky' crap."

Ensavlion laughed. "That's why the scene this morning with the amulet. Oh sure, Leo, you've seen the error of Steel City ways, sure you have."

"Damn it all, why this hostility from everyone? I've made clear my intention to fulfil the agreement of my contract. I'm going to do it, but why should I be pressured?"

Ensavlion was cold and pragmatic. "Because you're a coward. Oh, you may realize that you're not, but your section doesn't. Your team mates were swept away, and the correct thing to have done would have been to impart luck in a long and generous good-bye, and within a two-day to go down to the valley and wait. If you'd done that you'd have had every man and woman

223

of the section down there with you, waiting with you, making sure that your last days and weeks in the valley were spent with the best of friends. But no, you had to run, up into the hills. And two days ago Cal Reza died in a squall, and that was because of you, and so is it any wonder that your section would like to string your guts across the canyon from one edge to the other?"

Faulcon brooded silently for a moment or two, staring at the huge maps of the world, letting his gaze flicker disinterestedly from picture to map to screen and at length down to his spread hands, resting lightly on his thighs. "It's so bloody stupid," he said, trying to forget the two occasions when he had participated in, and insisted upon, this exact same rule of life, the compulsory death of one man and one woman after circumstances not dissimilar to those that had now made his own "suicide" imperative. He knew, and he repeatedly told himself, that there was no hesitation or doubt in his own mind that he would perform the act of willing self-destruction; but this need to be hurried, this denial of a man's right to pick his moment and place . . . this began to anger him. It especially angered him that he should be held responsible for a young rifter's death, or loss, by carelessness.

He repeated this to Ensavlion, who shook his head and then banged his desk with a flat hand and almost shouted at the resentful form of his junior. "Cal Reza went out into the valley thinking of you, thinking of bad luck, the bad luck that you had become. In other words he went out there with death on his mind, with his survival attitudes blurred; you know how it is, you've been around long enough. Reza was vulnerable, and a man is always ten times as vulnerable as he thinks he is."

Grimly, angrily, Faulcon accepted the reprimand, accepted the point. He felt an unaccustomed stubbornness jostling to remain the prime motivator of his behaviour, but gradually, breathing deeply and trying to rid himself of the sense of hurt and disloyalty he had received from his one-time friends, he came to experience a pleasant calm, a lingering moment of resignation. His willingness to face the time winds was re-

224

inforced, and the prospect seemed almost unworrying again . . . and exciting: the chance to find Lena and Kris, the chance for life beyond what appeared to be the dark wind of death.

Ensavlion seemed to observe the relaxation, for he too relaxed, toying with a small alien artifact that he used as a paperweight. "Is there any reason, any reason at all, why you can't go out to the valley now, and sit there and wait for a time wind?"

There was, but Faulcon found his mind choking on the idea of telling Ensavlion.

"I'm waiting," Ensavlion persisted, an edge of irritation showing in his voice. Faulcon refused to meet his gaze. There was perspiration on the Commander's face again, the sign of his growing tension. "Any reason, Leo, any reason at all? If there is I want to hear it."

Abruptly, tearing his gaze away from the corner of the room, Faulcon decided to be straight with his Commanding Officer. "One reason," he said. "I want to see Lena before I go. I think she'll be expecting me."

Ensavlion frowned, staring at Faulcon. The paperweight turned faster in his fingers, the harsh room-lights reflecting sporadically from the uneven surface. "Lena? I don't understand what you mean."

"The phantom," said Faulcon stiffly. "It's Lena. She survived the sweep of Othertime, so can I. I'm going to minimize the risks by talking to her first."

"The phantom is different things to different men. You know that." But Ensavlion was deeply curious, almost shaking with excitement.

"Do I? Kris saw the phantom that night he went out alone. I thought he'd seen me, from the elusive way he behaved afterwards, but it was Lena. It must have been Lena."

"You don't know that. The way I read it, Kris saw a phantom that reassured him about his brother Mark's survival. He saw someone who made it clear to him that beyond the time winds was life, survival . . . and Mark."

Fleetingly, Faulcon remembered that flickering, devastating

wave-front, the tiny, sprawled form of Kris Dojaan vanishing in an instant. He wondered where Kris had gone, and whether, moments later, he had struggled to his feet in an alien land: and he wondered what he had seen there.

To Ensavlion he said, "Then maybe there are many phantoms. Maybe you're right. But I saw Lena. I saw her as close to as you are to me now. And the young Lena saw her old self, and fell into the wind because of it. Don't even think of that, about its implications. There's something more than coincidence working here, Commander. It's just too easy to see the phantom, and recently it's been too easy to come *closer* to a phantom who turns out to be someone known to you."

"The travellers, you mean; playing games with us."

"Or something." Faulcon couldn't control the hint of a smile that he felt touch his lips; Ensavlion was in deadly earnest, his eyes bright, his body tense with expectation. "I keep asking myself what the hell was Kris up to? What was it about our encounter by the ocean that made him so secretive—or did he really not know he'd gone into the machine? He claimed to have had contact with Mark *after* Mark had been lost, but he never talked about any communication with Mark after he arrived here looking for the man. Games may be right, Commander— but Kris's games? Mark's games? Or something else's, something using the wind, hiding behind its destructive front. Maybe there's a whole world of time travelling beyond the wall of present."

"Of course there is; I *know* there is."

"Yes, but we also know the time winds can kill; perhaps they kill 90 per cent of the time. Perhaps someone, or something, only wants a *few* people to pass through them." He leaned back, watching Ensavlion, but seeing only the valley. "That's why I want to encounter the phantom before I go—I don't know what it is, what it means, but it means *something*. I'm sure of that. I want a head start on everyone else who gets sucked into the void. That makes sense, doesn't it?"

"Very good sense indeed," said Ensavlion. He stood up behind his desk and walked round to lean against the front edge of the table, close to Faulcon, folding his arms across his chest. "And I suppose you'll want to be alone when you try and see her?"

Faulcon concurred. "She'll not wait around while anyone else approaches. Why?"

Ensavlion said, "Because whether you like it or not, you're part of the Catchwind Mission now. When you go into the valley, I'm going with you. Talk to the phantom—to Lena—all you want; but when the wind comes to take you, you're going to have company."

Faulcon rose from his chair and faced Ensavlion. He felt confused. He had been afraid of the prospect of his solitary trip for so long that for a moment or two he could not adjust to the idea of his "ritual death" becoming a part of a larger mission. Then pleasure, and security, and the warmth of excitement washed through him, making him smile, making him relax. Trying not to let too much relief show through, he said, "I can't think of any better news I've had in months. Commander, we're going to take time apart at the seams."

Ensavlion grinned. "And we're going to be the second to do that. But we're not going to come back like the phantom, aged and withered. We're going to breach time, explore time, and we're going to walk up to Steel City afterwards and tell them a story that will blow their cosy world apart."

CHAPTER SIXTEEN

And yet, the strength of his resolve to commit himself, body and soul, to the time winds was still a strength tempered by doubt, by the nagging voice of fear. The unexpected and welcome ex-

citement of his visit to Ensavlion, the thrill of realizing that he
would be a part of an expeditionary force into Othertime, soon
passed away. It did not upset him that he could react so positively to the idea of a burden shared, for this is indeed what had
occurred to him: that what happened to him in Othertime
would happen to someone else as well; that the pleasure or
agony of the exploration would be received in company, and not
in solitary. Solitariness was the wall around his life that he
feared to contemplate, the hell within his soul. The manchanged
had significantly affected his attitude to aloneness, had reduced
his isolation by making him accept it, rather than resist it. But
the shadowy spectre of the Timelost chilled him, for he identified with the terrifying loneliness of men lost a billion years
from their own kind. With Ensavlion, no matter what happened,
no matter where he was flung, he would have the companion-
ship of another soul. This made the prospect bearable; it did
not alleviate the apprehension.

In a most impressive and determined fashion, Commander
Ensavlion immediately set about arranging for the first, and
most definite, plunge into the mysterious winds from Othertime.
He told Faulcon to leave all the preparations to him, and to get
out to the rift and seek out Lena. When he came back his r-suit
would be fully provisioned, serviced and ready to go. Faulcon
agreed to this and made his way from Steel City by byke, taking
only enough supplies of food and water for two days. He made
straight for the Riftwatch Station close to which, just days ago,
he had seen the phantom for the first time at close quarters.

The valley was changed now; where it curved through sixty
degrees, its wind-scoured bluffs and crags rising to obscure
vision from the long, straight tract that reached towards the
north-eastern horizon, here there was now an immense gate of
dull metal and dark patterning; although it did not span the rift
completely, it rose hundreds of feet above the dying vegetation
that here, and in its own time, covered the valley floor. It was
built into the rocks of the south wall, but sheered and broken
a good way from the north; like the rising immensity of a dam,

this gate watched him through the eyes of its doors, and the sparkling profusion of its tiny, circular windows.

Faulcon watched this bridge with interest. During the first day of his vigil on the rim of the canyon he saw movement in the body of the wall, the swift passage of some shape behind one of the open doorways. He rose from where he had been sitting and ran along the cliff top to where the span of the gate stretched away from him, and here he could see how wide was that wall, the width of a major roadway, and peppered with shafts and vents and small cylindrical structures. Braving the physical wind that blew strong and dangerous in the middle of the valley, Faulcon walked out across the gate, peering down into the gloomy interior of the structure, calling and shouting for Lena, and listening in vain for the hollow echo of his voice as it was sucked down into the alien place and lost. He returned to the edge of the valley and passed the night, frozen and uncomfortable, beneath the stars. Rift Station Shibano was close at hand, but he was apprehensive of asking for shelter; he was afraid of them refusing him.

He passed the second day in like fashion, walking slowly along the valley, riding to different access points, noticing, where he could, the new routes down that had formed since the last wind. For the most part he crouched within the span of the canyon, a few hundred yards from the cliff top, but close enough to the outer world to reach safety if a wind blew up. He had given up calling for Lena. He willed her to appear, but the canyon moved only with the dark shapes of rift suits, and the cumbersome and bored exploration by robots.

With two hours to go before the red twilight settled into black night he returned to his byke and, almost overwhelmed by his bitter disappointment, he rode back to Steel City. He ascended the access ramp into the towering, star-lit shape, and for a moment thought he must have approached the wrong entrance, for the door-seal failed to respond to his identity. He backed off a few yards and saw that he was in the right place. The sheer, curving wall of the traverse unit was a grey, monotonous surface above him, he a small, dark shape on the wide ramp, calling to be allowed inside.

The door remained closed.

He contacted the Watch on his mask speaker. He heard sour laughter, an obscenity, a curt instruction to get away to hell, and he knew that his disobedience of the unwritten rules of Steel City had reached to all corners of the installation. He was an outcast, now, and at the mercy of the world. He could not reach Ensavlion, although he tried, and his request to be put in touch with the man was greeted by a mechanical noise with a crude connotation. He was dirt in the eyes of the men of the Watch. Dirt was given no favours.

Resigned to his fate, and to a second night beneath Kamelios's brilliant spread of stars, he rode away from the City. Minutes later, as he debated where he should sleep for maximum comfort, he remembered the ruined Riftwatch Station, Eekhaut, and made his way there.

Station Eekhaut had been built too close to the edge of the valley. It had been constructed in the early days when the men who explored VanderZande's World still argued about how the geological structure of the world could be changed and bastardized by the phenomenon of time flux. They watched stratification and igneous insertion dancing hysterically before their eyes, and somehow it made no sense when considered against the might and axiom of Universal laws of conservation. It happened, though, and if Riftwatch Station Eekhaut had been built with an egocentric denial of the wind's true power, it had rapidly been taught the lesson of its lifetime; a gusting squall had ripped it in half, taking men and women with it, leaving the half-shell with the edge of metal as clean and smooth as if it had been machined; later, the valley edge had reappeared, three hundred yards of it, but the remains of the Station had not been a part of the refashioning.

Faulcon parked his byke in the shelter of the jutting dome; he walked through the gaping mouth, into what remained of the operations room, and found the doorway into the small sleeping quarters. He used the light from his byke, and with the door closed behind him, could fill the room with atmosphere from the still functioning air-supplies. He would not take the chance of failure while he was sleeping, but while awake, and sprawled on the floor, he took off his mask and enjoyed the smell of nearly natural air, just a certain staleness, the traces of animal life that had prowled here, reminding him that this was not home. It was all a part of taking risks, this breathing naturally, all part of putting survival in its place. He found his mind occupied with thoughts of survival, of the maintenance of the bodily status quo. He realized that his whole resistance to the rule of the rifters was a part of his enormous survival mechanism, his instinctive denial of the intellectual readiness to commit a self-sacrifice. And as he thought about this, as he allowed his mind to play with the words and images of the past days and weeks—even years—so he calmed in body and mind, found his own space and drifted. He was hidden here, tucked away from human eye, a man alone, and yet without having lost that recent gesture of friendship and support from Gulio Ensavlion. Faulcon was glad of this solitude, glad of the chance to let his mental defences down, and to look inside himself to see how he really was. . .

Afraid; truly afraid. Great. He was glad to meet his fear, to shake its hand, to let it wash through him. He liked the way his stomach churned, and the beat of his heart increased its pace. He acknowledged the residuum of his terror, and his unwillingness to die; he enjoyed acknowledging the cowardice in him.

Then there was his integrity, and his determination to live honourably. He had made the agreement when he had first come to VanderZande's World. He had thought it nonsensical at the time, agreeing that if his team mates died he would die too. But who ever considers the possibility of being forced by principle into suicide? He had been unable to envisage the necessity of his voluntary death, and the agreement had been easy to make, along with all the others. (And, of course, they had never talked in terms of "death", but of "going into the wind"). Now that fulfilling the terms of that agreement was a harsh reality staring him in the face, he resolved to honour it; he hated and resented those who had questioned his honour. He accepted both the questioning, and his resentment. He accepted that his fear had certainly made him pull the punch; there was right and wrong on both sides. Acknowledging this was a relief, and the pain of the last two days went slowly away.

But what would not go away were the words that he remembered from a time talking to Kris Dojaan; the youngster had brought to VanderZande's World a healthy excitement, a welcome expression of awe, and a nicely restrained cynicism for some of the wilder aspects of local life. Faulcon recollected only too clearly Kris's amazement when he had been told of the rule of suicide: "But it's unhuman; it's stupid!"

"It's an inhuman world, Kris. It's a hard world and it makes hard rules."

"I didn't say *in*human. I said *un*human. It doesn't sit right on man. It's wrong for man."

And Faulcon felt a moment's wry amusement as he remembered how that conversation had continued, how he had said to Kris that the whole world was wrong; it was a world of constant change and it changed man along with it. If you spent long here your body and mind became twisted and torn until sometimes you'd be walking when you were sitting and awake when you were asleep. Unless you fought it, that is, like they'd all fought it, resisting it, resisting until sometimes you would want to scream.

How had that conversation ended? Maddeningly, Faulcon realized that intoxication had made the exchange less of a conversation, more of a passing splutter of words. Why had that brief exchange insinuated itself into his awareness now? Was he trying to tell himself something? Faulcon grinned at that and sat up on the floor, stretching forward to test the stiffness of his back. He had been lying down for some minutes, and the floor was cold and hard. He was amused because all mental conversation was meaningful. It was too easy to dismiss that scattered memory, or imagery, or wordery that drifted through the waking mind as being mere day-dream indulgence. The fact was that internal conversations were often pointers towards important resolutions. And Faulcon knew that something about the valley, and the nature of Othertime, was disturbing him; it was not his fear; his fear was symptomatic of the uncertainty he felt, the feeling that he was committing himself improperly to the unknown, when in fact he should attack Othertime with considerably more foresight.

There had been another time when the word humanness had been brought up in angry dialogue; it had been those two days ago when he had gone to the lounge and had been attacked by his section colleagues. "You made an agreement, Faulcon . . . your integrity is on the line; you're betraying your very humanness."

Integrity maketh the man, he thought. I know that; I know the extent to which I can experience shame, and guilt, when I break an agreement, when I let my selfishness grow larger than my integrity, my basic humanness. *Opposite view:* for God's sake, what's more important, life or integrity? Certainly history is replete with suicide-warriors, and altruism of the highest order, the noble sacrifice for the greater cause, So what? What greater cause is served by my death now? This rule is based on fear; a man who dies to save his platoon advances a cause, the cause of more lives saved for the cost of one. The rule of suicide on VanderZande's World is a part of the luck/bad-luck obsession, the appeasement of something we have anthropomorphized: Old Lady Wind. Kris was right, it *is* stupid, a stupid rule, a senseless rule, but a rule that has now taken a grip upon us. Men *can* die if the rule is broken, because they are obsessed with the unfairness of a man like me who apparently flaunts the code of behaviour. It's called distraction, and distraction kills when the world is as unpredictably hostile as this one. But Kris was *right*. How simple to see the madness of suicide under these conditions; how hard to have seen it before. All that's keeping me determined to attack Old Lady Wind is my integrity; this is what's on trial here, my decency, my honour, my willingness to self-destruct for no other reason than that I have agreed that I would do so.

It was cold in the station, and he climbed to his feet, stretching his limbs to try and shiver some heat into his cooling flesh. He strapped his mask on and stepped out into the windy night. Movement was the best defence against cold, even though the night temperature was dropping rapidly towards a few degrees above freezing. As he walked towards the valley he noticed that all the moons were high; Merlin was full, and with Kytara, its twin, formed a strange, fascinating structure in the night sky, a double lens watching the world.

He kept well clear of the edge of the cliffs, for despite the glow of the moons, and the Galactic Centre, he found it difficult to judge the precipitous lip of the valley. As he walked he re-lived moments up on the plateau, in Hunderag Country: the warmth of the fire, and of his hosts, especially Allissia. He re-membered something she had said to him: you can work out reasons for anything, it's the human facility. Reasonableness can kill you quicker than anything. Reason is a liar.

Is that what he was doing now? Reasoning why it was good to be a coward, to break his word? Using reason to ease his conscience?

He remembered something else that the manchanged had said to him, that the quickest way to self-destruction was by resisting the basic nature of humanness. They had said that resistance in any form was an active statement for a point of view, and that if the opposite point of view showed up, then such a man would be trapped by it. Inevitability and acceptance allowed for freedom, for an escape from being manipulated whether by powerful men or circumstances.

He had become convinced that to simply accept what had to be was the best way to experience it, to live it, and to live throught it; all his "reasoning" was a form of resistance, and was a certain pointer to the inevitable failure of Leo Faulcon to sur-vive the time winds.

The sudden thought of the winds from time made him stop, listen keenly to the high howling of air currents above the canyon, and the distant moan of wind as it blew and gusted be-tween the eroded pinnacles of rock, and through the deep, winding gullies that riddled the lower valley walls.

234

He could not escape the fact that everything he thought and did was connected with his death, with his willing sacrifice of life to wind. That thought grew larger, twisted all about, seemed to come back at him again and again. Was it right that a man should be obsessed with his death when his death was all that tomorrow could promise? Of course it was. More reason, he said, more bloody reasonableness. A man alive should be concerned with life, not death. He could think of death after the event, when it didn't matter anyway. But that, he acknowledged, was not the human way. It might have been the way of the manchanged, but they were educated in the art of calm acceptance. To them both future and past were functions of the present; all were records, memories; past memories were true memories, whereas future memories; were flexible, changeable, all draining gradually towards the tight neck of time where the bubble of the present moment existed, declaring some records true, and most records fantasy, showing the way things were, no matter how things had been hoped for. And once something had occurred it was unchangeable, and therefore unremarkable. This was the manchanged, and Faulcon knew it was the true state of human-kind; but millions of years of intellect and concern had masked the deeper intuitive faculties, allowed man no space to breathe, save when he was discontent.

Death. Integrity. Discovery. Three factors in the complex equation that was Leo Faulcon, three factors that were not in balance, that did not add up, three factors that he thought about, and worried at, and as he attacked them so it seemed to him that he was watched; and that the watchers were testing him; and that he was a game to them, and this made him angry, very angry.

He turned around, staring into the darkness, looking up to the stars, then down to the vague patterns of light on metal that told of starlight on ruins. The wide chasm of dark before him was no invitation to him, was a sinister hidey hole for those to whom Leo Faulcon was a one man show, the raw meat of his existence on the table, prodded and dissected by inquisitive, alien minds.

He started to shake. Never in all his months on Kamelios had he felt the presence of the alien so strong, so close. He ran through the darkness and stumbled on a rock, jarring his toe painfully and sitting up, clutching his foot while he stared, wide-eyed, terrified, into the gloom. It was all about him, engulfing him, spreading dark limbs around his shivering body, drawing him into its maw. He rose to his feet, crying out as pain shot through his toe, and began to run back towards the starlit shape of the Station. The alien presence followed him, riding the air about him, moving effortlessly as he weaved and dodged, as if it rode upon his back and watched across his shoulders.

Abruptly he stopped. His heart was thundering and the blood in his temples was surging so hard, so fast, that his whole skull felt as if it would burst. His vision was bright, swirling, the stars moving through the sky in impossible patterns, the ground about him rippling and twisting, a carpet of living tissue. *This is madness. I'm generating all of this. There is nothing here at all.*

He dropped to a crouch and looked out towards the windswept canyon. He could see a ridged bluff of rock rising above the rim, and something shone steadily from a point half-way down the towering shape. The light, he knew, was just moonlight on a sheet of polished metal, a piece of wreckage cast onto the wall of the valley and waiting for the tide to whisk it away again. The claustrophobic presence of something alien had dissipated slightly; it seemed to him that he was watched from afar, again; that eyes were on him from within the canyon, peering over the sheer wall, shuffling restlessly as if waiting for his next move. He could hear its breathing, the noisy rhythmic flow of wind from east to west and back again, surging through the gullies and channels of the valley, whistling through the lung spaces between the crags and bluffs of time-scarred granite.

They are there, he thought. *This is not in my mind, not in my battered human psyche. They are really here, and they are watching me. . .*

Out of eye-shot, somewhere in the depths of the canyon, a

236

light glowed golden for a few seconds; he saw the brightness in the air above the valley, as if a match had been struck and flared up, before slowly dying again and leaving the place in gloomy darkness.

A night creature called its message through the black, a throaty gargling sound followed by a high-pitched clicking. From across the valley came an answering call, and Faulcon let his gaze follow the sound of wings beating hard as something launched itself towards its mate. He listened to the night sounds for about an hour, wondering if he had imagined the sudden flash of light, wondering if it would return, wondering what it had brought to the valley, what it had left below the rim.

The movement caught him by surprise. He had been staring straight ahead, half expecting something to appear before him. A human shape started through the moonlight to his left, dropped to a crouch so that he finally saw it only by the sheen of light on its mask.

"Lena?" he called gently, but was answered by the darting motion of the figure away from him, towards the valley's edge. He ran after her, picking his way carefully, straining to see a path, a safe place to step. He was belly flat and peering down the slope of the canyon before he knew it; and the phantom was some way below him, still moving away. Resigned to the danger he wormed over the edge and let his body slip and slide down until, some hundred yards or so away from the safety of the land above he came to a level ridge, and here he rested so that he might catch his breath.

I mustn't lose her!

Movement below him again and his heart fluttered; was she leading him down to the very bottom of the canyon? *I'll not be tricked. I'm going to stay right here.*

Tricked by whom, and to what ends, he wondered idly, as minutes passed and his body began to shake with cold. He *was* afraid of being tricked, and the thought of being tricked brought images of Kris Dojaan to mind. Never unwilling to entertain his idle thoughts in serious discussion, he asked himself, quite consciously, was Kris Dojaan tricked? Is that what I think?

He had no answers for himself, but was curious at the way he had first thought of himself as being on show, then had distinctly felt the presence of some alien awareness—perhaps nothing more than the closeness of Lena to him, before she gave herself away—and now started to think in terms of tricks, and games. . .

Movement; a rock dislodged and clattering for a few yards until its further downward progress was across a scrubby carpet of vegetation.

Again he called, "Lena? Are you there?" And this time he was answered by the frail voice of the phantom, "Hello, Leo. Aren't you cold?"

"Not now. I'm burning up. Where are you?"

"On the ledge. In front of you." He looked hard. There she was, crouched and hunched, watching him. He made no move to get closer; instinctively he wanted to hold her, to hug her, but the image of her whiskery, wrinkled face was hard and grim in his mind. The Lena he wanted back was *his* Lena; that she would ultimately end in the valley, chasing her young lover, was not as important to him as finding her and sharing time with her, time when she was young, time before whatever tragedy would bring her back to the valley as the wizened object of man's curiosity.

"Are they here?" he asked. Lena said nothing. Faulcon imagined she had not understood his question. "The aliens, the creatures that ride up and down time, watching us. Are they here? Our gaolers, our monitors, our guardians? I saw their machine, the golden colour of it, anyway. Are they here, Lena? Watching us now?"

There was a wind-disturbed silence for a moment, and Faulcon, his gaze somewhere out across the dark void, frowned, and turned back to the vaguely defined form of the phantom. Before he could speak again, or repeat what he had said, Lena's voice whispered, "But you *know* they're here. Didn't you feel them just a while back? Why ask me about what you already know?

238

They're always here, they always have been. The question is, why?"

"The question is why," he repeated. "That's a good question, Lena. But I don't have an answer, so perhaps, would you mind . . . could you answer that one yourself?"

"Can I ever answer anything you can't answer?"

Faulcon laughed, feeling a sudden intrusive chill through his clothing. "Not if you're a function of me, no. I had wondered about that. I'd wondered about the phantom, a figure that's always one of those enigmatic features of the landscape; so familiar in one respect that the wrongness tended to get over-looked. Everyone knows that the phantom changes; no one ever really bothered to try and link a healthy, rational, human nuts-and-bolts explanation to it."

"Does it need an explanation, Leo?"

"No, not really, not after a while. " Faulcon huddled down on the ledge, arms round his legs, chin resting on knees, eyes sad, yet resigned to what he felt, intuitively, was not a real encounter at all. "Kris was convinced you were his brother; I thought you were Kris; later you became Lena, and Lena saw herself in you at the same time as I saw Lena in you. We see what we want to see, or what our minds want to see. Isn't that right? There might be hundreds of phantoms in fact, but it's strange how no two ever show up at the same time. You're a sort of mind's eye symbol, a deep-rooted image. Something archaic, archetypal . . . the dead returned, the lost returned."

"Don't you find that interesting?"

"I don't understand how the mind works, Lena." He looked at her, and he felt moved to tears, and moved to shout. He felt angry. He had wanted denial; he had wanted reassurance; he had wanted evidence of her tangibility, of her realness; he had wanted to know that time was controllable; that somewhere she still lived, young, alive, passionate, waiting for him to reach her. "You're not real."

"What is real? How do you assess realness?"

"Measurability," he said without pause, "I can see you, but

that's not measuring. You're not physical; only physicalness can be measured."

"Aren't dreams real?"

"The fact of the dream, yes, the electrical activity; the events of the dream—the Lena factor—no, that's not real."

"How do you measure physicalness, Leo?"

"With instruments. Physicalness cannot be denied; physicalness is reality."

Her voice was a mocking whisper in his head, a tiresome distraction from his growing mood of depression and anxiety. "How do you measure the instruments, Leo? How can you measure real if you need to assume reality to measure it? Reality is what you see, Leo. There is only one realness, and that is what your mind tells you is real; there is a consensus, a general acceptance, that realness shared on a large scale is more real than realness observed alone. Don't question my realness, Leo, when nothing is real or unreal except inside your head. Don't you know that everything that happens to you is generated by you, everything you hear someone say is said by you, everything you see someone do is imagined by you—" *Audwyn's calm, insistent tone of voice! He recognized the shape of the words, even though they came in the frail voice of the phantom.* "—What does it matter if there *was* a state of existence in which an unconnected life-form actually altered the air, and made sound waves that communicated a word to you. If it doesn't happen in your head it doesn't happen. So whether or not I'm real, everything about me is you, and if there's one person in the Universe you should listen to, it's the ego-tripper inside your own skull."

Faulcon couldn't help smiling as he realized, abruptly, that he was recalling the words of his training supervisor, years back, when his whole attitude to perception and belief had been run through a mill of simple paradox, naïve logic and gradual argument, leaving him sometimes breathless, sometimes sceptical, sometimes angry, slowly more aware of how little he had actually *thought* about the nature of his own existence. The insights gained had rapidly fled; the human mind was too rigidly evolved to be changed by education, by the words of the great thinkers of ages and cultures going back to the beginning of Man; only over generations, only by social conditioning over hundreds of years, could the mind be made to expand, or contract, and to see round the corners of logic and reality, and thus travel outwards from its existentialist base.

"Are you alive?" he said finally, quietly, and the phantom answered, "I live."

Faulcon looked at her. "Can I ever get to Lena, to the Lena I knew?"

"Of course not. The past can never be recaptured. The Lena you knew was gone from you the instant she was gone."

"I meant", Faulcon insisted patiently, "the Lena who is young, not the Lena who is old. Can I ever get to her, get her back?"

The phantom made a sound that in the darkness Faulcon could not identify . . . laughter? Sadness? He wasn't sure. She said, "I was lost; I was alone; I grew old; the years; the aloneness; I grew old, then older; soon I will die; I was lost; I was lost. What is it you want, Leo? Do you want to wind me back, to reverse me like a car? Do you want to push me against the flow of time and watch the wrinkles fall away, and my breasts become firm again, and my legs lean and hard, and everything you liked about me reappear? Or do you imagine that there are millions of Lenas, all at different ages, from birth to death, and somehow you can walk into a room and pluck down the one you like, dust her off, put some clothes on her and take up where you left off? What is it you want, Leo? What is it you want to *do*?"

"I want Lena. I want the young and lovely girl who a few days ago was snatched from me, and who therefore is just a few days older than she was and can surely come back to me as young and lovely as she was."

"But I'm not young and lovely, Leo. I'm old, withered. Time has passed Lena by. Not your time, but her time. What makes you think that her time and your time are the same time? Where's the book of rules?"

"Oh God," Faulcon let his head fall forward, let a tear

form in his eyes. "You're a figment of my mind. So why am I even talking to you?"

The phantom laughed. "I reflect your confusion. I reflect your desperation to understand something, the winds . . . the time winds, the nature of time on VanderZande's World itself. You approach the study of time from a point of view that says: I don't have a clue about anything. That's not a good way to study anything, Leo. You have already decided that you are generating me, and that assumption has no room for the possibility of Lena actually existing and contributing to that generative imagery. You're so trapped in your neural pathways that whether or not you like it you are resisting the world that is trying to show you something. Have you thought of that?"

Faulcon looked up, wiped his hand across his eyes and started with surprise when his gloves hit his protective eyewear. "Okay, answer me this. What are the time winds?"

The phantom laughed again. "That's the wrong question, Leo. That's not the question at all."

"It's the question I came to Kamelios to help to answer. How can it be the wrong question?"

"It's the wrong question. Try again."

He said, "How do the time winds get generated?"

The sound of the phantom's humour, so reminiscent of her younger laughter, made Faulcon's stomach knot. "That's still the wrong question; what, how, why, what the hell does any of that matter, Leo?"

"I was about to ask *why* the time winds blow. I was about to get some motive into my questions. I thought you might find that more acceptable."

"Wrong question, Leo. Always the wrong question."

Exasperated, Faulcon shouted at her, "What question, then? For God's sake don't play games with me. What question should I be asking? Tell me!"

The phantom, he thought, had moved away a little, slipped out of what meagre view he had. At once he called, "Don't go. Please don't go."

"I'm not going. How can I go when I was never here?"

"I don't know what to do, Lena. I have to go to the winds. I have to, but I want to know . . . I want to know what to expect, how to handle them. I want to know how to survive them, how to find you."

"Poor Leo, can't ever let go. Can't ever let go. Didn't Allissia teach you anything?"

Faulcon was stunned. How could the phantom, Lena, how could she have known what he had done up on the plateau . . . he rose to his feet, staring at the crouched shape along the ledge. He felt cold, almost desperate. So she *was* a projection from his mind; she was not real at all. He had clung to the faint hope that she might have been. . .

The phantom said, "I can hear the clockwork, Leo. All that reasoning, all that explanation. She said that, so she must be this. She did that which means this is true, therefore that, therefore this, therefore that, therefore this. Give it up, Leo. Get rid of it. I'm old, old, old. I've had time to be everywhere, everywhen. I know all, Leo. And I know nothing. Every reason you come up with I can come up with a counter-reason. Reason is a liar. Natural knowing is all there is; natural knowing is the only truth."

Faulcon shivered and dropped to a crouch again to try to conserve his body warmth. He teetered a moment on the ledge, and felt a passing panic as he thought he was slipping; his eyes flickered out into the darkness, down to where the fiercest part of the time winds blew, and he thought of the next wind that would come, and of how he would be there, with Ensavlion, petrified, yet determined, and he would flicker in and out of objective vision, and then be gone. And people would wonder where he had gone to, to what age, what vast future, what bleak past.

"Nothing helps," he said quietly, almost self-pityingly. "The next wind that sweeps through the valley is my Charon, taking my soul; it will sweep me to hell and I shall have to go. I don't want to go, but I have no choice. I *have* to go into time, and I desperately want to know what to expect. My God, Lena, I feel like I'm being tested, torn every which-way. Surely there's

243

no reason for you not to tell me whether I can survive or not, whether it's death I face, or a new life?"

"If it's a test, Leo, surely it would be cheating to tell you that?"

"But a test for what? What the hell do the time winds mean to man, Lena—?"

"*That's* the question, Leo." She laughed delightedly, and moved away. "Or at least, it's part of it." Faulcon rose and walked towards her, but already she was darting through the darkness, down the slope, towards the sheer drop that he knew was below Station Eekhaut. Through the blackness her imagined voice came once more. "Never mind me, and what I am or represent. Think about Mark Dojaan, *think* about him for once in your life. Don't keep blocking him out. Think about a man who was so *different* to two people who were so close to him. Think about the sense of that, and then do what you need to do, and do it *alive*."

He called her name through the bluster of the night; over and over he called for her, but she was gone. Slowly, and sadly, he made his way back up the valley wall and into the cool shelter of the ruined Station.

At first break of dawn he rode back to the city, determined to gain access and to stand no nonsense from the entry Watch.

CHAPTER SEVENTEEN

Three hours later, Faulcon was uncomfortably seated in a small studio room, at the edge of the vast area of the records-unit; on a wide, curved screen before him there was a coloured picture of a sprawling farmhouse, built on the side of a hill. It overlooked a rich, cultivated valley, its crop well lit by the double yellow sun that was sinking towards the horizon of the world, Oster's Fall. Faulcon stared at the scene, trying to imagine the young Mark Dojaan running from house to barn, and then down the winding trackway that led to a low, rickety-looking fence demarking the area of cultivation. In his head a machine voice whispered facts about the farm. It was of little interest to Faulcon and he reached out to change the image on the screen; the words ceased, then began again as a new picture appeared.

Faulcon's knuckles stung as he straightened his fingers. He had not bothered to dress the grazes and cuts in his skin. The jagged wound across his palm had opened up again as well, and he had tied a white cloth about the gash. On the screen a picture of the Dojaans' parents had appeared, young people in brightly coloured clothes; they were standing at a gate, against a back-drop of strangely stunted trees; two boys swung on the gate, one taller, fairer than the other; both smiled broadly towards the camera.

Behind Faulcon the door of the studio room opened and closed; ignoring the machine-prattle about Mark Dojaan's early childhood, Faulcon glanced round, acknowledged Gulio Ensavlion as the man peered over Faulcon's shoulder, then sat down on the second chair, before the visual display console.

"I thought you were going to kill them," he said, and Faulcon grinned. "I enjoyed every punch, and I'll not hesitate to do the same again."

"I never knew you had such violence in you, Leo."

"I surprised myself," Faulcon conceded. He rubbed his bruised hands. "I had to get back into Steel City and I couldn't depend on you pulling strings to get the unofficial blockage stopped."

"I got you access to private files, didn't I? If you'd just asked, this morning. . ."

Faulcon glanced curtly at the older man. "If I'd asked, I'd have waited for days. I know you too well, Commander. You have a great talent for indecision." Ensavlion looked slightly stung by the unexpected vitriol in Faulcon's voice, but Faulcon went on, "With me around, Commander, there will be no chance to screw things up. I'm close to something, God knows what. I've spoken to Lena . . . I think; I've tapped my subconscious memories . . . I believe; in no time at all you and I will be changing the course of Kamelion history, I imagine." He smiled at Commander Ensavlion. "In other words, I'm quite determined in my confusion."

Ensavlion looked at the screen. "Mark Dojaan's records," he stated; "anything yet?" Faulcon shook his head, touched the change button and thereafter summoned images and spoken records quite fast.

He saw Mark Dojaan's history in fleeting glimpses. The machine voice was confusing, but after he had looked at the endless supply of photographs he could visually inspect the written records on the man. He would, if needs be, sit here for a week learning about Mark Dojaan, because somewhere in this file there had to be something to make clear what his mind-generated image of Lena had meant.

Ensavlion had been in the studio for no more than ten minutes when he came to what he was seeking.

The picture was of Mark Dojaan, a youthful-looking version, probably a teenager, sitting at a workbench, fiddling with something. The machine voice whispered, "Hobbies display; subject a keen musician and crystal artist; techniques learned from great great grandfather and inherited through paternal lines."

Faulcon leaned forward and stabbed a red button: further information.

A second picture appeared, a close-up of the first, Mark working with a small electric point, fashioning a human figure from a green shard of crystal, perhaps emerald. The picture changed, Mark and his brother Kris, still very young, working on a model of an Interstellar Liner, the Pan Galactic insignia clear on the hull; a third picture, a display of Mark Dojaan's artwork.

Quite literally, Ensavlion gasped; he leaned forward and stabbed a finger at the screen. "That's that bloody amulet!"

Faulcon put the display unit onto 'hold', and stared at the

star-shaped amulet that sat among the intricate and exotic carvings on the screen. "Well I'm damned," he said, and then, "Or am I damned?" and laughed.

Ensavlion was shaking his head. "So Kris was playing games with us all the time. He never found the amulet inside the machine, he brought it with him. Why would he do that, Leo?"

"I don't think he did," said Faulcon. "He came to Vander-Zande's World to find his brother. His brother found him: Mark left that amulet in the hulk for Kris to find. That's why Kris was so confident his brother was alive. It was a fine game; he didn't let on, of course; why should he? This was his private and personal trip, and that's why he could so happily face the prospect of a trip into time. Whatever Mark was, or is, up to, he couldn't show himself direct, but he wanted to contact Kris, and he used the jewellery he brought with him to the world . . . What was Mark's amulet, can you remember? Did he have one?"

Ensavlion thought for a moment. "It's a long time ago. I can't remember if I even saw one on the man."

Faulcon called up a picture of Mark Dojaan on Kamelios; he felt a passing chill as he found himself staring into that serenely confident face, the shock of fair hair falling across the forehead and nearly to his eyes, the smile just hinted at, the figure, photographed against a view from the city of the rift, so arrogant, so self-aware. Between the parted neck flaps of the shirt, a crystal fragment gleamed, and when Faulcon ordered a close-up he could see the hint of a star shape. The photograph had been taken on Mark's arrival, probably within the week, as soon as he had finished his basic training. Faulcon called up a second picture, and on this one it was readily apparent that Mark was wearing no amulet at all; and then, later still, a few months into his time on VanderZande's World he was wearing a spiral of metal, a real amulet, a real piece of luck. And here too he seemed to be showing the face that Faulcon remembered so well, the slyness, the self-centredness, the appearance of a man who is taking what he can. Mark Dojaan had really gone through the changes on Kamelios, and Faulcon felt a tinge of sadness about that. Why

247

sadness? He experienced the desire to cry, wondered about it. He thought it was because Kris had been a straight and genuine man, and Mark had perhaps once been the same; but Kamelios had beaten him down far more than most were beaten; it had wrenched Mark around and around and made him into something hard, something calculated, something whose greed was greater than any other consideration.

His empty words to Kris came back, words about how superficial the changes on Kamelios were, how no one was changed deep down. What a terrible self-deception that must have been. And Faulcon found himself wondering how deeply *he* had been changed, without him realizing the process, without him being aware of it. Should he draw his own file from the bank? Should he risk the watching of his earlier self, the sight of Leo Faulcon, the youthful Earthman who had followed his closest friend from New Triton to Kamelios, and thrown himself head-first into the restless tide of change, and had denied himself the luxury of intelligent appraisal as to what was going on within his skull, within his very soul?

He thought that he would not look at his own records. He concentrated on the screen again, on the image of Mark Dojaan, and when enough time had passed for him to treat the image as just that, and not as a haunting voice shouting abuse at him, so he checked to see whether the amulet had been among Mark's private possessions, after he had vanished; it had not. He had been carrying it with him on that fateful day. Faulcon summoned up the display of Mark's jewellery again, and settled back in his chair.

It was clear enough to him what must have happened. Kris and Mark had a closeness not measurable by traditional means; they were linked in spirit, a not unusual phenomenon, unusual only in that this linkage had worked through space and time, calling the younger boy to this place of Mark's "death". Kris had come, unsure, uneasy; but on his first expedition, watched from Othertime by his brother, he had been taken to a place where Mark could contact him, using a time-swept machine, and the amulet that he would have known from his days on

Oster's Fall. Faulcon remembered how quiet Kris had been, how secretive, how vaguely amused. He had tricked Faulcon and Ensavlion and even the Council into thinking this was a real discovery, and no one ever questioned the fact, because on Kamelios the world was full of junk.

He had played a game with Faulcon; he had made Faulcon touch the jewel and demonstrated its warmth. He was so confident of finding his brother, of sharing the experience of travel in time, that his childish humour had overtaken him. No wonder the interior structure of the thing had seemed so primitive, a silly colour-producing mechanism, and Steel City had not seen beyond the charade of alienness.

And only at the moment of decision, the final moment that he had been waiting for, the riding of the time winds, only then had he allowed a moment of doubt to surface, seeing that depthless black, and the swirl of change, he had been frightened . . . and Faulcon could not blame him for that.

"Mark is out there, in Othertime. My God, knowing that makes me feel quite dizzy. And not just Mark, surely not just Mark . . . all the timelost, all of the 'dead'. . . all the 'dead' of VanderZande's World."

Ensavlion had leaned forward onto the console, and sat awkwardly, staring vacantly past the screen, lost in his own thoughts. Faulcon watched emotion and concern walk across the man's features, the slightest of frowns, a movement of lips, the restless flicker of his eyes. At length Ensavlion said, "You make an assumption : you assume that it was Mark who put the amulet there. It is possible that Kris had the amulet himself, and was pretending to have discovered it. That *is* a possibility. It is possible further that it was not Mark who placed the jewel where his brother would find it, but the creatures who watch us. That is another possibility, is it not?"

Faulcon considered Ensavlion's careful words for a moment or two. On the screen the images of the jewels and carvings seemed to blur and flicker. "I don't think Kris brought the jewel with him. Something put it there. . ."

"But an alien, perhaps."

Faulcon recalled the presence of something, some force of watchfulness during the long night previous. "Yes. Perhaps. But even so, whether alien or human, it seemed a deliberate act, designed to make contact. Don't you see, Commander . . . ? It's a sign that time *is* occupied; it is evidence that time *is* under control on this world. If there are aliens, there can be men. Why not? Why should we doubt that men can survive in Other-time?"

Surely something, or someone, was communicating through time. On a world where time was periodically wrenched apart, where all hell let loose from past and future, it made good sense that creatures who understood the mechanism of the destructive forces of their Universe should patrol the ages, and make sure that intelligent life was not recklessly destroyed by its own, initial misunderstanding of the situation.

Lena, or whatever the manifestation had been, had hinted so strongly to him, hinted that he should think of Mark Dojaan, and she had been directing him to the evidence he needed that time was safe, that what was missing was the eloquence of communication between man and the guardians of VanderZande's World. He had seen the star jewel on Mark in the early days, and had forgotten it consciously; he had directed *himself* to the clue that time was safe! And time *was* safe. He knew that now, and the great weight of fear lifted from him.

CHAPTER EIGHTEEN

Think about a man who was so different to two people so close to him!

As Faulcon followed Ensavlion's rift-suited figure along the top of the valley towards the Riftwatch Station where the others waited, so he thought about that man, and about the difference. It was comforting to him; Mark was no longer the threatening, haunting presence in his past; rather, he had become the focus of his courage, his determination. The face of Mark Dojaan that he saw now was the youthful, pleasant face of a younger man, Mark as he had been two years ago; the resemblance between him and his brother Kris was close. And Kris was grinning at him too, and Faulcon knew that beyond time there would be no anger, no hostility. Fear and frustration had caused the row, the hurt, the tragedy. With Kris and Mark reunited all bad feeling would be transformed into support and closeness again. And Lena would be there. . .

What would happen to her that would bring her back to the valley, a wizened creature of indeterminate age. . . ?

The jarring thought chilled Faulcon as he paced along the cliff top. Even now, even in his contentment, he was uncertain about the phantom, about its nature. *Had* he spoken to Lena, to the real Lena, or had she been the phantom image of his confusion, a projection put up before his consciousness to help him resolve the conflicting facts and images in his own skull? The phantom *did* exist . . . there were physical records of that fact; but was Lena that phantom, or merely a convenient image for his ravaged psyche to grasp, and present to him? She had stepped into the valley when Kris had been lost, real, ancient, frightened. He had seen that.

His mouth felt dry. Ensavlion's rocking form some yards ahead progressed towards Station Epsilon with monotonous regularity, the dust rising from his feet, the reddening sun making his suit darken into a silhouette; dusk was two hours away. The valley was still.

He couldn't get the image of the aged Lena from his mind. He would find her, of course, and he would find her when she was young; there was no doubt in his mind about that. But would *something* happen, something that would allow her to live for years, when he had gone, and Kris had gone, and Mark had gone? How long, he wondered, would they have together?

I was alone; I grew old; I was lost. . .

The sad words sickened him; he slowed to a walk, then stopped. Ensavlion sensed the cessation of movement and turned. "Come on, don't hold things up. If there's a wind to-night, we'll be swimming in time before dawn. Come on, Leo."

Faulcon urged his suit forward into a gentle trot.

I was lost; I was alone.

That suggested that she had *not* found Faulcon. But then, he reminded himself firmly, the image in the rift that previous night was not necessarily the real Lena, the real phantom. It was Faulcon's own feeling of aloneness, of isolation, his feeling of fear that had put the sad words into the sad projection of his own mind last night. The real phantom was the last of them to survive their lives in Othertime, a life that might well—he clung to this hope!—bring them *all* back to Steel City at some short time in the future. That Lena would end her years in the valley, watching her younger self, in no way denied the certainty of their youthful rediscovery of their lives and passion and love.

He caught up with Ensavlion as they approached the bright Station, light spilling from its overlook window; Faulcon saw dark shapes inside, and as they approached the airlock so the door slid open, and the entry light winked on.

The Catchwind Team comprised eight men and four women, all of them with at least a year's experience on Kamelios, and all of them hardened and cynical about the valley and its remains. The one thing that linked them, and which tended to separate them from all other highly experienced rifters, was that the idea of *time* still fascinated them. They were determined to explore the furthest reaches of the world, both past and present. They had waited patiently for their Commanding Officer to give them the go-ahead, but after so long a wait, and so many delays, it was apparent to Faulcon, as indeed to many others, that they would soon take their fates into their own hands.

They had not heard of Faulcon's "cowardice", keeping them-selves fairly isolated from Steel City as they went about their normal routines of exploration and mapping while awaiting the word. They welcomed Faulcon pleasantly enough, most of them having seen him about, and two of them actually having spoken to him some months before. He was not a stranger; but he noticed how much of a stranger Ensavlion was to them. They were courteous to him, but distant. He stood apart from the sprawled or seated team, watching them, watching Faulcon, and then studying maps and notes. He spoke very little and seemed inordinately unrelaxed with any of the team save Faulcon himself.

For most of his waking hours, during the next three days, Ensavlion hovered above the monitoring screens and signal posts, watching the flickering lines and circular scans for a sign of a squall.

On a shimmering green screen, in a darkened room, bright yellow lines flickered briefly and faded; from a speaker there came staccato sounds, crackling sounds. They came in waves, sometimes quite dense, sometimes slowing down and then disappearing altogether. In the long moments of silence that followed, only Ensavlion's breathing could be heard; the screen remained blank, the speakers quiet. Then a flash, a yellow line, darting across the field of vision; then the sound of static, and silence again.

"What the hell *is* that?"

The man at the control turned slightly towards Faulcon and shrugged. "Wish to God I knew. I don't think anyone knows. It's one of the scanning features of the valley, but it doesn't have anything to do with a wind. Or a squall."

Faulcon said, "Something must be causing it ... something. . ."

"We've never found out what," said the man at the controls, reaching forward to gently stroke a strip of heat-sensitive green fabric. On the screen the scale magnified slightly. The man seemed satisfied and leaned back. Yellow lines flickered; noise crackled from speakers. Ensavlion leaned closer and shook his head, watching the enigma; not understanding.

Five days passed in this way, the valley quiet, the storm-winds pitching hard against the Station, blowing dust and debris against the walls; but never a squall from time; never a moment that could panic the Catchwind Mission into suiting up and racing down into the rift.

On the sixth day, shortly before VanderZande's blood-red dawn, a wind began to generate two hundred miles away in the west; within seconds it was blowing fast and furious through the valley, and Station Epsilon was alive with activity.

As the team moved out of the building and into the brightening day Faulcon sensed the disbelief in the group, the expectancy that Ensavlion would order the whole team back into the Station; he heard the words of several of them, the whispered agreement that this time there would be no going back. But Ensavlion was ahead of the team, a solitary figure fast-jumping down the valley towards the beginning of the sparkling ruins.

Faulcon opened all his communication channels and listened to the booming of the winds, and the whining of sirens, giving warning of the foul wind that approached. He found the sound excited him; his heart raced and he tasted salt on his lips. He began to run faster, jump further, and his abrupt motion spurred the rest of the team into a faster run. Soon they were gaunt figures, kicking up dust and slipping down the slopes as if they were a group of children, running to the water's edge.

Ensavlion fell behind, spoke to Faulcon through the radio. He was not breathless through effort, but was gasping with excitement, and the paternal hand that slapped Faulcon's rift suit hit with such force that Faulcon was glad of the armoured protection.

As they jumped on rocket power down hundred-foot gullies, and sheer faces, so the distant sky changed from red to a sombre black again, a frightening darkness in the bright day. The team stopped for a moment to watch and listen as the time winds thundered towards them.

Within minutes they were spreading out across the flatter ground at this chosen spot, where the walls of the valley were only a mile and a half apart, and the chaos of alien debris was confined to the edges of the deep valley; where they stood the land was flat and empty, ridged and raised in places, but still one of the most barren parts of the time valley.

Ensavlion's voice was firm and clipped as he called out orders:
"Spread out, keep in twos, when the wind hits don't move.
Keep your signal beacons on and sounding wherever we get to
and we'll hope to regroup at the other end of time."

As the dark wind swept closer, reaching high into the heavens
now, causing the day to darken substantially, so Faulcon and
Ensavlion stood together, twenty yards from each pair beside
them.

A deep calm took hold of Faulcon; he could hardly feel the
beat of his heart; he felt almost joyful as he watched the wind's
approach. Ensavlion was silent too, the man about to achieve
his dream, to plunge into the unknown and to come face to face
with those whom he had waited for, the creatures he had sought
during his long years on VanderZande's World. They would be
waiting for him, and Lena would be waiting for Faulcon himself. In this act of death there would be a discovery and a return
that would bring new life to their existence, new passion to
the emptiness that both he and Ensavlion had become.

Somewhere along the line of rifters a man shouted, another
man cried out in panic, concern tempered with excitement.
Distantly, towards the east, the landscape flickered and changed:
Faulcon saw a spire appear, growing out of the slope of the
valley, and in the flicker of an eye vanish again; a dark shape
remained there, something sombre and malevolent from the
more ancient past of Kamelios.

"Here she comes!" The universal statement of the obvious,
and now at last the blood in Faulcon's body began to surge,
the chemicals of his blood sharpening, adrenalin making him go
cold, tense, wide-eyed, wary.

Ensavlion repeated the statement, over and over again, and
each time the words rattled through Faulcon's transceiver so
that he could sense the rising pitch, the taint of fear, the beat
of fear, the rising storm of fear in Ensavlion's body and mind.
Here she comes . . . she comes . . . she comes. . . .

And elsewhere in the line of motionless black shapes a man
cried out, "God protect us . . . God watch us . . ." and a woman's

voice, calmer than her predecessor, shouting, "Into the wind forever, with luck . . . luck to us all."

Faulcon found his hand at the crystal shard that was tacked to the outside of his rift suit. He touched the jagged edge, and looked slightly to the left, and saw Ensavlion looking at him and smiling. Sweat tickled Faulcon's face, irritating him intensely, but the distraction was momentary. The wall of blackness, the vortex of time disruption, filled his eyes, his head, his Universe.

It swept towards them. The valley changed, he could see the change, see every detail, every shape and structure that came and went as the wave-front rolled through the valley, channelled towards the twelve who waited. He said, "Stay close," and he was surprised at the energy of his words, surprised almost at the words themselves. And Ensavlion's reply sank in, and was welcomed, although it said little: "I'd hold your hand, but it isn't done."

Faulcon heard himself laughing, a sound cut short as he licked salt and wetness from his upper lip. "Dear God, let her be there. . ."

"She'll be there, Leo. They'll all be there."

Thunder. The sensors on his rift suit reacted to the wind, screaming their siren warning above and through the sound of thunder, that bass booming that preceded the actual wind itself. The blackness was practically absolute in front of them, the light from behind lost in that depthless dark. Faulcon watched that blackness, trying to penetrate to the life beyond; he wondered, fleetingly, whether he looked into the future or into the past, or just into the void of space, or into the void of no-place and no-time. He sought a golden flare; he sought a tall and angular girl, walking towards him, her arms stretched out to hug him as he was bowled through the years into her love again.

There would have been seconds left, and as if his body and mind were reacting to the idea of death, he began to see, vividly and passionately, scenes and moments from his life; he could smell the smell of his home world; he could taste the food that his mother had cooked using the spices of Earth, ancient recipes, hot and sweet; he could feel the erotic silence of Lena's room, feel the smoothness of her body, taste her sweet breath; his tongue tickled as her own tongue darted into his mouth; perfume aroused him; laughter tormented him.

"Lena. . ."

Seconds. . .

He had a sudden, explicit vision of the time phantom, the wizened, stooped shape scurrying away from him as she had scurried from him a few nights before; it hurt for a moment, but his imagination was his worst enemy now, and that night when he had interacted with Kamelios to "see" Lena as the phantom, that had been imagination's triumph, his deeper, darker mind breaking through to him, pointing the way clear to this mission, showing how all along he had known that the time winds were not death winds, as long as one was taken complete; there was always that chance for death, like Kabazard must have died, but he could survive the actual *fact* of journeying through time.

Her words were the comforter. Think of a man who was so different to two people so close to him.

And he thought briefly of Kris Dojaan, and of Mark, and he knew that they too would be waiting for him, themselves reunited.

Seconds. . .

Think of a man. . .

I was lost; I was alone. . .

(the bitter memory of his own sadness, translated into imagery)

His suit shook as a powerful physical wind began to buffet him, trying to rock him; but the rift suit could stand against winds far more powerful than anything Kamelios could throw against them.

One of the team began to whine, expressing fear in his own personal way, but not moving, standing his ground. The voice grew until it was as loud as the shriek of sensor, overwhelming the booming and thundering of the raw wind itself. Others laughed or joked, or spoke aloud in words, lost against the howl

257

of the time wind, that Faulcon nevertheless intuited as being prayers. So many Gods, these days, so many deities being summoned for strength, for courage.

He said only, "Watch for me, Lena . . . watch over me, Allissia. . ."

How strange that he should invoke Allissia's name. He chilled—

Moments!

Allissia seemed to run towards him; he could see every detail of her, the round face, the smile, the hideous eyes, her thin gown pressed against her body by wind, her arms waving as she ran. She was saying something, and the words flooded back, jumbled, then clear.

Reason is a liar, she had said. *You can make reasons for anything . . . for anything. . .*

And Lena—the imagination's Lena—and the words he had said to himself: *the clockwork . . . all the clockwork . . .* figuring things out, rationalizing . . . you can get reasons for anything. . .

Reasons for living; reasons for dying; reasons to confront a danger confident of survival . . . of survival!

He felt suddenly sick; he experienced an upsurge of emotion, a sudden reliving of the fear of the alien he had experienced that evening when he had confronted his mind's image of Lena; he felt again that sense of being watched, and tried, and tested. . .

Reason is a liar. . .

Games! Games! Testing, trying, torturing. . .

Games!

There were less than seconds . . . there were only instants. And they had tricked him, after all his care, after all his bid for survival, they had tricked him into death, and he was about to die. . .

They were here: He could feel them, all around him . . . touching, probing, searching, questioning. . .

"A trick!" he screamed, his voice lost against the roar of the wind. "Ensavlion, they've tricked me, they've been playing with me all along, testing, testing me . . . Get out of here . . . *run!*"

He turned his suit and began to run; the motionlessness of the

258

·action was jarring, for his suit didn't move. Panicking, still crying out in desperation, he tried to shift the suit manually, but the bulky armour remained braced against the wind, facing it. The thought fled through Faulcon's mind : the damn suit is working against me . . . it *wants* to destroy me!

His panic, however, had reached through the few feet of distance between him and Ensavlion, and the Commander was turned and beginning to run. His howl of terror was one more note in the rising wail of sound. Faulcon turned his head and watched him moving away down the valley, but he was not running fast, and the arms of the suit were raised awkwardly; in seconds the suit had turned and was running its occupant about the valley in tight circles, like a hen without a head . . . like Leo Faulcon on his first trip down, all that time ago.

A sudden swirl of dust came between Faulcon and the dancing figure of Ensavlion; he looked back towards the wind, and the darkness reached past him, enveloping him. The thunder reached a deafening pitch, the whining of the rift-suit sensors seeming intolerably loud for just an instant.

The wind had struck.

He saw the valley as it had never been in the time of Steel City—green walled and sun-swept, with opalescent spires rising from the undulating sprawl of a living city; creatures and machines moved almost lazily about the whiteness, and as Faulcon watched—

Blackness, and a sudden silence, and

A rain-swept view, a dark gate, snarling faces carved in stone, and the procession of fire that marked a ceremony, or a war, or some unknown purpose—

And then the blackness was absolute, and the sound of life was gone; Faulcon was immersed in a silence so profound, so clean, so pure, that he felt at once shocked, and at peace; his body gave in to that silence and he found himself incapable of resistance, as if all of life and all of movement was a constant pull and push against sound, against music, and wind, and speech, and vibration, and with that universal noise gone, there was nothing for life to work against, and he began to evaporate, to drift, to disseminate. There was not even a ringing in his head, not even those neuronic echoes of the earthsounds that, instants before, had assaulted him.

He tried to cry Lena's name, but his voice was a soundless movement of lips and even that movement existed only within his mind; he tried to clench his teeth but there was no sensation; he tried to move his arms, but they were stretched out to infinity, great lazy sails, drifting through the void.

For an instant he fell, seeing no difference in the darkness, sensing only the way the blood shifted in his body, loving that moment's awareness of nerve ending, and pressure centre, loving the sensation; he twisted and turned, battered and buffeted by a feelingless, soundless wind; he spun, a leaf in the sky, a life on the wind; he drained upwards and down, his legs stretched to the ends of time, his head drawn out, and twined and twisted like a rope, then unravelled and whiplashed out so that his body undulated and snapped taut: no pain, no fear, no sensation other than that of the standing wave of sound, and light, the violin string struck and alive with energy, then snapped *taut,* and dead again, and drifting:

Colour now, but no colour he could relate to. Perhaps red, yet a bluish red, and swirling and changing, and something like red, yet not red, more—he thought, as thought faded, his last thought, the idle thought of a dying man—more the colour of laughter, streaked through with shades of tears, and the sparkling brightness of love, and here the tints and shades of childhood.

Through it all—last moments, last pulses of nerve and mind —through it all, the golden glow, the points, the faces, the lines, the twisting panels, the multi-dimensions of the pyramid, spanning space and time, and reaching into his eyes and ears and fingers and feet: the pyramid, the darting golden enigma, and Lena, yes, she was there, reaching to him, death-dream Lena, dying-thought Lena, long-dead Lena, so lost, so alone, so aching for the memories of her youthful lover, now falling after her, through the golden blackness, the silent roar of time, of endless time, of non-existent time, and downwards.

No touch, no temperature, no fear, no pain, no sound, no sight; and soon, as nothingness sucked all emotion from him, soon there was no thought, no sleep, no awareness, no existence. And it ended with peace.

CHAPTER NINETEEN

After the storm had passed, the valley lay almost uncannily quiet, its stillness seemed unnatural. Dark rain clouds had been gathering in the north, and they swept across the land, now, covering the world in a mournful grey and orange cloak; the rain came, fine and gentle at first, then more heavy, interspersed with thunder and electrical discharge. It rained for an hour, and because of tradition there were none who would venture out into the wet until it had passed completely.

The susurration of rain on steel faded and was gone; the sky brightened and the blazing disc of Altuxor peered through the dispersing clouds; above the valley, elusive red shapes, vortices and spirals, danced for a few minutes, insubstantial light-forms rejoicing in the passing of the rain.

Men moved out of Steel City, and from all the Riftwatch Stations, weaving and walking their way towards the valley. They came in rift suits, and in tractors, on air platforms and small copters; they came in ones and twos and sometimes in whole teams. They didn't hurry, but they were intrigued to know what time had left on the shores of their world.

The men from Station Epsilon were the first to arrive at the lip of the canyon; it was they who were closest to the Catch-wind Team, and they went down to search for the fragments of those who might not have made it, who might have been uncleanly swept by the time winds. They were surprised by what they saw through the magnifying plates on their suits. They were very surprised indeed.

A single rift suit stood in the deepest part of the valley, turned to face the direction of the wind, its legs braced apart, its form quite motionless. Of the others there was no sign. They had all been taken.

The identity of this lone survivor of the mission intrigued the rescue team that descended the rift for no more than a few minutes. Half-way down they could make out the markings on the suit.

Behind the face plate, staring out as if in wonderment, Leo Faulcon was at first thought to be dead. His staring eyes, the lips of his mouth parted as if crying, the cheeks tugged in as if withered, the crusting of salt down the sides of his nose and eyebrows, all showed the man had died of shock, and in terror. And yet, as the rescue team circled the frozen suit, so the expression on Faulcon's face changed, and the hint of a smile touched those twisted lips.

And then the eyes closed and the suit whirred for a second, powered two paces forward, its head bowed, its form finally sinking to its knees.

Faulcon was immediately hauled out of the back of the suit, and his shivering, ice-cold body wrapped carefully and taken up to the Station; from there he was transported to an infirmary in Steel City.

Hardly breathing, his heartbeat so slow that at times the pacemaker console was forced to squeeze a response out of the sluggish tissue, Faulcon lay in the coma for three days; his dreaming was monitored on an encephavid, something that would normally have required an authorization from Faulcon himself, but under the circumstances. . .

To begin with, the flickering images on the screen were quite lucid, showing a beach, a restless ocean, the movement of some bulky creature just below the surface. The image frequently broke up, corresponding to a dampening of the amplitude of various neural frequencies. When the activity returned, becoming more normal, the image returned. Faulcon responded to his own name with an image of his face; he responded to sudden noise in the room with an image of fear, the inside of a tiny chamber, windowless, doorless, dark shadows in the corners that moved about like ghosts.

It was after one of these fear-images that the basal image changed abruptly. The beach dissolved; Faulcon's alpha read-out began to fluctuate erratically, and his whole body began to tremble. When body and mind were calm again, the screen showed a picture of swirling clouds, brightly lit and colourfully confused; all the blues and reds of a *fiersig*, but stationary, now, and settled on a hillside.

Whilst the inside of the room remained quiet, colourful, intensely focused, outside, in the wider spaces of Steel City, there was mayhem. Word had leaked out that the coward Faulcon had *still* not made his sacrifice to the winds. That he might have been into the wind and come out again was not a possibility that anyone thought to entertain. His own section were the centre of the trouble. They tried to storm the hospital area, and were kept at bay by guards, whose numbers were tripled. Scenes of such anger had rarely been seen in Steel City. Faulcon's existence, his presence, was outrageous. It destroyed the smooth working of Section 8; it upset men and women on all levels. He was a core of bad luck in the city. There was public demand for his death, for his burning, for his ashes to be scattered in the valley.

Inside the room the men who watched and waited for Faulcon's return to consciousness were unmoved and unbothered by the noise and anger outside.

Within two days a second group had arisen, a quieter group who made their feelings felt in a peaceful way; to them, Faulcon was pure in spirit; he was God-given luck. They believed he had gone to the winds and returned; he was the turning point in the history of Man on VanderZande's World. The contradiction of emotions outside the hospital managed to cancel out the greater part of feeling; by the third day there was peace. Faulcon lay quietly, breathing once every minute, and behind

263

his closed eyes his pupils were wide, as if he watched a scene of great pleasure.

And yet, on the screen of the encephavid, there was nothing new, nothing but the image of a motionless *fiersig*, its colourful tenuosity hovering against a cleft in the hillside.

Had he gone into time, or had the wind avoided him? It seemed impossible that a man could be swept away by a time wind, only to be redeposited on precisely the same piece of ground that had been his waiting place; and yet Ensavlion, whose frantic form had been dancing only feet from Leo Faulcon, had gone, and the winds were not so precise that they could distinguish in the matter of a few paces.

At last one of the nurses picked up the crystal amulet, turned it about in her fingers and raised a question: had the amulet protected him? Had they found a way to survive the winds that had been available all the time, but had never been used as anything but a crude source of power? It was definitely a crystal of sun-dew.

Towards dusk on the third day someone came to a conclusion: "The crystal, in a way we don't as yet understand, has shielded the man from the effects of time. We can test that easily enough, but for the moment it seems a reasonable explanation. It would seem that Leo Faulcon never went into time. The winds ignored him."

Faulcon opened his eyes and smiled.

"Not true," he said, his voice soft, slightly hoarse; he struggled into a sitting position, propped on his elbows. He breathed deeply, almost gasping, almost hurt by the sudden indraught of sterile air. "I went into the wind, and I came back. They brought me back." He gasped for breath, beginning to laugh, and fell back onto his pillow. He stared at the ceiling. "They brought me back. My God, they really did . . . and now I can find her. I can find them all."

His eyes closed.

He slept again, fitfully, sporadically; while he was awake he said nothing, did nothing, just lay quietly, staring at the ceiling. When he slept he dreamed chaotic dreams, and only on occasion did the encephavid show a glimpse of hillside, and *fiersig,* or beach and rock, the images that had dominated his read-out for so many days.

One morning, when the nurse came in to inspect him, and to bathe his sleeping form, she found Leo Faulcon standing naked by his bed, his eyes not fully alert, his hands shaking. As she gently pressured him back to the bed he gripped her wrist. His eyes focused; the grip relaxed. "Get me my clothes."

"I can't do that, rifter. Not without the proper authority."

Faulcon conceded the point. He smiled, let go of the nurse completely, and began to run around the room. "I'm starving," he said abruptly, standing, hands on hips. He slapped his stomach and thighs. "I've lost more weight than is good for a man."

The nurse laughed, staring at his red-blotched body. "You've certainly got bony in the last few days. I'll get you some breakfast."

As she walked past him to the door he took her arm, leaned close to her. She blinked and recoiled a little as his breath was stale and sour. Faulcon knew this, but couldn't help his lack of freshness. He said, "Get me a suit; or a robe; or anything. And a doctor. I'm ready to leave."

He ate breakfast, sitting naked on his bed; he used the tray for mock modesty when the medical team swooped upon him, testing eyes, mind, heart and musculature. "May I leave now?"

By late afternoon he had been allowed his clothes, and, whilst being watched on the Steel City internal communication system, he was walking free through the plazas, corridors and lounges. No one took much notice of him; he was fortunate in not crossing paths with anyone who knew him well, and who might have drawn attention to him.

He refused, point blank, to talk about what had happened, not to the medical team, nor the psychologists . . . and not to the representatives of the council who pestered and plagued him. "All in good time," he said over and over again.

At the end of the day he went to the byke hangers and tried to sign out his rift-byke and a mask. He was refused. Angry, then canny, he found a corner, dropped a cushioning of under-suits into it, and sat down. He spent the rest of the evening and all of the night there, staring blankly ahead of him. Early in the morning two technicians approached him and informed him that exit clearance had arrived, and that he was free to depart from Steel City. He smiled at once, climbed to his feet, stretched and busied himself with preparations for a long journey. The technicians watched him, but made no move to interfere with him.

"I *will* be back," he said as he wheeled his byke to the exit ramp; he said it to the technicians, but he intended the moni-tors to hear him. For a while, at least, he felt he wanted to be alone, unfollowed, unwatched. All except for Ben Leuwentok, that is. For it was to Chalk Stack that he was headed, now, to find Ben, to talk to him, and to bring him up to Hunderag Country.

CHAPTER TWENTY

He skirted the valley, hardly glancing at it; the land steepened and the trackway wound away from the rift and up towards the chalk pinnacles which rose among the dense forestlands. Skag-bark and the threshing foliage of comb-fern had soon sur-rounded him, and he rode carefully, and alert, towards the semi-camouflaged hide where he was sure Leuwentok would be working.

Near by, quite suddenly, there was the sound of an animal panicking. A high-pitched cry was followed by a small, dark shape rushing headlong from the comb-fern, running across the track, then stopping. Faulcon braked hard and turned off the byke's motor. The silence was quite startling, although he became aware of the thrashing sounds in the distance, and the rustling of wind in the fragile branches of the skagbark.

An olgoi stood before him, its four eyes wide, its beaky jaws apart, gaping, drooling. Its whole body, supported on its muscular hind limbs, shook with fear as it stared at the human and his machine. In its tiny hands it was grasping the limp, probably dead, form of a slug-like forest animal. The olgoi's belly was not properly closed; glistening pink showed itself to Faulcon in a vertical gash from throat to crotch; fluid had dribbled down the olgoi's thighs.

The creature was beginning its mountain run. Almost unconsciously Faulcon glanced up and saw Merlin fully emerged from behind its permanent partner; in the bright day the moons were faint outlines, colourful. As Faulcon's gaze was distracted from the creature, so the olgoi snapped at its prey, biting and chewing a huge chunk of the shapeless mass in its mouth. Faulcon was concerned to pinpoint the gulgaroth that had at last released this little symbiont, but the big animal was probably a long way away, now, moving towards the valley, or to wherever it had chosen as its place of rest or death.

The olgoi swallowed, squawked, and vanished into the undergrowth, evident by its noisy passage for a few seconds before it had disappeared towards the far hills. "See you very soon," called Faulcon, and laughed.

"Well, if it isn't the olgoi hunter! Hello, Faulcon."

The voice caught Faulcon by surprise; he twisted round, looking back across his shoulder. Ben Leuwentok stood there, smiling from behind his thin mask; he carried a shoulder bag and camera, and was dressed in white and green safari clothes. He walked up to Faulcon and they shook hands.

"I was coming looking for you, Ben."

"I heard you'd been ignored by a time wind. You're a lucky man."

For a moment they exchanged a long, searching gaze. He knows, Faulcon thought. He had probably known all along. "I wasn't ignored," he said quietly. "They took me and they brought me back. In the wink of an eye, so I'm told. In the wink of an eye."

Leuwentok shrugged off his shoulder bag and put it on the ground. He closed up the camera, taking time about it, concentrating on the actions, although his mind was clearly elsewhere. "I was following the olgoi," he said. "Merlin's bright, now. The migration is beginning in a big way." He looked up at Faulcon. "How long did they keep you? Hours? Days?"

"I don't know. It seemed like no time at all, and yet I recall an age of floating in their minds. I was disembodied, and yet I could feel everything. I touched their hearts, their souls, their memories. I came closer, I think, than anyone has ever come. We exchanged thoughts, and I suspect it was for the first time, although they must have come close with Kris Dojaan."

Leuwentok looked up sharply. "That's a familiar name . . . Mark's brother?"

"That's right."

"I remember Mark. A vicious man, totally unprincipled."

"That's true," said Faulcon, "but it's not important. Mark was taken by the winds, but there was something that existed between his brother Kris and himself, an empathy that kept them in touch. . ."

Leuwentok was familiar with such rare, but undeniable, linkages. "Personality fifteen," he said, "ego links, instantaneous awareness of each other."

"That sort of thing. Kris knew his brother was here, and alive, and his dedication to the task of finding Mark was almost tangible. The creatures of this world responded to him almost at once—they tricked him with an amulet that was one of his brother's artistic creations; they convinced him to come into the wind because they made it seem as if his brother was waiting for him. And when they made contact with Kris, they made contact with me, and with Lena Tanoway. We should have been honoured—we were a special study to them."

Again Leuwentok fiddled with his camera before glancing at Faulcon. "Why are they doing it? And why did they let you go? And why have you picked me to tell this to? Why? Am I next?" His face was white behind his mask, his eyes wide, his demeanour that of a man suddenly afraid.

Faulcon laughed. "Get on the byke. There's something I want to show you."

Leuwentok obeyed, squeezing onto the saddle behind Faulcon's thin form. "Why you, Ben? Why not? You were very close to understanding the immense life-form that dominates Kamelios . . ." He punched the byke into action, shouting above the roar of the engine. "In fact, I suspect you knew all along. You certainly knew more than you let on last time I saw you."

"I have ideas, that's all."

"That's as may be." Faulcon guided the byke in a tight circle, cutting between shadowy trunks of skagbark. Leuwentok clung on too tightly for comfort. "There's another reason, though. I want you to come up to Hunderag Country with me. I want you to see what I see, and then you'll know everything. I might have to wait there a while, and it will be up to you to report to the *Magistar Colona* and the others."

As the byke lurched along the track, back towards the valley, Leuwentok shouted, "I don't mind that. I don't mind at all."

They came close to the gentle slopes of the valley; here, where the valley was nearly at its end, the span of the gorge was wider, but the drop was shallow. A few dusty, rather disappointing derelicts were scattered about the slopes and flatlands below: buildings, mostly, and unimpressive. The winds usually blew themselves out some way before this "beach", as the whole area was known.

As they stood, looking out across the rift, Faulcon said, "There."

"I've seen it before. Ruins." He looked at Faulcon.

"Not ruins," said Faulcon quickly, and tapped a finger against his temple. "Thoughts. Images. Dreams. Pictures from the mind of a creature that is several creatures in one, and which flows through this valley from one end to the other, almost a reflection of its own breath of life. It doesn't respond to the moons, or the daylight; it responds only to its own whim, rolling between the cliffs, seeking out the tiny life-forms that it has been watching for years—seconds by its own standards—and which it is still watching now."

Leuwentok was silent behind his mask for a while. He shook his head slowly, then, and Faulcon imagined that he was putting together pieces that had never quite fitted before. "I'd wondered about that. I thought the wind itself might be some by-product of the passage of the creatures: I always thought there were several creatures, I always thought of *them*. And I thought they moved through time, dragging these artifacts with them, and creating dream images. But I suppose they don't move in time at all."

"They aren't as tightly constrained by time, by the present moment as we are. But there is no span of billions of years. A moment to them is perhaps a few of our months, and they are free within that span of time. All of this, this whole valley, is a sort of crease in their ego; the ruins are the memories of other creatures that visited this world, and perhaps even lived here. There are even a few human ruins if you watch closely, a few human memories, twisted and changed just enough to make us blind to their real nature. Intelligent life has visited Kamelios for thousands of years, being taken in the same way as we have been taken. The creatures down there looked for memories, for life; they watched structures being built, and later they re-created them, made them into solid forms and beached them on the shores of their own collective mind."

"Tolpari," said Leuwentok. "Thought into substance. It never occurred to me. I was convinced that most of the strange manifestations were from an alien mind. But I linked the ruins with time, and accepted them as real."

"We all did. Very solid images, very real. They seemed something apart from the pyramid, and God, and the phantom."

"Tolpari *are* real. They're a phenomenon that some say we experienced on Earth more than we realized: space craft, figures, animals, all created by concentrated thought and given substance, and even life—*how* is something I couldn't tell you. They always decayed, though. The artifacts in Steel City haven't."

"Same principle, different intensity," said Faulcon, and thought of the very solid phantom, the one that showed up on photographs: turned on and off by the group mind that created it.

Leuwentok put his hands to his head and stood, for a minute or so, staring into the distance. Then he said, "But why are they doing all this, Faulcon? Why the tricks? Why these images? Are they trying to communicate in some way, throwing up echoes of our own minds?"

Faulcon relived that moment of close consciousness, floating so still, and feeling the contact of awareness, *becoming* for a while a part of the wind, seeing in an instant the longings and the memories of the natural inhabitants of VanderZande's World; he felt dizziness, a slight nausea; he felt his body teeter on the edge of the cliff, and stepped back, at the same time shaking his head to clear the sudden sensory assault that threatened to upset his equilibrium.

He said, "In one sense, yes. They *are* trying to communicate. Only their definition of communication isn't the same as ours. To them communication is part of reproduction, and it comes out simply as: 'Carry my life, my existence, my awareness, carry all of this, some mental part of me to *another* me on another world.' And part of that communication involved finding out the answer to a simple question: what will make a man die? What one thing would make us all sacrifice our lives to the wind when we happened across this creature's mate, a thousand light years away, a thousand years in the future. Was jealousy the key? Or passion? Intrigue? Curiosity? How they got us with curiosity! They gave us buildings, apparitions, life-forms—never an intelligent one, and how tantalizing *that* was—pyramids, they gave us anything and everything to whet our appetites for the unknown. They addled our brains to see what remained constant, what drive existed so deep rooted that they could find the 'lemming-factor', the all-jump-together button. They seemed to tune into the most psychically aware of us. Those without that particular openness of mind are probably dead. These creatures just didn't understand us, because they were responding almost instinctively, getting us ready to aid their reproduction. We're olgoi, Ben; messengers . . . To the wind-creatures we are star-travelling olgoi, to be primed with the seed of their lives and dispatched to other worlds, other winds, there to give up that seed—and our lives—in a splendid moment of 'mating'; mating not for the reproduction of the physical form of the creatures, but for communication . . . the spirit of life communicated to another of their kind, a replenishment, a linkage of existence. All of these last few years they have been working out what to prompt us to do, how to programme us to behave in a common way whenever we encounter their kind on other worlds. They sent phantoms, and they entered our heads with a different sort of phantom. They had us running about like headless chickens, pecking at enigma, seeking lost times."

Faulcon was breathless; he dropped to a crouch and dug out a small piece of stone from the earth, tossing it idly over the cliff and watching it roll away down the slopes. Leuwentok had wrapped his arms about his body, stood silent, intense. Faulcon thought he might have been afraid to speak, in case it should stop him fully understanding what Faulcon was saying, communicating what he had learned during his wild ride.

"Whatever Mark's brother, Kris, saw in the valley—he saw a phantom—and whoever it was, it made him more determined to go into the time winds because it reinforced his belief in the possibility of survival beyond them. The same happened to me. My own fear had to be overcome by *reason*, and at the last minute, as I was about to be caught by the trick, as I finally convinced myself that I *could* travel in time, I saw through it! The creature responded to that particular panic because it was like an enormous blast of mental energy—it was a communication as we understand it, and which they finally came to understand themselves. Quite suddenly they could see that we were not biological machines, that we no longer had some common, animalistic drive that was there for them to programme. An immense, intangible creature, trying to communicate with us: carry my life, my existence, carry the spirit of my life to others of my kind on other worlds. Only we couldn't do it; we're too diverse, too different from one another. The deep drives are just ghosts, now; phantoms. We've become a superficial race, aware of transient, passing things, fixed to a moment of time, busy evaluating our individual worlds. The deep world, the link between man and earth, has been destroyed by inutility. There was nothing for the creatures to grasp, to key into; nothing but scattered dreams, desires, images, different things to different men. They failed and failed. They trapped a few rifters, and killed many through misunderstanding. They found no key to the trapping of us all, and therefore no way to programme us to commit suicide, or at least 'union' on another world. Those failures that survived, those who were lost, they moved in their own way to a sleeping place, a long way from us, preserved because it didn't know what else to do with them.'"

"You know that for a fact?" Leuwentok's voice was unsteady.

"I know it."

"You've seen them? Where have you seen them?"

"In dreams, Ben. As yet only in dreams. But I want you to come up into Hunderag Country with me."

"I'll do that, Faulcon. You know me. I've worked for years to try and come to some sort of ecological understanding of Kamelios. I thought I'd got it. I understand the moons, the fauna, I thought I understood that mankind was responding to alien dreams, that our unfulfilled dreams and those of some creature, some entity, were interlinked, causing the chaos of Steel City and all its departments and failing scientific studies. I thought we were shallow creatures trapped by the deep drives, the ancient parts of our existences, the left-overs. Now you tell me that there are no deep parts. We are superficial creatures trapped by that superficiality: I want to know, I want to have, I want to touch, to experience . . . always I *want*. And I want to *know*. Is knowing such a superficial thing? Is knowledge so empty?"

Faulcon turned away from the valley, stretching his cramped limbs and leading the way back to the byke. As he walked he said, "I can't answer that, Ben. The manchanged made me realize something when I was with them last. They said that

273

natural knowing is the only knowing." He glanced at Leuwentok, who walked hunched and frowning beside him. "What you are born with, what you die with, that which is the very life you are. Natural knowing. All else, all we learn, all we strive for, all of that is garbage. Our species has lived for so long trying to find some reason to learn that we've now lost that ability to know without effort, to know naturally. Our friends in the valley, the creatures that are the wind, have never experienced anything like us, such empty things, such transient life-forms."

Leuwentok made a sound, perhaps a bitter laugh. "There's truth in that, and there's nonsense. Without science, without striving, we wouldn't be here, across the Galaxy from Earth, on an alien world; without disease."

"Or we would have been here a long time ago; without disease. We are an impatient, edgy species, Ben. We can't wait for things to happen; we have to *make* them happen. We've put our lives into *trying*; *trying* has become a religion to us, something honourable, and we've overlooked the fact that trying is *failing*. Ultimately our success, our understanding of our microcosm, comes generations late, and when it comes it is a truly superficial thing."

The byke had fallen over; together they heaved it upright, and brushed dirt from its panels. Leuwentok said, "I don't really believe that. How can I? I'm a 'modern' man. The Age of Roses is long since past for me." He shrugged his equipment pack onto his shoulders again, then hesitated and grinned, the mask wrinkling slightly. "A few minutes ago when you asked me to come with you, I was afraid. I felt horribly afraid." Faulcon said nothing, just watched the biologist. "So you see, Faulcon, I *do* believe what you said. Quite apparently I do, quite obviously. But I'll only admit it to you. I'm certainly not going to admit it to myself. How can I? I'm a modern man."

Faulcon tapped his temple twice, then laughed. "Get on the byke. First stop Overlook; then the Jaraquaths and the sort of food you've had nightmares about."

CHAPTER TWENTY-ONE

Allissia was working in the lower fields, digging furrows in the stony earth ready to take a new season's calcas. She saw them as they rode above the distant edge of the plateau, and for a moment manchanged and rifters regarded each other across the distance of half a mile or more. It was late in the day and the wind was strong, blowing hair and dust and sweet pollen from the high forests. Shading her eyes, Allissia finally decided that one of the pair was Leo Faulcon. She jumped up and down three or four times, then stopped, then jumped some more. She waved. Then she stared hard into the distance, puzzled as to why the figures on their weird-shaped machines had stopped so still.

Across the intervening land came the sudden, repeated roar of the bykes; one of the men waved and Allissia cried out delightedly, dropped tool and earth sack and turned to run and fetch her husband.

Audwyn was in the high field. Allissia ran through the village, stopping just for a moment in her own house to make sure that she had all the food she would need for the guests, and then she took off like an olgoi, bounding and tripping, through the skag-bark woods, and out into the busy field where harvesting was in progress.

Audwyn was close by. He stopped his work as Allissia shouted to him. Several of the manchanged gathered about her, their bodies reeking with the smell of sweat and dirt, their faces creased and content, but tired, very tired after this exertion. Audwyn wiped the earth from his blade, and kissed the cold steel. He laid the tool at the edge of the field, pointing inwards, the promise that the time he was absent from the harvest would be made up two-fold the next day. But there were none who resented his departure.

Audwyn loped ahead of the sprinting form of Allissia, and they reached the house in a panting race. Faulcon and Ben Leuwentok were waiting for them at the edge of the village, and the manchanged caught their breath and went to meet them.

"I've come to ask your help," said Faulcon, his voice tired as it sounded through his dusty, choked mask. Allissia took his arm, led him back to the house with Audwyn walking beside Leuwentok and hearing of the journey up to the plateau. Leuwentok seemed quite relaxed with the manchanged.

"Don't even talk," Allissia insisted, "until you've both eaten and we've drunk a toast to our pleasure at seeing you."

They seated themselves around the wide, wood table. The sight of food made Faulcon's mouth water, simple vegetables and boiled meat though it was. Leuwentok seemed slightly apprehensive of the meal, but relaxed more as Allissia allowed him a pre-taste, which he found, to his surprise, to be very tasty. Naturally enough they joined Audwyn in raising a mug of *calcare*, draining the sweet liquid and pressing hands to sternum as the burning went on and on, all the way from throat to fingertips. "Excellent brew," said Leuwentok, and removed his mask for a moment to smell the drink. They ate, then, and the meal that had taken scarce minutes to prepare, took scarce seconds to vanish from their plates.

When they had eaten their fill, and Audwyn and Allissia had taken a small meal for themselves, Faulcon suggested a stroll up to the high field to watch the harvest. Leuwentok had come over slightly queasy and decided to lie down for a few minutes. Faulcon and the others walked easily through the woods, listening to the scurrying movements of dusk creatures venturing into the deep, reddening shadows. From afar, from the mountain lands beyond this plateau, came the solitary, mournful howl of a female gulgaroth; the sound made Faulcon shiver. This was the time when the females came down from their mountain haunts, seeking the olgoi. It was not unknown for them to wander as far as the farms of the manchanged.

Audwyn had noticed Faulcon's sudden hesitation, the way

his head had lifted to regard the distant cry, the narrowness of his eyes behind the wide, clear-glass goggles. "Is that where you are to go, then? To the mountains?"

They were at the edge of the wood, now, and in the breezy dusk the fields glowed orange and moved in colourful rhythm before the gentle winds. All but a few of the manchanged were finished with the day's work, and stood in groups in the stubbly clearings, resting on their long-handled farm tools, or seated, arms around knees, staring into the setting sun and talking in quiet voices. They seemed unperturbed by the sporadic, but insistent, crying of the gulgaroth.

"The mountains," Faulcon agreed as he focused hard, intent upon the white peaks and the dark slopes that now seemed almost a part of the sky. "Not to the tops, certainly. Not to the snow. But to a deep valley that looks towards twin peaks. What is sleeping there is what I seek." He looked round at Audwyn, who was noticeably uneasy. The man's wide, staring eyes were rimmed with pink, and though he smiled, though he affected composure, Faulcon realized that the thought of a trek through the territories of the gulgaroth was deeply disturbing to him; or perhaps it was as simple as Audwyn having divined Faulcon's purpose in coming to the village first, and despite the manchanged philosophy that they were all far greater than the circumstances that affected their lives, he was nervous at the prospect of going into the valleys. Faulcon watched him carefully, wondering what spark of memory, what hint of the past, might have been nagging at Audwyn, making him respond with a very human fear.

There was no time for subtle suggestion. "I need a guide, Audwyn."

The manchanged smiled. "Of course. But you shall have two guides. Allissia must come." He reached for his wife and put his arm around her waist. Allissia melted against the tall man, and her eyes too showed the passing concern, the moment of fear before the fact of acceptance.

"What a confusing man you are," she said, and Faulcon

277

frowned his question. She shrugged almost imperceptibly. "The last time you were here you were seeking the courage to walk into the depths of the rift valley. Now you seek guides to the high lands."

"There is a connection," said Faulcon. "I went to the valley. I went without hesitation. I went with others, and together we faced the time winds, and together we travelled into their realm."

Audwyn and Allissia exchanged a startled glance. Audwyn shook his head, the transparent gesture of confusion, as he said, "You rode into time, on the wind? You went and you came back? How can that be?"

"I wasn't wanted," said Faulcon simply. "I suppose I was needed here. I was to have been a messenger, but I decided to keep my message to myself for a while. I wanted to see for myself where time's tide has been leaving its debris."

Audwyn looked back at the mountains. "The high land. Very well, we shall go and prepare to take you. The journey will be long and dangerous. It's the gulgaroths' time of seeking, and they are more vicious at this time of year." Faulcon, perhaps Audwyn too, remembered that occasion nearly a year ago when their respective paths had crossed that of a seeking gulgaroth, and Audwyn had escaped death by mere seconds.

Allissia had stepped ahead of Audwyn in understanding what Faulcon was searching for. She said, "The place where time has left its debris . . . to seek what sleeps there. The timelost. Is that what you mean?"

"There are no timelost," said Faulcon. "There are just those who are lost. And Lena is among them."

"I don't understand," said Allissia. "You were far-flung into time like the others of the timelost, and you are back . . . Were they all brought back to this world and this time?"

"Allissia, there is no time but the present; there never was a wind that blew from past to future, only a wind that blew memory and desire, and those things on a scale beyond our understanding, almost. Concrete memories, and heartfelt passion, and a desperate attempt at communication with those that were seen as couriers. The *lost* were taken into the fabric of creatures that fill the valleys and the deep seas. I don't know what was done to them, but they have been changed, more changed than you, much more. They were placed by the guardians of VanderZande's World in a valley, in the high land; they have been cared for, out of the way, asleep. The guardians have recognized the nature of their couriers at last, and I think they have realized that we are useless to them as such. It has taken a long time for them to come to this understanding, but now I think there will be a stop to the taking of men into the winds."

By their faces neither Audwyn nor Allissia could understand the flow of words from Faulcon. He smiled suddenly and began to walk back to the village, the manchanged following him closely.

Audwyn said, "I know the valley that looks towards twin peaks."

"I know you do." Faulcon glanced back; Audwyn was troubled, remembering something but not enough. When Faulcon said, "We must keep our eyes keen for lonely men," Audwyn almost jumped, his face whitening in a quite startling fashion.

Allissia did not know. She said, merely, "If your Lena is going to be so changed . . . why do you wish to find her again? Why not leave her in peace?"

Because I can't! Because I cannot control anything in my life, least of all my selfish concession to curiosity, even less my human need to complete the pattern, to see Lena again, to prove to myself that they really are what they say they are, these wind-creatures of Kamelios. Because without Lena I am a shadow; because with her, in whatever form she is, I can make a pretence of completeness; a part of my mind can rest again, the human part, the insecure part, the loving part.

"Because I am incomplete without her," he said aloud. The woodland area was noticeably darker than when they had walked up this way; night winds shifted the spidery branches against the red sky above.

279

"Are you not complete within yourself?" murmured Allissia, and when Faulcon looked over his shoulder, staring pointedly at her hand, clasped in the larger fingers of her husband, she grinned. "But I'm still an individual. Without Audwyn, if I were totally alone, I would live on, I would survive. I am complete within myself."

Faulcon shook his head, swinging down a steep bank by hanging onto the leaning trunk of a skagbark. He reached up to catch Allissia's hands as she jumped down; Audwyn descended on his rump. "It would seem that way, I suppose," said Faulcon. "Even as I followed Lena to VanderZande's World, even as I became obsessed with finding her again, even as I drew the friendship of . . . someone else, another man, drew it into me like life itself, still I thought that I was an individual, indulging the social rituals. But I don't think that now. When I hunted olgoi alone I felt not solitary but cut off, severed from some part of me that exists not in me but in you, in everyone. I'm a part of more than me, and Lena contains most of that which is outside of me. I'm incomplete without her. And I must find her."

After duskfall Faulcon stood at the edge of the village, listening to the sounds of night, watching the distant lights close to the rift valley, and the darkened heights of the mountains to the south. In the village there was a celebration somewhere; he could hear the sound of a weird string instrument, accompanying the awful clash of untrained voices. A blacksmith was mending tools, the sound of hammer on heated metal muffled behind the closed doors of his forge, but still punctuating the music. Faulcon could smell the odour of the coals; lifting his mask for a stinging moment he smelled the sickly odour of skagbark, and the pungent aroma of cooked food.

It was very cold and he was glad of the extra clothing he had brought on this trip. When Audwyn finally stepped from the house and walked through the village towards him, the man-changed's breath frosted. Faulcon watched him approach. Nothing had been said since their arrival back from the woodlands, and the high fields, but he had known that Audwyn would want to talk to him, quietly, privately.

"Your friend is very ill, I'm afraid."

"Ben? He'll get over it. Too much synthetic food is his problem."

Audwyn made no response except to say that Leuwentok would be unfit to travel the following day.

Faulcon said, "It isn't important. I think I'd prefer for just the two of us to go."

"Agreed," said Audwyn, and he tugged his coat tighter about his neck as a freezing wind suddenly sprang from the east. For a while nothing was said, Faulcon remaining quiet as the man-changed found the right moment to confirm the idea that must have been worrying at him. Above them, above the village, the moons were bright, Merlin the brightest of all, tugging at Faulcon's attention, catching his eye every time he looked around.

At last Audwyn reached out and took Faulcon's arm, leading him slowly into the lee of one of the houses, where the night was not quite so fierce. "What was my name?"

"Darak Iskaruul. I only had a few moments to scan the records; I saw your face and recognized you at once, but I had little time to read about you. As far as I can tell, all else that you remember of your time in Steel City is the same."

Audwyn hunched a little; he was angry, Faulcon could see that, and he was allowing that anger its full expression. "The same, except for the manner of my leaving. I didn't mind not knowing my name, but I don't understand why a false memory was given to me."

"But no one would have known where you came from. You were a wanderer, and someone suggested you had wandered up from the city, and that is what you remember. There was no deception, I'm sure of it."

Again silence, and then, "When was I lost? I came here five years ago."

"Then you must have slept for nearly a full year. Did you

arrive here in the spring, can you remember? When Merlin was full?"

Audwyn nodded and Faulcon smiled slightly. "The moon has a strong effect on animal life . . . and on man. When Merlin is full, and the olgoi are chasing up into the hills to fulfil their role as carriers of life, at that same time a few of the sleepers wake up and wander through the high lands as lonely men, choking their lives away. A few survive. Your colonies a long time ago must have found them and helped them, not knowing where they had come from, no doubt assuming they had come up from the rift valley. Perhaps the manchanged thought they were doing the right thing, saving the lonely men's lives, changing them, adapting them, allowing them to forget. Now it is done quite routinely. You remember quite a lot of your early life, but not the events that led you into a time wind. But you *are* beginning to remember something now; or am I wrong."

Audwyn straightened and shook his head, his gaze beyond Faulcon, out across the night lands below the plateau. "No, you're not wrong. I remember the valley where I slept. I remember it clearly . . . a bright light, like a *fiersig*, yes, a *fiersig*, hanging on the side of the valley. I passed through it and into the brilliant daylight, and saw the lights when I looked back. I remember choking and weeping and feeling as if I was going to die. . . And then a manchanged, a gatherer, covering my eyes and bathing them, and asking me where I'd come from, and would I like to become a part of their community, a part of this; and I can recall how welcome I found that suggestion, and how good it was to sleep in the Grey House, and to come closer to this world." It was too cold to stand talking any longer and they began to walk back to the house, to the warm fire, to a long night's rest. Audwyn said, "I had had no idea. Until you mentioned the valley looking towards two peaks I had remembered nothing. Allissia never knew. I think you're right, Leo; no one here knows where the lonely men really come from." He laughed gently. "It's ironic; some of the timelost have been among men for years, and none of us ever realized it."

282

In the house they found Leuwentok, wrapped in his bed roll and propped against the wall, white and uncomfortable, trying to conjure up a spell for sleep. Allissia was already preparing the packs for the long journey. She made no objection when Audwyn told her she would not be coming.

FINDING

It was not the valley that he remembered from his dream, but the clouds were low and the twin mountains hidden from view. It did not have the brightness, the freshness of the land he had experienced in his time of contact. It was drab and wet, the dark stones sombre and unpleasing, the plant life tangled and uncomfortable.

Yet Audwyn was quite confident that he knew where they were. Calmly, resisting Faulcon's assertions that they ought to travel further round to the east, he led the way down the difficult hillside, between boulders that towered high over their scrambling figures, and eventually out into an open space where Faulcon could see more of the spread of the valley. Without a word Audwyn waited for Faulcon to see the *fiersig*, and grinned as he heard the rifter's gasp of surprised delight.

Colours and shapes, almost static, hugging the earth below an overhang of rock: high on the far wall of the valley, a long climb away. There was a cave there, although its entrance could not be seen through the swirl of its guardian.

It was time for Faulcon to go on alone. Perhaps the creature in the great valley could have brought him here direct, but he had not wished that—he had needed Ben, and Audwyn, and Allissia, he had needed to draw something from them, to convey something to them; he had needed their company before he began the long wait for Lena. Now it was time for solitariness, time to lie down beside Lena's sleeping form and wait for her to stir, and wake.

Audwyn began to pitch the tent. He would wait for a few days and then go home again. Faulcon felt sure he would not be going home alone.

Audwyn was a tiny shape in the lower distance when Faulcon turned for the last time and waved to him. If the manchanged responded, Faulcon was unable to see. The *fiersig* was brightness around him and above him, and as he stepped into its insubstantial form he was immersed in colour and tranquillity; he felt a gentle embrace and knew they were with him. Deeper, through a place of darkness, he could see floating human figures.

He stepped towards them.

Julian May
The Many-Coloured Land £1.75

Book One in the Saga of the Exiles

The year 2034 was when a French physicist discovered a one-way
fixed-focus timewarp into the Rhone valley of six million years ago. By
the start of the 22nd century, there are those who seek to escape a
world of technological perfection–the misfits and mavericks of the
future, who pass through the doors of time and enter a battleground
of two warring races from a distant planet.

'Grips the reader and doesn't let go' VONDA McINTYRE

The Golden Torc £1.75

Book Two in the Saga of the Exiles

Exiled beyond the time-portal, six million years in the past the misfits
of the 22nd century become enmeshed in the age-old war between
two alien races. In this strange world, each year brings the ritual
Grand Combat between the tribal Firvulag and the decadent city-
dwelling Tanu, possessors of the mind-armouring necklet, the golden
torc.

'Altogether enchanting and engrossing . . . I was captivated by its
glamorous, sinister movement through the misty forests of Earth's true
past' FRITZ LEIBER

Orson Scott Card

A Planet called Treason £1.50

Lanik Mueller, heir to one of the richest Families on the planet of
Treason, is used to growing extra limbs – they are just removed and
the body heals within the hour. But when trans-sexual growth occurs,
he is banished from his militarist kingdom and doomed to wander the
strange planet for ever . . .

'Brimming with wonder-stimulating ideas and twists'
PUBLISHERS WEEKLY

Robert Holdstock
Earthwind 80p

'On the planet Aeran, the original colonists have undergone a drastic change: under the influence of some strange psychic force they have forgotten their identity and created a new culture – an exact reconstruction of the Stone Age society that flourished in Ireland 6,000 years ago . . . An absorbing and thought-provoking mystery tinged with mysticism' OXFORD TIMES

Alfred Bester
Golem [100] £1.75

'A major event . . . only the fourth novel by one of SF's greatest and most exciting writers. It's a fast paced page-turner with original concepts and lots of pizzazz' PUBLISHERS WEEKLY

'Outrageous, erratic, brilliant Bester is back' KIRKUS REVIEWS

Robert Silverberg
Lord Valentine's Castle £1.95

'In an archaic, feudal empire . . . Valentine, an itinerant juggler, discovers through dreams and portents that he is his namesake Lord Valentine, his body and throne stolen by a usurper. He sets out to win his throne back . . . Valentine and his companions trek across the forests and plains of Zimroel . . . to Alranroel with its Labyrinth and then to the heights of power at Castle Mount. Silverberg's invention is prodigious . . . a near-encyclopaedia of unnatural wonders and weird ecosystems. Silverberg, like a competent juggler, maintains his rhythm and his suspense to the end' TIMES LITERARY SUPPLEMENT

Science fiction

☐ The Hitch-Hiker's
Guide to the Galaxy
☐ The Restaurant at the
End of the Universe
⎱ Douglas Adams £1.25p

£1.25p

☐ Non-Stop   Brian Aldiss   60p
☐ 100 Great Science
Fiction Short
Short Stories   Isaac Asimov   £1.75p
☐ Golem 100   Alfred Bester   £1.75p
☐ A Planet Called Treason   Orson Scott Card   £1.50p
☐ Childhood's End   £1.50p
☐ Earthlight   £1.25p
☐ A Fall of Moondust   £1.50p
☐ The Fountains of
Paradise   £1.50p
☐ Imperial Earth   Arthur C. Clarke   £1.50p
☐ The Lion of Comarre   £1.75p
☐ Profiles of the Future   90p
☐ Rendezvous with
Rama   £1.50p
☐ The Twilight of
Briareus   Richard Cowper   £1.25p
☐ Clone   £1.25p
☐ The Green Hills of
Earth   Robert Heinlein   80p
☐ The Puppet Masters   80p
☐ The Stars of Albion   edited by
Robert Holdstock and
Christopher Priest   £1.20p

☐ Out of the Silent
Planet   £1.25p
☐ That Hideous Strength   C. S. Lewis   £1.50p
☐ Voyage to Venus   £1.00p
☐ Dreamsnake   Vonda McIntyre   95p
☐ The Many-Coloured
Land   Julian May   £1.75p
☐ The Golden Torc   £1.75p
☐ A Dream of Wessex   75p
☐ Indoctrinaire   Christopher Priest   75p
☐ The Space Machine   £1.50p

☐	Medusa's Children		70p
☐	Other Days, Other Eyes		75p
☐	Vertigo	Bob Shaw	95p
☐	Who Goes Here?		75p
☐	A Wreath of Stars		70p
☐	Capricorn Games		80p
☐	The Second Trip		£1.50p
☐	The Songs of Summer	Robert Silverberg	£1.25p
☐	Lord Valentine's Castle		£1.95p
☐	The Fenris Device		60p
☐	The Paradise Game		60p
☐	Promised Land	Brian Stableford	60p
☐	Rhapsody in Black		50p
☐	Swan Song		60p
☐	War Games		£1.50p
☐	10,000 Light-Years from Home	James Tiptree Jr	60p
☐	Up the Walls of the World		£1.20p
☐	The Time Machine	H. G. Wells	£1.25p
☐	War of the Worlds		£1.25p

All these books are available at your local bookshop or newsagent, or can be ordered direct from the publisher. Indicate the number of copies required and fill in the form below   5

....

Name_____
(Block letters please)

Address_____

_____

Send to Pan Books (CS Department), Cavaye Place, London SW10 9PG
Please enclose remittance to the value of the cover price plus:
35p for the first book plus 15p per copy for each additional book ordered
to a maximum charge of £1.25 to cover postage and packing
Applicable only in the UK

While every effort is made to keep prices low, it is sometimes
necessary to increase prices at short notice. Pan Books reserve
the right to show on covers and charge new retail prices which
may differ from those advertised in the text or elsewhere